A BookNest.eu Anthology

Art of War

Edited by
PETROS TRIANTAFYLLOU

Editor: Petros Triantafyllou
Copy Editor (all stories): Tim Marquitz
Cover Artist: John Anthony Di Giovanni
Interior Artist: Jason Deem
Cover Design and Interior Layout: STK·Kreations

Worldwide Rights.

Published by Booknest.eu
www.booknest.eu

Art of War is an anthology for charity, by BookNest.eu.
All proceeds will go to Médecins Sans Frontières
(Doctors Without Borders).

·CONTENTS·

FOREWORD

BRIAN D. ANDERSON

"I AM TIRED and sick of war. Its glory is all moonshine. It is only those who have neither fired a shot nor heard the shrieks and groans of the wounded, who cry aloud for blood, for vengeance, for desolation. War is hell." - William Tecumseh Sherman –

When I was asked to write this foreword, I was unsure how I should approach it. Or even if I were qualified to make the attempt. Many a great mind has written on this subject. From revered generals to spiritual leaders, war is a preoccupation of the human condition that has been explored in tremendous depth. Given this, I was more than a bit intimidated by the prospect of throwing my own two cents in. I am no general, nor a spiritual leader, and I have never considered myself among the great intellects of the world. But wars are not fought by great intellects. They are fought by soldiers. Men and women no different than myself. So rather than give in to self-doubt, I thought I would simply go talk to some soldiers. It felt like the right place to start.

I knew that my own perceptions of war had very little, if anything, to do with reality. After all, I've never been a soldier; never been close to a war in any significant way. And yet most of my books depict massive battles, where good and evil collide to determine the fate of the world. I practically sing songs of its righteousness and virtue. I use the most sinister and violent aspects of our nature to paint a picture of valor, bravery, and kinship. Even though I know that war is among the most reprehensible acts perpetrated by humankind, I have yet to find a better way to illustrate who and what we are as a species. Even never having been near one, its horrors are as familiar as they are terrifying. I shudder at the thought of sending our young to their deaths and yet am utterly transfixed by tales of bloody conflict and heroism. I curse as fools those who claim war to be glorious or say that it is a necessary and unavoidable evil. And yet I cannot tear my eyes away from the images splayed across my television screen. The more I thought on this, the more I felt as if I were a true hypocrite - hating war yet unable to stop writing about it.

It wasn't until I went on one of my visits to the VFW that I understood, at least in a small way, what was behind my fascination, and why I was right to use war and its horrors to display laudable and even beautiful images of humanity. For those of you who do not know, VFW stands for Veterans of Foreign Wars. Though a private club, it welcomes the public to visit – vets and non-vets alike. I've been going there for some time, favoring the company of older people with milder temperaments who are not prone to getting into bar brawls. When you walk through the door, it's not much to look at. Just a bar, a pool room, and a small hall where they hold the occasional minor event (dances, karaoke, and whatnot). The casual observer would see little more than a bar full of crusty old men speaking to one another in slurred voices over mugs of cheap beer. But I assure you that it is much more than that. In a very real way, these crusty old men are what gives war its virtue, if any is to be found.

With a plan in mind – or at least a vague idea where I would start – I jumped in the car and headed off. They know me pretty well there and were more than happy to give a "youngster" such as myself the skinny on war and what it was all about. In truth, I think they were excited that someone else beside the other vets wanted to hear their stories. These men have been going to the VFW for years; long enough to have told every story they know a hundred times over. A fresh set of ears was obviously welcome.

So, after buying several rounds and listening attentively for hours, I discovered a common thread woven into each story. But it was not what I expected. It seemed that regardless of the war in which they fought, none of them spoke a single word about the fighting itself. Very little suggested they were speaking about their time in the service. Except for the mention of officers and technical terms only a soldier would use, they could have been telling me about their time at college or a trip with friends. I heard about bar brawls, loose women, pranks they played, the trouble they found themselves in, even being arrested. But the words *enemy*, *firefight*, *bombs*, and *combat* never came up. What did this have to do with war? I wondered. Maybe they would come to it eventually. But they didn't. After the first try, I went home quite discouraged. I still had the option of watching a documentary or two and then faking my way through it, as if I knew what the hell I was talking about. But I shoved this aside and marshaled my determination. I had resolved to give this my best, and I intended to do precisely that. Perhaps I was approaching this from the wrong angle. I hadn't wanted to lead them in a specific direction, thinking spontaneity would be better, more genuine. But I had either been wide of the mark or hadn't given them enough time to arrive at that point. After all, they had decades of tales to tell, and I had only given it one day.

On the second trip, I was still reluctant to lead them where I thought I needed them to go. Don't get me wrong; I was thoroughly entertained. The stories they told were interesting, deeply personal, and often side-splittingly hilarious. And with men ranging in age from 55-95, I could have spent weeks – possibly months – and still not heard them all. But I didn't have that long. My deadline was fast approaching. So finally, I was forced to press the issue.

Initially, I had assumed that they were avoiding telling me about the actual fighting because the memories were too painful. And in many cases this assumption was proven accurate. However, there were a few who seemed unbothered and were willing to describe their combat experiences. But the stories were unvaryingly bland and lacked any flavor or depth. The vets appeared disinterested, and sounded as if they were reading from a dry textbook. And oddly, they didn't understand why I would care about it in the first place. After all, everyone knew about the fighting. Only *they* knew what happened in the in-between moments, when the bloodshed ceased and the bombs stopped falling.

I had hoped to hear of strategy and heroism, the adrenaline-fueled rage of battle, where the average soldier finds courage he never knew he possessed. Instead, I was regaled with accounts of frivolity and almost juvenile mischief-making. What little I had heard of battle I could have read from any book on the subject. No closer to my objective, I went home, again on the verge of giving up. It had seemed like a good idea at the time to use veterans as a resource. But maybe I should just go with my other idea and watch some documentaries or read a few books by famous generals. But that didn't feel right either.

On a whim, I read one of my early works, flipping forward until I reached one of the battle scenes. It was the first book I had written, and the prose left much to be desired. But it wasn't *that* which struck me. As the scene progressed, I came to realize what I had missed. I'd thought I had left the VFW empty-handed, when in fact they had given me everything

FOREWORD

I needed to understand why I, along with many other writers, use war as a vehicle to explain human nature in its entirety.

Soldiers don't concern themselves with geopolitics. They serve. They fight. For their country, true. But for the soldier standing beside them as well. In many cases they fought for their friends more than they fought for their country. Each story about some local girl they met or bar fights they were in was another layer to be revealed. Each word I was hearing was a slice of humanity in its purest form.

Taken individually, in the grand scheme of things, nothing they had said was of any particular significance – amusing anecdotes at best. Yet when patched together, even sitting at that greasy bar, drinking that cheap beer, I began to see a wealth I would have missed had I not taken on this assignment. It encouraged me to delve deeper. So I spent several more days listening with renewed vigor and excitement. But this time, I didn't ask them a thing. I simply listened to these men interact with each other. There was a bond between them that I imagine could be only formed through a mutual experience like war and service. I found myself feeling a stab of regret for not having served; unable to truly join in.

Still, I felt privileged to get to know them and that they were comfortable in my company. Whereas before they had been just a bunch of nice old men, they became much more to me. So I went home and began to write. Well, I confess that I deleted the first draft and started over. My initial attempt had focused on the generals and their strategies. I proposed that good leaders send their soldiers into battle with a heavy heart, understanding that some must be sacrificed to ensure others would survive…blah, blah, blah. That's what I get for trying to be clever – I end up sounding pretentious and ignorant. I had forgotten one of the rules for good writing: Write what you know. I had learned about soldiers from soldiers. I would stick to that. Anyone with even a mild sense of human emotion can extrapolate depth and suffering from the burden of command and inject it into a fictional character. But only *I* was lucky enough to have heard the stories these men had recounted for me. I had a completely new perspective from which to write. And I would use it.

To my own credit, the way I had described in my books the hardships of warfare and its implications for an impact on life and civilization had been accurate. And I had even hit the nail on the head when it came to the camaraderie among those who had been through combat together. But now I could delve deeper into the heart of war. I could show things in a way that previously would not have occurred to me. Where before it was shine without substance, now I could create a greater degree of realism.

As fantasy authors, we imagine worlds that cannot possibly exist. We write books meant to transport the reader from the mundane into the fantastical. And yet we build our stories on a foundation of what we know firsthand – things that exist as a reality in our own dangerous and often confusing world. We try to explain the human condition in a way that provides our audience with the full scope of experiences and emotions. War accomplishes this as does nothing else. Our earliest tales are about conflict. We have been simultaneously fascinated and repulsed for as long as humankind has had the means to pass along knowledge from one generation to the next.

As much as we desire the end of all war, there is no denying that it is stitched inseparably into the fabric of who we are. And were there to be an end, I believe the tales would continue to thrive and retain their allure.

As I was concluding this foreword, I realized that there was one element I had neglected to mention: the reason for this anthology being put together in the first place. Through it all, the aftermath of battle is often forgotten. The victory is won, the enemy defeated, and all rejoice. Cue the music. But it doesn't end there in the real world.

Real war creates poverty, hunger, and disease on a massive scale. Ravaged towns and shattered lives are left in its wake. When this humanitarian crisis arises, who is there to care for those who have had everything stripped away? It is the doctors, the nurses, the volunteers willing to risk their lives to lend a hand. They walk bravely into the heart of danger bearing no weapon or any protection to speak of. And why? Because they know that they are needed.

Learning that Doctors Without Borders would be the beneficiary of the anthology filled me with a sense of pride. That as much as anything was worth the hours spent laboring over this piece. I was already aware of this organization and knew a bit about what they did through friends who had participated. But I took some time and looked into it a bit more. These men and women are simply amazing. They sacrifice their time and put their skills to use in places I would be terrified to even think about going. I am honored to be a part of this, and hope that my meager contribution in some way inspires whoever reads this to learn more about what they can do to help.

Brian D. Anderson

.

THE BREAKING OF THE SKY

ED McDONALD

This story takes place in the same world as The Raven's Mark series, and is set long before the events of the first book. No prior knowledge of Blackwing *is required.*

IT WASN'T REACHING the war-torn border-town that bothered me. It was the box.

The saying went that only three kinds of people hired on with a Blackwing captain: the stupid, the greedy, and the desperate.

Mama Gil was greedy enough. The rings squeezed onto her bloodless fingers were artless chunks of tarnished gold, her riding gear silk instead of leather, and her horse had probably once almost won a big race. At a distance, she might have been a lady rather than a groom, but up close you saw that, for all her glitz, there was no substance to her. Just a tacky woman that stank of horse shit as she tried to continue her perpetually second-place existence.

Peralli was desperate enough. The magistrate had been set to stretch his neck on account of what he'd done to them dogs, and the law normally said you could do whatever the fuck you want with a dog, so whatever he'd done with them it had to be pretty fucking bad. I didn't like Peralli, but he was a mean bastard, stewed with spite and baked full of kill, and when we'd got into a scrap with the drudge, I'd run and hid behind him all the same.

That meant I was probably the stupid one. I had no idea why she'd taken me. I weren't a true fighter, didn't work the horses well, neither. Flotsam, tossed into her stream and swept along with the flow.

"What do you think's in the box?" Mama Gil asked. Seated beside me on the wagon's driving platform, she was painting her lips with something sticky and purple. Some high-ranking noble had got his face boxed by a prince and suddenly the fashion was to mask it up like he did. I was country-born. Never understood fashion.

"Best not to ask," Peralli said, walking alongside. His voice rustled. Dry leaves, silk on silk. An unkind voice. A killing voice. "Best not to think, even. Let her keep it to herself." Peralli scared me.

"What do you think?" Mama Gil asked.

"Diamonds maybe?" I suggested. It was a stupid suggestion. Couldn't envisage anyone bringing wealth out here into the war zone. I'd never seen diamonds, but they was more costly than gold, and there was no sense in paying gold for something small. Whatever was in that box, it was big. Big, and locked down on the wagon in an iron sarcophagus, chains binding it down. The wagon was drawn by eight horses, shire breeds from the western states. Biggest damn horses you could ever lay eyes on. The cargo was only six by four by five, pig iron, rough cast, but even if it had been solid, that didn't explain why the horses struggled to get it moving. Like it was heavier than lead. Much, much heavier. And it wasn't that they weren't eager. No sooner than Mama Gil got them hitched, they started straining away. Like they knew something about it and wanted gone.

"Diamonds? You're an idiot," Mama Gil said. "Ain't no diamonds here. This is war, not a country ball."

"Is this war?" I asked. It seemed to me that mostly it had been driving a wagon so far. Nothing to write home about, if I'd been able to write, that was.

"Blackwing don't care for wealth. They only care for serving their master," Peralli rustled. "Whatever's in that box, it serves her master's purpose. And his purpose is war."

"*Our* purpose," Mama Gil said. She clinked her fat rings together, reminding herself of the little bit of the world she'd managed to gather to herself. We were hired hands, not Blackwing. She was a gaudy fool.

Peralli gave her a look that said he'd enjoy doing to her whatever it was he'd done to them dogs. I looked away.

Three idiots, scraps of disbanded companies seeking work on the edge of a war that wasn't going to be over any time soon. Been going on for a century or more. Life choices had been simple in the valley: you farmed or you went soldier. I could have stayed a farmer, if I'd had the energy. Could have been a tailor when my folks got me the apprenticeship, if I'd had the will to stick it. Could even have been a father if I'd had the balls to stick around and answer the scowls of both sisters. Not to mention the fury of their pa.

Now, I had to wonder whether I'd got myself mixed up in a cess pit that didn't need stirring. I hadn't any real fighting skills, not really, and I hadn't Mama Gil's way with the horses neither. Mama Gil had said that I'd just been brought along because I had a pretty face and, sometimes, I wondered if she was right. I didn't fit in here.

The box was bad news, and everyone felt it. I looked down at me knuckles, the ones I'd tapped against the box. Just wanted to see if it was hollow. Best not to think about it. Best not to look at my hand. The colours were wrong. Greens, browns. They smelled bad, soured milk and baby shit. Keep them hidden. Tucked away.

"Alright. Far enough."

I reined in the horses and was glad to be able to jump down from the driver's seat. The stink of onion perfume on Mama Gil's neck hadn't been worse than the old tobacco on her breath, but it wasn't just her odours. I'd been able to feel the box at my back. Day by day, I'd got used to it, feeling like it knew I was there. Ahead of it. Watching me.

Stupid thing to think about a box.

"This place is a shit-sty," Mama Gil said as she began to uncouple the horses. We'd rolled right into the centre of a little town, a nowhere place of bean-farming, corn, and heavily fortified walls. A front-line fortification between Clear and Adrogorsk. Mama Gil never liked any place we wound up. Maybe that was why she joined up with Captain Narada. Serve a Blackwing captain, see the world, fight the Deep Kings. Right.

"Andlass." Peralli rustled. "Frontier town. Nearest enemy outpost is forty miles east." He was scanning the little crowd of locals who had rolled up to offer us things. Cakes, wine, meat on sticks. The town was fortified, and the people here were well used to soldiers rolling in and out. There's a way with soldiers, a casual kind of knowing you might as well make the best of things, but beneath it, the town was tense as a cat. They knew that soon the fighting was going to engulf them for real. People were going to die.

People had already died.

Living and dying, over a box. Drudge rangers had tried to take it from us, twice, on the journey east. Bodies stinking in the dirt for nothing but a box. It was the way of war. Somewhere, a general in his finery wrote numbers into a log-book, the tallies of the dead and the nearly dead. And he dipped the end of a sausage in mustard and just before he passed the morsel into his mouth, he wondered whether he could get away with not providing any reinforcements to replace the casualties. If he didn't, he could afford gold tassels on his next uniform. And then he would eat his sausage, and enjoy his mustard, and someone like me got orders to drag a box halfway across the states.

The box stood alone in the centre of the town's marketplace. Peralli did the work and the horses, uncoupled, moved away with all the speed that four legs could muster. As they clopped away, I noticed that their hindquarters afflicted with some kind of sickness. Mottled green and brown flesh where fur had fallen away in patches. Must have been a trick of the light, but I'd have sworn they was steaming. Couldn't be. Trick of the light.

Captain Narada stood watching the box. She was fierce, scarred, and brutal as winter starvation. Every bone stood out, bulging eyes trying to escape her face. Escape was what she'd offered me, freedom from the dumb corn-daughter that had let me plough her fields for a year, not to mention her equally ploughed sister. Corn-girl had been accommodating. Her sister had been the same, and it was bloody bad luck that they both missed their bloods the same month.

I wasn't even sure you could get two girls into that way in one month, but then they'd been teaching me an awful lot of other things as well. I still didn't believe in the magic spot they talked about. If it was there, I'd have found it.

The captain was sad. You wouldn't see it, behind all that ink and spit n' grit, but there was something missing. Something broken. You saw that a lot in the older fighters. Only, you didn't see many older fighters. The war didn't go easy on anyone when age started slowing them down.

"You three," Captain Narada said, snapping from sad to stern in a grasshopper's leap. "You done good. Good work. Good job. Done good."

She blinked a few times. She didn't seem all that together, but I dunno what I ever expected from a Blackwing captain. She looked us over. Thinking. When her mismatched eyes settled on me, I couldn't have felt smaller. They roamed on.

"Gil, you're discharged," she said. She stood there in silence. Mama Gil looked like she didn't know what to say. We'd never had to fall out at the end of a day before.

"Permanent like?" Mama Gil asked.

"Yes." Narada said it as though it were insignificant. A trifle. That she hadn't just dragged us all out here to a war-torn frontier for nowt.

"You said we'd make a quarter each," Mama Gil said. Nervous. You had to hand it to Mama, she had balls the size of coconuts under her skirt. We'd all got taken on with the promise of cash, but I'd not have been able to ask for it. Not direct.

"There's a satchel on my horse," Narada said. Bored. Barely glancing up, as though a fly had got past the nets. "Take whatever you think's fair. All of it, if you want."

Mama Gil's tongue ran across sticky-purple lips. More than the quarter we'd been promised? Was it possible? She was already imagining the bloodstone earrings, the silver, the opium. She practically ran. Narada looked to Peralli.

"I have another task for you," she said. "When she's done taking her share, go get my horse. I want you to ride as fast as you can back west. There's a small town we passed through, Valengrad. Go there and await further instruction."

Peralli was a killer, and spirits alone knew what he'd done with those dogs. But he listened, blank-faced and dead-eyed, and when she was done talking, he turned and walked away. I hadn't liked Mama Gil and her clutching hands. I had definitely not liked Peralli and his grave-dust whispers. But now, I stood alone with Blackwing Captain Narada, and that was worse. How would she dismiss me? She stood looking at me for a moment, and as her mis-coloured eyes regarded me from beneath the corvid tattooed over her face and the scabbed, cracked flesh across it, I saw her properly for the first time. Not as an employer, to be obeyed, or as a servant of the Nameless, to be feared. As the person she should have been in some other life. She was younger than I'd realised. A handful of years past twenty. Dark hair, cut at the jaw. Not a natural prettiness, but the snub nose and buck teeth could have worked for some unambitious clerk.

"You come with me," she said. My heart did a little shudder in my chest. Was all well and good imagining her without that bird inked onto her face, but that wasn't the story we were living in.

Captain Narada led me away from the box, which she didn't seem to care she'd simply left, abandoned on its wagon in the middle of the market. She moved with slow purpose. Soldiers filled the streets, whether from the steady garrison or the company that had just rolled in, and townsfolk was doing their best to persuade them to part with a coin or two. Narada paid them no attention, looked upwards as she walked.

"Beautiful sky, isn't it?" she said.

She'd said little to me that wasn't an order or a reprimand since she took me on. I didn't know how to respond. Narada almost looked happy looking up into the fading sky. Maybe this was the spot the girls had been going on about.

The setting sun soaked the western horizon peach and amber, colour bleeding to colour. To the east, the lingering blue was dense, stately. No stars yet. All three moons rode high tonight, and that rarest of occurrences was taking place; all three had waxed to fullness. I'd been so preoccupied worrying about the rotting knuckles that I'd barely looked up all day. I almost glanced down at them now but caught myself in time. No point worrying at something you can't fix. I'd said that to the corn-girls.

Narada led me to an inn. A common place, nothing fancy, but clean enough considering that soldiers tramped mud in every day.

"Sit," she said. I didn't want to. I didn't like what was happening. It hadn't felt so exposed when Mama Gil and Peralli were around, but alone with the captain, I felt cold. Isolated, though the inn was busy with drinkers. I sat.

"Ma'am, may I be excused?" I asked. Instantly regretted it.

"No," she said. "I'll need you, later on. Have a drink."

We ordered drinks. Summer ale, citrus flavours. I decided that whatever she needed me for was going to be deeply unpleasant, so I might as well at least get drunker than shit so as she wouldn't scare me so much. The bar-boy brought the beer, but Captain Narada ordered liquor, drank it neat from a tin cup. She didn't talk to me, just knocked it back like it were water. Tough constitution, that girl. My head was swimming before hers, and in the absence of conversation, I hadn't nothing to do but drink anyway.

"Your hand bothering you?" she asked eventually. I'd forgotten to keep it beneath the table, and she'd seen the green and brown mottling spreading out from my knuckles.

"It's nothing," I said. Pulled down my sleeve. Captain Narada snorted, a little drunk snort of derision.

"'Course it's something."

She peeled down one of her long gloves, showed me. Hand and forearm were swamp-dirt green from finger to elbow. The smell rolled out, and drinkers at other tables suddenly took notice.

"Shouldn't have touched the box," Captain Narada said. "I did tell you. But then, the boss told me as well, so I guess we both done fucked that up. It won't be the thing that kills you, though, if you're worried 'bout that." That didn't make me feel any better.

"You think the drudge will come overrun the border?"

"No, I don't," Narada said. "There's a whole lot of them. More than anyone realises, truth is. They're coming, but they'll not be the ones to kill us. We got the cargo, and that's going to change everything. Change the fucking world. Cheers to that."

She raised her cup. Didn't wait for me to clink it before she slugged it back.

"What's the cargo?" I said. I hadn't meant to ask it. I realised even as the words left my lips that she was hardly going to spill her master's secrets to me.

"It's the end," she said. Secrets be damned, it seemed. "Or the start off it, anyway." She leaned in very close, close enough that I could see every pore on her face. She spoke in a drunk whisper. "It's the heart of something from the void. Something very evil, very ancient. We'll open the box tomorrow and let it free."

I had no idea what a voidling was, but I suppose at about that point, I probably began to understand. I were never a smart one, but I looked at Captain Narada's darkened arm and hoped that Mama Gil was making the most of her money. By now, she'd be spending it on tawdry, second-best silks.

Somewhere after the fifth, or maybe seventh, cup of beer, I found that the captain's hand was somewhere it shouldn't have been, and despite the booze, she was a woman and I'd always had a thing for women who weren't too fussy. She led me up the stairs and told a bunch of soldiers to get out of their room, and they done it right away on account of her being Blackwing. They gave me fearful looks as they went by, maybe sympathy. She dragged me across to the bed, and there I had a moment of real fear, but then she was pressed hard up against me and the fear dissolved into a desperate, time-shortened desire. She kissed with the lack of skill that says that this was the first time she'd ever kissed anyone, but there was something that excited me about her efforts. She'd not done the other bits either, but she was a fast learner.

Afterwards, she didn't lie in the bed but, instead, stood looking out the window at the moon-bright sky. Her skinny body was speckled with scars, a real lot for someone so young.

"Come back to bed," I said. "You'll catch a cold."

But she didn't. Didn't say a single word to me, just stared out at the midnight sky as though it were the last time she'd ever get to see a moon or a star. She dressed without looking at me, but it wasn't shame or regret. She'd simply stopped paying me attention, like she'd forgotten I was there at all. Maybe in the act of lovemaking, she'd paid just as little.

When she was dressed, she belted on her sword, then went to the mirror and brushed her hair vey carefully. Got the collar of her jacket straight, brushed down the sleeves. Readied herself to look her best. Took a deep breath, and out she went.

The dawn was cold, the blankets rough, the night fading into memory. Bells were ringing, battle-bells, the call to arms. Voices clamoured in the streets, and they all said one thing only: war is here. My first thought was to find Peralli and get behind him, but he was gone, and it wouldn't have helped anyway. The inn was empty, not even the landlord had stayed. The streets flowed with human rivers. People were fleeing.

"The drudge are coming," one man nearly screamed at me. "Half a million of the bastards. Half a million drudge. And they're bringing Kings!" He was swept away by the current.

I could have joined them, I suppose, but I knew it wasn't going to make a difference. A timeless sense of lonely acceptance had taken over me. I found myself back in the market square, where the box sat on its wagon bed. Captain Narada sat alongside it, watching the swollen moons.

"Is it true?" I said. "The Deep Kings are going to come here?"

Narada didn't take her eyes from the moons.

"Here. North. South. Everywhere. They've made these new creatures. They— It doesn't matter. It's not relevant."

"Why did you pick me?" I asked. Captain Narada looked at me, and spirits, but she was young. Everyone was young that morning.

"I needed a pretty face," she said. "You've done what I needed you for. You can go now, if you want to run."

I saw everything in her expression there. The fear. The burden of knowledge. The weight of responsibility.

"Is there any point running?" I asked. Narada looked at me a moment, then shrugged.

"No."

"Will Peralli get away?"

"I doubt it. He's a good fighter, and the war will need good fighters, even after today. But no. I gave him the chance, but unless he sprouted wings during the night and flew then…no. But I thought I might as well give him the chance."

We sat in silence for a while, shared a smoke. The bells clanged, clanged, clanged, and people passed by with arm-loads of possessions or shouldered bows, pikes, as they headed to muster around the walls. I couldn't help playing with my fingers. The rot had spread across my hand, into my other fingers, along the veins in my wrist. One of my fingers came away, painless, rotten through. I dropped it onto the floor. It didn't seem to matter anymore, and in a way, I was glad that it wasn't my own stupidity that was going to kill me.

"And you?" I said. "Why are you here?" But the crow inked across Narada's face told the real story there, and she didn't need to answer me.

"Help me open it," she said. We jumped up onto the wagon bed, and Narada did something that caused the black-iron box to groan. It took both of us to pry away the lid, and I felt my remaining fingers and my palms sizzling, burning against the cold metal. When it was done, and exposed, we sat back down. I'd never seen anything like it before. Maybe no living man had. I could already feel the wrongness of it, the raw power and magic beginning to emanate. Poison in the air. It was huge, and alive, and it silently promised me oblivion.

I could have stayed with the fattening corn-daughters, but I'd never done anything to make their lives better. I could have played a different game, maybe, tried to be a better man. But here I was, at the end of the world, and although I was as scared as I'd ever been in my life, there was a dismal satisfaction to knowing that everyone else was going to die with me. A selfish thought, maybe.

Narada reached out and took my hand. The moons all looked very, very bright. From the voidling's heart behind me, I dreamed of terror and screaming and the hatred of living things. Somewhere distant, a general dipped a sausage in mustard and looked at the day's reports. More soldiers or gold tassets?

Above us, the sky buckled. Flexed. Howled a long, sonorous cry of anguish as reality began to twist and turn.

"Is this really war?" I asked.

"It's not war, no," she said. "It's only misery."

The weapon ignited, and nightmare blossomed incandescent and burning as the sky began to tear itself apart.

THE LAST ARROW

MITCHELL HOGAN

FROM ATOP THE battlements, Heikir reached for another arrow and launched it into the teeming horde below. The feral stench rising from the besieging jukari was so pungent it seemed to have substance, and it made him retch. Metal clanged as weapons struck primitive shields, and he could hear snatches of the guttural chant the creatures screamed throughout their assault. Torches held in their clawed hands cast lurid orange glows, which seethed as the creatures moved. Howls of bloodlust and anger broached the night, from both sides.

Another arrow. Nock. Loose.

And another.

His fingers were rubbed raw, even calloused as they were from weeks of fighting.

The fortress of Kascunir's first line of defense was the wall of Skaitha, composed of seamed granite forty yards high. It snaked for almost two miles across the entrance of the Soras Pass, which the fortress blocked. Skaitha had been lost the first day of the siege, jukari swarming over stone that had been untouched by nonhuman hands until now. Truula, the second wall, two hundred yards distant, had fallen shortly after due to the sheer weight of jukari numbers and corrosive vormag sorcery.

During the years of peace, a city had grown up around the citadel and between the first and second walls. The screams of those who'd made their homes there had lasted long into the night and through the next day. The jukari were worse than animals, and the dead were a source of food.

That left only another two hundred yards of clear killing ground between the third wall of Angem, and then the citadel of Kascunir itself.

Heikir and his squad of archers had heard rumors the lord commander had abandoned his plan to retake the second wall. Clearly, there was a limit to what his sorcerers could do, so it was also said, and here on the border of the Desolate Lands you had to work with what you were given—or what you took with blood and sweat and death.

Makeshift ladders of branches and stripped timbers thudded against the wall. Jukari scrambled over each other to reach the top, where they were cut down by swords and pierced by spears. The creatures were a full yard taller than a grown man, with skin of mottled gray and heads covered with thick black hair. Slanted yellow eyes peered out above beak-like noses.

Tortured wails reached Heikir's ears as on the wall far to his left archers and soldiers writhed in agony. Arcane concussions hammered bodies, tore their own sorcerers shields to smoke. Coruscating fire slicked across the battlements, igniting flesh and breaking bones like straw, before the defenders' sorcerers repulsed the attack.

Horrified, Heikir tore his gaze from the charred corpses littering the gutted section of wall.

There were murmurs from behind as a sorcerer walked along the wall, dispensing crafted arrows with red feather fletching. Heikir turned to grab three, and as he did, a black-shafted arrow slammed into Rafnar beside him. The young man grunted and staggered back, blood oozing from the wound in his chest. His mouth opened, frothed crimson, and he dropped to the stones. Hands dragged the archer away and another stepped forward to take his place, a too-young boy with wide eyes and trembling hands.

A lucky shot for the jukari, not so lucky for Rafnar. But then again, the defenders had fought for so long, even the unlucky incidents seemed a regular occurrence.

Heikir nocked one of the red-fletched arrows and waited for the command to loose. When it came, his joined a few dozen others, trailing incandescent lines of sorcerous power.

They exploded where they struck, throwing up chunks of earth and hurling jukari from their feet. The concussive impact blasts reached Heikir's ears a moment later.

Another red arrow. Nock. Loose.

More sorcerous fire enveloped the attacking creatures, and agonized howls split the night.

Whimpering like beaten dogs, the jukari retreated.

But lingering behind were smaller, darker figures cloaked in arcane shields upon which dazzling motes erupted when struck by arrows. These creatures had survived the sorcerous onslaught and stood unmoved. Vormag. Sorcerers in their own right.

Unbowed.

Uncowed.

HEIKIR STARED IN revulsion at the morsel of charred rat-meat Bersi handed him. Although it was stringy and rank, he shoved it into his mouth and chewed. His empty stomach had ceased growling weeks ago, as if it had given up hope of ever being full again.

"There's no seconds," joked Bersi, drawing a guffaw from Ulrik, another of their squad of archers.

Outside, a cold rain tumbled from a gray sky. Drops plinked into the pots and pans the soldiers had set out to catch what they could to drink. Ulrik made a round and poured a portion into everyone's cup.

Heikir sipped his slowly. They collected enough to drink, but not to bathe with. He knew he must have reeked as much as everyone else, and his head was constantly itchy from lice.

Bersi used a wooden spoon to stir a pot atop a small cookfire that gave off too much smoke and struggled to bring the gruel to a boil. Heikir wasn't sure what was simmering inside, but it wasn't likely to be substantial. Only the spiders in their corner webs were getting fatter—from the flies the jukari bought with them.

What he wouldn't give to be back on his farm and eating his fill while his wife, Svea, bustled about their kitchen. By the ancestors, how he ached for her. He wished he'd never seen the soldiers who came to his farm and conscripted him to help defend Kascunir.

"It's all right," he'd told Svea, not knowing, believing the soldiers' lie that he'd be home in a few weeks once the threat was over.

He'd been a fool.

With nothing solid to sustain the archers, even their shit had become watery and foul. Sores crusted their lips, and their skin was unhealthily dull, broken only by eruptions of red spots. Heikir worried at a loose tooth that hadn't been moving at the beginning of the siege. He wanted to stand and take in some night air, but his body and limbs ached, and he couldn't be bothered.

Their squad of archers huddled on the ground floor of one of the towers close by the main gate of Angem. The rest of the archers were billeted somewhere close by as they were the first to the walls whenever the jukari attacked. Lord Commander Adryan had given a speech when the monstrous horde first approached, declaring that the creatures would soon tire and leave them alone.

That had been fifty-three days ago.

Inside the unprepared fortress, supplies had been exhausted quickly. The frequent riots were quelled violently by the lord commander's black-clad soldiers—his supposedly elite force named the Steel Fist. So far, Heikir hadn't seen them fight the jukari.

"Where's Rafnar?" Heikir asked. "Is he alive?"

"They took him into the citadel and he hasn't come out," said Bersi.

Heikir glanced at Bersi, but the cobbler remained tight-lipped. "Why are they taking all the wounded inside? Treat them out here, I say. No point dragging them all over the place."

The rest of the squad remained silent, staring into the meager fire.

HEIKIR, BERSI, AND Ulrik lifted the wagon tongue and struggled to drag the wagon toward the others blocking this side of Angem's gates. A horse or a mule would have made their task a breeze, but those had been the first to be eaten once it was clear the jukari weren't leaving. The gates were constructed of massive timbers with metal plates nailed to the outside to render them immune to fire and some sorcery. A single sorcerer sat a little way off, staring at the crack in the center of the double gate. *Was it slightly wider than yesterday?* Her eyes were blank and sweat dripped from her brow.

Ulrik slipped, and the weight of the wagon caused both Heikir and Bersi to lose their grip. The wooden tongue crashed to the cobbles, and a squad leader shouted at them to stop messing about and get it up against the others.

"Sorry," said Ulrik. "I'm tired."

"We all are," Heikir said. "Come on. Wouldn't want these soldiers to break a sweat by coming to scold us in this heat."

They picked up the tongue again and, this time, made it to the gate without incident. As best they could, they jammed the cart against the others and dusted their hands while they took a breather.

Heikir glanced at the sorcerer, but she hadn't moved. She wouldn't until someone came from the citadel to relieve her. Violet tendrils latched to the outside of the gate like tentacles: Vormag sorcerers were attempting to thrust the entrance open. The lord commander had ordered wagons and barrels of oil and timbers to be stacked against the gate to lend it added weight, and if the vormag managed to force the gates, then the defenders could ignite the pile and set it burning for days.

Heikir noted the sorcerer's clean hair bound in braids, her clear skin, physique plump and in sharp contrast to the emaciated appearance of the archers and the common soldiers.

A hand squeezed his shoulder. Bersi.

"Don't think about it," the man said. "They're protecting us."

"We're all dying."

"Maybe the jukari will give up."

Heikir laughed. "Would you? We're on our last legs. Suffer until we're dead, is that our lot?"

"Would you rather die fighting? I thought you were a farmer, not a warrior."

"I'm just a normal man. But I know injustice when I see it. I know when we're being used."

"Forget it, and don't let them catch you spreading dissent."

"Or what?"

"Maybe you'll follow Ossur."

Ossur had been an archer in a squad stationed on the next tower over. He'd been a big, belligerent lad, and too quick to mouth off. He'd spread rumors about the nobles and sorcerers surviving off the dead soldiers, and one night he'd disappeared. Vanished as if he'd never existed.

A notice was posted that he'd deserted, but where to? There was nowhere to go.

In Heikir's mind, Ossur's disappearance had solidified the rumors into more than gossip. Hoarding provisions was one thing, but fallen soldiers—their comrades—supplementing the nobles' meals?

Heikir felt his gorge rise at the very thought and swallowed sour spit. Now, no one spoke of the possibility except in hushed whispers in the dead of night.

The fallen soldiers were supposedly interred in the catacombs beneath the citadel. The lord commander claimed it was the best that could be managed considering the jukari had overrun the cemetery outside the walls.

If he hadn't seen with his own eyes that the nobles and sorcerers weren't exactly starving, he'd have been inclined to believe the story. It rankled him, how those that did the fighting suffered deprivation while their *betters* lacked for nothing. His arms were thinner already, and his bow became harder to draw every day. Soon, he wouldn't be able to shoot arrows as far. Already, a couple in his squad were struggling, and for what? To fight and die and be devoured by monsters from either side?

Jukari or noble seemed the same to Heikir at that moment.

And while the creatures outside the walls persisted, there would be no respite.

No victory for the defenders.

"YOU GOING BACK to farming after this?" asked Bersi, who was repairing one of Heikir's boots with cobbling tools he'd brought along with him.

Heikir looked up from his bow, which he was rubbing with wax to protect it from moisture. "I don't know anything else. And it's a good life. Will be hard work for a while though. My wife, she—" his throat closed for a moment, and he coughed to clear it, "she can't do the hard work after she lost the baby. The physiker said she mightn't be able to have another…but we're trying."

"Trying is the best part! My wife should keep my business running. She's as good a cobbler as me. Ouch!" He sucked on his thumb, which he'd pricked on a needle. With a wry smile, he continued, "Better, actually, but don't you tell anyone I said that! It'll be good to get back. To make something, rather than…this." He rose and handed Heikir his boot back.

"How much do I owe you?"

"A couple of cabbages and some carrots when we get discharged. A dozen eggs, too, if you don't mind."

Heikir laughed, but the thought of his farm overwhelmed him, and his mirth turned to tears. Bersi squeezed his shoulder as Heikir hid his shameful weeping behind a hand.

Ulrik shifted from his position by the tower doorway. He lay on a pile of rags he used as a bed when they weren't fighting or laboring. "I get to go back to being an apprentice bricklayer. It's boring work, but once I finish my apprenticeship, the pay's good. One day, I'll build my own house."

"Or maybe you can join the rat-catchers' guild," quipped Bersi. "You've learned a lot about the vermin here!"

Heikir smiled. "He still can't catch the fat ones."

"There ain't any!" Ulrik laughed.

After their laughter died away, none of them spoke, as if breaking the companionable silence would bring the horrible reality of their situation crashing back down. Ulrik stirred himself and brought a pan of rainwater around to top up their cups.

"Ancestors, Heikir!" blurted Ulrik. "You've got a red fletch in your quiver. You're supposed to hand the leftovers back."

"I know. I always do." Heikir checked his quiver to find Ulrik was correct. Among the standard arrows, whose quality was deteriorating as quickly as the defenders' strength, stood one with red feathers.

"Don't touch it! It might explode."

"Don't be stupid. They need a sorcerer to—"

"Then why are the crafting runes on the shaft glowing?"

Heikir leaped to his feet, the gleaming shaft cradled in his hands. He ran a few steps and then stopped. What should he do with it?

Laughter from the others made Heikir realize he'd been had.

"Right, I'm taking it back now."

"And get a whipping?" said Bersi. "Your back will be bloody, and then what'll happen? You think you can heal on the rations we get? You'll join the other corpses in the catacombs."

Heikir clenched his jaw and ground his teeth. "They ain't going to eat—"

"Shh! Fool."

HEIKIR WOKE TO the sound of Ulrik coughing, a coarse bark torn from his lungs and throat. Pale light filtered through the doorway, indicating dawn was already here. It seemed like Heikir had only just lain down.

Ulrik hacked into a rag, then stared at the cloth. "There's blood," he said dully.

"Shit," said Bersi.

"You'll be all right," Heiki said, with as much conviction as he could muster. He wouldn't be. A soldier they hadn't known had begun coughing two days ago and been taken into the citadel for treatment. So far, he hadn't returned.

"They ain't taking me," said Ulrik. "I won't go."

"You can still draw a bow," Heikir agreed. "We'll tell them that."

The captain's morning inspection would happen soon. If Ulrik coughed when she was doing her rounds…

They drank some water, and Bersi passed around chunks of cheese covered with a fuzzy layer of green mold.

"Eat up," he said, "that's the last of it."

Heikir looked at the furry chunk, and then gagged at the wet dirt taste as he chewed. A few mouthfuls of water and he felt better, but only just. Some swore the mold helped prevent sickness, but he wasn't so sure. He'd probably be dead before finding out.

Svea. He missed the sight of her brown hair, her touch, the way she dusted her hands of flour and smiled at him when making bread. He wished there was a way to get his wife a message. To let her know he was all right and not to worry. It wasn't the truth, but it might ease her pain until she found out he wasn't ever coming home.

A sharp pain erupted in Heikir's bowels, and he staggered from the tower clutching his sides. He barely made it to the jakes they'd set up in a nearby building, and almost tripped over his own feet when he dropped his trousers.

It was a good half an hourglass before he made it back to his squad. His innards burned like fire and his watery waste had made him retch.

"You all right?" asked Bersi when he returned.

"Never better," managed Heikir with a wan smile.

"Don't give in to despair, Heikir. We'll get through this. You'll see. You owe me them cabbages and carrots, remember. And don't forget the eggs. You're not getting out of it that easily."

He didn't reply, though was grateful for Bersi's words. He needed to get out of here. Wanted to go somewhere far away. Take his beloved Svea with him. Sell the farm and move. This fighting, the horror of it, had beaten him down. He'd do anything to end it.

It was said the immortal god-emperor had died a few months ago defeating a great evil, saving the empire he'd created. Perhaps that was why the jukari were here: they sensed weakness.

THE JUKARI ATTACKED again that night.

Heikir, Bersi, Ulrik and the remainder of their squad manned the walls, pressed up against the battlements and ducking under the fierce assault of black jukari shafts, which descended like sleeting rain.

During a lull in the fighting, Heikir went below with Ulrik to bring up bundles of arrows. They were on their second trip when Ulrik stopped at the top of the stair in full view of the jukari and broke into a fit of coughing. His eyes bulged, and he clutched at a wall to steady himself. A black shaft struck the ground beside him, sparks skittering from the impact, and the arrow ricocheted off over the wall and into the street below.

"Get down!" said Bersi.

Heikir dropped his bundles of arrows and dove for the protection of the battlements. Ulrik took a step, then doubled over as another cough racked his thin frame.

There was a sickening *thump* as a jukari shaft hammered into Ulrik's side and penetrated deep into his chest. He collapsed, blood leaking onto the stone.

Heikir stood to help him, but Bersi pulled him down just as another three shafts struck sparks from the stone around Ulrik's lifeless form.

"Archers ready!" came the command.

Heikir tore his eyes from Ulrik and looked toward his discarded bow beside Bersi. He picked the weapon up with trembling hands.

Ulrik dead.

Another of his friends gone.

Their squad had started with ten and was down to only five survivors.

Survivors. That was all they were. Not defenders. Not heroes.

When he was dead, no one would care or remember, except his sweet Svea.

The rest of the attack passed in a blur for Heikir.

Dimly, he remembered loosing arrow after arrow. Drinking stale water from a tin cup that was handed to him. More men and women dying around him from both jukari arrows and vormag sorcery, which snaked over the walls in glittering violet lines.

The jukari never seemed to thin until they melted away behind Truula, back from where they'd come. Many stood on the second wall's battlements, yellow eyes watching the defenders.

Heikir and Bersi sat there exhausted, fingers bleeding. Heikir noticed squads of soldiers marching up the stairs, evacuating the severely injured and ferrying the dead into the citadel.

Three of the lord commander's black-armored soldiers of the Steel Fist came for Ulrik, and Heikir stirred himself. He planted his feet wide, standing between the soldiers and the corpse.

"No! You'll not take him."

"Lord commander's orders. Try to stop us and you'll be whipped for insubordination."

Bersi grabbed Heikir by the arms. "Let them. I don't want to lose anyone else today. We've suffered enough."

Heikir's sudden burst of strength left as quickly as it had come. "Aye," he said wearily. "We've suffered enough."

When the corpse was gone, they descended the stairs and made their way along the inside of the wall to their tower. Heikir glanced at the northern gates.

The gap between them looked to have widened a finger's width. A young sorcerer sat in the usual position, but his mouth gaped, and he'd torn open the top buttons of his shirt, as if he were overheating and needed cool air on his skin. To his side lay a crafted amulet, misshapen and melted.

HEIKIR SAT BY his belongings and imagined he could still smell Svea's scent on his blanket. He held the sorcerer's red-fletched arrow in his hands, its runes glowing a soft yellow in the darkness.

"You'd better take that back soon. Best to do it now."

"I will, Bersi." All he needed to do was get this over with, and then he could rest.

He rose and grabbed his bow, leaving his quiver. The glowing runes on the sorcerers' arrow kept catching his eye as he walked through the darkness.

What was the point of all of this? It was madness. They were starving and being whittled away one by one.

Maybe the lord commander was hoping to hold out until one of the Mahruse Empire's armies arrived and their powerful warlocks turned the tide of battle.

No, no one was coming, that was obvious. The only wonder was the lord commander and his nobles and sorcerers hadn't yet found a way to slink away to safety.

Heikir trudged along shadowed streets away from his tower, toward the citadel. The street opened into a paved square, from which rose another tower. This one was unmanned but commanded a view of the northern gate from atop its high battlements. If the gate broke open, sorcerers would be stationed here to flay the creatures as they tried to get through, or so he imagined. He was no strategist, just a farmer.

He stopped then, a chill night breeze caressing his lank hair and sallow skin. The tower door was open.

His hands gripped his bow and the arrow until his fingers ached. Heikir had to slow his breathing and force himself to relax. Without a conscious decision, his feet found the doorway and began to ascend the stairway. His lungs and thighs burned by the time he reached the top.

Countless stars pierced the night sky, and he let them shine upon his upturned face as he breathed deeply of the cold air. Heikir turned to face the west and imagined he could float, out over the city, across the walls, and all the way to Svea.

He moved to the northern parapet. It was a good seventy yards to the ground and two hundred yards from here to the gates. But he was standing on a higher vantage, and really there was no difficulty to the shot.

Heikir nocked the sorcerous arrow and aimed. Drew a breath, released a little, held it, then loosed.

Glowing runes traced an arc against the night. Descended to strike a barrel of oil.

There was a flash of orange and a thunderous crack. Flames leapt up and swirled across the wagons piled against the gates. Shouts of alarm reached him. The sorcerer stationed there stood, limned in the flames' orange glow. He turned and pointed up at the tower.

Heikir watched the conflagration intensify as wood crackled and damp timber hissed and whistled. In no time, the gates were ablaze and the stone walls around them glowed red with heat.

He saw archers and soldiers already heading toward the citadel. It might be crowded, but they would at least stand a better chance if they worked together to repel the jukari and vormag or wait them out until help arrived. They'd have plenty of time until the blaze burned itself out and the jukari breached the wall.

Boots thumped up the stairs toward him. The lord commander's soldiers, presumably. And they wouldn't be merciful.

Heikir dropped his bow and stepped onto the parapet.

"I'm sorry, Svea," he said.

He looked up at the stars again and leaned forward.

Wind whipped at his now-baggy shirt and trousers.

Gray stone rushed to greet him.

DEAR MENELAUS

LAURA M. HUGHES

I DON'T WISH to waste any more time on you than I must, but there are some things that have to be said. Fear not—I shall try and use small words (and large letters). I sincerely hope you're able to pry your thoughts away from wine, wenches and war for long enough to read what I have to say.

Actually, it's about the latter—war—that I wish to speak. You and I both know that history is written by victors. The winners, the aggressors, the strong. Which means that the history of war—and of most things—is written by men. Men like you. You say it is an art. You lie. There is no art of war. Only war.

The *start* of war, now, that's something worth debating. For instance, you say I launched a thousand ships. I say: did I? Really? Apologies; not me, but my *face*. Quite the feat! As though I slathered myself with makeup and then trudged along the beach, slapping buttocks and calling encouragement to those fine, brave Greek captains of yours.

But *surely* this cannot be true, because you—and others like you—have always insisted that war is a *man's* game.

But you see, that possessiveness is also your downfall, at least where logic is concerned. For if women are not allowed to be players—only pieces—how then can we be held accountable for the result? For the consequences of the ultimate 'man's game'?

Therein lies part of the problem. That word: *game*. You look at your kingdom and see naught but pawns and territories, imagined slights and dreamed-of victories. You seek pieces, but never peace. You make the rules and you set the board and you wait. Because with men like you in seats of power, there is no such thing as peace. Only waiting.

Yes, dear husband, I know all about the oath you signed. You and the other kings. In your eagerness to preen, and maim, and kill, you signed the Oath of Tyndareus—a brotherly bond with a pretext flimsier than the papyrus on which you wrote it. (And named after your fellow king—oh, how that must have grated at your ego!)

Swearing to find—and revenge—insult where none is intended, the lot of you displayed an inflated sense of self-worth and an ego that would make Narcissus blush. You men—and your insistence that war is the heart's blood of humanity - would plot Apollo's course with yourselves at the centre, and without regard for the chaos and ruin the rest of the world would suffer in consequence.

Is it any wonder I fled across the ocean with the only man in the Aegean who thinks differently? The only man who cries my name with more passion than he does Ares'?

Though I admire her staying power, I have not Penelope's patience, and for good reason. Monogamy is all well and good if you've had the fortune to choose your own spouse. When you've been bartered for, though—like livestock at the market—you'll soon learn that fidelity is overrated, and that marriage—much like war—is no more or less than the proverbial desire for more cattle.

Life is choice. We are the decisions we make. Your soldiers fight and die because you teach them that that is their only path to glory. As though spilling blood beneath Ares' uncaring eye is somehow more honorable than hunting the boar that feeds your family, or sowing the crop that feeds your village.

'For Ares!', you cry as you embark on your gleeful slaughter. 'For glory!', you shout. 'For Greece!' Perhaps you should stop calling others to war, and instead listen to the cries of those left behind.

I have never gone to war. Of course I haven't (it's a man's game, remember? I'm not allowed to play). I have read about war, and I have heard of war, but I have never done it. Still, I can well imagine that sensation of victory, the visceral thrill of success, even if I cannot claim to understand it. Why then must those of you who seek it cloud your intent and invent false purpose? Why not call it what it is?

You say glory, necessity, pride; I say barbarity, greed, arrogance. War is a search for glory, for that particular sense of joy and satisfaction that comes from staking one's life on the outcome of a gamble. The search for a cheap thrill, with a cost too dear for Midas, and on a pretext that more or less amounts to 'My neighbour has a thing. I want it'.

Helen of Troy. Helen of Sparta. Why can't any of you just say 'Helen'?

No cattle we, the women of Sparta. Not the cowering prey, but the watching hunter. Not the way of Thetis, but of Artemis. We bear arms as well as children and stand fearless toe to toe 'gainst mighty Ajax or brave Achilles.

And yet, for me, the path of Demeter, of Hera. For why kill and die for a stranger when you can live and love for a person?

I can almost see you frowning, husband. Still you wonder why any woman would choose a short but happy life over a long and miserable one. That failure—nay, refusal—to understand speaks to a deficiency in your character, not mine, and 'tis pointless for me to speak any more about it. Suffice to say that it is small wonder to me that joy and passion should win victorious over the domestic strictures set down by a council of walking phalluses such as yourself.

Calm yourself, husband. You think I am saying that men are *entirely* to blame? No. Athena, Aphrodite and the rest are just as guilty in their own ways. But did we compel those brave, foolish souls to embark across a sea of blood? I think not. That, dear husband, is on you, and others like you.

I imagine you're well into your cups by now, so I'll keep the rest short. Fear not, I'm almost done.

While Athena might scorn and Ares may scoff, I say that war—and glory, and honour—is not about whether you fall in a blaze of glory, or shrivel up and die of old age. Nor is it about whether you get to drive a chariot between adoring crowds, or just rot by the roadside. Really, it's about where you stand in line for the Styx—front, or back?

I doubt I'm the only one in no rush to jump the queue to Hades; to meet the lord on his throne of bones, with his cloak of souls and crown of skulls. But by all means, continue to waste the lives of those loyal to you. Continue to fill the underworld—and the ferryman's pockets—and don't even bother trying to wash away the blood of thousands that already stains your hands. Meanwhile, I'll be over here, growing old in comfort, warmed by my home's hearth and my lover's gentle arms.

So carry on, dear. And when the ships' shadows creep over the horizon; when the chariots thunder across the sand, and fire rains down from the sky, ask yourself: which would be the better way to die?

WARBORN

C.T. PHIPPS

I AWOKE INSIDE the summoning circle. The moons were high in the sky, and the stars shimmered even as the air was cold and unforgiving. I was in the middle of a cornfield where a larger circle had been cleared away to create the demonic sigil in secret. I had never been summoned before, at least before my death, so I was a trifle disorientated. I mean, I'd barely completed my transformation into a war demon.

It took a moment for me to even register the pretty blonde-haired woman wearing a simple black and white Purifier's dress with an apron and a long loose-fitting coif. She looked to be about nineteen, and I found myself reminded of my first wife. I'd found her with our children with another man after I'd returned from a five-year-campaign. She'd told me how I'd abandoned her, how she hated me, and how I had no place in my home or in the lives of our offspring. I'd taken it...poorly.

Do not judge this woman by she whose murder damned you, I thought. *Regrets didn't save you from the Seven Circles.*

Looking her up and down, I noticed she held the decapitated form of a chicken in her hand and that the circle was made of blood.

"Oh, that's just offensive," I said, frowning.

"What?" the woman said, blinking.

"Summoned *with a chicken,*" I said, chuckling. "Oh, the men in the Iron Garrison will laugh about this tonight."

"Iron Garrison?" the woman asked.

"Where the damned soldiers who fight forever are garrisoned," I told her. "The Northmen think of it as their paradise. I think of it as simply continuing life as I did it before."

"I do not understand," the woman said, a little too innocent to be believed. "What do you—"

"It doesn't matter," I said, dryly. "So, what do you want for your soul?"

"What?" the woman said again.

I rolled my eyes. "This conversation is on the verge of becoming very dull. You have created a Daemon's Circle in the middle of a corn field and made a blood offering, pitiful as that may be. I'm assuming you're not doing so just to see if it would work, Goodwoman—"

The woman looked behind her, clearly not having expected it to work. "Laura."

"Goodwoman Laura," I said. "There are three kinds of payment you can offer in a demon contract. Your soul, blood, or—"

Goodwoman Laura then started undressing, at first with reluctance, then with a bit of excitement even as she looked me over. Before long, the Purifier was nude before me. It was not an unpleasant sight, even though I had my pick of the women of the World Below as the Hell of War was next to the Hell of Lust. The Archons in Heaven hated the body and, between the two sins, I was surprised anyone over the age of twelve went to the Four Paradises.

"Ah," I said. "Well, I suppose that will do. What do you want?"

Goodwoman Laura smiled, and it was a somewhat devilish look. I'd seen the same one on countless women across the empire. Life was not particularly kind to daughters, housewives, and women in general among the peasant class. The discovery you had the attention of a demon (a process that hammered out the flaws of Earthly ugliness) made the sale of oneself an all-too-easy transaction. It made me wonder if the witch-hunters would do better to hang and burn less witches and simply find them better husbands.

"I want you to kill my parents," Goodwoman Laura said.

I burst out laughing.

Goodwoman Laura lost her smile. "This is not funny."

"It is, actually," I said, shaking my head with amusement. "I'm sorry, Laura, but you really don't need me for this. I've killed thousands, sacked cities, and tortured my fair share of nobles who thought they were invincible—and that was before I died. All you need for this is some mushrooms or maybe a knife while they sleep."

Goodwoman Laura stared at me. "They're Warborn."

I lost all mirth. "Ah, yes, well, that is a different matter."

"I'll tell you everything I know," Goodwoman Laura said. "They're—"

I shook my head. "Payment first."

ONE MIGHT THINK me callous for taking advantage of a young woman who was clearly driven by dread, and you would be right. However, I have a defense: I'm a demon. The Archons saw fit to condemn me for the life I'd led, and when I prayed for forgiveness, they denied me a chance at atonement. I would never see my children again or be able to do anything but evil, so I did what evil was enjoyable.

Laura, at least, did not seem to mind and squealed underneath my care. I did not feed on her life-force, much, but made a point of establishing a witch's bond between us. She believed she could simply pray away the use of black magic, and I was amused at her naiveté. Even so, I decided I would help her. Warborn were a threat us all.

Even demons.

"It happened when my father and mother were scavenging after the village was sacked," Laura said, lying naked against my body in the middle of the summoning circle. "The empress' army rolled on through and—"

"You don't need to explain more," I said, able to guess the story. War never changed. Whether it was the enemy or your side, armies often went hungry in the Telllarus Kingdoms. If there were villages nearby, they invariably didn't stay hungry for long. It was human nature to put yourself and your mates first over some random peasants.

"I want to." Laura blinked, then moved forward with her story. "They found Priest Hardwin's home held many treasures. They were things from his days when he worked as a state inquisitor. He had many books of magic and objects taken from the witches he killed. Things he'd hidden and my parents hoped to sell."

"Of course. That would explain why you have a book for summoning demons."

Laura looked away. "My mom could read a little. One of the spells in one of the books talked about summoning beings like you—"

"Warborn are not like me," I corrected. "Not in the slightest."

Laura looked down. "No."

Laura paused. "Whenever our neighbors' fortunes weakened, ours increased. I live in a two-story house and my parents own all of the farms for the next ten miles. I did not question it when it was good."

"And people started killing each other," I said simply.

Laura nodded. "My father was made chief of the rebuilt village and learned to talk to the others. He assembled an army from the surrounding villages and had no trouble starting to loot them. It turned into a full-fledged revolt."

"For the purposes of making your father a petty king," I said. "That's how it works. Warborn are the remains of demons slain by the Archdemon of War if they cannot master their hunger. The Warborn are consigned to the pits as their need for slaughter would otherwise destroy the world. Then there would be no war at all. Their ghosts can be summoned by the blackest of magic. They offer much more, seemingly for much less, until their appetites swell out of control. Unlike proper demons, such as myself, who keep a more measured feeding."

"I see," Laura said, clearly not buying any of it.

"What did they charge?" I asked, deciding to illustrate the differences between us.

"My baby brother," Laura said. "They told me he died in the night."

I wished such an act surprised me, but it was fairly typical for wannabe sorcerers and witches. "Let me guess, your father's rebellion had a lot of success in the beginning but gradually became more violent until the surrounding countryside turned against it and was annihilated. Perhaps with the help of the Grand Temple since, for all their hypocrisy, they know the stench of demons when it appears before them."

"Yes."

"And you?"

"I hid," Laura said, sighing. "I hid far away until the fighting was over. Nothing is left where I grew up. Nothing but the monsters."

"No," I said, not quite believing her explanation. It was a little too pat. "They can't be killed by mortal means, and the Grand Temple is not what it once was. They'll dither for decades over whether it's moral to summon an Archon to cleanse this place and just quarantine it until they hope the demon leaves on its own. Mortal prayers have no power over Warborn."

"Can you banish these evil spirits from them?" Laura asked.

"No," I said honestly. "Death is the only release."

Laura lowered her head. "I understand."

"Show me where they're staying," I said, wondering if I actually had a chance in, well, hell, of defeating them.

THE WARBORN HADN'T chosen to hide their presence and were still living in the former domicile. Goodwoman Laura's home was indeed quite luxurious for a Purifier's, or at least had been before a supernatural rot had caused the place to become a twisted shell of its former self. The two-story manor house overlooked a courtyard with a marble fountain and had a carriage house with two barracks for farm workers.

It must have been beautiful.

Once.

Whereas most places tainted by the damned were cold, dead, and dark, the decaying manor was covered in ivy and fungus. Strange lights circled around it in the form of will-o-wisps, the creatures fleeing from my presence as if I was a hungry beast. Finally, there was an unnatural heat to the air so that, even in the middle of autumn, it felt like a sweltering summer day. Laura had, wisely, chosen to stay away from this place.

Using magic to cover myself in black demon leather armor with a silky cloak and hood, I drew forth my glowing daemonsteel sword, the one that gave my family its name. I raised it into the air and spoke with a resounding bellow. "Twicedead, I compel you to come forth and face me. I have been summoned by one of the mortals of this world to send you back to our god."

There were formalities to be observed when dealing with fellow demons, even scum like the Warborn.

Two voices, low and soothing, but *wrong*, spoke from the house. "Eric Hellsword, we work the will of our master. Take the whore born from our hosts' flesh and be gone."

"No," I said. They knew my name, that wasn't good. It meant their power had grown to the point they could perceive the shape of my true name. It would allow them to strike at me harder than most demons.

"For what purpose do you stop us?" One of the Warborn, a female, cackled.

"I don't like you," I said, shrugging. "That is my law, doing whatever I wish because I will it."

"So be it," the Warborn said together.

The rotting bodies of what I presumed to be Laura's parents shambled out of the front door. They had fungus growing across half of their bodies even as hideous insect-like wings burst out of their backs while tiny legs and tentacles grew out of their chests. Neither wore clothes, and their eyes had rotted out, replaced instead with glowing embers.

"You can't beat me," I said, wondering why they'd even try. "Go back to your master and leave these poor mortals alone."

My sense of hypocrisy grew even more. After all, they were preying on these people no differently than I was their host's daughter.

The Warborn continued speaking as one. "Hundreds of souls exist in us, spared from Hell by becoming our fodder. They will give us the power to destroy you. You are not the Archdemon of Hell but an up-jumped ghost with some of his trinkets."

I shrugged. "You have me there. At least I'm not making pretenses of mercy when I'm a shitstain feasting on souls."

The two bodies snapped together as the manor house tore itself from its foundation, then smashed together into a twenty-foot-tall human-sized form that absorbed the pair into its *chest*. I blinked, watching the process as I realized the fungus was a medium for them to animate it. Hundreds of souls, probably most of the now-damned army they'd recruited, wailed from its interior.

"PREPARE FOR PERDITIO—" The merged Warborn didn't have a chance to finish its speech before I slammed my sword into the ground and started draining away souls from its body. I was a demon, too, after all, and what was stolen by one could be stolen by another.

"No!" The merged Warborn hissed, charging forward.

I took advantage of my smaller size to grab my blade from the ground, duck between its legs, and make a running jump onto the creature's back. Jamming my blade into its spine, I began to feast on the spirits within. The spirits I absorbed cried out in terror even as I could sense very little of their original selves remained, only mindlessly obedient drones for the merged Warborn. I drew on their power, and then blasted the merged Warborn with spells of death and living darkness. It threw me from its back, but it was already at less than half its power.

While I was much stronger.

"Thief, they worship us!" the merged Warborn cried out.

"And they fear me," I said, chuckling. "This is war, and whoever is strongest, smartest, and luckiest gets the spoils."

The battle ended in a decidedly anticlimactic manner. The Warborn took a few steps back and crumbled into a pile of brick, wood, fungus, and slime. I called forth their spirits into my sword and bound them for return to the pit.

While disappointing as a battle, it was a profitable one. A few hundred souls were mere pocket change in the Great Celestial War, but these could be easily molded into demons ready to serve my cause. That was when I was struck by a blast of glowing white light from behind.

I GROANED AS I got up, finding myself once more in a binding circle. Goodwoman Laura was standing outside of the circle, holding a finely crafted staff with a crystal on top. A young man, maybe twenty, lie just outside the circle. His throat had been slit, and his blood currently powered what was surrounding me.

I smirked. "A compatriot or victim?"

Laura snorted. "Just a man from the village who believed I could save it."

"That staff is a mark of an inquisitor," I said, chuckling. "Not the kind to be held by a nineteen-year-old farmer's daughter."

"I have a youthful face," Laura said, smiling. "I was sent by the empress to deal with this matter when her soldiers failed."

"So, they weren't your parents?" I asked.

"They were," Laura said, sighing. "I just left out the part where I was Inquisitor Hardwin's apprentice. The inquisitor general was less than pleased to find one of his agents was the daughter of petty demonologists, especially when she was working on similar areas of study, so he sent me to clean up their mess."

I stood up. "And you thought the best method was to summon a demon?"

"As you say, the Grand Temple is hesitant about summoning Archons these days," Laura said. "Perhaps because they know they would judge their corruption. Instead, I thought it best to fight evil with evil."

"I suppose this is the best place to test such things," I said, looking back. "Isolated, superstitious, and with a host of corpses to justify whatever atrocities worked here."

"Indeed," Laura said.

"What about the payment?" I asked, cheekily. She could have summoned me without it and bound me with a blood sacrifice instead.

"I always wanted to fuck a demon." Laura smirked. "I have orders to bind you and bring you to the general. I was already working on carrying forth Inquisitor Hardin's work when I was summoned before him. This should prove demonology is a discipline which can be used for good."

I sighed. Such a brilliant mind as hers was wasted in the Inquisition. "You're not the first to think so."

"My masters have said as much. I think otherwise. Soon, the empress and inquisitor general will have an army of your kind to fight for them. To bring order to the world and unite the Telllarus kingdoms."

I sighed. "I'm afraid you have a new master now."

Laura was about to rebut when I reached into her and used the mark I placed on her, plus the fact my essence was inside her, to stop her heart. The binding circle died with her before I walked over to her corpse and placed my hand over her breast.

"Arise," I said. "I have need of an agent like you. I will claim your soul either way, but you can serve me as a creature of evil or be one of the many foot soldiers used as cannon fodder eternally on the Fields of Despair. I am sorry to say that will be the last choice you will have for a long time. Centuries at least."

Laura's eyes opened, now glowing. Her teeth like knives. A Bruxa. She'd made her choice.

"Where now?" Laura spoke, her voice empty of all emotion. It would be years until the demon inside her became able to approximate who she was.

"Deliver the late Goodwoman Laura's experiments to the Inquisition," I said. "It's good to spread such knowledge. Then we'll go wherever wars are fought. We do not need to spread it but merely feed."

"Yes, master."

THE GREATEST BATTLE

JOHN GWYNNE

The Year 7 of the Age of Lore, Hunter's Moon

CORBAN CRAWLED THROUGH the undergrowth, the earthy scent of moss and mulch thick around him as he worked his way between trees wide as a tower. By the angle of sunlight filtering through the tree-top canopy above, it was around high-sun, but in Forn Forest, it was only ever varying degrees of twilight and shadow. Insects and worms scraped and slithered over his hands, up the sleeves of his tunic. Behind him, he heard the rustle and squelch of his companions following through the saturated ground, a whispered curse from one of them as they snagged on a branch of thorns. He carried on, elbows and knees levering him through the forest litter, thick-growing fern and vine.

Slowly, it dawned on him that something had changed, was different.

He paused, tried to control the sound of his breathing, which seemed deafening to him. Figures caught up with him, one either side.

'Why is there always the unpleasant part before a fight,' Farrell muttered. 'Running for days, or sitting in the snow, shivering, or crawling through this muck—'

'Or listening to Farrell whining,' Dath said from the other side of Corban.

'You're not doing this with a war-hammer strapped across your back.' Farrell grunted.

'No one forced you to choose a weapon that is roughly the weight of a full-grown draig,' Dath whispered back.

'Quiet.' Corban hissed. 'Can you hear anything?'

Dath and Farrell were silent for long moments.

'No,' they both whispered.

'Exactly,' Corban said. That was what had changed. None of the usual sounds of the forest, insects whirring or chirping, birds singing. Things hunting and being hunted, dying. Nothing. Silence hung in the air, un-natural and malignant.

'We are close,' Corban said. He drew in a deep breath, calming his nerves, cinched tighter the buckles that strapped his round shield across his back and set off again, squirming and crawling his way through the perpetual twilight of Forn Forest.

The trees thinned for a while, giving way to thorn-thick shrubs that made the task of crawling through the undergrowth even harder. Then a tree appeared before Corban, roots breaking through the ground, thicker than Farrell's chest, the trunk of the tree wide as a barn.

'We're here,' Corban whispered, crawling to the tree and rising onto his knees, shifting his weight and sitting with his back to the gnarled oak. 'This is where Craf said to meet him.'

Dath and Farrell caught up with Corban, Dath swearing as his unstrung bow got tangled in another snare of vine.

'Now, we wait,' Corban told his two friends.

They checked their weapons, loosened blades in scabbards, then Farrell dug inside a pouch on his belt, producing a slab of cheese.

'Anyone?' he said, offering the cheese.

'How can you eat at a time like this?' Dath said, lips curling disdainfully.

'Don't like fighting on an empty stomach.' Farrell shrugged as he took a knife from his belt and carved a chunk.

'Seems you don't like doing anything on an empty stomach,' Dath said, pointedly looking at Farrell's belly, which was beginning to hang over his belt.

Farrell opened his mouth for a sharp retort, then seemed to think about it and shrugged again. 'Fair point,' he said.

Movement drew Corban's eye, a shadow at the edge of his vision, shifting in the murk of the forest. Corban stared, saw it solidify and take shape.

Storm.

'I was wondering where she was,' Dath said as a huge wolven emerged from the gloom, tall and broad, silvery fur streaked with black and grey and latticed with old scars. She padded over to them, silent as mist, and loomed over Corban, bent her head and gave his face a lick. Corban stroked her cheek, tugged on one of the prodigious canines that protruded a hand span from her jaws.

'Good to see you, girl,' he said.

'Always feel better with her around,' Dath sighed.

'She's never far,' Corban said, 'whether you can see her or no.'

Storm cocked her head, ears twitching.

A sound, somewhere above.

'What's that?' Corban asked.

His friends listened.

The forest was still eerily silent, but there was a sound, high above, a rustling in the branches that suggested it was more than just the wind.

'Dath's knees knocking,' Farrell said, chuckling at his own joke.

'All feel fear, the hero and the coward,' Dath intoned.

'Aye, but it's what we do about it that matters,' Farrell finished.

Corban felt the familiar stab of grief and loss at those words. They had been recited so often through the years that they had become a mantra to him, but he never forgot who had said them to him, first of all.

Gar, my friend. I miss you still. Time heals, Cywen told me, but when it comes to you, it hasn't.

Somehow, that sense of loss felt greater today, its edge sharper.

Perhaps it is because Coralen is not with me. How I miss her, too, when we have spent so many years at each other's side.

The sound above grew louder.

A dark smudge shifted amidst the shadowed branches, and then a bird was spiralling down to them. A crow, feather's black as charcoal, scruffy and poking in all directions. It landed on Storm's back, and she growled, low and menacing.

'*Sorry*,' the bird squawked and hopped off to land on Farrell's knee.

'Ouch,' Farrell muttered, but he didn't shoo the bird off. Instead, he cut another slab of cheese and offered it to the old crow.

'Hello, Craf,' Dath said, and the bird bobbed his head.

Corban held back his impatience, his wanting to know. He knew Craf too well where food was concerned.

Craf took the cheese and gulped it down. '*Thank you*,' he cawed.

'Welcome.' Farrell grunted.

'Well?' Corban said.

'*Kadoshim there*,' the bird croaked, shaking and ruffling his feathers. '*Craf scared.*'

'You're a brave bird,' Corban soothed, stroked Craf's chest. 'How many?'

'*Craf see seven. Maybe more. And men.*'

'How many men?' Farrell asked.

'*Lots*,' Craf croaked.

They all knew that Craf couldn't count past twenty, so it could mean a score, it could mean a hundred.

Not incredibly helpful.

'Show us,' Corban said.

With a grumble, Craf hopped off Farrell's knee and beat his wings, flapping away and landing on a branch in the next tree. Corban, Dath, and Farrell crawled after him, Storm slinking into the shadows, becoming a silvery blur.

They followed Craf like that for a while, as he flew from branch to branch, waiting for them to catch up through the undergrowth. Then Craf landed on a rotted tree-stump atop a ridge. When they reached him, Craf was pulling a slug the size of Corban's thumb from the stump and slurping it down.

Storm came and lay beside Corban.

'*There*,' Craf said, pointing with his beak.

They were situated upon the top of a ridge, a steep incline dropping thirty or forty paces down to a gully, levelling out into a shadow-filled glade. At its far edge, a sheer cliff of granite reared, higher than the ridge Corban and his companions lie upon. There was a deeper shadow of a cave at the cliff's base.

In the glade, figures moved, men and women, dressed in leather and fur, short-swords and bucklers strapped to their belts, the glint of warrior-rings in beards and braids.

'Vin Thalun.' Dath hissed. 'Thought we'd seen the last of them.'

'Like flies to dung.' Farrell growled.

Corban counted eighteen.

A fire-pit burned in the glade, pots bubbling over it, fat dripping from a carcass turning on a spit, a willow-screen about it to shield the flames from prying eyes.

Something passed between the warriors in the glade, all turning to look at the cave in the cliff face.

Figures emerged, taller than those spread around the glade. There were seven of them, their faces all sharp angles and piercing eyes, clothed in chainmail and leather, swords at their hips, some with spears in their fists. They moved with effortless grace, a shifting of movement upon their backs, leathery wings furled and looking like high-arched cloaks. More Vin Thalun followed behind them, at least a dozen.

'Kadoshim,' Corban said, and he felt a silent growl vibrating deep in the cavity of Storm's chest.

'Cheeky bastards,' Farrell snarled, 'to build a den so close to Dun Seren.'

'It's clever,' Corban said. 'Who would think to look so close to our doorstep when we have been spreading our hunt ever wider.'

'They won't feel so clever when my hammer starts crushing their skulls,' Farrell said, slipping the huge weapon from his back.

'We ready?' Corban asked as he unstrapped a gauntlet from his belt, curved knives like talons stitched into the hardened leather at the knuckles. He strapped it to his left hand, loosened his sword in its scabbard.

Dath was stringing his bow, stabbing arrows from his quiver into the soft turf. 'Ready as I'll ever be,' he said. He rolled his shoulders, adjusting the curved sword strapped across his back.

'Craf, go find Sig and Veradis, tell them to follow the noise. And not to linger.'

'*Be careful,*' Craf muttered, and with a whisper of wings, he was gone.

'Guards?' Corban said to Dath. He had the best eyes amongst them and a talent for finding and silencing unwanted eyes.

'One there,' Dath whispered, pointing. A shadow halfway down the slope to the gully, 'and there,' further away, on the far side of the glade amidst the trees.

'Storm,' Corban whispered, pointing to the guard furthest away. The wolven stood and loped into the gloom.

'Wait for my signal,' Corban said.

'I'll come with you,' Farrell said.

Corban raised an eyebrow. 'Might as well have brought Sig and her bear if you come down that slope with me now,' Corban said. 'You weren't built for stealth.'

'I'm your shieldman,' Farrell protested.

'Aye, and so's Dath. You'll both be at my side when it counts. I know that.' Corban winked at his friends, and then slipped over the ridge.

'Truth and Courage,' he heard them whisper after him.

He picked his way down the slope, edging around the guard, taking his time with each footstep, each shift of weight.

Ten paces from the guard, a man, streaks of grey in his warrior-braid and beard, a bearskin cloak pulled tight about him. A tall spear was held loosely in one hand, leaning propped against his shoulder. Corban could smell sweat and grease.

He waited, breathing slow and silent. The emergence of the Kadoshim down in the glade had drawn the warrior's attention. Another three paces closer.

A twig snapped.

The warrior twisted, instantly alert, his spear-point lowering, levelled at the darkness.

A *whirring* sound, an impact, and an arrow-head sprouted through the guard's throat, blood jetting.

He opened his mouth to scream, only a gurgling choke came out.

Corban covered the last few paces in a single bound, grabbed the wavering spear-shaft with his right hand, tugged the warrior towards him, rammed his wolven-clawed gauntlet into the man's lower jaw, his momentum driving the claws deep, felt them grate on skull.

A flurry of muscular spasms, a last gurgle, and the warrior was sinking, already dead, Corban lowering him gently into thick foliage. Crouching, breath rapid, heart pounding. He pulled on his claws, withdrawing them slowly. Took a moment, then peered over the bushes to look down into the glade.

One of the Kadoshim was speaking, black hair pulled tight and tied at his nape, the warriors in the glade all focused upon him.

No one heard.

A sound away to their left, a rustle and snapping, a grunt. The Kadoshim talking paused, head cocking like some predatory bird, all in the glade suddenly alert.

The Kadoshim gestured, one of his companions unfurling their wings and taking to the air with slow, powerful beats. It flew towards the sound, a handful of warriors following, iron glinting as weapons were drawn.

'Truth and Courage,' Corban whispered to himself, stood, setting his feet, hefted his stolen spear for half a heartbeat, judging the weight and balancing point, then it was flying, struck the Kadoshim in the air, a meaty *thunk* as the spear-tip burst through chainmail, the crack of bone as ribs shattered, and pierced deep into flesh.

The Kadoshim shrieked, wings flapping frantically as it lurched in the air, half-falling to a heap on the ground.

A horrified silence as warriors spun around, staring in all directions into the darkness.

One stumbled backwards and fell, an arrow in her belly.

The Kadoshim who had been speaking saw Corban halfway down the ridge, yelled a warning, pointing even as it drew its sword, wings snapping open. Other Kadoshim leaped into the air, wings beating, hovering as they searched for enemies. None thought one lone man would be fool enough to attack them.

Not one man. Three, and a wolven.

Corban put one fist around his hand-and-a-half sword, red-leather hilt sweat-stained, a familiar, perfect fit to his fist, the other hand gripping the scabbard, and he drew, held his blade two handed, in a high guard.

Stooping Falcon, he heard Gar's voice in his head.

'TRUTH AND COURAGE,' Corban yelled and launched himself down the slope. Warriors moved towards him, though some were hesitant, eyes scanning the darkness and ridge behind him. Another whirring noise, like a host of angry hornets, and another Kadoshim was spiralling from the air, crunching to the ground.

A crashing from above, sounding like a bull careening down the ridge, and Farrell appeared, his great war-hammer in his fists, and he bellowed Corban's battle-cry, surging down the slope like an avalanche.

Corban hit the first row of warriors, sword arcing diagonally down, slicing through a face and chest, let the momentum drag him down, turning him around, felt a trio of blows *thud* into the shield across his back, and then he was amongst them, switching to a one-handed grip on his sword, knees bent, still spinning, slicing in a straight arc, through leather and flesh, opening a belly, his other hand slashing across a face, cleaving through an eyeball, cartilage and jaw. Intestines spilled from the opened belly, their owner stumbling, a high-pitched screeching as he tripped in his own entrails, the other warrior falling away, grasping at the red ruin that had been his face.

Keep moving, Corban told himself, knowing that to stand still and face these veteran warriors would be to die.

Cannot give them time. Speed, chaos, fear were his allies. He shouldered forwards, levered his shield-rim into a face, mashed lips, teeth flying as he ducked and spun away, onwards, through the heaving mass of warriors as they tried to marshal themselves.

An impact, screams, the sound of bones breaking, one man crashing to the ground, another spinning through the air, and Farrell was in the glade, bellowing, war-hammer swinging around his head.

Another warrior falling, an arrow piercing her eye.

Corban ploughed on, disoriented, moving he hoped towards the Kadoshim. He caught a stabbing sword between his wolven-claws, twisted, stabbed with his own sword into an open mouth, severed spine, ripped his blade free in a spray of teeth and blood, kicked the dying man away.

A shadow above him, instinctively he ducked, air whistling as a sword slashed where his head had been. He twisted on his feet, knew the Kadoshim was above, angling to get behind him.

A blow to his leg, red-fire pain lancing along his thigh, and he stumbled, heard Farrell bellow his name as he dropped to one knee under a torrent of blows. Slashed at a knee with his claws, swung his sword in guard across his body, iron sparking, trusted his shield to protect his back.

A scream, a body collapsing in front of him, half his face pulped, space opening up. Farrell, standing over him, swinging his war-hammer in a looping circle.

Corban staggered to his feet, saw a circle of warriors about them, dead scattered about the glade, Kadoshim hovering in the air above them, snarling, spears and swords glinting.

Still too many.

Farrell shifted to Corban's side, the both of them turning, slowly, waiting.

'TRUTH AND COURAGE,' a battle-cry rang out, a figure leaping from the foliage, curved sword in hand, slashing at a warrior's back, slicing another across the throat as warriors turned, then Dath was with them, breathing heavily, sword dripping red.

'Thought you were to stay on the ridge, keep picking them off,' Farrell said in a grunt.

'I know. I got carried away,' Dath answered. 'Don't tell Kulla,' he added.

Their enemy closed around them, a score at least still standing, edging closer. A spear stabbed at Farrell, Corban swatting it away, another slicing at Dath, who swayed, chopped the spear-head from the shaft.

The circle about them tightened.

A snapping of undergrowth, a savage snarling, and something burst from the trees. Storm, all fur and muscle and bloodied teeth, crashed into the warriors moving on Corban, sent two of them hurtling through the air, stood over another, jaws clamping around a throat, a savage wrench and spray of blood, a scream cut short. Then she was padding to Corban's side, facing outwards, snarling as the enemy closed the gap in their circle.

'Is it you, Bright Star?' one of the Kadoshim said, voice sibilant. His eyes flittered from Storm to the arm-ring coiled around Corban's bicep, two wolven-heads at each end.

Corban answered with a savage grin.

'What a fool, to come with so few.' The Kadoshim grinned in return.

Above the Kadoshim, Corban saw something small and dark, circling.

'That's what your Calidus said,' Corban snarled, 'before I took his head.'

'Kill them,' the Kadoshim screamed, levelling his sword.

The enemy moved closer, cautiously, no mad rush from these veterans, all searching for an opening, sharp iron poised, tightening their circle. Five Kadoshim spiralled above them, ever closer.

A vibration in the ground, Corban feeling it through his boots, a rumbling in the forest, growing rapidly louder. Branches snapping, and then timber and foliage was exploding into the glade, and a monstrous form was exploding from the woods, a giant bear, jaws wide as it let out a roar that shook trees and rattled bones. A swipe of one of its paws eviscerated the warrior unfortunate enough to be closest.

Upon its back was sat a giantess, fair hair bound in a thick warrior-braid, tattoos spiralling up her muscled arms. She was clothed in chain-mail, a longsword gripped in her fists. She leaned in her saddle, swung her blade, sliced a wing from a Kadoshim, sending it screeching to the ground, where her bear stamped the screaming into abrupt silence.

A warrior emerged from behind the bear, serious faced with short-cropped hair, a round shield upon one arm with a white, four-pointed star painted upon it, a short sword in his fist. He strode forwards, nodded to Corban. Then more warriors swarmed from around either side of the bear, all with the same round shields and short swords. They came together with a concussive thunderclap as lines were formed and shields thudded together, forming two shieldwalls on the bear's flanks.

The enemy scattered, running in all directions.

Storm leaped after them, a fox amongst chickens, dealing death with tooth and claw, Farrell and Dath smashing and cutting men down as they tried to escape.

Corban unclipped a folded net at his belt, weighted at each corner with lead balls, shook it out, swung it around his head and threw, the net snaring a Kadoshim, lead balls looping around it, tightening, constricting its wings. The Kadoshim plummeted to the ground, Corban striding forwards, a sharp thrust of his sword and it stopped struggling, blood, a widening pool staining the grass.

And then, as suddenly as that, it was all over.

The giantess rode her bear deeper into the glade, threw a leg over her saddle and slid to the ground, striding to Corban, the serious-faced warrior at her side.

'Well-met, Sig, Veradis.' Corban nodded to them.

'You could have come quicker,' Dath said as he joined them.

Craf flapped down from above, landing on the dead Kadoshim at Corban's feet.

'*Craf told Sig, faster, faster,*' the crow squawked, then pecked a strip of flesh from the dead Kadoshim's cheek.

Sig glowered at the crow. 'You take too many risks,' she rumbled at Corban, a frown on her broad face.

'All's well as ends well, as our friend Tahir is fond of saying,' Corban said, smiling at the two of them.

'Sig's right,' Veradis said. 'Cywen would have my head if anything happened to you.'

'It was the only way,' Corban said. 'They needed distracting and holding here while Sig and her bear smashed a way through the forest. Think they would have heard you coming, otherwise.'

'Huh.' Sig grunted begrudgingly, not looking entirely appeased.

'Agreed,' Veradis said, 'but why do you always have to go first. You are too important.'

'I'll not shirk from danger and ask another to take my place,' Corban said, returning Veradis' serious stare with his own.

'And that's why we love you so much,' Farrell said, wrapping a big arm around Corban and ruffling his hair.

'*Corban, Corban,*' came a cry from above, all of them looking up, even old Craf. A bird appeared above them, a white crow, spiralling down in a flurry of feathers.

'*Rab,*' Craf croaked, '*why you here?*'

The white crow alighted next to Craf, dipped its head to the old crow, ran his beak along Craf's black-feathered wing as if he were bowing.

'*Cywen sent Rab. Said, get Corban.*'

'Why, Rab?' Corban said, crouching down to look at the white-feathered crow.

'*Coralen needs Corban,*' Rab said. '*Cywen said hurry.*'

Corban's heart lurched in his chest.

'*Cywen said HURRY,*' Rab screeched, flapping his wings.

'Take Hammer,' Sig said, sweeping Corban up into her arms and striding over to her huge bear, then hoisting him into the saddle.

TREES THINNED AND then faded around Corban as the giant bear, Hammer, lumbered onto broad meadows that undulated between the forest and his home, Dun Seren. Storm loped alongside them, a bone-coloured blur, and Rab flew ahead, squawking encouragements for greater speed. Dawn had recently come, the world painted in pinks and amber hues, and then Corban saw the tower of Dun Seren in the distance, grey stone glistening in the rising sun.

'Well done, Hammer,' he said, patting her thick neck. They'd covered a three-day journey on horseback in a day and a half. 'Nearly there, now.'

As if understanding his words, or maybe it was just the pleasure of seeing home, Hammer seemed to increase her speed, which was already prodigious.

Meadows rolled by and, soon, Corban was passing half-built walls of stone, marking the new Rowan Field that was being built, an enormous training ground for the warriors of the Order of the Bright Star, men and women carrying stone calling out to him, waving. And then Hammer was climbing the gentle hill that Dun Seren stood upon, shambling through the arched-stone gate and into a huge courtyard.

Before the bear had properly stopped, Corban was leaping from her back and sprinting across the courtyard, up wide stone steps towards the open doors of the feast-hall. Storm kept pace with him, red tongue lolling.

A dark-haired woman stood at the top of the steps, petitely built, her belly heavy with child, four bairns of various sizes swarming around her legs.

Kulla, Dath's wife, with their ever-growing warband of children. She was also one of the most skilled sword-masters Corban had ever known.

'Where is she?' Corban gasped.

'The healer's tower,' Kulla said. 'You must hurry.'

Corban sped up.

'My Dath?' Kulla called behind him.

'He's fine, showed great courage, he's half-a-day behind me,' Corban called over his shoulder, then he was through the feast-hall, veering right, and climbing spiralling steps up a tower. His heart pounded like a drum in his head, breath a wheezing gasp, even though he'd run for days at a time before.

A scream echoed along a corridor, and he froze, felt his heart in his throat, fear, a coiled serpent slithering in his gut.

Storm whined beside him.

Another scream, high-pitched and lingering.

Corban sprinted down the corridor, hammered on a closed door.

A new sound, muffled crying.

Footsteps, the door opening. Cywen, his sister stood there, her frame blocking his view of the room, black hair tied back with its famous streak of white, dark tear stains on her cheek like tattoos marking where she had wept tears of blood on the day of Wrath.

'You're too late,' she said.

More crying, behind her. High-pitched.

Cywen stepped aside, revealing a bed, a woman laying upon it, Coralen, Corban's wife.

Her eyes were closed, her red hair dark with sweat, blankets upon her stained with blood.

My Cora.

Then a bundle on her chest squirmed, cried again.

Coralen's eyes flickered open.

'Why do you have to be late for everything,' Cywen said beside him, a grin splitting her face.

Corban stood there a moment, dumbfounded, speechless, then his legs were moving and he was at Coralen's side, kneeling, crying, kissing her, his tears wet on her cheeks, mingling with her own tears, Coralen's hand rising weakly to cup his cheek.

'Say hello to your daughter,' Coralen said, a tired smile and shining eyes as she lifted the bundle to him.

A pink face looked up at him, serious dark eyes, completely bald.

Storm licked a tiny foot poking from the blanket, and the baby wrinkled her nose and gurgled.

Corban took her gently, almost reverently, held her close to his chest, gazing down at his baby through tear filled eyes.

'Hello, my darling Brina,' he said.

THIS WAR OF OURS

TIMANDRA WHITECASTLE

THINGS I'VE LOST:

Daddy

my home

my favorite socks

my favorite red dress

my special pillow on which I never had nightmares

Auntie Neko

Uncle Loran

our home in the basement of the broken house

my tail

It was the leafless time in the forest, and Mother made me put her gray mittens on, which I immediately used to wipe my nose. She tutted, but didn't mention it, and pulled the woolly cap deeper into my face before her hands settled on my shoulders.

"Things are going to change fast, little Sparrow," she said. "It'll be spring soon. So, what do we have to do?"

"Look for its signs?" I sniffed.

"That's right." She squeezed my shoulders tightly. "But right now, in the winter forest, what do we need to be?"

"Silent?"

"Silent." She nodded grimly. "Were you silent?"

"I was silent," I started. "I was very silent! It was Bug. He made the noise."

I pointed a finger at the sling with which Mother carried my little brother on her back. His little kobold face peeked out, little piggy eyes nearly hooded by the too-large cap he wore—my old cap—and the rest of him bundled in cloth.

"Din't!" he insisted. "Sparra did."

"Did not!"

"Sparra spoked Bug."

"Poked Bug," Mother corrected wearily. "She poked you. Didn't you, Sparrow?"

"No." This was true. I had pinched his little porky leg, strapped tightly around Mother's waist. Pinching is not poking.

He could walk already. But she still carried him on her back because (she said) he couldn't keep up with our pace, and I wasn't allowed to go piggyback on her back because I was too big. And Barras couldn't carry me, either. "Unfair!"

She sighed.

Barras cleared his throat. "We need to get moving. The Wildcat's infantry must have secured the town already and sent for the Falconidae to drop their bombs."

"Peace, Barras. One more moment." Mother raised her hand, then turned back to me. "Give me your arm, Sparrow."

I pressed my lips tight together and tried not to sob. Sobbing made too much noise. Noise could betray our position. Noise could get us killed. Mother had said so a thousand times. I stretched out my arm, tears rolling down my cheek.

"It was Bug," I whispered as she pushed up the many layers of sleeves, exposing my scrawny brown skin to the cold. "Bug made the noise."

"Because you poked him." Her sharp talon's edge was chill against my flesh, making the tiny hairs on my arm rise. "In this war of ours," Mother said quietly, "we must learn how to be silent."

She looked into my eyes before drawing a straight line across my arm, parallel to the other three faint lines.

"We must be stealthy. We must be silent," she intoned as we watched the blood well up. Mother rubbed the salt into the cut with her thumb, and while I squirmed, biting down hard on my lip, I didn't make a noise.

"Good. It's done. You will remember. You will learn," she said, wagging her finger, then straightened with a grimace. Bug was getting heavy. *He should walk,* I thought. Mother hugged me tightly and left her embrace with a quick kiss on my forehead. A wet cold spot like a snowflake's kiss.

"Things will change soon, little Sparrow." Her voice broke, and I looked away. I pulled the sleeves back down over my stinging pain, cuffing my hot tears. Too many things had changed already, and I hated it and wished it would stop. Barras clapped his large hand on my shoulder.

"Come on, soldier. Let's go."

IN THE FOREST, Mother teaches me there was always war. War against the elements, war against hunger, war against winter itself, for the leafless time in the forest makes war on us all, she says. Regardless of kind.

And it makes us war against each other. There was always war, she whispers to Barras when she thinks I'm asleep, but now it has changed. Our wars had spectacle, they had ritual, they had art. Now, there is only mess.

"No." Barras growls. "It's only that the war has changed us. Else we could see that creatures claiming that war has an art must be held accountable for what happens in it."

She says nothing in response.

Mother and Barras have always been good friends. When Daddy was still alive, we'd stay at Uncle Barras and Aunt Melli's dacha by the lake on quiet summer evenings. The grown-ups would sit and talk about the last war, the war they fought together, while we children would play, weaving through the trees, sneaking up on one another, hiding and seeking until we fell exhausted into the laps of our mothers and slept. In peace.

When the bombs first hit our town, it was suddenly only Mother and me. She dragged me to the dacha, and we stayed there for a few nights, mourning, until Uncle Barras had stood on the doorstep one day. Alone. His left trouser leg hung in tatters. Empty.

"Town's crawling with spiders," he said, swaying on his crutch. "It's a siege."

"But where else can we go?" Mother asked him. "It's the only home we know."

"There's a place I know. If we lie low, scavenge for supplies, we might endure. They won't stay long. Nightly shelling gets expensive, and you know it."

Their voices angry whispers, the stink of alcohol underlining every harsh gesture. I was silent. I made no noise, and so they thought I slept.

But I couldn't. I couldn't close my eyes.

My special pillow was still in the house where Daddy died.

WE MET AUNT Neko and Uncle Loran later, when we were in our basement home. Loran was sick and Neko wounded, and they stumbled in on us by accident, looking for medicine, blundering on the ground level, tripping over the washing line Mother had hung there. It was the time when I still fitted in my favorite red dress. But not for much longer.

Uncle Loran used to be a star show flyer. I recognized his face from the posters that hung in the grocery store near our old home. Aunt Neko was his lady. They had a small space for themselves; a curtain partitioned off a corner in the basement. But Aunt Neko was always sad and angry. She couldn't stay silent. Maybe that's why she left.

Mother was pregnant with Bug by then. And when he was born, my red dress didn't fit me anymore. Mother made Bug one set of baby clothes from it.

Bug has never been silent.

Maybe that's why Uncle Loran left one night. Maybe he went after Aunt Neko. But maybe he died. I hope not, but he's gone anyway, even if he managed to survive. The town grew emptier by the day. And by night.

"That's good news for scouting," Mother said, the smile on her face too bright. She stretched out her hand, and I took it. She adjusted the baby sling around her and checked to see if Bug was still asleep.

"Don't take the kids out there," Barras said in a low voice from his chair. The sheen of a stray moonbeam alighted on his blackened revolver. "You should leave them here with me. That'd be safer." He paused, then tapped his gun. "I can protect them. I would protect them with my life."

Mother's smile wavered. "I know, Barras, but I can't." Her hand clutched mine, pulling me closer. "They're all I have left now."

Barras grunted, and as though that was a sign, we left.

At the threshold of the broken house, Mother raised her arms and flapped her wings, pulling the night's shadows around her shoulders like a well-worn cloak. Bug was wrapped in it, and I hated him for that. She waited patiently until I had roughly thrust my own arms into an overcoat of darkness, blending in with the surrounding gloom.

We stalked the town for supplies, always silent, always wary, picking through the leftover lives in the husks of houses. One time, we heard a creak in the floorboards from above. Mother quickly shoved a small stash of medicine we had found into her satchel, and we left through the shards of the window just as the long snout of a rifle peered into the kitchen we were leaving.

I had been silent. I had made no noise. I wanted her to take me in her arms and be proud of me. But her arms were always filled with Bug. She mouthed, "*Well done*," instead, and planted a kiss on my brow.

That wasn't the time when I lost my tail. I lost my tail on a later scouting trip, when the nightly town was alive and lit in the center, and sounds of laughter and screaming and shots rippled through the watchful silence. Mother and I lay still on our bellies on wet roof tiles, slick with moss, Bug on Mother's back.

"We need to warn Barras," Mother said, tugging on the edges of her spell to make sure it held in the drizzle. "Come along."

She glided down from the roof like a ghost, arms spread out wide, her wings speckled with star dust, and she landed with the touch of a feather. And I—

I slipped.

My own spell slid from my grasp as I clattered down the roof. The world tumbled around me, only to come to a sudden stop.

I cried out.

My tail was caught in a split beam, and I hung from it, winded by the pain. Far below, the ground awaited me, and though I struggled, I found no purchase. The wooden splinter cracked farther, and I jolted downwards.

Lights blinded me as the night burst into day, and an alarm sounded, deafeningly close.

Then shots, ricocheting off the roof like the *ting! ting!* of glasses raised in celebration.

THIS WAR OF OURS

For a moment, I thought I was alone. I panicked. I thought she had left me, and I screamed for my mother.

She came, nearly running up the wall.

"Hold on to me," she said, the roof's edge in one hand. Her other showed her talons ready. "Hold on to me, Sparrow!"

I dug my face deep into her shoulder, breathing in her scent, and with one deft slash of her talon, my tail was lost. But I-I was free.

Boots pounded nearby.

"The Nightwitch! Get the Nightwitch!"

A spurt of gunfire accompanied the shouts. My mother held me tightly to her chest. I could hear her heart thundering as she wrapped all three of us in her shadows and ran, casting balls of darkness behind her blindly to confuse our pursuers. We were hounded by the Wildcat soldiers until suddenly we weren't. And we went home to Barras in the basement, who stitched up the remnants of my tail and stroked my head in my mother's lap.

It was the only time I made a noise and she didn't cut my arm for it. She didn't have to.

The nightly raids continued, closer and closer to the decrepit house where we hid, and though Bug's constant noise was muffled by the siren's wail, it was time to leave.

WE RAN IN the early morning hours. We ran through the mists curling in the empty streets filled with potholes and craters. We ran past the lake with Uncle Barras' dacha. We ran for days. We ran despite the morning hoarfrost that covered our eyelashes and the winter that was trying to kill us, trying to lull us to an eternal sleep.

But the winter wood—the leafless time—knows no mercy and no cover, and so we ran into a small patrol of Wildcats.

Mother raised her arms and conjured up a spell, a cover under which we could hide and sneak around them, our hearts pumping rapidly at the proximity of the enemy creatures, our breath misting before our mouths, nearly betraying our position.

One of the Wildcats was on the radio just behind the trees we crept towards. He talked rapidly, a smoke hanging from his lips, but as we tiptoed past, he stopped mid-sentence.

We halted, too.

I was crushed between Mother, holding her enchantment, and Barras, holding his revolver just an inch from the Wildcat's eyes. I was so close that I could see the cat's pupils in the yellow iris dilating, then narrowing.

"What is it?" the tinny voice on the radio asked.

"Thought I felt something move..." the Wildcat murmured more to himself, and I saw his whiskers dance nervously.

My hand moved of its own accord, reaching out for the warmth of my mother. Only Bug was in the way. I pinched him angrily, and he protested.

Mother's spell broke, a shot banged loudly, and the Wildcat operator tumbled into the midst of his patrol as dead as a dormouse as we appeared before them.

Mother swept down upon them, her razor-sharp talons flashing forth again and again, as they shouted that it was *the Nightwitch! The Nightwitch was on them!* Barras' gun roared another six times next to me.

In seconds, it was over.

Mother pressed her lips tightly together in displeasure as the tinny radio voice called in other troops to assist. There had been an attack by the Nightwitch, and she stamped her foot down onto the radio until it broke.

MY ARM STILL stung from the cut, and the clotting blood stuck to my innermost sleeve. Another scar I would carry. It would not be my last, or deepest.

Mother and I conjured up a screening spell around the four of us as we wove our path through the dense forest. To where exactly, I don't think even the grown-ups knew. Where do you go when there's nowhere safe left?

The forest was overrun with Wildcat troops. They were everywhere, easily recognizable in their flashy gear, the deep brown reddish stripes. Most of them weren't even actual Wildcats. I saw all kinds of creatures in the Wildcat uniform—thin tails, short tails, bushy tails—teeth filed to look serrated, cannibal mouths dripping with the unaccustomed blood.

We tiptoed by the rumble of their tanks as they flattened the trees, as their engineers reinforced bridges to hold the weight of their heavy artillery, their anti-aircraft guns, their womenfolk barking curses and orders at the jumble of child soldiers, squirrels, raccoons, foxes, all trying to be Wildcats.

Mother took my hand when we snuck past the youngest, playing war, playing hide and seek. She held my hand tight. She crushed it.

But even the Nightwitch couldn't hold an enchantment for days on end. Even the hardiest, most enduring love of mothers couldn't protect her young indefinitely, and so we stumbled on together until we couldn't keep going anymore. And, exhausted, we fell down, my head on Mother's shoulder, Bug in her arms, and slept.

And were found.

Barras shot once from the revolver at his hip, and with the sound, mother jolted awake, jumped up, and conjured her wings and talons to tear at our attackers' faces. Bug started to wail, and I stood over him, swishing my patchy cloak of darkness over us, trying to remain unseen.

The enemies moved quickly, feinting and striking, snarling and growling—now Barras had managed to pull himself upright on his remaining leg—each attack coming faster and harder than the one before. A Wildcat snapped and twisted around Mother, as though to trap her in one last embrace, but she gouged out his eye with her beak, shining red in the twilight.

Fierce, she turned to us, her children, and snatched us up to flee, my hand in her hand, Bug on her hip. But we slowed her down, and as we ran, a Wildcat launched himself at us, claws finding soft tissue, the force of his attack carrying us down, tumbling down a natural dell, down into a clear-running brook.

I gasped for breath, clambering out of the water to the safety of the other bank, and Mother followed, pushing me up.

Her face was torn and ugly, and I had never seen it that way before. I stared.

"Quick, Sparrow, move up!" She held me up to scrabble on top of the bank with both of her arms. "Quickly, now!"

With both her arms.

"Where's Bug?" I asked.

She looked over her shoulder into the water, filling quickly with red swirls, and her face broke.

"We lost him," she said.

Barras crashed over the embankment and hobbled over to where we pulled ourselves onto steady ground.

"Bug?" He saw my mother's face.

"We lost him," she repeated.

But she was wrong.

NOT FAR FROM the brook, Barras found a shallow dip filled with drifts of autumn leaves, and we hid in them, burrowing deep as Mother cast a spell on the eyes of any who came near. She held me close, clutched to her chest, racked with silent sobs, while Barras held us both.

Because Bug wasn't lost. He was alive and making noise, as always. He screamed for Mother for hours, until he grew weary and whimpered. And we listened to his anguish for hours in the deathly silence of the forest.

In the evening, mist rose from the brook, and Barras lay on his stomach, peering through the gloom.

"I see no one out there," he said, "but that doesn't mean it's safe."

A wail went up once more, and Bug began calling for Mother again, choking on sobs, fearful and alone.

"It's too quiet." Barras stared into the quickly-gathering twilight. His voice was low, dead, while Bug's cries echoed against the banks. "Surely they wouldn't leave him there alone when they could take him in for training as one of their own. What a prize. The Nightwitch's son."

Mother didn't seem to be listening. She caressed my face, and I was safe and warm in her arms, which I had missed for such a long time.

"My little Sparrow," she said, smiling, her eyes tender and moist. "You're not so little anymore, are you? You worked your own concealment spell, protecting Bug, and you did it so, so well."

She hugged me. I hugged her back.

"It's a trap," Barras said plainly. "They want you to go back."

"I know," Mother said, my head nestled beneath her chin. I could feel her hoarse voice. She began to rock me gently and hummed a lullaby just as she used to do with Bug. With me. Before. Before this war of ours demanded silence.

I closed my eyes and breathed in her scent.

"You can't go over there, Freya," Barras rumbled from afar. "You can't. Think of Sparrow. She still needs you."

I did.

I needed her. I always wanted her to be near like this.

"Remember, little Sparrow," I heard her whisper as I drifted close to sleep. "Things change, my love."

Darkness took me, filled with the terrible screams of my little brother. And then came silence.

THINGS I'VE LOST:

Daddy

my home

my favorite socks

my favorite red dress

my special pillow on which I never had nightmares

Auntie Neko

Uncle Loran

our home in the basement of the broken house

my tail

Uncle Barras

my brother Bug

my mother

SHADOWS IN THE MIST

SUE TINGEY

WE REACHED THE brow of the hill overlooking the battlefield just before dawn. We were too late—it was long over.

A foggy pall hung over the killing fields, swirling in ghostly, damp clouds, bringing to mind the early morning mists that often covered the churchyards of my homeland; the difference being the lack of birdsong and the stench of death and burned flesh.

'We make camp here,' Curt said. 'Get a couple of hours sleep, and once the mist clears, we can go down and see if there're any survivors.'

Ragnor spat on the ground. 'Not much chance of that, I'm thinking.'

Curt didn't bother to reply. If our men had been victorious, they would have been here waiting for us and in raucous form. Sadly, they were not, which meant only one thing, they had been slaughtered. Our opponents, the men from the north, weren't just satisfied with victory, they scoured the battlefields for the wounded and dying and, with a blade to the guts, slit them open, pulled out their innards, and left them to die a slow and painful death. As we were too late to join the fight, our job would be to see the mortally wounded on their way.

We all dismounted and saw to our animals before curling up around a hastily made fire. We were hungry, but even more tired, though I doubted any of us slept more than a few minutes at a time. Every single sound had us reaching for a dagger or sword. In the end, I gave in and started cooking up some chow. It would be a good breakfast. I'd caught us a few rabbits the previous morning and still had some root vegetables from when we'd started our journey.

'Morning, young'un.' I started at the sudden barking voice from behind me.

'Kelso,' I said, flashing him a smile, which was at odds with the dagger in my hand.

'Sorry, did I make you jump?' he said, laughing.

I tucked the dagger back under my cloak, close to hand but not obvious. 'Breakfast will be a while yet,' I told him.

He hunkered down beside me. 'I can wait.'

'There's some brew.' I gestured with my head to the steaming cauldron hanging over the fire.

'Don't mind if I do.'

I ladled some into a mug and passed it to him. He took a swig and closed his eyes for a moment, savouring the honey and herb infused beverage that had ensured, if not the friendship, the goodwill of the other men. 'Ahh, this is *so* good.'

I carried on cooking while he looked on and, from behind us, I could hear some of the others stirring, no doubt awoken by the aroma of cooking meat. One by one they joined us, all accepting a brew while they waited for their breakfast. The sun was warming our backs by the time I'd finished cleaning the dishes.

We formed two groups. Curt led the main party down to the west of the battleground while the rest of us spread out to the east. Strangely enough, the mist that obscured the valley below us hadn't diminished. If anything, it had thickened into a grey soup.

As we started down the hillside, Kelso, who was leading us, raised his hand, drawing us to a halt.

'Is it me or can you see something moving around down there?'

Drew sheltered his eyes from the sun with his hand and squinted into the mist. 'No, I... Yes, yes, now you mention it.' He leaned forward on his mare, peering into the grey.

'You're imagining things.' Ragnor laughed. 'There's nothing down there but the dead and carrion crows.'

Kelso's lips twisted into a sour grimace. 'Crows you say? Can you hear the cawing of crows? Can you hear *anything* down there?'

Drew shivered and hugged himself. He was younger than Kelso and Ragnor. They were old warhorses, but even so, Drew had over ten years on me.

I stared down the hill, past the main group, into the shifting clouds of fog, and I *did* see something. I was sure I could see dark shadows drifting through the murk, sometimes stopping to stoop down then rise up again to continue on their way.

Drew glanced at Kelso, his cheeks pallid and beads of moisture forming on his brow and top lip. 'You're right. There is something down there.'

Ragnor snorted. '*Something*? What do you mean *something*?'

'I can see shadows,' Drew said.

Kelso's hand dropped to his dagger. 'So can I.'

Ragnor raised his eyes to the heavens. 'This is what comes of filling the youngsters' heads with superstitious nonsense,' he said. 'Come on. We're falling behind.' He patted the neck of his horse and started after the others.

Drew and I exchanged a glance. I shrugged and urged my mare on. We were already a fair way behind Curt and his party. They had become nothing more than blurs within the mist. The further down into the valley we went, the murkier it became. We could no longer see farther than a few feet ahead of us and, within the mist, every sound was muffled.

'I don't like it,' Drew said, leaning close to me so he wouldn't be heard by the others. 'There's something unnatural about this.'

I wasn't about to argue. Now and then, I thought I caught glimpses of movement ahead of us. We reached the bottom of the valley and it wasn't long before the dead began to slow our progress as we picked our way through them, searching for the living.

'This is pointless,' Drew muttered after about twenty minutes.

We'd all dropped down off our horses by then as it was easier to check the bodies, or what was left of them. Never before had I seen such carnage.

'If we find just one poor soul needing our help, it'll be worth it,' Kelso said to a grunt from Ragnor.

'I've never seen anything like this before,' he said. 'There's nothing here but body parts.'

I kept quiet. I hated the overloud way our voices sounded. It was almost as though the mist was making a wall around us, not letting sound in nor letting it out. Then a voice cried out, a scream abruptly silenced, proving me wrong. I'd heard that all right. We all had.

'What the...?' Ragnor said but was silenced by another scream and the cries of a panicked horse.

I glanced at the men around me. They all looked as fearful as I felt.

'Remount!' Ragnor ordered.

We all clambered back onto our steeds. 'What should we do?' Drew asked.

'Carry on across the valley and up the other side.'

'Ragnor!' a voice shouted. 'Ragnor, can you hear me?'

'Curt?'

'Turn back and get out of here now!' he shouted. 'Get out while you can!'

Drew's scared eyes met mine. He looked as though he was ready to bolt. Kelso stood in his stirrups, squinting into the mist.

'Curt, where are you?' Ragnor shouted.

'Get out. Get—'

He never finished, cut off mid-sentence. Then there was silence, the only sounds being our own ragged breathing.

'We can't leave them,' Kelso said.

'It was a direct order,' Drew said.

Ragnor gave a grunt. 'Curt would never leave us.'

'But he said—' Drew started to argue but was silenced by an angry glare from Ragnor.

'Fall in line, draw your weapons, and we'll head in their direction.'

'We don't *know* their direction,' Drew said.

'They should be ahead and slightly to the west of us,' Kelso said.

Another scream rang out, a horse's. It was a terrible sound full of pain and fear, and it was too much for Drew. He swung his steed around and bolted back the way we'd come.

'For the love of all the gods,' Ragnor said, and then uttered a profanity.

'Stupid young bugger,' Kelso muttered.

I held my tongue. I didn't blame Drew one little bit, but I wasn't about to condone his actions either. We were soldiers, we were comrades, and we were family, and I'd rather die than let a single one of our small group down.

From behind us, came a terrible cry. 'Help me! Help me... Please help!' Drew's pleading ended in a bloodcurdling shriek mirrored by his mare.

Ragnor and Kelso moved their horses alongside mine. 'We stick close together,' Ragnor said and urged his horse on. Kelso and I had no alternative but to follow his lead.

We rode in a tight line, knees almost touching. We weren't even making a pretence of searching for any who lived. There was something wrong with this place, and deep in my heart, I didn't believe we'd ever make it to the other side.

Now and then, shadows would glide through the mist ahead of us but never close enough to see anything other than dark stains in the milky murk.

'Did you hear that?' Kelso asked.

We all stopped, sitting up in our saddles and glancing around.

'I...' Ragnor started to say but was silenced by a moan coming from just ahead of us. His hand went to the hilt of his dagger.

'Ahhh,' another moan.

'Who's there?' Ragnor called out.

'Ahhh!'

Ragnor gestured with his hand that we should move on. We glanced around, searching for movement, listening for the slightest sound or indication of life. Another groan so close we were almost upon him, whoever he was.

'Stay mounted,' Ragnor said, swinging himself off his steed.

He walked slightly ahead of us, head bent and moving from left to right and back again, searching. He abruptly stopped and crouched. I heard another moan, but this time I was sure it came from Ragnor.

'Oh, dear father,' he murmured and, turning his head, threw up.

Kelso and I exchanged a glance and, as one, we slid off our mounts. Ragnor had dropped to his knees.

'Ragnor?' I said, moving to his side. 'What...?' and then I saw. My throat closed up and, for a moment, the world swayed around me. It was only Kelso's hand on my shoulder that stopped me from falling. 'What happened to him?'

Ragnor staggered to his feet, swiping his hand across his mouth. 'I told you to stay on your beasts.'

'What happened to him?' I asked again, unable to tear my eyes away from what remained of the man who'd once been our leader.

'Ahh,' Curt groaned again, though how he lived I couldn't comprehend.

Raw black caverns, rimmed with red, stared up at us from where his eyes had once been. Dark blood, the colour of molasses, coated his chin, and when he groaned again, I could see his tongue was gone, too. And these weren't the worst of his injuries. His body below the waist was missing. All that remained were the blue-grey strings of his guts spilling onto the mud.

I felt a tear slip down my cheek as Ragnor pulled his sword. With one swipe, it was all over.

'What do we do now?' Kelso asked. 'Go back or carry on?'

'We look for our comrades,' Ragnor said. 'We find them and, if necessary, put them out of their misery.'

'What did that to him?' I asked.

'Northern scum lurking in the mist,' Ragnor said.

Kelso and I exchanged a look. The man had been ripped in half. The northerners were big and strong, but not strong enough to do that to a human body.

We got back on our horses and carried on. Every now and then, we saw movement in the mist. Sometimes dark figures that languidly glided across in front of us and at others shadows, moving impossibly fast.

Then the whispering started.

At first, I thought it was a breath of breeze blowing through the valley, it was so soft, or maybe the twittering of birds. Ragnor and Kelso looked from side to side so I was sure they could hear it, too.

Kelso.

A whisper slithered through the mist like a snake.

Ragnor.

Another call bringing to mind fine, silken spider webs.

Christian.

My name followed by tinkling laughter. Like before, we rode in a tight line, so close we were almost on top of each other.

Ragnor, Kelso, Christian.

Still they called, and the movement within the mist became more obvious, as did the whispering of our names. Sometimes, the voices sounded feminine, and at others, almost childish. All the same, they filled me with mounting dread.

'It can't be much further now,' Kelso said. 'I feel like we've been riding for hours.'

I turned his way about to agree with him when there was a whooshing sound and a grunt from my other side and when I looked back Ragnor was gone. His horse whinnied and bucked, its eyes wild and scared.

'Kelso!' I hissed. 'Ragnor's gone.'

'What?' he said, and from behind him, something black reared up within the murk. He was swept off his horse backwards and disappeared.

'Kelso! I shouted. 'Ragnor!'

Christian, Christian!

I drew my dagger, looking this way and that. Then up ahead, a line of dark figures wafted towards me. I drew to a halt. My mare, Shiva, stomped her hooves nervously. The other two stopped, snorting and snuffling with eyes rolling.

Christian, Christian. Come with us, Christian.

Arms stretched towards me as the shadows drifted closer and closer. Soon, they'd be upon me and, in my head, I saw mouths full of pointed teeth and hands tipped with sharp talons.

I slapped Shiva on the rump and leaned forward, screaming, 'Ride,' hoping the other two poor creatures would run with me. They did.

We raced straight at the creatures coming towards us, and I was sure they were creatures now. Humans faced with three fine pieces of horseflesh charging towards them would have scattered.

Then we were upon them. I felt hands reaching for me. Something grasped hold of my arm and saddle, hanging on. I swiped down with my dagger and was rewarded with a high-pitched shriek. One of the horses screamed, and I felt, rather than saw, Kelso's steed go down and disappear behind me.

Shiva raced onwards, Ragnor's ride, Jet, getting ahead of us, and then we were going upwards. We had reached the other side of the valley. The mist began to thin. I didn't slow. I didn't dare. The safety of broad daylight was in sight, but I didn't dare believe, I didn't dare hope. Then we powered out of the mist, and I could feel the sun on my face and a breeze ruffling my hair. I didn't stop until we reached the top of the rise.

I patted Shiva on the neck, and she stomped her feet, snorting puffs of steam. 'Good girl,' I told her.

Ragnor's mare trotted back to stand beside us and nuzzled at my shoulder. I supposed, as far as she was concerned, there was safety in numbers. I scratched her forehead as I looked into the mist below us. From the top of the hill, the valley looked like a lake of heaving storm clouds.

'Come on, girls,' I said. 'Let's get away from here.'

I rode down the other side of the hill and kept going, trying to put as much distance between me and the valley before nightfall. I didn't stop until we reached a shallow river where the horses could take a drink.

It was here that I slid off Shiva and reached for the water skin hanging from my saddlebag. I caught a glimpse of something white caught up under my saddle. As I leaned forward to take a look, Jet gave a whinny distracting me. I glanced away—

—and something grasped my wrist, sharp nails digging into my flesh.

I shrieked, falling backwards onto my rump. Then I saw the thing holding onto me so tightly, and I screamed as I fumbled desperately within the folds of my cloak for my dagger. Before I could find it, the thing fell from me, dropping to the ground. Long, bone white fingers clenched and unclenched in jerky spasms, as if the hand and severed forearm had a life of its own. I scrambled away from it and jumped to my feet, heart pounding and my breath coming in short gasps.

'Dear God, dear God,' I heard myself saying again and again.

For a few moments more, the hand scrabbled at the dirt, ivory talons gouging the earth in its death throes, as I hoped they were. Then, with a final shudder, the fingers curled in on themselves. A gout of something as black as treacle oozed out of the stump, and it flopped flat on the ground.

I stood staring down at it while my heart calmed and I stopped shaking. 'What in the name of all the gods?' I muttered to myself, and then remembered hacking madly at something that had grabbed at me within the mist.

I moved a little closer, but not too close. I reached out with my dagger and gave it a prod. Nothing. I pressed the tip of my blade into it. More black goo erupted from the wound and, with a hiss and a puff of smoke, it erupted into flames, burning as bright as the sun until there was nothing left but dust.

Gradually, I could breathe again without gasping like a grounded fish. When I could, I said a brief prayer for the souls of my lost friends and took the time to look over the horses, checking in and under the saddlebags and saddles. When I was sure there were no more unwanted passengers, I remounted and made my way east.

I'd had enough of death—I was going home.

THE ART: POST WAR

RJ BARKER

IT WAS THE Grand Sycophant Oroestes who brought the artist Milon of Honsa across the seas from his faraway land to paint the great and terrible King Hattaran of Murast. What greater honour could there be for the greatest warrior the world had ever known than to be painted by the greatest painter the world had ever known?

None, of course, and it was the job of a grand sycophant to know such things.

Now, friend, I have heard of the painting, it is a terrible thing. A picture so real that it feels like Hattaran lives again, that his armies may move across continents, cities will fall in fire and pain, and those who love will find what is dearest to them taken, sullied, and destroyed. But you, to come here across the sands, to pass through destruction and the rubble and to travel up the Shard Road of Murast, you must indeed be a true lover of art. But though you walk now through a wasteland, do you know that we, the people of Murast, were once the greatest art lovers in the known world? Indeed, Hattaran himself brought the best and the brightest artists back to his mighty capital to ply their trade among the gentle towers of our city.

Of course, we see none of that.

And how, Milon, do you achieve such vibrant colours in your pictures?

It is in the application of materials, Grand Sycophant Oroestes. It is all in the application of materials.

It is strange that you must look upon a ruin where I see what once was, a city overflowing with beauty and fat with plenty. Those few who scratch a living here now mourn the days when every stall was overflowing with produce brought from all over the world. A man who is hungry quickly forgets fear, just as a man who is frightened quickly forgets hunger. We forget too quickly in any case, and quicker than ever in the case of Hattaran of Murast. Oh, he is seen as a monster, and he was a terrible thing to behold, but he loved beauty also. For a time, Murast was a wonderful place to be, though few books from his reign survive to tell us different.

Of course, we had books, friend. Of course.

When I was young, the libraries of Murast were famed, they were ripe with knowledge. It is said the tribesman who once travelled the forests around Murast, bringing us the food and milk from their beasts, all died on the sword because Hattaran needed vellum. Huge herds of goats were driven through the city to provide enough vellum for our writers, playwrights, and poets to scrawl their thoughts upon. One could not go past a street corner without encountering a poet or writer reading from their latest opus. We had so many writers in Murast that some of the greatest names to have ever written starved on our streets, ignored. No, we had no shortage of books in our time, but all that is lost now, burned.

I see you bring me no vellum to paint upon. Do you not have any in this huge city?

No, Milon, for a writer found a form of poetry that was beautiful while making no sense, and King Hattaran could not understand this, and he thought on it for days and weeks until he decided that if he did not understand, then the people would not understand, and he decreed no one should write these poems any more. But the poets did not listen and tracts lampooning Hattaran appeared on the walls. For that, he had a great pyre made of all the books and scrolls in the city's libraries and gathered together all the writers and threw them into it. You will struggle to find vellum here now as it is the sign of a writer, and writers in Murast are burned alive.

No mind, Grand Sycophant Oroestes, I will source my own materials.

Now, are you thirsty, friend? You will hear the running of water and you may follow that to find a spring. Cup your hands and drink deep for water is scarce in the ruins of Murast. The sun beats down and steals the moisture from even our skin. Pots? Oh, once we had such pots. Hattaran worked a hundred thousand slaves to death to build a causeway across the bay of Urlay and lay waste to the land of Beckan so he had access to their clay mines. What was done with that clay was astounding, my friend. Porcelain so fine and thin you could see your hand through it. The pots were made to look like every animal you can imagine. Clever jugs of birds, which spouted water from their beaks, snakes, cats, fish, and more. Our potters competed to make the tallest and thinnest vessels imaginable. Such fine handles you have never seen, clay made to do things that seemed impossible: bowls that rang like bells when touched and likenesses of men and women that, if they had not been so still, you would have taken to be real. In fact, I knew a man who fell in love with a clay likeness of a woman. It was a famous story but, of course, it is lost now.

By the well are some shards and hollowed bones that may hold water if you do not wish to use your hands. I would be grateful if you brought me a little water, for to talk makes me thirst.

Ah no, we have nothing to put your paints in. See the path we walk along? Well, Hattaran found himself displeased with the potters. He believed they were mocking his manhood with their new shapes. He had learnt from his experience with the poets and did not give the potters time to turn on him. He is a great man who is not afraid to make hard decisions. He had every pot in Murast smashed on this road. Then he had horses drag the potters over the road of shards to flay skin from their backs. When he was satisfied that the blood and screams had taught the artists of the city to appreciate him, the potters were thrown into their own kilns to roast. It was a very fine lesson our king taught us.

No mind, Grand Sycophant Oroestes, I will source my own materials.

You say you are starved of colour and your eyes thirst to see the famed colours of Milon's painting, though it is a terrible thing? I understand that need, sand and crumbling sandstone provide little for the eye to feast upon.

So little was left of beautiful Murast when her enemies fell upon her, my friend, though I do not blame them for their anger. How could I? Once Murast was a riot of colour, beauty was everywhere. Our king even loved to paint himself. So much so that the great and terrible Hattaran besieged the city of Varim purely for its painters. He stood his army outside the city for three months until the starving people overthrew the government and opened the gates for him. You will hear he murdered everyone in the city, but it is not true. Hattaran was not a man to waste anything, and although he only wanted the painters, he did not abandon the rest of the city. Those who were well enough, he sent to mine clay, and the rest he did kill, out of mercy, deeming it cruel to leave them to starve in the empty city. The artists he brought back, and they painted our city in honour of their redeemer. It was a magical place then, huge vats of paint kept in the central courtyard before the Palace of Skulls. Pools of every colour under the sun, and the stories of Hattaran's conquests did bloody dances across the walls of Murast. It was said, even those taken in war and brought in chains to die before the palace were thankful for their fate because they had at least lived to see the walls of Murast.

I do not doubt there was some truth in that.

Paints? Ah, the great sadness of Murast is that some of the painters King Hattaran was kind enough to bring to his city became decadent. They created art of such strangeness that it bothered the king, worried at him like a dog will worry at a corpse, and so the king, in his great and terrible wisdom, had them drowned in the paint vats and all the paint was spoiled.

No mind, Grand Sycophant Oroestes, I will source my own materials.

Do you carry an instrument, friend? Many who ply the arts also love music. I do, and I miss it. Murast once sang as loudly as any city. Great halls were built, which threw sound from their gates, sending it echoing through the streets until it mixed with the sound of instruments that fell from the many other halls. At each and every corner in Murast, a man could hear a different symphony, and the birds themselves wept with jealousy over Murast and her songs. Every type of instrument was played here, friend. King Hattaran loved music so much that he brought down the great forest, which once surrounded Murast, to build his fleet and take the island of Voisi where the greatest harpists lived.

But do not take up your instrument for me, friend, it may be best not to play, lest you wake ghosts, which sleep in the ruins, and that would be a terrible thing.

Music? Ah, sadly not, the wise and mighty Hattaran decreed his people must be happy and, as such, all music played in Murast must also be happy. But the Harpists of Voisi could not obey, and they betrayed great Hattaran by loving their old home more than they loved Murast. Their songs wept out minor keys, and Hattaran, in his righteous anger, had all the musicians of Murast strangled with harp strings and forbid any to as much as whistle on pain of death. You will have seen the street of hanging on your way here, of course. It is difficult for a man not to make any music.

No mind, Grand Sycophant Oroestes, I will make my own music.

But Hattaran...

Will make allowances, I am sure.

The stone feet, friend?

You will find many such things in the ruins of Murast. Hattaran brought artists from every land he conquered but he had no need to bring sculptors. Murast was always a city of sculpture, our buildings were decked with faces and figures, our squares with glorious statues that reached for the sky. In the early days of Hattaran's rule, we celebrated his conquests in marble and quartz, in bronze and iron. We beat our enemies' weapons into images of their subjugation, we destroyed cities, made their people slaves, and had them bring the stones of their homes to us so we could create a huge likeness of our warrior leader. Vast it was, throwing a shadow over the whole city like a sundial, and you could tell the time wherever you were by looking for Hattaran's shadow. But it was cold in that shadow, friend, and it had a weight we never realised until it was too late. Sculpture was the only artform he did not destroy as he became older. I think he could not stand to see himself maimed in any way. We had to wait for our enemies to truly bring down Hattaran and banish his shadow. But the sculpture here was astounding once, friend. We had started to leave behind the human form and experiment in more and more abstract forms but...well...

That ended.

The sculptors of Murast? Oh, they live, but they no longer sculpt I am afraid. Hattaran found their more experimental forms difficult to understand, and then found his own meaning in it, found mockery in it. He had their eyes put out, as punishment.

And yet they live?

My son was a sculptor, Milon. I begged for his life.

And now, you bring me to paint your king?

I am the Grand Sycophant of Hattaran, Milon of Honsa, and I have heard much of your work. You are the greatest at what you do, are you not?

Oh yes, Oroestes, yes, I am that.

I have heard it said, friend, that the screams from Hattaran's chambers went on for a week but no one dared intrude. After all, screams from Hattaran's chambers were nothing new. Only when there had been silence for another week did anyone dare enter the king's bedchamber. Oroestes led them in, and of the painter, Milon of Honsa, there was no sign. All that remained of King Hattaran was his throne, sticky with dried blood and discarded flesh, and the painting. Of course, all know of the flesh portraiture of Honsa now, how the artists take apart the subject to create a likeness of his soul. Paint bowls made from bones, paint from flesh, canvas from skin, music from screams, sculptures of agony, a history written in blood; but none did then.

None except Oroestes.

What became of him?

He died when Murast fell, like most did. The victors knew of Hattaran's cruelty, so all who were well or able-bodied, they put to death, and all who were not, they judged as victims of Hattaran's cruelty and took them away from this place. All except me. I remained to guard a painting I have never seen and never will. Hattaran put out my eyes for my craft, you see, and only my father's begging kept me alive. So, I stay here to guard his vengeance.

Now, are you sure you wish to see it? Absolutely sure? For I am assured it is a terrible thing.

THE FOX AND THE BOWMAN

SEBASTIEN DE CASTELL

THE FAINT CREAK of the bow let Thomas know he'd drawn it as far as the yew would allow before breaking. *Two hundred yards at least,* he thought, and prayed his position atop the hill would help him bridge the distance. If he couldn't hit Sir Hamond's armoured hide from here, then all of his sacrifice would have been for nought. Thomas squinted, just barely able to make out the golden eagle crest on Sir Hamond's tabard. Letting out one last breath, he aimed for the dead centre of that eagle and hoped a sudden wind didn't take his arrow astray.

"That's an odd sort of bird you're hunting tonight," a voice called out.

Thomas spun around. "Who's there?" He trained his bow on a man of middle years stepping out from behind the trees.

"I'm not entirely sure it's legal to shoot a bird of that particular type, and I'm positive it won't taste very good." The man's hair and short, neatly trimmed beard were reddish brown, almost russet in colour, framing angular features and a cocky smile. His long leather coat fringed in silver fur at the collar marked him as a foreigner, at least from these parts. Glinting rings, each bearing colourful gemstones, decorated long, manicured fingers. The man might have been a wealthy merchant, or perhaps a minor noble, but what mattered most was that he was a witness to Thomas's impending crime.

"Don't come any closer!" Thomas said. "Go back the way you came, forget you were ever here, and I'll let you live." He did his best to muster the tone of an angry soldier, but what came out was a quivering mess.

"Now why on earth would I want to do that?" the nobleman asked. He walked casually over to the edge of the outcropping next to where Thomas knelt, seemingly unconcerned that he might soon find an arrow in his belly. "It's not the worst plan I've ever seen," he said, idly looking down at the scene below. "Sir Hamond goes down to that little cottage every evening, I imagine? Perhaps to meet with a secret lover?" Without turning his gaze, the nobleman reached out a finger and casually brushed the tip of Thomas's arrow. "Shooting from this height might even give you enough speed and force to pierce that armour." He removed his finger and tapped it against his lips. "Good thinking. I always say, 'if you're going to commit a murder, a hill makes a very discrete accomplice.'"

"Who said anything about murder? I'm just out here—"

The nobleman held up a hand. "Please, Thomas, let's have no lies between us. Lies are the least elegant form of deception."

"Who are you? How do you know my name?"

The man bowed low and said, "You may call me Master Reynard."

"Reynard? Sounds French."

"Well, I'm not, so let that be some consolation. Funny you should mention the French, though, as they're a key part of our new plan."

"Plan? What plan?"

"You want revenge, don't you? This Sir Hamond of the dependable virility just confiscated some small portion of your family's farmland, didn't he?"

"He's taken more than half!" Thomas cried. His arm was growing stiff and tired from trying to keep the bow drawn. He took a few steps back away from the man and eased the tension on the bow, keeping the arrow nocked and ready. "He's ruined my father."

Reynard nodded sagely, though not particularly sympathetically. "Yes, that is the way of knights, isn't it. They take whatever they want under the authority of the king or some earl or even God when they feel the need."

Thomas had to blink the tears from his eyes. He didn't want to show weakness in front of this Reynard, whoever he was, but the wound was still too fresh. His father had always been such a strong man. Fearless, or so Thomas had always believed. To see him on his knees, begging and pleading like a child… "Please, sir, may we keep just a little bit more, grace be to God?"

"It was a trick," Thomas said. "A dirty trick. They changed the day the taxes were due and said my father was late in paying. There would be a fine. But we had nothing left to give so they took over half our land."

"Well then, perhaps you and I should play our own."

"I don't care about tricks. I want revenge on the knight."

Reynard tilted his head as though his hearing was impaired. "What's that, you say?"

Thomas knew this might be some kind of trap, and yet, it would be cowardice to deny the vow he had made only days ago. "I want revenge on the knight."

Reynard seemed to mutter to himself, repeating Thomas's words one syllable at a time as if trying to decipher a foreign language. "I have this… friend," he said at last. "His name is Wetiko."

"Wet-tea-who?"

"Close enough. Anyway, my…let's call him my colleague. He's quite taken with knights like Sir Hamond, with their armour and their big swords and their lances." Reynard began fanning himself with his hand like a nobleman's wife threatening to faint from the summer heat. "They're oh so mighty. So very daunting. Practically indestructible."

The man made it seem like a joke, but Thomas had seen how imposing Sir Hamond had been, standing over everyone in the village in his armour. He might as well have been a hundred men. "Your friend isn't far wrong."

Reynard arched an eyebrow. "Whose side are you on? No, wait, don't answer that yet." He closed his eyes and waved a hand in the air as if dismissing a thought. "The point is, they offend me."

"Offend you?"

He nodded vigorously. "Bad enough when they were wandering around in chain mail. Now they've started in with full plate!" He placed his fists on his hips and turned his head, striking a majestic pose. "They look like pompous metal statues of themselves."

Thomas wasn't sure how to respond. Statues or not, those steel breast-plates could resist an archer's arrow, which was what made Thomas's plan to revenge himself against Sir Hammond so precarious. "I suppose the armourer's art progresses like anything else."

Reynard seized on the words. "Progress! Progress! Progress!" He shouted, and began thumping one foot after the other in a rhythmic march. "Always this *progress* plods on and on, day after day, year after year, century after…" He stopped and turned to Thomas. "It's just so boring, isn't it?"

"I'm not sure there's anything you can do to stop it. New things almost always win against older things, don't they?"

"You sound like Wetiko," Reynard said, drawing himself up haughtily. "It doesn't suit you. Perhaps you want to take his side of the wager?"

"What wager?"

Reynard's dropped the pose and smiled. "He made a wager with me. About you, in fact."

"About me? Why would this Weah-tee…whatever his name is, why would he care about me? Or Sir Hamond for that matter?"

Reynard winked conspiratorially as if he and Thomas were suddenly back on the same side. "Well, it's possible I might have led him into it. Regardless, he bet me that you would never kill the knight. He thinks men like your Sir Hamond down there will rule the battlefield for hundreds of years."

"Sir Hamond won't be ruling anything for long," Thomas replied, anger flashing hot inside his chest. "I'm going to kill him."

Reynard looked surprised. "Oh, really? I'm sorry, here I thought you said you wanted revenge on the knight."

"I do, damn you. What better revenge than to take his life? It'll teach them to fear us. They won't try to take our land again if they—"

Reynard held up a hand. "I'm sorry, Thomas, I'm going to have to stop you there. You're starting to bore me. Shall I show you exactly what's going to happen when you fire your little arrow down on poor, unsuspecting Sir Hamond?"

Thomas watched as Reynard knelt down on and picked up some loose dirt from the ground. "You see this?" Reynard asked.

"It's just dirt."

"Dirt," Reynard said mockingly. "Dirt? It's the earth. It carries the history of everything that happened and everything that will happen upon it." He paused for a moment and looked down at the contents of his hand. "Actually, now that you mention it, it does rather look like dirt, doesn't it? Nothing very interesting there…" His gaze returned to Thomas. "Ah, but when the wind carries it? Then it becomes something much more interesting." Reynard blew into his hand, spraying its contents into Thomas's eyes. The young archer tried to get his bow back up and drawn but before he could take aim, his head began to swim, and he stumbled back.

"Damn you, I'll—"

His ears filled with the sound of horses. A dozen of them. They're coming for me…I have to run! But Thomas realized he was already running, through a clearing past the bridge that crossed into Ferney. It was mid-day, the sun above beating down on him as if pointing the way for his pursuers. He felt thirsty…so thirsty. How long have I been running? Days? No, weeks. Ever since they'd hanged his father. He could still see the body swinging from the tree, hear the cries of his sisters trying desperately to cut him down.

Wait…when had his father died? Wednesday. It was Wednesday the week after Thomas had shot Sir Hamond. The knight's family had assumed it had been Thomas's father, and even when Thomas himself had confessed to the crime, they'd still hanged the old man. Then they'd come after Thomas.

Closer, damn it…the horses are getting closer. Someone barked an order and the twang of a crossbow sang in the air. Something burned into Thomas's back. The sun is so hot…why is it so hot all of a sudden? He began to feel faint as the ground rose up to greet him.

"Enough," Reynard said, clapping his hands once with the sound of a branch breaking in a windstorm.

Thomas shook the dirt from his eyes. It was late—near dark. He was back on the hill. "What did you do to me?" he demanded, raising the bow and training the arrow on the man in the long coat.

"Me? Nothing at all. The wind, though, she showed you why your plan isn't going to work."

Thomas felt sick. Whatever this man's trick, there was some truth to it. Thomas could throw away his own life, but what about his father? His sisters? Yet if he walked away now, Sir Hamond would just go about rutting with his mistress and nothing would change. The knights would go on taking what they wanted, leaving destruction in their wake. "Good God in Heaven," Thomas pleaded. "What am I to do?"

Reynard hopped up from the ground where he'd been kneeling.

"Funny you should ask, Thomas. I believe I mentioned a certain plan of mine?"

He speaks as if he were my friend, Thomas thought. But he smiles like a wolf. No, not a wolf, a fox. "Will this plan of yours get me my revenge?"

"A thousand times over."

Thomas considered those words. He would have happily settled for getting his revenge once over, but a thousand times might be alright, too. "What would I have to do?"

Reynard beckoned to Thomas and walked back from the edge of the hill towards the small lake a few yards away where Thomas used to swim as a boy. Reynard pointed to the water.

"Am I supposed to drown Sir Hamond?" Thomas asked.

"Of course not, silly man. You're not going to kill him at all."

"I'm not?"

"No, you're going to join him."

"Join him? Join him at what?" Thomas asked.

Reynard sat down cross-legged next to the edge of the water, dipped in a finger, and began swirling it around. "In a few weeks' time Sir Hamond is going to be coming back to your village. He'll be looking for conscripts to fight under his command in a lovely little spot called Sluys."

"Sluys? Never heard of it."

"It's in France."

"I knew it," Thomas said. "I knew you were French. No way in hell am I going to France to fight for Sir Hamond. You're trying to trick me!"

Reynard gave a small sigh. "I promise you three things, Thomas. First, I'm not French. Second, you're going to Sluys along with many, many other men to fight under Sir Hamond. Third, I am indeed playing a trick on you. But this is how you're going to get your revenge."

Thomas didn't fancy the idea of being in a war, though his father had fought a few years before under the banner of King Edward. "More chaos and madness than a man needs to see in one lifetime," his father had said. Then an idea came to him. It was sort of ingenious, actually. "Ah, I understand now. I'll go to France and then find a way to kill Sir Hamond on the battlefield. If I pick the right time and place, I can do it without being discovered."

Reynard was nodding and smiling, his eyes far away. Then he focused on Thomas. "What? No, of course not. You won't be killing Sir Hamond in Sluys."

"Then what will I be doing?"

"This!" Reynard leaned down and tilted his head so that his lips were close to the surface of the water. He blew on it, very hard, and little droplets began to spin up out of the lake, flying into Thomas's eyes. Thomas tried to blink to them away, but when he opened his eyes again, he saw water all around him.

A boat. I'm on a boat. He could feel the rocking motion of the boards under his feet. There were men next to him, rough peasants like himself, for the most part—holding longbows like his own. They were crammed together on an English ship like far too many rats packed so tightly none of them could flee. Thomas felt seasick, as he had every day since they'd left the coast.

Good Lord, why did I ever listen to that fox-faced bastard? Why did I come all the way to France just to die on a boat without ever avenging myself on Hamond. Damn you, Reynard. You tricked me!

"There!" the man next to him shouted, his voice full of panic.

Thomas looked off one side to see the French ship nearly two hundred yards away. It was full of men with crossbows. Genoese mercenaries hired by the French knights, Thomas knew, though he wasn't sure how he knew.

The crossbowmen took aim for the English ship. Several of the men standing next to Thomas tried desperately to get down low, fearing the hundred bolts that were being fired from a hundred crossbows. From behind, Sir Hamond swore at the archers to get up, but most of them cowered. Thomas didn't flinch, though. They're too far away, he realized. No crossbow can match the range of a proper longbow. "They can't hit us!" he shouted, and nocked an arrow. He aimed a little high to compensate for the distance and fired. A moment later, a Genoese mercenary fell back into his fellows, the shaft of Thomas's arrow protruding from his chest. A roar went up from the men next to Thomas, and they drew their own bows. Soon the English archers were firing volley after volley, faster and farther than the French troops could hope to match. We're winning! Thomas thought. We're going to…

"Alright, alright," Reynard said, shattering the image.

Thomas opened his eyes and ran his fingers through the short beard he'd kept ever since the war in Sluys. "Sorry. Must've nodded off."

Reynard was sitting next to him, his back leaning against the same tree. "You really do like to pat yourself on the back about that tiny bit of gallantry, don't you?"

"Actually, I was just thinking back to when we first met, five years ago on this very hill when you convinced me not to shoot Sir Hamond but, instead, to follow him to France."

"I convinced you?" Reynard said, he looked up at a passing flight of birds. "I'm quite sure it was all your idea, wasn't it?"

"Don't start with me," Thomas said, jabbing a finger at Reynard. "I won't fall for your tricks a second time."

"Tricks? Me?" Reynard reached out a hand and patted Thomas's new wool cloak. When his hand came back up, it was holding a bag of coins.

"Give those back!" Thomas said, reaching for the bag. "They're mine."

Reynard skipped out of reach. "Given to you by a grateful Sir Hamond, as I recall." He tossed the bag of coins back to Thomas. "I thought it was a lovely speech, didn't you? I mean, the one he gave at your village, all about your skill with the bow and your courage. Your father looked as proud as if someone had just pinned angel's wings to your back."

Thomas looked at the bag of coins in his hand. "So that was your grand plan? For me to trade my revenge against Sir Hamond for a little praise and a few coins?"

Reynard was watching a butterfly land on a blue flower and humming absently. He stopped to look at Thomas. "What? Coins? Of course not. What do I care about whether you have money or not? No, my friend, our plan is much more ambitious."

"Then—"

Reynard picked up a pair of small stones from ground and stood to hold them up to the sun to examine them. "Sir Hamond will be coming back to your village next week. He's going to ask to see you personally."

"So, that's when I kill him?" Thomas asked.

"No, you're going to follow him again." Reynard knelt down and began striking the two stones together.

"Where?"

"It's called Crécy."

"Great," Thomas said. "I suppose that's in France, too. So what's in Cressy?"

Reynard banged the stones until a little spark flew off and a small pile of dried leaves began to smoulder. "More French knights. You're going to fight for Sir Hamond again under the banner of Edward, Prince of Wales."

Thomas shook his head. "The Black Prince? Why would—"

Reynard leaned in closer to the burning leaves, seemingly disappointed at the paltry flame. He puffed three times on them, and the fire grew until small embers began to float up into the air. Thomas watched, fascinated, as a tiny bit of leaf rose up, never losing its soft, red glow. When it reached the height of his head, it landed in his left eye, burning it.

Before Thomas could wipe it away, the ember became brighter and brighter until it took over the sun. Light. Nothing but whiteness.

Thomas opened his eyes. Why did the sun always seem so much brighter in France? It forced him to squint and played hell with his aim. His legs were stiff and aching, too, both from the long march and from the endless waiting. Why, oh, why had he listened to Reynard a second time?

"They're here!" a voice called out.

Thomas turned and nearly bolted when he saw the knights coming. Hundreds of them on warhorses, barely three hundred yards away, charging straight for Thomas and the two hundred archers standing with him in a V-formation.

"God help us," someone screamed.

Thomas forced himself to stand his ground. He was leading this group of archers, and they were looking to him for guidance. He raised his bow and let loose an arrow into the French horde. The knight in front went down, his horse knocking two others off balance. The other English archers fired, too, and watched as their shafts began to break the French charge. "Again!" Thomas shouted. "And again!" he called out.

Sometimes the arrows would manage to pierce the steel plate, other times they broke off. But many of them hit the weaker places between the steel, and others struck the horses themselves, sending the knights careening to the ground.

"Loose," Thomas said, and his men did. Wave after wave. "Again." He repeated the call over and over until the sound of his own voice became oddly faint in his ears…

"Have a nice nap?"

He opened his eyes and saw Reynard kneeling next to him, building up a small fire in nearly the same spot as he had two years before. Thomas reached out and warmed his hands near the flames. It was strangely comforting, he reflected, to meet back here every few years with his strange acquaintance. "I was just thinking back to the battle. The one in Crécy."

"And?"

Thomas smiled. "And you know, I think I've quite gotten the hang of this war thing."

"You do all right," Reynard said with a little chuckle. "Especially for someone who very nearly died on that ridge in Poitiers."

"Poitiers? I've never been to Poitiers." Thomas rose to his feet. "Don't tell me that's another damnable French town. No, Reynard, I'm not going back to—"

Reynard blew into the fire and a little fragment of floated up into Thomas's right eye. Strangely, it didn't hurt at all this time.

Another fire, but this one from the hearth. "I'm back at home," Thomas said. He rubbed a hand over the spot between his shoulder and his breast-bone where the sword thrust he'd taken in Poitiers still ached sometimes. What a fight that was! But Thomas and his archers had acquitted themselves well in the end, he thought.

"Of course you're home, dear," a woman's voice said.

Thomas turned from where he stood by the hearth and saw Elizabeth. She was braiding those long black tresses of hers. He loved to watch her as she worked at it so patiently. Who knew he'd find someone like her? Years ago, he'd always assumed he'd marry Sarah, who'd lived in the cottage next to his father's. Others might not find Elizabeth as pretty as Sarah was, but what she stirred in Thomas was as deep as the ocean itself.

Something tugged at his leg, and his gaze went to the source of the pulling. A boy. My Boy.

"Tomorrow, right?" William asked. "You promised you'd teach me the longbow tomorrow. For my birthday."

Thomas looked up at his wife. She hadn't been fond of the idea of an eight year-old boy trying to learn the longbow. It had taken months for Thomas to fashion something light enough that he was confident William could use it, but still...

"Oh, I suppose it's fine," Elizabeth said. Then she grinned at her son. "But if you're going to be a big hunter, then you'd better shoot something bigger than a pigeon for supper."

William shook his head. "I don't want to shoot pigeons. I want to shoot Frenchmen, like father. I'm going to be a hero just like him."

"Tomorrow," Thomas said. He walked over to the soft chair he'd made last summer and sat down heavily. "For now, this hero needs a little nap." He let his eyes drift closed, warmed more by the closeness of his wife and son than by the fire itself.

"Nice family," a voice said.

Thomas woke up with a start. "Damn you, Reynard. Do you drug me every time we meet?"

Reynard kicked dirt over the leaves to put out the small flame. "Your dreams sound perfectly pleasant. How is William, by the way?"

Thomas smiled. "Sixteen and already the best archer in the county. Robert's coming along, too, and Elizabeth is pregnant with our third."

"Sounds delightful," Reynard said in a voice that made it quite clear he couldn't care less.

Thomas pushed himself up from the ground. "So, it's over, then, this trick of yours? You fooled me into fighting in three wars, and in exchange, I got a family and a nice cottage? You must really hate the French, Reynard."

"I don't give one whit about the French. Besides, it seems to me that you got a fair trade in return, doesn't it?"

It was, Thomas knew, more than fair. He loved his family, and, truth be told, he was proud of his service in the wars. A life that could have been about nothing more than scraping the next season's meagre crops from the dirt had become one of plenty.

And yet…

Even after all these years, there was still a knot in Thomas's stomach when he thought back to the day Sir Hamond had taken half his father's lands. Some wounds never seemed to truly heal. "When do I get to kill Sir Hamond?" he asked.

Reynard was deeply occupied in carefully arranging a leaf on the ground. "Hmm? Oh, him." He shrugged. "You don't kill him. Actually, you end up reasonably good friends with Hamond, all things considered. He gifts your family with quite a substantial plot of land and, when you die, it's he who pays for the bronze plaque on the cathedral floor in

Cragston that will bear your name. It'll be quite pretty, and say, 'Here lies Thomas of Braiden, The Archer.' Your sons and daughters will be buried there, too, with their names alongside yours. And everyone who visits the cathedral will look at the plaque and wonder, who was this man they called the archer?"

It was a remarkable thing, Thomas thought, but the casual, almost dismissive way Reynard said it made him angry. "So all those years ago when you told me you'd bet this Wetiko person that I would kill Sir Hamond, it was really just a trick to get me to live a better life?"

Reynard put down the small squirrel he'd been gently petting and gave Thomas a look of utter disbelief. "Are you absolutely mad?" He asked. "You think I care one whit about whether you have money or family or fame? I thought we agreed this was about revenge."

"You're not making any sense!" Thomas shouted. "What the hell do you mean by revenge? This was all a trick!"

"Of course it was a trick. Look at the wind."

Frustrated, Thomas turned to stare at the breeze blowing the leaves on the trees. "Fine, I'm looking at the wind."

"Not the leaves, silly. The wind."

"No one can see the wind," Thomas said, turning back to Reynard. "It's—"

Reynard blew straight into Thomas's eyes. Suddenly, Thomas could see the years flying past him. Springs and summers and falls and winters, spinning `round and `round. The grass grew and died and grew again as fifty years passed by. Then the air became still, and Thomas looked out onto a wide field between two forests. "Another battle," he said, trying to sound unimpressed. This time Thomas wasn't even part of the battle, he was above it. But what he saw horrified him: French soldiers, thousands upon thousands of them, marching against a force of Englishmen barely one quarter their number. Over a thousand knights on horseback charging English longbowmen. The archers were terrified, certain they faced steel-helmeted death coming right for them. Thomas tried to call out to them, to encourage them. Fight, he wanted to say. We're archers. Longbowmen. We fear no knights! Then he saw a dark-haired young man, standing there in the midst of the other archers, standing firm and shouting the very words Thomas had longed to speak. The young man fired an arrow three hundred yards into the neck of a French knight. Without a moment's hesitation, he nocked another arrow and fired again, and again, and again, and…

"Who was that man?" Thomas asked, still watching the battle unfold.

"Your grandson," Reynard answered.

"My grandson? But…"

"The year is 1415, as your people will reckon it. The place is a lovely field surrounded by woodland called Agincourt."

"And the knights?" Thomas asked. "There were so many of them!"

"Destroyed. Utterly. Thousands of wealthy men in armour, convinced they can't be defeated, taken apart by peasants with sticks and lengths of string."

Thinking back to the young, dark-haired man, standing so tall and brave amongst all those other archers brought a flush of pride to Thomas's heart. "So what we started, all those years ago…it wins the war for us in this Agincourt place you showed me?" Thomas turned to see Reynard gesticulating wildly in an effort to coax a caterpillar to go left instead of right along a ridge of soil.

"What? No, of course not. Wars are complicated things. Lots of moving parts. Like legs on a centipede or…a caterpillar." The fox-faced man seemed to find that funny. "Besides, what do I care about which country wins or loses a war? The whole thing is silly if you think about it."

"Then—"

"The knights. They're the ones who truly lose that battle." Reynard grinned. "Well, the knights and Wetiko, of course."

"The knights? Won't there just be others to replace them?"

Reynard shook his head, though Thomas wasn't entirely clear whether it was in response to his question or to the new direction the caterpillar was taking.

"The knights will disappear from this world not long after Agincourt," Reynard said. "And I will have proven once and for all that all this progress nonsense Wetiko prattles on about means nothing compared to the wild ways of the world."

The wild ways of the world. Certainly life had proven itself to be unpredictable, but Thomas couldn't imagine a world without knights, strutting about in their armour, cutting people down and taking whatever they wanted. No, he realized suddenly. I really can see it now. "So that's been your plan all along. Even though I never got to kill Sir Hamond…"

Reynard raised a finger in the air. "You were very clear with me, Thomas. You said, 'I want revenge on the knight.'" He smiled. "You didn't say which one. Wetiko was equally clear when he said, 'The boy will never kill the knight.'"

All those years, Thomas thought, and despite himself, he nearly broke out laughing. But then he saw Reynard's features become grim, and for the first time, Thomas thought the other man might be capable of violence.

"They are vain, and violent, these malicious worms in their steel carapaces. They hide behind words like honour and chivalry even as they wreak havoc—and not the good kind, mind you—on the earth and all her children. I've watched them pillage and murder their way across one continent and into another, all the while telling themselves it's a god's work they do. They offend me. Wetiko thought his little metal men couldn't be stopped. Well, you and I and your heirs will prove him wrong."

Thomas felt his knees go a little weak from the enormity of it all. "So, all those years ago when you told me to go fight in Sluys, that caused the end of the knights? Forever?"

Reynard laughed. "Oh, it's never quite as simple as that, Thomas. But you've been a part of it. An important part. A truly admirable trick requires many pieces—all in their perfect place—to work its magic." Reynard gave a grin then, and for a moment, with his russet hair and pointy features, looked more fox than man. "And this, I'm sure you'll agree, has been a most magnificent trick."

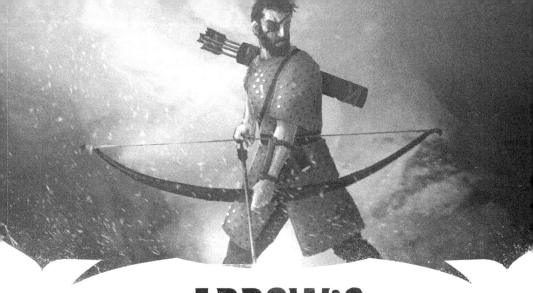

ARROW'S WRATH

CHARLES F. BOND

MACKELL HELD KANNARRA by the hips ready to help her into the cart. She laughed at his touch and looked into his eyes. They were the green of the ocean, and her hair the red of a Black Baccara rose flowing behind her lithe shoulders.

In her glare, Mackell saw the reflection of her final strained efforts, and the blood-soaked babe fall from her body. It had her nose; precisely the same nose, in miniature. It was both weird and wonderful at the same time. And then he knew, knew how much he loved her. Had he heard it in a ballad somewhere, that when one could see their unborn in the other's eyes, their love was real. True, most songs were stories, make-believe, yet somewhere, that line had stayed and spoken straight to his heart.

He sucked in a breath, tasting her scent, remembering the afternoon and the feel of her warm and naked body next to his, and smiled.

At the sight of his grin, her lips curled, and she giggled, staring, alluring and wanting, into his eyes. Those eyes sprang wide, shocked. In the same instant, droplets of fine warmth touched his chest where his shirt was half-buttoned. His gaze fell to her neck, the one he'd been kissing not long before, and saw an ashen arrowhead protruding from it. Blood ran along its edge, drops forming at the tip and falling.

Kannarra reached up, touching the dart, choking out a muffled cry, gasping for breath. She coughed and gargled, coughed and gargled, her body trembling. Her knees buckled, and it took all his might to get his stunned body to gently lower her to the ground, the grass around them splattered with crimson droplets: her life's fluid.

The longest any good archer could shoot an arrow, and hit target, was 350 metres. There was one other, beside himself, who bested this. He had the Dragon's Sight, and could strike a spinning coin at 400 metres, kill prey half a mile away.

Kannarra lay in his arms, coughing and spitting more blood. Her lips mouthed words, which sounded like, "Eye ugg ooo." She was leaving him, and there was nothing he could do to stop it. In all the battles he'd fought, men died from such wounds, far swifter. Was this her showing resigned strength, or had time slowed somehow? A voice at the back of his mind told him to remove the arrow, even though all his training had taught him never to do so. He didn't want to let her go, wanted her here as long as possible, but that was selfish. All he could do for her was help her pass swifter. He reached to the back of the arrow near her hair, placed his other hand behind her neck, fingers either side of the shaft. 'I will always love you,' he told her. And then yanked hard, removing the arrow. Three short gasps, and then she slumped, still.

She was gone.

The killing dart in his hands, he felt its smooth, almost enamelled, slenderness. It was weighted in its centre, better for covering longer distances, and was made from trees across the seas. He gripped it hard.

On the death of a loved one, any man would yell the name of their lost, struck tight by bereavement. He did not. He looked up at the arrow, looked across the valley knowing the direction of flight, and with his left eye, his only one, saw a leaf flutter to the ground, stripped, no doubt, from the arrow's passing as it had been loosed.

'Valean,' he yelled, drawing out the last syllable. It was all he needed to say. The other would know Mackell would not rest until his sword pushed through Valean's heart.

With tears streaming his cheeks, he pulled Kannarra close, hugged her tight one last time, then rose and lifted her into the cart. He moved to step up into the driver's seat, changed his mind, and leapt onto his steed, and rode back to the fortress.

LORNE CASTLE, THE enemy fort, stood against a cliff, so well-constructed it looked part of the natural surroundings. Its outer walls were taller than the tallest tree, a dome of protection against the mightiest army. On this side, the east, the Forest of Fair Chance, as it had been renamed, stretched almost to the castle gates, ending 200 metres from stone. As expected, the woodland was littered with lookouts, perched among high boughs and concealed within crevices in boles: not the numbers calculated, much less. Among the Ninety men Mackell had gathered were loggers and trackers. They swept the woodland ahead, making short work of the lookouts, guiding archers to those hidden high.

Sixty marched from the forest in tight formation, obscuring the view of a log, no taller than a man, twice the thickness of an elephant's foot. As they approached 150 metres, shouts were heard high among the crenellations and arrows were loosed into the air.

'Shields high.' As one the band halted and lifted their shields. No ordinary shields of wood, these were square and encrusted in slate, harder for arrowheads to penetrate.

The shields were interlaced, preventing gaps, and no arrows got through. They moved on, shields up. Thrice more they were showered in shafts, some making it through where a man slipped, men sustaining minor scrapes.

At the gates, they stopped two metres short. The gates were set within an arch a metre wide, giving them some relief from above. They came closer together, keeping shields tight over their heads, others to each flank, forming a tunnel. At the head, three men were allowed out and emptied small jars of oil they'd brought, covering half a metre of the bottom of the huge doors, all the while those above threw rocks of all sizes, none bigger than a man's head.

Once the jars were empty, the three retreated within their makeshift tunnel. At a command, they all stepped forward three paces, extending their formation, showing almost the entire trunk they'd brought. Those above would see it as a much longer log.

From up high came the command they knew would follow. 'Oil!'

At the last, before being soaked, the forward half of the tunnel changed position, forming an overlapping slant. When the oil hit, it ran down the slant, covering the area at the foot of the gates. When no more oil came down, the party moved hastily back, just as a fire arrow shot down from the high walls. As it struck, another from within the woodland, loosed at the sight of their retreat, stabbed the base of the doors.

'Noooo,' a shout came from above as they realised their mistake. It was too late, the oil caught and, soon, flames licked the great doors.

It would take an age, but now all they had to do was wait.

As the men found the cover of the trees, all the while being harried by more arrows, those who'd stayed hidden in thicket and thorn took this as their sign and let arrows fly of their own, taking the high archers by surprise.

THE FIVE CROUCHED within the fringes of the forest, like deer before dusk. Here the forest had been cut away, leaving a mile-long expanse of nothing, disallowing a surprise attack. The wall, while tall, was shorter than Mackell remembered. It seemed to shrink a little more each time he visited. Its smoothness like ice sugared in the setting sun behind them.

All along the parapet, he saw men standing watch on the crenellations. On this, the open western wall, there should have been more than the handful he was seeing now. He put this down to men having been moved to the east. Good. His ninety were in place. At the thought, billows of smoke rose on the opposite side. It had started. The lookouts on this side moved in the direction of the eastern wall.

'Let's move.'

He leapt and sprinted across the plain, keeping a close eye above. With no watchmen, they made it to the wall's base unseen.

Where the main fortified wall of the castle met the sheer rock of the cliff, a small, cave-like tunnel had been burrowed beneath the foundations of the defensive wall. A fox had dug it out long ago and found a home to rear her cubs. When a guardsman found them, his father had the family slaughtered, much to his young self's dismay. The channel so small, it seemed no one deemed it consequential enough to fill. Even if it had been, this was still his best chance at getting in. They each rummaged their cloaks to bring out the metal plating they'd brought for this very reason and began using the makeshift earth movers to enlarge the hole. With battle taunts and orders being shouted, and the last cries of the dying, none would hear their scraping.

Soon, the gap was large enough and Mackell shuffled through.

This portion of the structure was buttressed. In his older body, it was a tight fit, but he managed to climb, and did so without delay. Unable to look down, he was assured he was being followed when he felt a brisk brush of hand on his lower leg; accidental or assuring he was uncertain.

He heard laughter, too: a young lad's voice, sounding not too long after its breaking. Then he heard naked feet slapping stone, coming closer.

Looking upwards as he climbed, he stopped when the young man's naked form came into view, holding what his father had bestowed him in one hand.

'Come on,' the young man said, head twisted over one shoulder, 'try it. No one will know. I do it all the time.'

Knowing what was coming, he closed his eyes and looked straight ahead. The trickle of liquid hit the outer buttress and flowed down to soak the back of his cloak. Spray-back glistened his hair.

'Attagirl,' the boy cooed above as the flow stopped.

He heard her feet hit stone, and stayed as he was, waiting for the girl to empty her bladder.

He'd done the same when he occupied the room above, stopping only when he'd spied light shining through the slit below and the fox had moved in.

He waited after the girl stopped. Heard their pattering feet move into the chamber, and then inched his way upwards.

Soon, he heard playful laughter and soft pleasure moans from the girl.

A shame a youngster had taken his old haunt, he thought, as he reached the ledge. Taking a peek, he saw the girl straddling the lad on the bed, her back to him, no one else in the room. Then slowly, silently, he crawled over the ledge. Keeping low, he stalked to the bed. In one fluid motion, he reached around the girl's head, clasping her mouth, pulled his short blade, stabbing it into the young man's throat, splitting his Adam's apple, moving through his brain, and penetrating his soft skull. The young man's body flailed on the bed, twitched twice, then went still.

Beneath his fingers, he felt the girl's attempt at a scream. She jerked forward as a rapier blade burst from her chest, below her left breast, piercing the gland. Blood gushed from the wound, covering her lover's dead face.

It made up a little for the piss soaking his back and buttocks.

To get to his target, he had to move like a mouse, silent and swift. At the door, he lay flat on his chest and looked through the narrow gap between wood and stone, searching the flanks either side. Seeing no boots, he jumped up, opened the door, and moved out into the passage.

The small party moved on unhindered. They passed his brother's old room, its door left ajar. The next was his parent's old quarters, this door firmly shut. They continued. In the diminishing light, the corridor was dark. What little light there was filtered through arrow slits, creating ghost-like doors of light, which they passed through, dust particles dancing in their wake.

'You weren't supposed to be here so soon.' The voice came from behind. He knew it well.

Turning, he saw Valean push back a portion of wall, a narrow door. It had been painted in pattern to look like the wall, and once Valean had it in place, it was hard to notice.

Valean's gaze shifted from one man to the next. Those eyes showed a scintilla of surprise. Valean held it well. There was no bow across his back.

'Take him,' Mackell said.

The four jumped Valean, who offered small resistance.

When Gurrin and Karrick, the more muscular of the quintet had him in their grasps, Gurrin said, 'Where to?'

'His quarters,' Mackell said, 'I'm guessing our folks' old rooms?'

Valean nodded.

The room had changed completely. Not in appearance, that was still as Mackell remembered, and though the bed, not a four poster, was new, this wasn't it either. It *felt* different, invaded perhaps, certainly not his parents' old bed-chamber. He stifled the urge to shiver, feeling unnerved by the place. To the left of the central bed, a single easy chair stood. Gurrin and Karrick moved towards it.

'No,' Mackell said, 'make him stand, as the rest of us will.' Valean's words when he'd snuck out of his hidden door filtered back. 'What did you mean about being here so soon?'

'What? No hello, how are you, brother? Just—'

'Don't call me that, we haven't been that in a long time.' Mackell reached for his missing eye automatically, covering his patch with the palm of one hand.

Valean, not the slightest taken aback, continued, 'just straight to it, without the small talk, eh?'

Gurrin punched his ribs, hard. 'Not the time for that. Just answer the fucking questions or the blows go lower, got it?'

Valean glared up at Gurrin, opened his mouth as if to remonstrate, then closed it, reconsidering. Instead, he said, 'Well you weren't. The plan was to attack while you were in mourning. You were supposed to be too stupefied for anything but seeing her body put to the ground, before coming here. And come I knew you would, for me.'

Attack and *mourning* were the two words he heard above the others. He remembered the lack of guards outside the door of the boy and the lover he'd slain, the scarcity of lookouts on the wall. King Thorrin was on the march.

'Knowing I'd come, why are you here and not surrounded by many more men?'

'You mean why am I not with the others, attacking your fort. Simple, I am done with all that. I'm spent.'

'Don't like battles no more, I hardly believe that.'

'Believe what you will, it's true.' Valean's eyes fell on the bed. Mackell followed his gaze and, for the first time, saw the filled travel sack. 'I'm heading south, as far south as south goes.'

'You always did abhor the winter.'

'Besides, had I been with the others, you would have found me, and nothing and no one would have stood in your way to getting to me. You five are a force to be reckoned with, I know that. That said, even with one eye, you are still the greatest archer the realms have ever known, my elder. You best even me, you know the bow so well. You would have sought my face among thousands, even the ten who are…' he looked up, calculating, 'about now knocking your fort's doors. You would have stuck me with a dart long before the fighting started. No, I was hoping you would have had to battle your way out, giving me the time to get away. But here you are.' Valean spoke in resignation. He knew his fate.

On the opposite side of the bed to the chair, a bow rested against the wall, a filled dun-leather quiver by its side. Mackell moved to it, picked up the bow, chose a random arrow, and nocked it. He turned, aiming the point at Valean's right eye.

Seeing his own bow pulled back with an arrow pointed at his skull, a fire rekindled in Valean's eyes. It was the ultimate insult to any warrior to be killed by his own weapon. 'Mackell, think what you are doing. Whatever you say, we are still br… We are still siblings.'

'You stopped being that the moment you killed our parents. You had your reasons, and I forgave you that.'

'You forgave me?'

'I let you live. The moment you let loose your arrow that killed Kannarra, you became my prey.'

'Fine, but not like this. Let us dance.'

Mackell pulled back the bow string, then let loose.

The instant Valean saw what was coming, he flinched aside, not quick enough, but enough to alter where the arrow struck. Instead of going directly through his eye, it struck him in the corner, slicing a feather's notch out of the bridge of his nose. Mackell saw it all in slow motion. The right eye got shoved aside, leaving the socket. In some cases, not all, whether human or beast, the shock of a projectile cutting through the brain makes the eyes pop out. That is not, he decided, what caused Valean's right eye to come out—the arrow itself did that—it was what caused his left one to leap from its den, however. It happened instantly, the eye coming out quick as Jack from his box, then drooped and hung on sinuous threads. Valean's head snapped back, and his body kicked out.

CHARLES F. BOND

Gurrin and Karrick let him fall to the floor. He watched Valean die, convulsing and twisting and coughing up blood.

THEY FOUND THEIR mounts tethered where they'd left them. Seated in his saddle, Mackell spurred his steed on, facing southwest. Deep in thought, he halted his horse, the others stopping around him.

'Mackell?' Bethod asked. 'You change your mind, wanna go back and break some bones to save our king?'

'No. Even when it's his own daughter to avenge, he wouldn't come out. He *is* the coward people whisper him to be. I saw it in his eyes.'

'Then what is it? Whatever it is, you know we have your back.'

He didn't need the others to show their acquiescence, he knew it to be true.

'Valean may have fired the killer shot, but King Thorrin would have given the order. I want his life, too.'

'Then we go. Even if we have to fight our way in, we'll have him.'

Mackell had a better idea. He heeled his horse's flanks. The others followed.

MACKELL WATCHED AHEAD, attentive to every shadow cast by the few fires that burned throughout the camp.

A new moon had aided in their secret return to Massern Keep. Its walls looked unscathed, judging by the dim light flickering off its surface from the nearest campfire. King Thorrin was renowned in his use of fire in all his battles, and come morning the walls would be swathed in scorch marks. And now the army lie in wait. This was no ordinary siege, however. They would not be waiting long before striking a new volley of attack. They would harry those inside all night long, Mackell knew.

There looked to be 3000 three-man coned tents, all ocean-green (the colour of Thorin's ancestry), arrayed in a dome. In the centre stood a square nine-man tent, of which would hold only one, Thorrin. A fire burned outside its elaborate entrance to warm the occupant. He hoped the ruler would show face soon, yet would wait until dawn if he had to.

Behind, Mackell heard the faintest of muffled voices, and the four around him scuttled off in different directions.

Focus unhindered, the point of the arrow nocked in Valean's bow was locked on the flame outside Thorrin's tent, half pulled back.

A flap moved inside the tent's entrance, and the king of Lorne Castle emerged. He strolled to the fire, hands in front, seeking warmth, and stood. Men saw his appearance and gathered, forming a circle around the fire. The ruler looked to be talking to those who'd joined him. Good. It meant his intended target would stay in one place, making this an easy enough procedure.

Mackell could feel a breeze on his left ear. Wetting his lips, he turned his head that way and could judge the strength of the wind. He had no idea of the accuracy of these strange arrows for he'd never fired one before. He had been studying its weight since leaving Valean's body, and with its heavy centre, knew it would mean a higher flight path than what he was used to. He only hoped he'd judge it well for he had one chance alone. One shot, for should an arrow come down and miss, his quarry would know he was under attack and flee into the shadows, which were mere steps from his current position. One shot.

He aimed high, pulled back the bowstring, wet his lips once more, and double-checked the wind's speed, re-adjusted his aim, and let loose.

The arrow left the string with great ease and made no sound in flight. Unable to see its path, Mackell reached down and fumbled for another arrow lying by his side. It in hand, he nocked and took aim. As he watched the fire, he saw the arrow enter the light of the burning wood, coming straight down. To his elation and astonishment, it struck the enemy king in his chest, the descent not as straight as he'd first thought. With the shaft buried deep in Thorrin's torso he went down on his back. Before the man went down, Mackell had noted a dark stain growing from the wound, discolouring his blue satin shirt.

With his remaining eye, Mackell could see very clearly the man on the floor writhe. Not dead. He aimed again, looking closely at the king's nose jutting above his brows beyond, and loosed.

Men surrounded their fallen and lifted his head slightly off the ground. Damn.

Yet it was to Mackell's advantage. The arrow entered the light and dug deep into Thorrin's forehead, jolting his body once, before his mouth dropped open as he expelled his last breath.

Mackell lifted from his sitting position, thought about dropping the bow, and shouldered it instead.

He found the others farther down the slope, surrounding two men lying face up on the ground, one with throat slit, the other a bulging bruise to his temple ready to burst: the mark of Gurrin's war-hammer which now rested on Gurrin's shoulder.

With no words needed, the five descended the hillock heading north. They, unlike most, preferred the cold.

'What about Kannarra?' Gurrin asked. 'I mean, don't you want to see her put to the ground?'

Mackell faced his friend as they walked. 'I have her in here,' he pointed to his heart, 'and up here,' he gestured to his head, 'and there she will always be. I have no desire to see her final resting place, and no need to visit it.'

Mackell and Gurrin were the only singles among the group. The others had wives and small children. They met them two miles north, a place they'd agreed upon before setting for Lorne Castle, and with greetings out of the way, they ushered their two horses, each drawing a single cart, and moved slowly into the cooling night. The echoed explosions of fiery fultons blasting the stone of their former homes' walls, diminished with each step they trod.

HARD LESSONS

MICHAEL R. MILLER

A short story from the world of The Dragon's Blade *by Michael R. Miller*

ORDERS CAME BEFORE dawn for the retreat, yet no reason was given. First light broke when they were already upon the road south. Scythe stole an apprehensive glance back at the great fort of the Nest, already fading into the semi-distance. He'd felt safe behind those thick walls, unreachable atop its tall towers. Out on the Crucidal Road, he felt dangerously exposed, even with a legion of dragons and thousands of human troops around him. His lingering stare earned him a shove from the hunter behind.

"Can't slow down, son," the man gasped. "Gotta keep up the pace."

Scythe faced forwards and quickened his step until he was back in sync with the others. Already, he was breathing heavily and a throb in his abdomen warned of a stitch in the making. He probably shouldn't have wolfed down that breakfast.

Yet half a day later, he was glad he'd eaten something. The dragons hadn't slowed down and showed no signs of doing so. Scythe could still make them out ahead of the human column, the light shining off their golden armour. They looked so magnificent, though the reflections made it hard to stare for long. He shifted his gaze downwards, watching his feet move to the tuneless beat, focusing on drawing his next breath; his next one; the next one.

"It's too hot," he whispered through parched lips, as though his word alone could drive away the baking sun. Someone handed him a water skin and he nearly choked in his eagerness. The skin was pulled from his grasp even as he tried to take a second gulp. He walked on.

"Won't they slow down?" he asked to no one in particular.

No one answered.

Scythe blinked, stumbled, and staggered sideways. Another strong hand kept him on his feet, and he struggled on for a while more, though how long he could not say. Everything was bleary. The world had turned to an orange haze, the dragons now nothing but a glittering blur at the edge of sight.

He stumbled again, this time falling forwards. The road rushed to meet him. His cheek met blistering stones and a puff of dust rose to sting at his eyes. At least he wasn't moving now. It may even have been pleasant had everything not also been fading to blackness.

SCYTHE SLOWLY OPENED his eyes. For a second, he thought no time had passed. The light was still orange and flickering, then he realised there was a neat little fire with dark figures moving around it.

Was I out for the whole march? What must they think of me?

He sat up too quickly, winced, and clutched his throbbing head.

"Here," a voice said. A woman's, that much he could tell. A second later and a heavy pouch landed in his lap, the contents sloshing inside. "Get as much of that down you as you can."

"Am I ill?" Scythe asked.

The woman hissed a laugh. "Just drink. Take it in sips, mind. Don't need you retching everywhere."

Scythe fumbled with the skin for a moment before managing to take a mouthful. Nothing had tasted so sweet and wonderful in all his life.

About halfway through the skin, he felt more human. His vision refocused, and the woman came into sharper relief before him. She wore the yellow-brown leather armour of a huntress from the Golden Crescent, with hair so short it barely covered her ears. She seemed olde,r too, more hardened and experienced. Perhaps a captain? But no, a captain wouldn't be looking after him.

"Are you a healer?"

"No," she said, unhelpfully. "Keep drinking that."

Scythe did. The silence grew awkward, at least to him, though the huntress didn't mind. She trimmed the ruffled fletching on her arrows, cutting with a well-practised rapidity, and blew the cuttings away.

"You're very good at that," Scythe said.

She raised an eyebrow. "And why wouldn't I be?"

"No reason. Just that, even after basic training, a lot of hunters still don't get it right. My dad's a fletcher, you see."

She blew away another sliver of cut feather. "Is he indeed? Good job that. Wish my parents had been exempt."

"I'm sorry," Scythe said.

"Long time ago, kid." She eyed him again. "Have you finished drinking that?"

Scythe took another gulp, larger than intended, and half-choked. The huntress tutted and returned to her arrows.

Emerging from his episode, Scythe spluttered, "Who are you? If you helped me, I've not even said thank you yet. That was wrong. So, thank you. My name is Scythe, by the way."

"No need for names."

"Why?"

"Just adds attachment. Best not to be out here."

"But what should I call you?"

"You don't have to call me anything," she said. She placed her final arrow into her quiver, laid it down beside her bow, turned to face him fully, and stretched out a hand meaningfully towards the water skin. Scythe noticed something as he placed it in her hand.

"Your finger—"

"Is missing, yes," she said. Despite the missing forefinger, her grip on the water skin was surprisingly strong. She took it from Scythe, threw back her head, and drained the last of it. "What, not going to say sorry for that as well?"

"I don't know who to say sorry to."

She smirked. "How about some food?"

"Please," Scythe said, his stomach groaning in anticipation. The huntress threw an apprehensive glance around, then rummaged in something under her travelling cloak. Seconds later, she emerged and tossed a chunk of hard bread and even harder cheese his way.

"Eat quickly, too," she said.

Scythe chewed the bread and cheese into a bland ash which took some effort to swallow. Army rations were one thing he'd probably never enjoy about it all.

"Are you sure you're not a healer," he asked between mouthfuls.

"As certain as I have four fingers."

"It's just, why are you helping me then?"

She wrinkled her nose, not quite meeting his eye. "Those less injured get to look after the injured. Anyway, now you're up you can go find your squad."

"What, right now?"

"Better now than when we're scrambling to march again."

"We won't do the same tomorrow, surely?"

She laughed again. "You haven't been out here long, have you?"

Scythe shook his head. "Ship dropped us close to the Nest. That was two weeks ago."

"Two whole weeks." She whistled sarcastically. "Bloody veteran you are."

Scythe jumped to his feet. He didn't have to sit and be belittled. "I've gone through the training, just like every other hunter. I'm just as capable as you." He brandished the remainder of his cheese at her like a knife, small chunks flying off of the end.

"Sit down, you idiot."

Scythe ignored her and crossed the few short steps to her piled equipment, including the travelling cloak. "Why are you hiding this anyway, unless you're hoarding food? That's against regulations."

The look she gave him might have cracked stone, made all the more chilling from the dancing light of the fire. Scythe realised he'd gone too far and began to back away. He'd just have to go find his squad after all and—

He hit something solid as he turned. Staggering backwards, Scythe found that that something was a man. A regular soldier, judging by the mail shirt, with tree trunk legs, a wild beard and a cruel smile. An equally unsavoury fellow stood beside him like a menacing twin.

"Bit o' food about here is there?" one of them said.

"Got some there in his hand," the other said, lunging for Scythe.

Scythe just managed to sidestep the man, but his back was now painfully close to the fire. Sweat gathered at the back of his neck and brow, and not entirely from the heat of the flames. The men were closing in on him.

"Stop," Scythe said meekly. He tried to resist but his assailant forced his hands behind his back with ease and plucked the cheese from his weak fingers.

"Lovely that," the man said, smacking his lips. "Right, Griz, find this dolt's stash."

"That's enough," the huntress said. She was on her feet, her bow in hand.

The second man, Griz, hesitated. "Didn't see you was there."

"And now you have," she said. She pulled an arrow, notched, and drew it faster than Scythe ever could, even with his hand still whole. "Try some other fire."

A tense second passed, and then Scythe's captor released him.

"C'mon," the man said to his companion. "The bitch has a new pup."

The pair left and the huntress kept her arrow trained on their backs until they were at a safe distance. Scythe rubbed his smarting wrists from where the brute had held him, avoiding the huntress's eye. He faced the ground instead, so embarrassed he'd quite like to pass out again.

Before he could react, the woman had grabbed his arm and was hauling him back to where he'd been sitting. "No wandering off tonight," she said, shoving him down. Scythe hit the ground with a jolt and let loose a gasp of pain. She shook her head at him as she sat back down. "Since when did hunter training forgo common sense for rule stickling."

"I just…I just…" but he trailed off, thinking it best he just keep his mouth shut this time.

She grabbed him by the shoulder and forced him to face her. "Hunters are trained to survive. Out here, it's the same thing, only different rules. Your squad mates will die quicker than you get to know them. The demons don't feel fear like wolves or bears or other creatures you might have faced back home. The dragons will leave you behind if you don't keep up. And half the humans on your side are the thieves, the rapists, and the murderers. Not many friends out here, kid. You just survive, okay?" She let him go and turned away, her chest rising and falling heavily.

"I'm sorry," Scythe said.

"It's alright. I haven't forgotten what it's like to be new out here."

Scythe peered off for a moment, looking to the dark world beyond their fire in the direction the two men had walked off in. He'd met plenty of soldiers before now; in the capital, on the ship, at the Nest. None had been like them.

"Murderers and rapists are sent to the eastern front?"

"Harsher sentence than a cell, that's for sure," the huntress said.

"But why? Recruitment hasn't been a problem."

"The army isn't made of criminals, lad. Just a good chunk of it."

"Doesn't it bother you?"

She shrugged. "It is what it is. For all I know, old Griz and Talp there were wrongfully accused. Maybe King Arkus' new war taxes left them broke, and they stole to feed their families." She smirked again, seeing the look of incredulity on Scythe's face. "Maybe, but not those two. They're as crooked as they come."

Scythe sighed. "It's just…not what I was expecting."

"And what were you expecting?"

"Something…something more. Something nobler, I suppose."

"Hmm," she mused. "The king sends us the scum of his dungeons to help defend humanity, but he doesn't force a single one of his pampered chevaliers to sail east. Now that bothers me."

Scythe considered this. He supposed he hadn't seen any of the knights since leaving the ship. There'd been so much going on, he hadn't really noticed their absence. Now this huntress brought it up, it did seem glaring.

"In fairness, don't the dragons bear the brunt of the fighting? They're better suited for it after all."

The huntress snorted. "If they're so damned tough, why do they need us? Take that march today, what was the point in that?"

"We were retreating?"

"Retreating from what?" she said. "We had a battle with the demons long before you arrived. They tried to take the Nest but we beat them soundly back. So why leave?"

Scythe bit his lip, but was sure of one thing. The dragons knew their war craft. They wouldn't make a foolish decision. "I'm sure they have good reasons."

"You really are new out here, kid." She looked around again. "How about another bite to eat?"

Scythe sat up straighter. "Go on."

"Look at you breaking the rules," she said. "Just be subtler." She ferreted around in her bag and pulled out and unwrapped two strips of salted pork. She really had meant a bite to eat. There wasn't a lot, but he hadn't seen much meat since boarding the ship and was grateful for it. Its deliciousness lasted for a few brief seconds. He savoured it. Gulped it down.

Then felt horrible.

A sense of dread clouded his thoughts. This wasn't what he imagined it would be like. Scrounging for food from one stranger and nearly beaten by others.

"Mum didn't want me to become a hunter," he said. "She wanted me to stay and help dad in the workshop."

"Clearly you disagreed."

"I packed up as soon as I turned sixteen and could join. I wasn't very nice about it, looking back." A vivid memory of his crying mother running after him through the streets blazed painfully before him.

"You can miss home, Scythe. It's allowed."

"I only just got here."

"That's when we miss it most," she said. "You should take a boat to the Dales rather than the capital when you get leave."

"If I make it that long."

"You'll make it," she said. Something behind Scythe drew her attention, and her eyes widened in alarm. "Lie down and pretend you're still out. Now!"

"What?" Scythe spluttered.

"Just do it." She shoved him down. "You're dead to world, hear me? Don't move a muscle."

Scythe did as he was told, long past the point of questioning her. The crackle of the fire magnified as he focused on his hearing, tuning into the world around him as hunters were taught to do. After a moment, he began to hear the stirrings at the other campfires. Low voices talking in hurried whispers, heavy feet pressing into the earth. He even felt the pulse through the ground as he honed in on it. A small group were now heading their way. The huntress got to her feet to meet them.

"Can I help you, Legate?" she asked.

"What's wrong with this one?"

"He's seriously dehydrated from your forced march." She sounded bold, considering she was speaking to the head of a dragon legion.

"The humans are to move camp one league to the north. Can he walk?"

"Does it look like it?" she said. "And nobody moves camp during the night, what's going on. North is back the way we came."

Scythe couldn't help it any longer. He risked opening an eye by a fraction. Towering over the huntress was a dragon warrior, his wide shoulders draped in a crimson cloak, his torso armoured in golden plate. A plumed helmet topped his head and his expression was grim as a morning after the bottle. Flanking the legate were two dragon legionnaires, equally well-armoured and standing as though carved from stone.

"Orders from the prince," the legate said. "I don't relish having to partake in spreading the word, human, but time is of the essence. Get him up and get moving."

"He can't just *get up*." She snarled. "What are the rest of the wounded doing?"

"Taking up my legionaries in order to move them," said the legate. He turned to one of his men. "Pick him up."

The huntress took a step between Scythe and the dragons. "Wait.

I need to pack his gear properly."

"Do it quickly," the legate said. "Onto the next fire," he added to his companions, "I'll send someone back for the whelp. You have ten minutes." The dragons stomped off.

Scythe let his breath go, unaware he'd even been holding it. What was going on? This didn't feel right.

The huntress knelt by his side, busying herself with pretending to pack up some equipment.

"They're gone," Scythe whispered. "You don't have to—"

"Don't speak. I'm giving you the food," she said, barely moving her lips.

"What? That's yours."

"Shhh. Just don't eat it all at once."

"You can't—"

"I can, I am, and you'll be fine," she said.

"Won't you need it?"

She paused in her work, looked to him, then returned to her task. "Last time this happened I lost my finger." She hesitated again. "Find me after, if you like."

But her voice didn't fill Scythe with confidence. He wanted to say more, do more, but didn't know what. He was utterly out of his depth.

She tied a knot with an air of finality. "You're dead to the world, remember? Give one hint you're okay and they'll send you marching to the front." She glanced behind her, then snapped her attention back to him, a fervour in her eyes. "Don't let that happen."

"Why are you helping me so much?" Scythe said.

She leaned in closer, so that no one else could possibly hear her words. "I have a soft spot for idiots like you. Try and live. Go home. You've still got a home to go back to."

"What's your name?" Scythe said, louder than he ought to but he had to know.

"My name's Aifa." But before Scythe could say more, she scrambled to her feet. He closed his eyes to feign his ill constitution and, soon enough, a pair of rough hands were lifting him up. He felt his knapsack, bow, quiver, and sword get piled on top of his limp form, followed by the bobbing up and down of movement.

He never had a chance to say it.

Thank you, Aifa. He nigh on sang it in his mind. He wanted her to hear him somehow across the rapidly growing distance between them. *Thank you for saving my life.*

SCYTHE FEIGNED UNCONSCIOUSNESS for what felt like hours. Inside, he fought a desperate battle with himself, pitting his relief at not being sent to front against his guilt for not being there. Aifa's behaviour had been worrying. Clearly, she thought something terrible would happen. Could he really just lie here in the dark, eyes screwed shut as though he could block out the world? Could he run from it all?

Sleep claimed him before he decided. When he woke again, he was surrounded by the sick and wounded; the *true* sick and wounded. Missing limbs, blood-stained cloth wrapped wounds, the sickly smell of rot and decay. His being here was a lie. And it was cowardly.

Gingerly, he got up and tried to slip away. He didn't have to try hard, no one was paying much attention to him. Beyond the rows of the dead and dying, he could see some dragons facing north, their backs turned to him. Some were pointing north and, against the bright sky of the morning, Scythe saw smoke rising. Not the thick black smoke of a fire, but the wispy, guttering smoke he'd heard came from demon blood.

A battle raged.

Scythe made it to the where the dragons were standing, just beyond the camp's boundaries. A wide flat plain lay before them, a perfect spot for a pitched battle with plenty of room to manoeuvre. So then, why weren't these dragons up there in the thick of the fighting? Ahead, he couldn't see any signs that the dragons were there at all. What he did see horrified him.

Humans fleeing, running, hobbling, or crawling in desperate flights from the vast horde of writhing darkness that was the demon army.

Mad senses of duty and honour flared in Scythe's chest, and he darted forward, weapon-less but intending to do his part nonetheless. About ten strides out, a hand grabbed him by the collar and lifted him bodily from the ground. The dragon walked him back to their line and set him down between two strong legionaries.

"No use you running out there," the dragon brooded. "Not after doing so well in escaping it."

"Why aren't you helping?" Scythe said.

"Following our prince's orders," the dragon said. He looked to Scythe as though he were stupid for not understanding. "Prince Darnuir wished to draw the demons out for a fight. They learnt their lesson at the Nest."

"And we were the bait," Scythe said. His whole body sagged.

"There," another dragon exclaimed, pointing to the south east this time. "The prince arrives."

Scythe whipped around. There, moving like a herd of golden bulls, a legion of dragons charged into view. They would have outstripped horses the way they pushed themselves. From the southwest, another legion emerged. Together, they swept up the battlefield, causing the earth to quake, and reached the battle in half a minute. The columns of shining gold pivoted right and left, slamming into the exposed demon flanks with impunity.

"Glorious," sighed the dragon nearest Scythe.

"Hail the prince," another called.

"Hail Darnuir!"

Scythe wanted to vomit. He did. And while he clutched to his heaving gut, his awe of the dragons became the very bile in his throat. So, this was the dragon prowess he'd heard so much about. This was the dragons' art of war.

HARD LESSONS

From the Author

I hope you enjoyed this short tale set in the world of *Dragon's Blade*. As you can see, though I draw on many traditional elements of fantasy, I don't do so in the usual ways. A fast paced epic fantasy awaits those who wish to delve deeper into my world with book 1, *The Dragon's Blade: The Reborn King*. It is this Dragon Prince, Darnuir, who takes the leading role in the trilogy, and he has a lot to make up for.

Arrogant. Scornful. Full of Pride. Darnuir cares little about the damage he's done to the faltering alliance against the demonic forces of the Shadow. He thinks himself invincible - right up till a mortal wound forces him to undergo a dangerous rebirthing spell, leaving him a helpless babe in human hands. Twenty years pass and with the alliance between humanity, dragons, and fairies fracturing, Darnuir will have to uncover the secrets of his past, seek redemption for his sins, and rally the disparate races if they are to survive.

Only Darnuir can do this. For he's the last member of the royal bloodline and only he can wield the Dragon's Blade...

Amazon US link
www.amazon.com/dp/B06WRVZLJ2

Amazon UK link
www.amazon.co.uk/dp/B06WRVZLJ2

For those about to delve into my books, I thank you, and hope you enjoy!

Michael R. Miller

A BATTLE FOR ELUCAME

RB WATKINSON

THEIR TORCHES FLARED, burning the walls and ceiling as they trotted faster down the narrowing tunnel. Closing fast, the boots of the Murecken soldiers and blood-priests pounded their pursuit, now certain of their quarry.

"Spirits! They're close." Leah's heart hammered with equal measures of fear and nervous energy. "Only fifty yards behind us, if that."

"It's a big group, too. Must be fifty or sixty of them." Richa stopped next to Leah, panting hard. He tugged at the fake iron collar around his neck. "Bollocks, but I hate wearing this blasted thing. It feels too damned real."

"That's why we've got to wear them." Using her Wealdan-sight, Leah studied the glowing wire-like Wefan-patterns running within the rock near the tunnel's end. She spotted, the area where the Wefan-patterns changed minutely and knew Uncle Kharad stood just two feet from her, but she sensed neither him nor his magik. His Wealdan-cloak camouflaged him and the entrance to the smaller cave too well, along with a whole lot of Freed itching to get their blades into the Murecken.

"Are they there?"

"Yes." Leah nodded.

"Good," Richa answered, patting the hilt of his short sword. "Looking forward to using my new weapon."

"Hurry, you two." Joff stood in the cavern's entrance, her bald head washed with green light. "Get in and be bait. You know your roles."

In the cavern, the torchlight didn't quite reach the ceiling. Up there, clumps of luminous fungi grew, filling the cavern with their strange glow. For these lowest levels of Elucame, it seemed almost bright.

THE WORK WAS quick and bloody.

Leah tugged her knife out from between the blood-priest's ribs and ripped the Blodstan from his neck. Already boiling with smoke-like tentacles of Ascian, she threw the lumpy red gem as far and fast as she could. The Freed had learned to get rid of the Blodstans after realising the Murecken channelled their Ascian, or blood-magik, through them. The gems also healed wounds fast, making it hard to kill the bastards.

Leah watched the life bleed from the man's eyes. Whenever she could, she'd snatch that breath of time to see death steal a blood-priest's spirit.

Staying low, she moved on, careful of her footing on the uneven floor, her feet whispering over the dust and blood. She spotted a blood-priest wrestling with one of the newer Freed, Torig. The priest's whip and two fingers lay in a pool of blood on the floor. The combatant's grunted, red-faced, veins protruding, each gripping the others' wrists, daggers in their other hands, all slippery with blood. Blood-magik coiled from the blood-priest's Blodstan, slow to respond to his need, which meant he was weak in the Ascian. Leah's knife found its way between his ribs, puncturing a lung, piercing his heart.

"I had him, Leah," Torig complained.

"You did," Leah agreed. Ignoring Torig, she crouched and ripped the Blodstan from the dying priest's neck. The link gone, its magik died as it flew across the cavern. She stared into his confused eyes. "Not what you lot expected was it? To be beaten by a bunch of ex-slaves? You arrogant bastards had it coming, and you'll get more of it."

Warned by a change in the air, Leah rolled toward her attacker's legs, dodging the sword that came for her. Surprised, the Murecken soldier overbalanced, an opportunity she used to slice through the back of his knee. Screaming, he toppled, and Leah left him for Torig to finish. She searched for the next Murecken, wanting, needing it to be another blood-priest.

Leah spotted Uncle Kharad and Alan working together at the upper entrance to the cavern, stopping any Murecken from escaping that way. Uncle Kharad blocked the blood-magik of the priests, and Alan cut them down with his sword, a method that'd proven an efficient and safer way to fight against the Murecken. Most of the Freed now fought in pairs.

NO MORE THAN half a day later—measured by the hunger in her belly—the screams and crash of battle ended, replaced by the groans and cries of the wounded and dying. With others of the Freed, Leah helped any wounded Murecken reach the path to their god, Murak, and marked them all with the clawed hands of long dead writhen to make it look like the creatures had rebelled against their masters. She wondered if the ploy would fool the Murecken for much longer.

Leah found a ledge of rock in the least bloody corner of the cave and began cleaning her knives. She'd barely started when Lance, a fair-haired boy a year or so younger than her, scuttled over. She'd killed a blood-priest, pulling him along like a dog on a chain not long ago, and Lance followed her about like an annoying puppy ever since. Sitting next to her, he looked up, his blue eyes crowded with terror. She sighed and rolled her eyes as he crept under her arm and pressed his head against her chest. Maybe the sound of her heart comforted the annoying brat. His narrow shoulders heaved, and Leah let him stay.

"Wonder how they're doin' in the other caves and tunnels." Richa hunkered down nearby. "Six ambushes in one go. Alan and Kharad are getting' ambitious. Spectacular bit of Wealdan-magik goin' on down at the other end of the cavern, too."

"We'll know soon enough how well it all went," Joff said. She slid down with a bump on Leah's other side and started cleaning her short sword. "And Alan's right, we've no time left to be careful anymore. We've got to free all the other slaves and captives fast and kill as many blood-priests as we can before they get wise to the fact there are so many of us Freed. And that it's not the writhen that're attacking their patrols."

"I'm happy to kill as many damned blood-priests as needed." Leah had lost count of the number she'd killed a while back.

"We know, Leah. We know," Joff said, sighing.

"You got a problem with me, Joff?" Leah slitted her eyes at him.

"No, Leah." Joff shrugged. "It's just you get so focused on killing blood-priests, you forget other Freed might be about or needing help. One day, you're going to get someone else killed, is all."

"One day?" Leah snorted. "In case you haven't noticed, there are no days here, Joff."

"Just one never-endin', bloody killing-filled night," Richa muttered. "I dream of the sky. Day or night, doesn't matter to me. I need to see the big blue again."

"It's what we're fighting for," Joff agreed. "These battles are small parts of a long war we're fighting, but at the end of it, we'll all be free to see the sky again."

"That's the truth," Leah agreed. "And I'm fighting for it as much as anyone."

"We saw a Mid-priest escorting a wagon bound for the armoury yesterday when we were scouting." Richa began working a whetstone along the blade of his short sword. "Looks like he's got himself a cushy new job."

"You had to tell her, Richa?" Joff scowled at him. "You know—"

"Who, Richa?" Leah interrupted.

"It was him. Tall, skinny, with snaggleteeth." Richa shrugged, glancing Joff's way. "She'd have found out soon enough, Joff."

"Mid-priest Wenst. Bastard!" Leah scowled. The blood-priest had hurt her bad her first night in Elucame, more than once, and he'd promised to do it again. He'd gone by the time Alan and her cousin, Watt, had found her and led her to the Freed. As soon as Kharad broke her slave collar with his Wealdan-magik, she'd made an oath to find and hurt Mid-priest Wenst. When she was done, she'd kill him.

"There were Mid-priests here." Joff leaned back, her eyes closed, weariness dragging her narrow face down to her chest. "Fair bit of blood-magik was thrown around down at the lower tunnel entrance. It's still burning."

"Weren't you listenin'? Half of that magik was Wealdan. Watt and his team were throwing as much at the Murecken as they were at us, if not more." Richa slapped his hand against his chest in a salute. "Fuckin' awesome, those Wealdan-warriors. Spirits! If only I'd more than a drop of Wealdan in my blood."

Leah squashed the flare of jealousy she felt, wishing for the umpteenth time she'd her cousin's skills. She could Wealdan-heal a bit, and had the Wealdan-sight, too—a useful skill down in the pitch-dark bowels of Elucame. For fighting, though, she relied on her knives. She'd practiced hard with them since the day she became one of the Freed.

She pulled out a knife and twirled it into the air, then wove it through her fingers. It thrilled her every time she cut a Murecken's throat. His gurgling breaths, his spurting blood, the thud as he collapsed to the ground, the sight of death stealing into his eyes. And all of it up close and personal. Leah didn't think she'd get the same thrill from throwing Wealdan-fire at a blood-priest, with his death a distant thing.

"I'll go when the magik has dissipated. I've no urgent need to get burned," Leah lied. She'd a burning desire to hunt the stinking, rat-bollocked bastard Wenst right now, but she wanted to do it alone.

"This lure and ambush trick won't work many more times," Joff said, yawning. "They'll get wise to it soon enough."

"Yeah, even the Murecken can't stay that stupid," Richa added.

"What we've got to do is trap the bastards in their lairs, then kill them all in one go." Leah flicked the knife into the air again, snatched it by the blade, flipped it, and slipped it back into its sheath. "It's the only way."

"The only time you get lots of them together is when they've their arses in the air, prayin' to their soddin' god, Murak." Richa laughed. "We could spear every one of them 'tween the cheeks then."

"I'm sure Alan and Kharad are planning for it," Joff said.

The whistle sounded, three short bursts.

Leah shook Lance's shoulder. "It's finished for now. Up you get."

Lance looked around, dazed.

"You'll get used to it soon," Joff said.

"You will," Leah agreed. She had. Fighting the stinking bastards was better than shaking in fear at what they might do should they ever take her again. She'd stick herself with a blade before she ever let that happen.

"Especially if you keep following Leah," Joff said. "Her paths are littered with the dead, and always will be until she finds the one she's really after."

"Even that won't stop our Leah," Richa added. "She's got a taste for killin' nothin' else will ever satisfy."

"Shut up, you two," Leah grumbled. It was true enough, though. Her mother would shiver at what she'd become, but her mother was long dead. "You're being idiots, scaring the boy like that."

"I'm not a boy. Not no more." Lance blinked and struggled to his feet, then his face turned red, and he reached behind to feel his trousers. He looked at his hand, then at Leah, his face all misery.

"It's no disgrace," Leah said, understanding. She'd pissed herself the first time she'd faced a writhen with nothing but knives to keep its claws and teeth from tearing into her flesh. "A lot people fill their pants their first battle. Know the tunnel my Uncle Kharad was hiding in? There's a pool you can wash in not far down it."

Leah stood and watched the boy move off, his steps awkward. She turned toward the fading magik-made fires. "I'm going to find a way to the Mid-priest sector. I've waited long enough. Like you said, Joff, I'll not stop until I've killed that bastard. Mid-priest Wenst is going to be fed his own bollocks."

"Are you mad?" Richa sat up, looking to Joff for backup. "Kharad said there was no way up to the Temple Quarter that the Murecken don't already know about. The whole place is heavily guarded."

"It's suicide, Leah," Joff added. "Alan has a plan for the big push into the Temple Quarter. He and Kharad have worked on it for a while now. You don't want to spoil their plans by doing something to alert the Murecken, do you?"

"Alan and his plans are taking too blasted long. And Kharad can't have covered every inch of the place. Even he hasn't been Freed long enough for that." Leah scowled and opened her Wealdan. The patterns of Wefan sprang up all around her. It was bright in the flesh of her friends, in the fungi, in the rock, though faded in the dead scattered across the cavern. "I'm a scout, aren't I? Best one the Freed have got. For Alan and Kharad's plan to work, we'll need a secret way up to the Temple Quarter, and who better to find it?"

"We'll come with you." Richa began to lever himself up.

"I'll be faster on my own. You've not got the Wealdan-sight, you'll just flounder about behind me," Leah said, already turning away. Alan and Kharad, the leaders of the Freed, were good men but too slow and careful. "I'll make a new map for Alan. He's always wanting more maps."

Leah picked her way past bodies of men, tadige, and writhen. There was even a dead lacert—no, two.

Good.

The blood-magik had burned away the fungus, and apart from the odd red flame guttering on clothing, the tunnel was dark. It didn't matter to her, though, not with her Wealdan-sight showing her the way.

LEAH PRESSED BACK into the crack in the tunnel wall, shallowed her breathing, and prayed the guards had no lacerts with them. The spirits were with her. Four, five, six Murecken guards marched past. No lacerts, not even any writhen, though that was no surprise. Fewer patrols took writhen along with them now so many ambushes seemed to be the work of the twisted creatures. She grinned, touching the bone handles of the knives she'd liberated from Elucame's armoury a while back.

As the soldiers passed her hiding place, Leah felt the need to knife them all but knew she couldn't take on so many. Not by herself. She worked in the dark, sneaked up from behind, cut a throat, holed a lung, skewered a brain. Freed scouts like her preferred knife work, it was their way of fighting. It wasn't noble or heroic like the swordsmen with their face-to-face battles, but it was effective. Anyway, they didn't have the time nor the luxury for heroics. Not down here in the tunnels and caves of Elucame, weighed down by the Ruel Mountains, surrounded by the enemy. The thump of boots faded into the darkness as did the flickering torches.

Leah knew Joff and Richa understood her need to kill Wenst. The blood-priest had been more powerful than her once, but she'd learned a lot since then. When she found the blood-sucking bastard, she'd show him just how much she'd learned.

She continued through the pitch-dark of Elucame's bowels, with the patterns of Wefan in the rock guiding her. When she came to a vertical crevice, or *chimney* as Alan called them, she began climbing. It stank of piss, so she knew it'd lead to a more populated area of Elucame.

Spirits! Hope no one thinks to use it for a while longer.

With her hands pressed against one side, and her feet jammed against the other, she inched her way up. Alan had taught her and Watt how to climb a chimney when the three of them had first arrived in Elucame. They'd hidden up one when the blood-priests came to their Holding Cave to cull the slaves.

The stink got worse the higher she got, but she lucked out. No one pissed on her and the chimney opened onto a wide, bright tunnel. Burning torches set in fancy iron brackets, fixed into the walls every ten yards or so, lit the tunnel and the doors lining it. Leah waited, her eyes at ground level, listening. On the door opposite, above the painted number fifty-six, a burning mountain was carved into the dark wood. The sign of their god, Murak. Her heart lurched when she realised she'd reached the Temple District. A distant bell rang with hard, deep clangs.

Leah froze. Someone was climbing up behind her, panting like a dog on a hot day. She looked between her legs into the vague darkness and saw a face appear.

"What in Murak's hells are you doing here?"

Lance looked up at her, his smile faltering. "I followed you."

"Obviously," Leah said with a hiss. "Why's the question I want an answer to."

"I want to help you," he whispered, his face screwed up, but he set his jaw. Stubborn boy. "I want to learn."

"You'd have helped me by staying with the others, blast it!" Leah shook her head. How was she going to look after the boy and do what she meant to do? "Stay here, don't move, and I'll be back soon as I can."

"But—"

"No blasted 'buts,' boy. You're not even wearing your collar. What if a Murecken sees you?"

Heart pounding, hands shaking, her knuckles white from their grip on the ledge, she ignored Lance's whimpers and pulled herself out of the piss-hole. She stepped into the tunnel too fast, without that last look around every scout should take. She barely had time to lean against the wall and pretend she was waiting before a priest spotted her.

"What are you doing here, slave?" The Low-priest came to a stop in front of her, tapping the handle of his blood-magik whip against his thigh.

"I'm waiting for Mid-priest Wenst," Leah answered. Arms folded across her chest, she bowed low, though her body screamed to launch itself at the blood-priest. "I have a message for him from the armoury."

The knives she'd stolen from said armoury were the message, one this priest would get a word or two from if he didn't let her pass.

"Can't you read? You're waiting by the wrong door. His is thirty-two, back toward the Temple. This end of the tunnel is for the Low-priests," the young man said. His face twisted as he glanced over his shoulder. "He wasn't far behind me. He could be back in his rooms by now."

She frowned, watching the priest hurry down the tunnel. Soon as he'd gone, Leah ran to door thirty-two, checked no one was coming, and tried the handle.

"Damn!" It was locked. The stamp of boots announced someone approaching. Leah adjusted her clothing and her hair and stood in a way she knew would appeal to him—frightened, small, young.

Then Leah saw him. Tall, skinny, snaggletoothed. Nothing to fear. Not the man of her nightmares—not anymore.

"Mid-priest Wenst?" she said, keeping her voice high, child-like. She bowed low, arms folded, though her feet were set ready for a leap. For attack or escape, she didn't know yet. "I've a message for you from the armoury."

"A message, slave?" Wenst looked her up and down. He liked what he saw. Leah's skin crawled.

She nodded, thanking the spirits he didn't recognise her. He opened his door and indicated Leah go in ahead of him. "Tell me in here."

She squeezed past him, his scent reminding her of her first night in Elucame. She'd woken to find Wenst in the doorway to her cell, a ghoulish figure painted green by glowing fungi. Deep in the marrow of her bones, Leah had known the look in his eyes meant no good.

Leah shuffled through the doorway, hunching her shoulders, taking in everything.

The room was a surprise. Ornate, with tapestries hiding the walls and plush carpets scattered with enormous silk cushions. Through an arch, Leah saw a large, velvet-curtained, four-poster bed.

They both turned at a yell. A boy leaped onto Wenst's back, a small knife reaching for the blood-priest's throat.

"No!" Leah ran forward, her hands reaching to grab Lance, anger filling her at the thought of someone else killing Wenst.

Before she could get there, the blood-priest snatched hold of Lance's wrist, twisting and pulling so bones snapped, and the boy fell screaming to the floor. Leah shot forward and pulled Lance away from Wenst, sheltering him with her body.

"You bloody idiot, Lance!" The words were out of Leah's mouth before she could think.

"How interesting. A slave-boy without his iron collar," Wenst drawled. He stepped closer, his blood-magik whip live with growing tentacles of oily, red-tinted smoke. "Are you slaves becoming…organised?"

Leah stiffened, fear filling her. She had to finish this fast. Keeping her back to Wenst, Leah whispered into Lance's ear. "I know it hurts, but stop crying and listen. Soon as I move, you've got to run like Murak's demons are after you and get back down that piss-hole. Got it?"

Lance snuffled down his tears and nodded. Leah prayed to the spirits he'd do as he'd been told.

"I should thank your leaders for sending children," Mid-priest Wenst said, smiling. "It gives me the opportunity for an enjoyable hour or two. Always a pleasure after a hard day's work."

Leah moved. Giving Lance a push, she rolled towards Wenst's legs, her knives out. She heard the crackle of blood-magik and Lance scream, but then the door slammed, so she guessed he must've escaped. Curling an arm, she sliced a blade across the back of Wenst's knee, her blood thrilling at the blood-priest's shriek. Twisting, she leaped toward him, punched one blade up between his jaw bones, the other between his ribs. She then tore through his trousers and cut, and cut again, into the meat that dangled there.

His voice stolen by welling blood, Wenst gurgled and folded to the floor. Tentacles of blood-magik spilled from his Blodstan, writhing towards his wounds. She ripped the red gem from his neck and threw it into a corner of the room.

"Recognise me, rat-face? Now you get to die slow and hurt as much as you made me hurt."

Leah stared at Wenst's confused eyes as his life bled out. Why didn't she feel jubilant? Or satisfaction at fulfilling her oath? She just felt empty and dull.

A whimper had Leah turning for the door. Lance lay in a crumpled heap, the blood-magik whip in his blackened hand. Its magik might be gone now, but burns smoked all over the boy's body where its lashes had cut into his flesh. Unlike most of the others, the burn circling his throat hadn't cauterised. Blood pumped onto the floor.

"I got it off him, Leah," Lance croaked. "Told you I could help."

Leah, there in an instant, pressed her hand against his throat. She summoned her Wealdan, tried to heal the wound, but it was too deep. He'd already lost too much blood. She wasn't strong enough.

"Spirits, Lance! Why couldn't you just do what I'd told you?" She cradled him against her chest, where he'd hear the beat of her heart.

Leah held Lance long after death came in to steal the light from his eyes.

"I'm sorry," she whispered. For the first time since she'd been captured by the Murecken all those months ago, Leah cried.

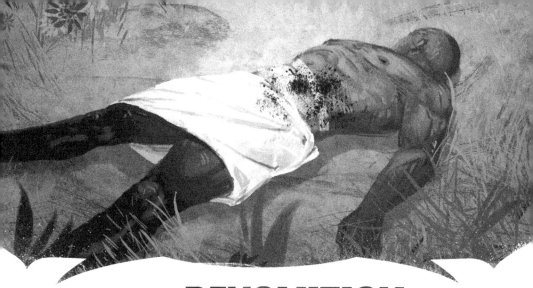

THE REVOLUTION CHANGED EVERYONE

D. THOURSON PALMER

EVEN AS THE water runs clear over her hands, rushing downstream cold and once again unsullied, Camule's stomach turns over at the lingering scent. Kneeling, she clenches her fists and breathes with the mud on the bank seeping cool and sticky through her skirt. Her eyes squeeze as hard as her hands. Sometimes a fever kills, she reminds herself. For mercy. To save many at the cost of one. She'd gone upwind, so she wonders if it's just her imagination making the bile in her guts swirl and churn and not the wafting stench of blood and early rot riding high on an undercurrent of powder and smoke.

After several breaths—two or twenty, she's not sure—the pounding in her ears and the growl in her bones gives way to the soft burble of water, the buzz of mosquitoes circling. Echoing from downriver, outside the city, comes the sound of steel and the *pop* of muskets. Here, though, there's humid breeze stirring the palms and the boughs of the *kapok* trees. There's wet earth and the clean scent of leaves and the nipping spice of bark. The blood-smell is gone.

She opens her eyes, takes up her cleaned tools: knife and razors, clamps and thin spoons and long needles of different sizes. She packs them into her satchel and levers herself upright. Her back tightens, weak from leaning over and squatting and crouching for long hours, day after day, and she moves slow in anticipation of the crack she knows is coming from her spine. There's resistance, then the little *pop*, and she straightens fully.

Halfway back, the sight of a shadow making its way toward her through the sunlit gold-green of the undergrowth stops her. She waits, recognizing the broad-shouldered silhouette. Esube bends his wiry frame nearly double to pass beneath a bough, then comes up with a grin on his scarred lips.

"There you are." He blows out a sigh, then pats his chest and glances around as if he were just taking the air.

Camule masks the deep breath she must take before she trusts her voice. "Got worried about me? I was only gone a moment."

"You were gone longer than that. He's awake."

"What? How long?"

"The time it took me to find you. I came right away." Esube motions for her to precede him back along the path.

"Did he say anything?" Camule forces her voice to steadiness.

"Not yet. He's not going anywhere in his state."

Her jaw relaxes. As they walk, she glances behind her and sees the back of Esube's bald head. Even this far from the fighting, he walks backwards at the end of a line. Old habits. She understands. She takes another deep breath and faces ahead. "And the others?"

Esube makes a noise. "Better, thanks to you."

Camule walks on a few steps without answering. Ahead, she can hear the nearness of them, their voices whisper-calling, the occasional moan of pain.

"What do you think did that to them?" Esube says.

"Animal. Jag, maybe" She shrugs, even though he's watching behind them.

"But a big one."

She grunts in response.

"They're resting now, though. Seem more balanced. I think you got them past the worst of it. Clean work as always, *Nageh*."

She chuckles, returns the formality. "Thank you, *Nageh-tiem*." Her humor is gone as soon as the words leave her mouth.

Her brow is slick with sweat again by the time she reaches the camp, with Esube still walking on his heels behind her. A sentry leaning in the deep shade beneath a tree nods, idly turning a blowgun in his fingers. Others glance up at her arrival—her assistants, the priestess, the haggard fighters, pausing at their half-packed tents or where they're loading the bundles onto donkeys and long-nosed *cobaras* or into the wagon. She had lingered longer than she'd thought by the river.

Men and women in bandages sit in the shade, waiting. Some of them look up with sunken eyes, sallow skin and smile at her, spent grins of appreciation. Others stare at the sudden, linen-wrapped termination of an arm, a leg, and do not notice her passing.

Her people, in smocks and skirts spattered with drops in a narrow spectrum of red to dried-up brown, are inventorying bundles and preparing the wounded fighters for the walk back to safety. The bright green, stylized patches on her companion Leeches' arms are a mockery for the task still ahead. No healer can dress the wound she must see to. She worries her patient has been awake too long, long enough to talk, and she can't remember if she poured two drams of Dream Honey into his ear or one. Two drams would kill anyone else, but him? No, she must have given him two.

The fighters smoke and mutter together outside the hospital tent containing the three scouts Esube had spoken of, the ones she'd cleaned up and stitched up and who were now resting. Some tobacco would be just the thing right then. Something to calm her trembling hands. She could get a cigarette easily. The soldiers look up and grin or nod at the sight of her. Everyone but the wounded likes a leech. But Camule can't bring herself to meet their grateful smiles. She makes for one of the sailcloth-walled tents center camp, where Miss Palomo stands wringing her white hands and sweating like a horse after a two-mile. Her face is red, but it's always red. "What's wrong?" Camule asks.

"He's awake." Palomo's accent is almost too thick for most of the *Olino* to cut through, but Camule has grown used to her tripping syllables and shallow vowels. The foreigner wipes sweat from her brow and leads Camule into the little white canvas room.

There's no ceiling, so there's plenty of light inside. The man lying on a bloody bed of palm fronds is holding bound hands to his stomach, which Camule only recently wrapped with cotton strips. The strips are already crimson, brighter than the dirt under her feet. His ankles are bound and weighted with a stone. They seldom bind the wounded. Bindings were for prisoners, and until they left Camule and her team's care, they were patients.

The man is, or was, called the Cutterman, but only Camule knows that.

Tivu crouches at Cutterman's head, holding his shoulders flat to earth as he strains to curl himself into a ball. Camule kneels at his side and pulls her tools from her satchel. Her back aches. She controls her voice, looks only at her patient. "Has he said anything?"

"Don't think he can."

Her ears strain for any hint of guile in sweet Tivu's voice. Would he even know how to lie? Camule feels Esube behind her, feels Palomo circling to the other side of the wounded man. The prickly, back-of-the-neck feeling of someone's eyes on her. She doesn't look up. Can't. It's just her imagination. Or is it Palomo, watching? The foreigner spends too much time staring and silent, and she smiles too much. No, she's just nervous about speaking Olino correctly. Camule brings her gaze back into focus on her patient. Her burden.

Veins and tendons bulge in Cutterman's neck and forehead. He's lighter of skin than Camule or Esube's cool near-onyx, but still an islander. *Avuntu*, from one of the Orange Islands up north, but to anyone else, just another of the queen's partisans.

"Did you find his insignia?" It'd be unusual if she didn't ask. Camule pulls his hands away from his wound "Hold these, please." She grunts as he resists, but Esube and Tivu manage to take his arms up over his head so she can look at the dressing.

"None on him."

She knows. It's in her pocket. She curses inside. Forgot to throw it in the river in her haste to get the blood off her, get the stink out of her nostrils. She'd forgotten how potent the blood could be. The whole tent reeks of him, makes her skin itch.

"Any information? His regiment, name?"

"Nothing, *Nageh*." Tivu sounds frustrated, but Camule doesn't allow herself the sigh of relief that presses up in her chest.

Cutterman's eyes open. Red and bleary, they roll to and fro, and he thrashes for a moment in Tivu and Esube's grip. They raise their voices at the sudden movement and hold him. Camule helps. Cutterman's muscles bulge and strain beneath her fingers, sweat-slick skin and hard knots and cords beneath, too powerful for his frame, too powerful for someone who'd been torn open halfway to his spine an hour before. A yowl escapes his throat, and Camule prays to Iisha.

"Hey." She grips his chin and forces his face to hers. "Easy. You're safe." Careful. If he's awake, better hope he's awake enough. She tries Avuntu, the language flushing more bad memories into the open. "Easy, soldier." His eyes meet hers and go wide. Careful. Warn him. "*Owali yoto.*"

She uses an Avuntu phrase only used upon a first meeting. "You're in an Olino camp. Don't give them a reason to harm you."

He stares, trying to sit up but gasping, bare chest heaving beneath her hands. His eyes search hers. His stink of blood and fear-sweat sends her stomach rolling again. The mouth, the full lips, twist for a moment. Furrows trench his forehead down the middle in recognition. He's about to speak. To give it away. Does Palomo understand Avuntu? Esube does.

Then he falls back, and his face goes blank and tired. "*Owali yoto.*" He winces and lets out another yowl, loud, wild. Tivu and Palomo jump. Cutterman's guts seeming to clench as he tries to curl up again. They hold him, and he strains, panting. "Please, water."

Esube moves beside her, unstopping a gourd. Camule catches his hand, and he looks at her. She's squeezing his wrist. Too hard. She releases him and tries to keep her voice authoritative and unafraid.

"Are you the only one left?"

Esube whispers. "Iisha's sake, Cam. He just woke up. He doesn't even know."

"Drown Iisha." Tivu gasps at the blasphemy. Blood smell's gnawing her patience. She feels a wash of guilt as Esube's color deepens, but she buries it with her other stores. Guilt can be ignored. Avuntu again. "Are you the only one left? Is there anyone else?"

Esube's voice is gentler. "We found you with your squad. They're dead. I'm sorry." Cutterman stares and Esube goes on. "We heard one of our scout whistles and went to investigate. They chased off whatever it was that attacked your troupe, but not before it got them, too. Almost killed them. Only you and the three of ours survived. I'm sorry."

The man on the ground opens his eyes again and meets Camule's. "They're dead?" He chuckles, cringes at his pain.

"Did you see what did it?" Tivu asks.

"Not now, Tivu," Esube says. "What's your name?"

"Are you the last one?" Camule says over him. She fumbles between three languages for a moment, unable to draw up the right one. "Are there any more? Did anyone get away?"

"Cam, now? Give him a moment."

Palomo clears her throat. "Command expects us to reach Shobasa by nightfall. There's been fighting all day. Can't we ask him whatever needs asking there?"

Tivu grunts. "Not that far."

"Far enough." Palomo slaps a mosquito on her red neck. A sudden, fresh bloom of blood-smell fills the confined space.

Camule snaps, "Now. We find out now. I need you to tell me if you're the last one."

"He needs water," Esube says again.

She and Gia disagree as one. "With that gut wound, it could kill him," the foreigner says.

Camule raises a hand. She holds the gourd before Cutterman's face and flicks his temple. His eyes open and settle on the gourd.

"When you were attacked," she says carefully. Cutterman meets her eyes.

"It was an animal," Esube says. "A jaguar, or dogs?"

Camule knows what it was. Once she'd seen the rips, the gnawed flesh, the claw-cuts on their stomachs, she'd known. Once she'd recognized the man who lie covered in blood and still breathing among them, she'd known. And she'd cursed the three wounded scouts for surviving.

"It was a beast." She uses the Avuntu word that also could mean *monster*. "I need to know if anyone got away. If there are any more wounded out there. Anyone like you. Then water."

Cutterman breathes, stares at her. His nostrils flare, but an awful smile crawls its way across his sweat-sheened face. His teeth are bordered in red. "Am I going to die?"

Camule feels the bones, the ribs in his side, quiver beneath his skin. They twitch and then begin, slowly, moving, traveling like waves—the big, slow, portentous waves that come into the coast far ahead of a typhoon. They roll, and her fingers rise over them like ships cresting a swell, then fall into the troughs between as his body changes.

She looks at Tivu, but he hasn't noticed yet. Her hands subconsciously dig into his side, as if she could hold back what's happening. The smell thickens. She doubts any of the others can taste it. A sharp, acid stink rises out of his sweat, cat piss and burned hair. The smell triggers something in her—the fear, the animal before a predator. Her fingertips prickle, but she forces the feeling back.

Beneath her hand, his ribs are moving. She whispers. "Just tell me."

The teeth flash in a grin. "I should've killed you. My children'll find you."

Camule blinks, nods. "Lift him." Tivu obliges, and she tilts the gourd to Cutterman's lips. His eyes widen and, beneath his skin, the muscles and bones rearranging themselves slow. He slurps and chokes and drinks, his throat pulsing like a tide.

"*Nageh* Camule!" Palomo's voice rises. Tivu makes a low, surprised noise. Esube, though, is watching Camule from one eye.

Camule speaks Olino. "Listen, you three. The healing art is leeches and pus and fever. Sometimes a fever kills for mercy." While Cutterman's eyes close in bliss, Camule picks up her blade from beside her. A shame, so recently washed. She pushes it between the knobby bones where his neck meets his shoulders. It's a quick, sure motion, a surgeon's cut. There's a moment of resistance, then slow, steady pressure. Gia's jaw works, and Esube lowers his eyes. Tivu makes the same noise, a step lower.

Cutterman twitches. His eyes open, already dead as glass. Camule gives a twist-*must be sure*-and slides the blade back out. Blood wells from the cut.

"He was going to die anyway. The wound had caught his guts. The blood sickness would have made a fever, and it would've got him tonight or the day after." Gia nods while Tivu lowers the lifeless shoulders to the ground. "We leave him for the jungle." They nod in understanding, except

Gia who has never accepted the practice. "Pack up."

A cough at the flap of the canvas tent. Camule looks around from where she's still kneeling.

One of her *nageh-tiem*. "*Nageh* Camule? The other three..."

Camule's stomach leaps to her throat. She starts to rise, but the *nageh-tiem* raises an open palm, a gesture for her to slow. "They're dead. None of them made it."

The tears come, without trying, and she lowers her gaze to the dirt. Esube's voice. "How?"

"*Nageh* Camule, there's nothing more you could have done. They went peaceful, all asleep."

WHILE THE OTHERS work, Camule finds the fighter captain and informs him she'll catch up to them at command in Shobasa in two days, though in truth, she's got no idea. The captain asks no questions, thankfully. Esube will be tougher. She approaches him as he finishes binding up the canvas, leaving the dead Cutterman exposed in a flattened clearing on his bloody palm leaves.

"I've got to go off a bit," she says. From the corner of her eye, she watches Cutterman's body, seeking, but not seeing. Esube looks shocked, but she continues "You go on. Get Gia and the other leeches to Shobasa."

"Why?"

"I'll catch up soon."

Esube faces her, folds his arms. "That man knew you."

She returns his stare. "He was delirious."

"Like damn-all he was. He said he should've killed you."

"Yeah. He's from the other side."

He waits. Sighs. "I'm going with you. Wherever you're going."

"Go with the others. That's an order."

"Then court martial me once we get back."

"Don't be difficult."

"Why?"

"Because you're just making my day harder. Thing's going to be how it's going to be."

"I'm going with you. It's as simple as that. Or you can come back with the rest of us."

She considers her answer. His deep brown eyes glint like a polished musket stock. "Why'd you try to hide what hurt that man?" Before she answers, "It was no animal that got him. I saw when you checked the dressing. It was a machete. Someone tried to kill him before they all died."

She waits, but so does he, and Shobasa is far enough without lingering. "Fine. We'll talk about it once we get to command. But I need to sleep. I'll be in the wagon."

ONCE THEY'RE UNDERWAY, Camule slips out of her wagon and into the brush and flattens herself into the undergrowth. Grasses and leaves rustle in the shifting, stifling air beneath the trees. She lies there for a long time while millipedes and ants crawl over her hands and the damp soaks into her clothes. Once she can no longer hear the healers and wounded and their guards, she rises and heads back to the cleared campsite.

Finally alone, she casts about for a likely place, spotting a fallen tree and a mass of vines and fallen palm fronds a few yards off the trampled path. She crouches beside the rotten trunk and digs beneath it in the loamy soil with her hands. Opening her satchel, she removes three empty vials of Dream Honey from a covered pocket. These she places in the hole as if in burial, laying them gently side-by-side, and then covers with dirt and jungle debris. Soon, there's naught to be seen but wet leaves and bark, and she rises and continues.

In the abandoned camp, the trees and undergrowth are hacked back, the smell of palm sap and spicy *ilibo* brush coiling around her. Below it, though, is the blood, and the other thing, the acid stink, growing stronger. She makes her way past the palm bark lean-tos, knowing she's making too much noise, listening and watching for any stragglers from the leech-and-soldier company. In the south, *pops* and heavy *thud-booms* roll against a sky darkening to nightshade, the sounds coming faster, louder. There will be wounded. Work to do. She hopes her *nageh-tiem* arrive safely and in time to help where they can. She finds the trampled clearing and Cutterman's body and approaches as if stalking, or hiding.

He's in the same position they left him, but he seems bigger. The shadows of dusk slip over him as the sun sinks. He's breathing. She can't see it, but she can smell it, smell the sour, thin current grazing his parted lips. Each pinched exhalation stronger than the last. She draws closer and the acid predator smell burns her eyes, making them water. It stings inside her nose, gets in the back of her throat, cloying. All her effort goes to surrounding the fear, the fight-and-kill response that threatens to change her, breaking it, driving it down, muscling it back. Meanwhile, Cutterman's skin stretches. As she nears, the bones in his wrists, rested across his middle, *crack* as his arms rearrange and the hands lengthen.

The revolution changed everyone. Mostly it peeled back layers to show what's underneath. Some survived while others *thrived*. It changed everyone.

Some more than others, she thinks as she stands above Cutterman, above a kind of kin. She watches beads of blood appear and swell at the tips of his fingers. The beads collapse as the claws coming up from inside him break their perilous films and push and curl out of his skin. The smell fills her consciousness as the colors of the world fade to grays. *Some more than others,* as her own claws prick like needles from the insides of her fingertips, then slide out. A memento from the time, long ago, when the Cutterman didn't kill her.

Stomach knotted, she remains on her knees and holds it all back 'til there's nothing left but ache after she hacks his head off with her machete.

Must be sure. Must be sure.

When she can stand, she faces the jungle. *My children'll find you.* The revolution changes everyone, but mostly, it peels back layers. Shows what's underneath. Camule started as a healer, but survival made her the leech, the pus. The fever.

MISPLACED HEROISM

ANDREW ROWE

Chapter I – Elsewhere

I REMEMBER THE moment when the light consumed me. I'd been nursing my coffee addiction while browsing the internet, attention consumed by U.S. Marines fighting ten trillion lions on /r/whowouldwin.

Hilarious.

I had taken one final sip when white light emerged from my screen, blinding me.

When I reopened my eyes, I saw a medieval throne room.

Given that I wasn't high, sleeping, or LARPing, I noted this circumstance to be unusual.

I was ringed by hooded, wizard-looking figures. Etched into the floor between them and me was a geometric figure that glowed with a pale blue light. It faded as I watched.

Either someone had decided to turn off the EL-wire, or it was magic fading away.

Beyond the ring of hooded figures were dozens of armored soldiers and a handful of other people. The one who drew my attention immediately was, of course, the woman sitting on the throne.

She was in the regalest garb I'd ever seen, highlighted by a ridiculous crown that covered the entire top of her head and proceeded a couple of feet upward. It looked like it weighed about thirty pounds. I pitied her poor neck.

The woman on the throne raised her voice above the clamor that had erupted upon my arrival. "Silence!" Her voice struck the room like a hammer.

Everyone got real quiet.

When she seemed sure she had my attention, she spoke again.

"Greetings, chosen hero. I am Queen Valerie of Generia. You have been summoned to our land in a time of great need."

I nodded amiably. This was exactly the kind of scenario I'd probably encounter if I experienced some kind of psychotic break.

The queen continued. "For many years, our land has been besieged by the forces of the Demon King. Though the forces of good—humans, elves, and dwarves—banded together against this onslaught, we have been pushed back to our last bastion of hope. The city of Aegis, in which we stand."

Wow. This was an *implausibly* generic setup.

The demon king's name was the Demon King? Really?

"The demon armies have nearly reached our city walls. Within one month, they will be upon us. Desperate for any solution, our wizards have divined an answer, a chosen hero, summoned from another world, with the strength and wisdom to lead us to victory over the demons."

I nodded once more. "And your wizards cast some sort of spell designed to summon the optimal hero for your situation?"

She glanced at her wizards.

One of them, a traditional grey-bearded man who seemed to be wearing a pointed hat *under* his hood, turned to the queen. "Erm, no, your grace. We, uh, left it to the, uh, prophecy to determine who would be best."

Meaning they summoned me at random.

I barely managed to stop myself from face-palming.

The queen seemed cheered by this, however. "Ah, yes. The power of prophecy has guided us all. Surely, this one is the hero who was promised, but I must ask you, hero, will you help us?"

This is a terrible idea.

They really should have summoned a mechanical engineer. The old "giving guns to the Romans" strategy is probably appropriate, but I have no idea how to implement that.

I looked around the room awkwardly. Everyone was looking at me with hopeful stares: the soldiers, the few nobles, the bearded wizard, even the queen.

"Of course, your grace. What sort of hero would refuse?"

I'll have to fall back on what I know.

It wasn't arrogance that led me to agree, nor any real belief that I could lead their armies to victory. It was, rather, that I doubted the confused-looking wizards surrounding me would be able to send me back home safely.

Beating the demon army seemed like a better bet.

"Thank you, hero." There were many sighs of relief. "My kingdom's resources are at your disposal while you prepare for your battle against the demon king."

"Wait, what?"

FIVE MINUTES LATER, after vehemently clarifying that I had no intention of fighting any demon kings in personal combat...

"To start with, I'm going to need a map of the area with troop positions and numbers. For our side, at least, though ideally for both. How strong are these demons individually?"

"They vary significantly, but on average, about as strong as three of our soldiers."

"And I presume the demon king is stronger than an ordinary demon?"

"Oh, yes. Thousands of times stronger. He has destroyed cities single-handedly."

Lovely.

"I'll need an idea of where he's located and if he's going to be leading his troops personally. Also, any sort of files you have on his generals, lieutenants, and other important forces."

The queen nodded. "Anything else?"

"Several things. How do our numbers compare to theirs?"

"We are outnumbered at least one hundred to one."

Even guns probably wouldn't be enough of a force multiplier to handle that. Tanks and aircraft, maybe.

Assuming bullets even work on demons.

The queen gestured to a noble at her side. "Begin those preparations. Anything else?"

"I'll need information on demon strengths and weaknesses. In addition, I'll need to know who our strongest troops are, as well as what other resources we have at our disposal. Magic, items, that sort of thing. Can you summon other people from my world?"

The hat-and-cloak wizard answered me. "Nay, Lord Hero. It took months of saving our magical resources for a single summoning spell. We have very little left, and certainly not enough to summon a person."

I considered that. "What about an object?"

"Something small."

"How small?"

"About the size of a dagger."

I nodded. "How hard is it for you to teleport something that's already here? Say, to transport someone or something directly into the midst of the enemy army?"

A series of gasps erupted from the wizards around me. "Surely, you don't intend to fight the entire enemy army from within!"

I waved my hands. "Nothing like that. More like teleporting a small object. Would that be possible?"

"With appropriate preparations, yes. We could send a person, a small object, or both."

Okay, a "vials of deadly pathogen" plan is potentially viable, presuming that demons are susceptible to diseases. I'll need to find out more about their physiology, as well as local human culture, before I go to that kind of extreme. There's too much of a risk that it would either fail or backfire to start with that route.

If the morality of that approach bothered me, well, murdering an army was going to be bad regardless of how we did it. And there was no doubt that murder was the best strategy here. We could not possibly survive a straight fight with hundred-to-one odds.

"I'm going to need a better understanding of your magic in general. Would it be possible to teach me the fundamentals within a few days?"

"Perhaps, but if your soul is not properly attuned, you may not be able to cast powerful spells."

"That's not the important part."

SEVEN DAYS PASSED.

We had an estimated twenty remaining before the demon army arrived.

Speaking of demons, I learned they could be hurt by both conventional weapons and magic, except for the strongest ones. Only magical weapons, holy magic, and powerful spells worked on greater demons.

Mages were, unfortunately, in short supply.

Everything was.

The mighty kingdom of Aegis had about ten thousand troops. This was, by their kingdom's standards, quite a lot.

It was smaller than the student population of my college.

And it certainly wasn't going to stop an army of one *million* demons for very long.

In terms of advantages, we had walls blessed by one of the ancient gods, Reinforcia, in the early days of the world. Hopefully, those would hold up against serious bombardment.

We had about fifty trained wizards in total, although roughly half of those were apprentices. There was no requirement for a *magical spark* or that sort of thing here. Anyone could learn the local magic with effort, and basic battle magic could be learned in a week. It was more powerful or specialized magic that had serious requirements.

I instructed the wizards to begin teaching classes to the army as quickly as possible.

Demons were critically weak against holy magic. We only had a few holy mages, and they were apparently on the front lines, trying to hold back the demon army as long as possible. I was informed they were all too deep in combat to be summoned back here.

I recommended the local wizards begin studying holy magic as soon as possible, but it seemed that would be difficult without a teacher, a book, or an object to study. I couldn't plan on getting any additional holy mages easily.

I tried to tour the city. I'd been assigned guards, and they were stubborn about keeping me confined to the palace itself. They feared that demon assassins would strike if I moved into an area that wasn't secure. Apparently, they'd lost several important figures that way.

Including, I learned after some pressing, the *first* hero they had summoned.

I was, in fact, the fifth and final attempt at a prophesized savior. Every other summoned *hero* had died some terrible death, and relatively quickly.

Given that explanation, I grudgingly accepted their protectiveness, even if it kept me from doing a visual check of the state of the walls and siege engines.

I'd have to trust that, as well as a number of other things, to the people of Aegis.

"IN CONCLUSION, COMBINING magical types is possible, but only for a mage who is capable of wielding both types at the level necessary to generate an effect of the appropriate type."

"So, you'd need to be third level in both fire magic and lightning magic to turn a fire ball spell into a lightning ball?"

"Correct."

Two more days passed. My rudimentary magical education was progressing. I'd managed—to my delight—to conjure a flame about the size a lighter could produce.

If I was going to die, at least I'd die as a goddamn sorcerer.

I picked up a few other basic spells. "Frosty Beam," "Read Language," "Loud Noise," that sort of thing.

My favorite was a basic Comprehension spell. Every time I cast it on something—an object, or a person—it would tell me a tiny bit of new information about it.

This mostly consisted of useless trivia.

"Comprehension."

This is a sword.

"Comprehension."

This sword is called an arming sword.

"Comprehension."

The arming sword was first invented by—

"Comprehension."

This sword weighs exactly 1 pound and four ounces.

Nevertheless, I could cast the spell easily and repeatedly, and that had certain uses.

In spite of my excitement at learning magic, I found the limitations of it were severe. Magic was split into levels in a suspiciously RPG-like fashion. Nine levels, to be precise. Plus, a tenth *mythical* level that obviously existed.

At the moment, the spells I could cast wouldn't even qualify as level one. The demon king was presumed to be able to cast ninth level spells easily, and his generals were probably in the seventh or eighth range.

The local wizards were able to cast levels two to four spells on their own. Only three of them could cast fifth level spells, and one was just starting to push himself to the point of casting sixth.

The differences in spell power for each level were exponential.

A first level fire spell was probably around the danger level of a handgun.

A second level spell was more like a high-powered rifle. Or, on the utility side, things like causing rainfall or levitating someone.

A fifth level spell could rain fire from the sky or cause a minor natural disaster.

A ninth level spell? Looking at nuclear bomb territory. And not a small one.

So, in summary, we were hilariously outgunned in terms of magic, as well.

I found out that there were elixirs to boost magical ability, and I started drinking them by the gallon for every element.

Once I found out there were physical enhancement elixirs, I started drinking those, too.

Give me all of the permanent stat increases. All of them.

The kingdom also had a limited supply of magic items available, including an incomplete set of legendary equipment they expected me to wear for my confrontation with the demon lord.

Incomplete, of course, because the demon lord had pried some of the pieces off the *last* hero's body before the wizards had managed to teleport his corpse back.

Also, the legendary holy sword was kind of...bent.

They assured me it would still work just fine.

I didn't like the odds of that. I did, however, graciously accept the equipment for three reasons.

One, to boost morale.

Two, because it looked slick on me.

And three, because the sword was imbued with holy magic. I wanted to figure out how holy magic worked.

"Comprehension."

This is a sword.

"Comprehension."

This was once considered a holy sword.

"Comprehension."

This was called a holy sword because it was invested with holy magic.

I sighed.

This was going to take a while.

WHILE SPENDING AN absolutely absurd amount of time spamming the Comprehension spell, I picked up on a few important things.

The sword had once been imbued with the power of a divine goddess. A goddess who was also divine sounded redundant to me, but I couldn't exactly snark at the spell effect. Or the sword, for that matter, which I had learned was currently useless, though it still had a bit of holy magic dormant inside.

It was, at least theoretically, possible to repair using powerful enough holy magic.

From my magic lessons, I figured out how to draw some of the power out of a magical item to use. While I hated the idea of damaging the sword further, it was the only item available that had holy magic in it. The divine goddess was apparently pretty stingy with blessings.

It took me a couple days to figure out how to use the basics of holy magic from studying the sword, but I considered that a worthwhile investment. The sword had several holy spells imbued in it, such as "Holy Light" and "Bless Weapon," which had stopped working.

Both were effective against demons. I learned how to cast both.

I wasn't just studying holy magic for days, of course. I was also studying the art of enchanting items, as well as going over various tactical documents. Demon strengths and weaknesses, battle histories, that sort of thing.

I learned that most demons looked pretty much like humans. There were minor discrepancies, though. Horns were the most common. Some demons also had claws, wings, tails, or the like. More powerful demons actually looked *more* human-like, which sounded strange to me. Still, I had to assume it was reliable information.

I kept to my bedroom for my studies. It was a nice room, if lacking indoor plumbing. In spite of my guards' insistence on caution, I'd convinced them to leave me alone while I was inside.

When the ninja appeared in my room, I knew I had made a terrible mistake.

The ninja dropped from my ceiling, as ninjas do, and paused for a moment before rushing toward the holy sword that lay in a corner of the room.

"Nope," I declared, and hurled a tiny blast of fire in the ninja's direction.

This was my second mistake.

The ninja dodged easily and turned to face me. He said something in a language I couldn't understand.

That was a little confusing, since I had understood everyone here so far. Was he speaking the demon language, maybe?

Either way, he was talking, so I tried to talk as well. I raised my hands and said, "You can't have that. I'm still using it." I was defiant, like a brave and valorous hero.

He replied with another foreign statement, followed by a thrown knife aimed at my arm. Both came across as rude.

I caught the knife between two fingers and shook my head. Those physical power enhancing elixirs had done their job.

Now? I was pretty damn fast.

I closed the distance in a blink, throwing a punch.

Apparently, he was pretty fast, too. He dodged and my fist hit the wall, smashing stone apart. Which was cool, but kind of inconvenient, because my hand got stuck.

He reached for the sword's hilt.

I threw my other hand up. "Holy light."

A blast of golden light smashed into the ninja's face. He staggered back, blinded.

Blinded, but not burned.

As He stumbled, the ninja flung something to the ground. A plume of smoke rose from where it landed. Then he was gone.

Huh.

From that point forward, the holy sword never left my side.

But that wasn't the most important lesson I had learned.

MY MAIN PREPARATIONS after that focused on enchantments. Nearly any spell that could be cast could be turned into an enchantment.

I convinced one of the most powerful mages to enchant an item with a teleport effect for me — it couldn't be used often, but it would be a key component of my plan.

ONE WEEK BEFORE the demon army was set to arrive, I was summoned for audience with the queen. Fortunately, I was allowed a few minutes to prepare for the meeting.

She gazed down at me benevolently. "Great hero, the final battle approaches. Will you share with me your plans?"

It was a little earlier than I would have liked, but pretty close to when I'd expected to talk to her.

I'd already given some of the basics to the army gradually over time.

I'd decided against summoning a vial of a deadly pathogen. Instead, though a series of complex divination spells, I managed to target an eReader with a large collection of engineering books saved on it. I'd kept the device to myself, reading what I could from the books and silently thanking the anonymous donor, who was far better prepared for this scenario than I had been.

Initially, I had been planning to use that information to build an airship powered by air magic. The theory behind it was sound and, sur-prisingly, few demons were capable of flight or ranged attacks that could get above the clouds.

From there, I'd planned on bombardment with blessed explosives.

The encounter with the ninja had changed my mind.

"I have a question for you first."

"Of course, Hero. You may ask what you wish?"

I nodded, adjusting my stance. "You're the demon king, right?"

The *queen* stared at me for several moments. Then she laughed. "What gave me away? It was the hat, right?" She tapped on the absurdly large crown, which was presumably hiding her horns.

The hooded men and armored guards around me stepped closer. The guards pointed their halberds—so cool—at me.

"Mostly the hats," I admitted.

"Everyone here has been covering their head around me. That, and you wouldn't let me see the city at all. Then there's the suspicious lack of holy magic, the main weakness of demons."

I shook my head. "The thing that really gave it away was when some-one came to retrieve the holy sword. I used holy light magic on them, and it didn't hurt them at all, meaning they were human. It was possible they were just from some separate human faction, but everyone here being demons made a lot more sense."

"Well then," The demon king sighed, "that makes this awkward, doesn't it?"

I nodded. "Humor me by answering another question. Why summon me? Is the human city better defended than you claimed?"

"It is, though only slightly. We were hoping you would prove to be a counter to the tactics of their summoned hero, who has managed to hold us at bay for months with advanced technology."

"Advanced technology?"

"Indeed. Our spies refer to their hero as a *mechanical engineer.*"

Figures. Well, at least this implies that the real humans are smarter than these demonic caricatures of them.

"Well then, I must have been a disappointment."

"Oh, not at all. By seeing your patterns of research, we've been able to learn a great deal about what their summoned hero's moves might be and extrapolate how quickly their magical knowledge may have advanced. I have been cautious about entering the fray personally due to their new hero's presence, but after seeing your growth, I know I have nothing to fear."

That was rather rude, but I still had one more question. One born of tradition. "Well, you understand this puts me an uncomfortable position. I don't suppose you feel like offering me half the world if I work with you?"

"How delightful. You would have made an excellent demon. But no," she shook her head. "I'm afraid this is the end of our relationship."

The guards inched closer, preparing to strike.

I snapped my fingers.

The sound of thunder crashed in the distance. "You might want to hold off on that."

They took a step back.

"What have you done?" The demon king demanded.

"So, I've been studying magic for quite a while here, and I realized it was pretty simple to combine spells. I'll spare you the boring details. I found a second level spell called "Create Rain" and combined it with "Holy Light" to make "Holy Rain.""

The demon king stood and shouted to the guards. "Get everyone indoors, immediately!"

I folded my arms patiently as guards rushed out of the room. "Now, as you know, rain spells can last quite a long time. Sometimes days. And from what I could tell of the structure of this castle? It looks like a bit of a flood risk."

The demon king glared at me. "What is it that you want?"

"It's quite simple, actually. I'm going to leave here in a few moments. You will not pursue me. When, and *only* when, I am comfortably inside the human city, will I cancel the spell. If you kill me, the spell will just continue to run its course, and I think you'll find that killing me would be a little more difficult than you might have expected earlier."

I drew the sword at my side, just a little. It gleamed once again with holy light.

"You should not have been able to repair that so quickly. Your observers claimed you could not have learned higher than second-level magic."

I scratched my chin. "Looks like you've learned a valuable lesson. Humans can be pretty devious, too."

The demon king glared at me.

"Well? Do you agree to my terms?"

"I..." The demon king spat. "How can I be certain you will end the spell when you reach the human kingdom?"

I grinned. "I guess you're just going to have to trust me."

And with that, I clicked my heels to trigger the teleportation effect, and I was outside the city.

I ran as fast as I could. I hoped that anger and frustration might keep the demon king busy for a few more minutes.

It wasn't raining, of course.

I hadn't even managed to master first-level water magic, let alone second.

I had, however, mastered the level zero "Loud Noise" spell.

I hadn't managed to fix the holy sword, either. Casting "Bless Weapon" on the broken sword made it look pretty impressive, at least when it was only halfway out of the sheath and you couldn't tell it was still damaged.

I ran until the teleportation effect recharged, then teleported again, taking me all the way to the human city's gates. Fortunately, they didn't open fire at me immediately.

"Who are you?" a guard shouted down as I waved.

"Nobody important," I shouted back, "Just a hero, summoned to save the world."

VIOLET

MAZARKIS WILLIAMS

VIOLET TRIED TO burrow under the traveler's cloak and hide from the morning sun. She wanted to wrap it around herself again and fill her nose with the sandalwood scent that colored her dreams. But her fingers curled around handfuls of straw instead, and its sunny fragrance opened her eyes. His horse had gone. Her apron lay folded on the floor where she had left it. Violet brushed the dry stalks from her hair and looked out into the daylight.

The sun shone bright on the apple trees and on the gray-stoned house, yet visions of the night lingered in her mind. The traveler had conjured the Gardens of the Moon in Borann, his hands moving to a silent incantation. Her skin had tingled as he wound the magic into flowers and twinkling stars.

Violet tied on her apron and looked around the small barn. Something was missing. But what? There had been nothing here in the first place. Halfway in a dream, she found the outhouse, and then the kitchen.

"Any gold?" Her mother did not turn to ask the question, occupied as she was with braiding the morning's bread.

"Sorry," said Violet. The kitchen looked smaller than before, and bare. She edged past the table and sat by the fire.

"Aii," said her mother. "Well, he brought some fine salt."

Violet watched the flames.

"Maybe his seed will take," said her mother. "That would be a fine gift."

Violet's sister, Thia, had given birth to a straw-gotten boy six years ago. He entered the kitchen at that moment, his light, foreign hair tousled from sleep. "Is there milk?"

When Violet failed to reply, her mother said, "No, lovie. Vi forgot to milk the cow."

On the board, brown and twisted lengths of dough lay side by side like great worms. Violet ate bread with honey every morning, but she had no appetite for it now. Everything looked the wrong color, hollowed out and dull.

"Did he say anything?" she asked.

"The traveler? Just goodbye and thank you for the Shelter." Her mother took the loaves and pushed them into a notch beside the fire.

Violet rubbed her arms. The sense of loss settled over her shoulders, its namelessness prickling at her skin. She wished she could remember. "I think he took something of mine."

Her mother rubbed some flour from her apron. She appraised Violet's clothing, the Circle of the Martyr around her neck. "I see nothing amiss."

"Something important." Violet tapped the table with her fingers. Something not from her, but *of* her. She sat up, panic suddenly twisting round her gut.

Her mother's blue gaze flitted around the room to settle on Violet once again. "Scattered, you are." She sighed. "Well, nothing to cure you but some work. Take some of the salt up to the Perry house. We owe them still for the spice they gave to us."

"All right." But first, she went to her room. In a drawer, she kept a portrait of her sister, smaller than the palm of her hand. A traveling craftsman painted it the year before Thia died. He probably fathered her second baby, the one that killed her. Mother and child now lay just beyond the apple trees, in a hollow where ladyslippers grew. Violet slipped the portrait into her pocket. It made her feel somewhat whole again. She ran to the kitchen and threw open the trap door to the cellar.

"What are you doing now, girl?" her mother cried out, but Violet climbed down anyway and took two apples. She wanted only apples today. That and the plump orange fruit of Storian nights, the fruit that filled the air with spice and honey. Aromas were harder to conjure, he had said. More magic was required. It had flowed over her like a river, warm and vital.

Violet ran back up the stairs and gathered the salt.

Her mother shook her head. "If it weren't for that Circle, who knows what wildness you'd get into."

"Yes, Mother."

But her mother had not finished. "The special ones are hard to let go, but Shelter is our tradition. Everyone gets something, and nobody asks for more. Now go. Walk him off."

Violet turned that over in her mind as she stepped out. She had never thought of asking for more. Her life was small: milk the cow, haul the water, teach the boy. Only the travelers ever altered the slow pattern of the seasons. None had ever taken something from her before.

"I'm nothing but an entertainer," he had said. "A purveyor of cheap tricks. But to each person I try to bring something new."

He had spoken true. He had tricked her.

She made her way to where the road forked. To the left, a path led up the hill to the Perry house. To the right lay the way to Derman, where the traveler had likely gone. She turned right. Ten steps more and she began to run. She ran until her legs trembled and her chest felt tight as a fence-knot. She slowed to a walk, shaking not from exertion but from her own reckless will.

In Derman, Violet passed fruit sellers at their stalls and wove between the sheep on the main road. A hostel rose two stories above the street, its windows small and dark like secrets. In its shadow, a burly man buckled a saddle around a horse. The traveler's horse. Violet's heart lifted in relief. This would not be a difficult thing after all. She put down the cup and crossed the street to tap the hostler's big shoulder. "I'm looking for a traveler. His hair is long and his eyes are the color of the sky. He wears a red cloak with a golden crest." Her cheeks felt hot when she was done. "And this is his horse." She bit her lip.

The hostler nodded in a bored sort of way. "The magician."

She had not thought of describing him so simply. "Is he here?"

Now the hostler shook his head. "Nah, he traded horses with me. This one caught a stone. Had to make it to Peyne, he said."

It seemed the color drained from the sky. The city, full of hope just a moment before, now seemed empty of all but filth and sharp voices. "Martyr bless you," she said, turning away.

She had to follow him. She had known that even before she left home. The missing piece of her pulled like a needle with string. The harbor town of Peyne lay six days' walk away, but she had no choice. She traded the salt for a bit of cheese and some more apples. The sun rose hot over the road, and Violet regretted that she had no water flask.

When the sun settled to the west, a grower's cart pulled alongside her. An older man leaned out, his Circle hanging loosely around his thin neck.

"Martyr's blessings," he said, and she bowed her head at him.

He kept pace with her a while, then offered his water flask in a shy sort of way.

"Martyr bless you," she said as she accepted it.

"If you need a ride, I'm going all the way to Peyne."

"Sir, you're very kind." He stopped the wagon, and she climbed up in the back. The man continued driving and said nothing more. She lay down and closed her eyes.

The traveler drank his ale. Many voices called out around him, but he sat alone. She watched him, waiting for him to reveal what he had taken. But he only reached in his cloak, pulled out a bit of cheese, and chewed it as he stared into the distance.

Violet woke. She felt sorry to have left her mother with no warning. Her nephew would need his learning, and the cow her milking. But she could not go back until she had restitution. She prayed to the god to provide for them until her return.

As for herself, the grower was kind. Three nights she slept on his cart while he made camp on the side of the road. On the fourth day, he stopped outside Peyne. "Martyr protect you," he said, making the sign of the god over Violet's head.

"Thank you," she replied. "You are generous."

The grower put his hands together in the way of prayer. "I treat each person I meet as if they were the Martyr himself."

The principle of Shelter, the rule of her people. Violet felt her eyes fill with tears.

PEYNE WAS SO large she could not see it all from one place. The smell of fish hung over the buildings like a cloud. Every passing face looked ruddy and chapped. At the bottom of the hill, she could see the harbor, its masts swaying like wheat in the wind, and beyond that, a horizon of blue.

Across that water lay the heart of the empire, and the queen. Beyond her protected city, the Peresine aggressors burned and ravaged the countryside. Violet had heard tales, but such things never touched her own quiet corner of the world. Violet's peaceful lands supplied the food for the royal army, and their peaceful ways soothed all those who sought comfort. It was the way of things.

Violet wandered the streets, finding more hostels than she could count. Men and women in bright colors jostled her out of their way. Beggars pulled at her skirts. Fortune tellers and witches pitched their wares at every corner, as if their gifts were not rare as love-blooms with nine petals, or rare as the faeries who stole sleepers from their places beneath the trees and fed them honeyed wine. Faeries who showed these unwitting souls all the wonders of their realm, until the captives could not leave without fading away from grief.

Violet did not ask for her fortune.

At midday, she spotted a pair of men in red cloaks and followed them to a large stone inn. Several men sat around the tables, drinks in their hands, none of them the traveler. The air felt good and fresh. She stood a little straighter.

One of the men smiled at her over the suds of his ale. She smiled back and approached his table.

"...but the messenger didn't get there in time," a man next to him was saying. He wore a crest like that of the traveler's.

"Are you saying we lost the whole battle?" asked the man who had smiled at her.

"That's what I'm telling you. The Green Hills were too distant. Even the fastest rider couldn't warn them in time."

"Martyr's blessings." Violet pressed her hands together in polite greeting.

The speaker gave her an odd look. Clearly a foreigner. He wore no Circle.

"If I may, I wondered about your crest, there," she said. "What does it mean?"

"Magician's Guild," he said, giving her the once-over and apparently finding her lacking. "We fight the war for you. One would think you'd recognize us."

"The war? But do you know an illusionist who—"

A big-nosed man behind the bar beckoned her by waving a filthy rag in the air.

"Excuse me," she said to the magician. She crossed the dim room and nodded to the barkeep. "Martyr's blessings."

"Are you plying a trade in here? Just so's you know, I always get a share."

"Trade?" Violet shook her head. "I'm looking for a magician."

"You'll have to be more specific, now," he said with a laugh.

She tried to think of the most practical way to describe the traveler. "He makes illusions. He travels and brings back what he sees."

"Has a soft little voice like this?" asked the barkeep, exaggerating with a drawn-out purr.

The imitation was accurate and dug at her ears. "I suppose."

"I know `im. He stays here without paying. Shows me things, see?" He winked and threw the rag over his shoulder as if it were the edge of a gilded cape.

Violet kept silent for a moment, imagining what kinds of illusions the barkeep might favor. "Where is he?"

"Well now, nothing's free, nothing's free in Peyne. I imagine you to be a hospitable girl." He leaned over the counter, his gaze somewhere below her Circle. "Ain't you a grower?"

"I am." Violet leaned away from his greedy eyes.

"Growers are hospitable, ain't they? Shelter and all?"

He did not understand the principle. Or he meant not to. She shook her head. "I can't."

"Come now. Barn whore ain't no different from a city whore. Both of yous do your milking." He laughed. "Come now. I think I'm feeling the Martyr risin' in me. Do me a service, now."

They stared at one another across the counter. She felt the eyes of the other men at her back.

He drew away. "Well now, it ain't like I'm trying to kill your ma. Forget about it. Ain't no fun in that."

She turned away, her face red with shame. Somehow, he had managed to make the principle of Shelter sound filthy.

"Hey," one of the magicians called out. "You're looking for Simon. His ship left yesterday. Over the sea, queenside."

Violet nodded. "Thank you," she said, walking to the door.

The bartender regained his humor, shouting out for the other men to hear. "Now wait there, missy, you can't stay here with me? Ah come on now, the real thing is better than pretend!"

Violet did not answer, hurrying out the door, his words coming after her.

"You gonna chase after him? There's a war on, you know!"

She leaned against the wall outside and covered her mouth with her hands. Tears ran over her fingers. Something in the power the traveler spun, the power that had wrapped her and warmed her, had also robbed her, drawn her to this godless place. Simon would pay for this.

In time, she stopped shaking. As mad as it was, there was no question she would follow Simon, but she required money for her fare. Violet examined her clothes and the contents of her pocket. She had nothing to sell worth a sea passage. Except... Her fingers went to the band around her throat. It was unthinkable to sell her Circle. She had never been without the Martyr's protection. And yet she had been wearing it when Simon managed to steal a piece of her. It had not protected her then. Why would it protect her across the sea?

Violet stopped in front of a jeweler's and prayed, "Martyr forgive me." She opened the door and entered the dim shop.

The jeweler and his wife sat behind a dusty counter. Ten Circles of various sizes hung on the wall behind them.

"What is it, child?" the woman asked. "Do you need your band adjusted?"

"No," said Violet, taking a deep breath. "I need to sell it."

The woman made a sound of horror, pushed back her chair, and stalked out of the room. The jeweler wasn't angry, though. He rubbed his beard and considered her Circle. "What brings you to this madness?"

"I need to go across the sea." She raised her chin.

A whistling noise escaped his throat. "Not the safest place to go without protection."

Violet reached up and, after a brief hesitation, undid the latch of her Circle and tossed it on the counter.

He turned it with one finger. "You're lucky, or unlucky. The war has made gold hard to come by. I'll give you five degs."

Violet clenched and unclenched her fists. She had no sense of the Circle's worth, or of the cost of sea passage. It looked so strange and lonely on the counter, instead of being part of her neck.

The man gave her a sharp look. "That's my offer. Five degs would get you across the sea."

"Five degs." Violet pushed the Circle at him.

He pushed a stack of coins her way along with a little pouch on a string. "Martyr be with you anyway," he said. "If you come back before the end of the day, we can trade again. Lots of people change their view after a day without their Circle. But tomorrow, I melt it."

Violet nodded, but the choice had been made. She put the money in the pouch, and the pouch in her pocket, and pushed her way through the door to the noisy street. Her neck felt strange and light, but she was not scared: she was driven. Simon had left her with a burning need to be whole again. She would give up the Martyr's protection for that. She pulled up her collar and moved on.

Violet walked downhill, toward the smell of the sea. On the docks the wind bit through her clothes and the stench made her head swim. Some of the sailors would not talk to her when they saw she had no Circle. Bad luck, they said, but she tried and tried again. By midday, she found a foreign ship making the crossing. The price was two and a half degs. The jeweler had not deceived her. She found her place below decks, surprised by the darkness and the number of people. Her countrymen crushed together, on bunks, on the floor, and on barrels.

A middle-aged man with a scarred forehead was telling a story. "… and so the captain called for us to move forward. I had my sword—"

A young man interrupted. "The captain said to advance just because of the mage?"

The old soldier waved a hand. "Of course. The mages knew what was happening with all the battles in my day."

A woman with gray hair shook her head. "If mages could do that, we wouldn't be losing against the Peresine. Tell the story and don't make things up."

The soldier hit his knee with annoyance. "But I am! The mage told us the enemy was trying to sneak away." He looked up, saw Violet and her bare neck, and sneered. "Get away from here, you!"

Shocked, Violet backed away and found a hammock in the corner. By selling her Circle, she had separated herself from her countrymen. Would the kind grower who had taken her to Peyne react in the same way? Wrapping her fingers around Thia's portrait, she listened to the wash of the sea.

Simon stood on the deck of a boat. "What do you want?" he asked.
"What you took from me."
He frowned and crossed his arms. "What's that?"
She found she could not answer.

She woke, feeling a tingling of her skin. She felt as if she had a breath of fresh air, though all was as dark and dank as before. She ate one more apple, savoring the taste of home, feeling the touch of her mother's voice and the chubby fingers of her nephew. She saw the sun rising over the fields and the rain turning the house-stones purple. She smelled rising bread and freshly cut hay. All the things that had seemed so wrong on the day she left had begun to seem so right. And yet, if she returned, she would have to give up on what she had lost.

No. She could not do it.

On the fourth night, she dreamed of soldiers in green jackets. They marched and divided, making two parallel paths around a narrow valley. There would be fighting, she knew. She saw another man in green who looked at her and asked her a question. She shook her head. She could not understand his words. He looked angry. Screaming echoed in her ears. Had the fighting begun? Something hit her forehead. Violet opened her eyes, but all was black. She was falling, sliding across wet planks. She put her hands forward, searching in the blackness for something to hang onto. The ship groaned like a wounded animal. Water sprayed from between the boards. Salt pinched her tongue and burned her eyes. Finally, she caught up against something metal and wrapped her arms around it, shouting to the Martyr for protection. The other passengers screamed, their possessions tumbling everywhere.

Light spilled in from the upper deck. Someone had opened the trap door and stood on the ladder shouting up.

"That's the one!" The gray-haired woman pointed at Violet, her face sharpened by shadows. "She's bad luck! No Circle!"

"She brought the storm on us!" A young woman with a screaming baby in her arms gave Violet an accusing glare.

"Please, I never…" Violet struggled to find enough balance to stand up.

"Take her!"

Two men stepped forward, but the boat lurched, tilting back on its stern, and they stumbled, cursing. Violet grabbed onto a pole just as a barrel came loose from its ties and rolled between the hammocks. The passengers scrambled to get out of its way and the boat now plunged forward, bow down. In the confusion, something hit Violet from behind. She saw her own hands letting go of the pole, and the deck, moving again, rising up to hit her in the chest.

Simon stood on a bridge, watching the river below. He looked up at her with a start. "You're close," he said. "Where are you?"

Violet came to wedged between some crates. Calm waters lapped against the side of the boat. Efficient shouts and quick, measured footsteps carried from the top deck. The other passengers spoke to one another in cheerful voices. The storm was over. She tried to lift her head, but the world spun.

She was alive and in the port of Arnot. He was close now. She could feel it. The thought of his magic made her mouth tingle. She reached for her last apple, but it had gone, probably falling from her pocket during the storm. Thia! She gasped and shoved her fingers deeper. Her hand closed around the little portrait. It was still there, and her money, too. She let out her breath.

When at last she could rise and climb the ladder, she found the deck crowded with passengers. She kept away from them, standing close to a group of red-haired sailors. She waited a long time to disembark. Each person had to be interviewed by a white-haired official with a black tome. Violet felt dizzy and leaned over the rail. *Soon,* she thought. Soon everything would be back to normal. She had only to find Simon. The sun beat down on her hair. The mast's shadow grew by inches, but most passengers still waited. They began to jostle one another trying to get to the front of the line. Violet stayed at the back.

When she got to the end of the gangway, she pulled her collar up around her neck.

The white-haired man looked at her and frowned. "Where did you come from?"

"The fields around Derman City," she said.

He wrote in his book. "Name?"

"Violet Hanady."

He wrote this down also. "Destination?"

"Well, I don't know, sir. I'm following someone who stole from me, but I'm not sure where he went."

He looked up at her and pressed his lips together. "He took your Circle?"

Violet put a hand over her naked throat. It would not be a lie if she did not answer. "Can you help me, sir?"

He twisted the quill between his fingers.

"If he came here," she went on, "you must have written his name in your book. And his destination. Then I'd know where to go."

"What kind of young woman chases after a thief?" He shook his head. "You should go home and get another Circle made."

"Please, sir, whatever you say, I'm not going back."

He sighed and looked her up and down. She imagined how she must look: dirty, bruised, and disheveled. "Have you any means?" he asked.

"Means? Oh…" Violet pulled a deg from her pouch. He grabbed it up and slipped it into his chest pocket.

"He must have come in yesterday," she prompted.

He flipped through the pages. "I need his name."

Violet frowned. Why had she not thought of that? She remembered the traveler and the way his words rode up and down like a song. The way his breath fell against her cheek as he slept. Mages had no family, no possessions, and no life other than service to the queen. But they kept their names. And then his appeared in her mind, bright as sun on water. "Simon Marriett Jaines." The dock shook under her feet. She felt as if the ship might tumble over on top of her.

The official did not notice. He concentrated on his book. "Korban," he said. "Mr. Jaines went on to Korban."

"Thank you." Violet straightened her dress and took tiny steps to the end of the dock. Korban was the center of the queendom, where the palace rose over the Gardens without End and the buildings were whiter than snow. Sheltering travelers had described it to her. But not Simon.

She would find him, but first she had to understand what was gone. She tried to piece it together like the feathered edges of a torn skirt. Somehow, he left her a different person than he had found her, a person who no longer fit, wearing someone else's clothes. She lifted Thia's portrait and studied her sister's lovely face. She appeared so peaceful and wise. "What am I forgetting, Thia?"

Thia didn't answer, so she tucked the portrait away and entered the city. Violet walked with care, finding her body sore and her head woozy from being tossed about on the ship. Arnot was much like Peyne, except there were even more foreigners without Circles. She wished her hair were red or yellow, so that nobody thought it was strange she was not consecrated. She chose a foreigner to show her which road led to Korban and another to sell her cheese and a bit of bread. Sarna was more expensive than Peyne, and the food took almost all her remaining money.

Violet walked until the sky turned lavender and her legs ached. She thought about her warm bed, or how comfortable it would be to nestle in a pile of straw. But she could not ask for Shelter. Without her Circle, she would be considered bad luck just as she had on the ship. Though the god demanded that all travelers be welcomed no matter what, few people ever did so in practice. There were consequences to the choice she had made.

She lay against a rock, feeling the cold ocean air against her cheeks. This land felt stranger in the darkness than it had under the sun. She watched a man gallop by in a white cloak. His banner snapped in his wake, black on yellow, a raven on a branch. A royal messenger. She wondered if he brought news of the front.

A twig snapped somewhere in the forest. She huddled, shaking, waiting for the next sound. She clutched her portrait of Thia. Thia had always been so strong.

Only at sunrise did Violet relax and drift into sleep.

Simon waited for her at the top of a hill. "Where are you?" he asked. Behind him stood the man in green, the one who spoke a strange language and moved with an army. His face twisted in hatred.

Violet woke, her heart pounding. She had never felt so threatened by a dream before. But it had not been Simon. It had been the man in green who frightened her.

That day, her body ached and her throat burned with thirst. She began to wonder why she had come. To find what she had lost, she had given up everything else. What madness had caused her to make herself an outcast, to exile herself from her home?

At midday, a stream of growers flowed onto the road from the forest. They had bundles and carts full of animals, furniture, barrels, blankets— their entire households, or as much as they could carry or pull. Their faces were drawn and tired and their shoes were worn. One family seemed to disagree which direction to take. Violet watched them, one hand covering her throat.

A young woman with blue-black hair nodded Violet's way. "Martyr's blessings," she called out.

Violet nodded, not daring to come any closer.

"Please, how many days to Arnot?"

"One...just one," said Violet. Her voice surprised her, ragged and coarse from thirst.

The woman motioned toward her face. "What happened to you?"

"A storm...on my ship. I fell."

The growers murmured amongst themselves. "We came farther north than we intended," the woman said to Violet. "We've been walking for weeks, and Korban would be four more days. We'll go to Arnot." She motioned behind her, to the east. "Peresine," she explained. "Our homes are the new battlefield."

"I'm sorry," said Violet.

An old man with a ragged hat nodded her way. "Time was, mages didn't let anybody in. They saw everything, eye to eye, like this." He pointed at his own eye with an emphatic nod.

The woman next to him smiled. "You're welcome to join us."

"Thank you, but I am going the other way."

Waving, the growers headed down the road. Violet walked in the opposite direction, head down. By twilight, her head felt so heavy that she could not walk any more. She curled up beneath a pine but slept only in fits and starts.

As she lay in the darkness, her waking memories drew sharper. In one, Simon rubbed his chin with the back of his hand. In another, he laughed, throwing his body backwards like a child.

Morning found her digging crumbs of cheese from a pocket that somehow had become muddy. She kept an eye on the sides of the road for berries or the tops of wild onions. Thirst hollowed her throat. The memory of the apple she had lost tortured her. She kept on, no longer knowing why. At noon, she found a field of purple flowers and recognized them as pepper blooms. She ate a handful of petals and found a few drops of rainwater in the hollow of a rock. Temporarily sated, she curled up in the grass to sleep.

Simon stood on the bridge again. "What did you do?"

"Me? This is all your fault," she said.

He shook his head. "I think we are—"

Behind him, she saw the man in the green uniform. He spoke to her again, strange words, and raised his fists at Simon. "Look out!" she cried.

Violet woke to the sound of whispers and childish giggles. Thinking her nephew had sneaked into her bed, she reached out and touched the child's hair. But the boy jerked back with a curse and moved away. She opened her eyes and looked out into the morning sun. Five boys ran across the flowered field, shrieking at one another.

With horror, she reached into her pocket. Her money, as little as it was, had been stolen. But that was not what scared her the most.

Thia's portrait was also missing.

"No!" Violet rose to her feet, head spinning. She tried to run but stumbled over her skirts. "Come back!"

The boys waved at her as they disappeared into the woods.

"Come back! Please!" She lifted her dress and went after them. Her body ached, and every step echoed in her head like thunder. She tried to run, but she limped and tripped instead. By the time she got to the woods, the boys were nowhere in sight. Their gleeful shouts and catcalls echoed through the trees. She followed their voices. Branches whipped across her face and thorns cut her ankles, but she walked on. This was her fault for giving up her Circle, her protection. Because of her choices, her last link to Thia and to home were gone.

"What do you want?" the traveler had asked her, running his finger along her cheek. A lone piece of straw stuck to his hair.

Violet shrugged. "I don't want anything. Except maybe to see my sister Thia again." She looked into his eyes to see them crinkle with sorrow.

"I can't do that," he said, "but I can show you other things."

She remembered the touch of his lips, light and firm, and the way he cradled her head with one hand as the magic rose around them.

At twilight, Violet stumbled across a stream. She fell to her knees and shoveled the water into her mouth with her hands. She drank until her stomach twisted into cramps, and then she crawled through the mud to a clearing. She lay on the blanket of pine needles, eyes on the darkening sky. She no longer understood why she had come, or why she had given up so much to do it. Only the memory of magic kept her heart beating now. Whatever more the world wanted, she would give it. She no longer cared.

In the morning, Violet did not move. She kept her vigil by the stream. It began to rain, and she let the water flow over her. The stream rose and gushed over her feet, and yet she did not move.

She heard the rider before she saw him. The horse was nearly silent as it picked its way through the trees. But the rider breathed with deep gasps and wheezes. Sometimes he groaned, staring up at the sky. Blood soaked his white cloak. Violet forced herself to her feet. His royal banner was missing, but she recognized the messenger she had seen before. As he passed, she reached out for him, and he for her.

She helped him to lie down in the clearing, though it was wet. She cupped some water in her hands and brought it to him, but he knocked it away. "The queen," he said. "She must be told…" He coughed red blood that spattered over her dress.

Violet held his hand and waited. Soon, he began again. "Ships at Thunder Bay. Siege weapons…men…the east is a trick. She must send the troops…" He pushed himself up on an elbow. "Take my horse."

One glance at the horse told Violet it could not go any farther that day. "Rest now," she said, the tears on her cheeks blending with the rain. She brought him some more water.

After a moment, he moved again and said, "The Martyr put you here in the forest."

"No." She shook her head. "It is all misfortune and foolishness. I am changed, and live outside the Martyr's blessing now."

"You were changed, or you changed yourself?" It was the last thing he said. Violet sat by him until the sun went down. The messenger took his last shuddering breath as full night fell. Violet stayed with him.

As soon as the horse was ready, she would carry his message. It did not matter that they might not listen to a ragged girl with no Circle. It seemed absurd that she had lost everything, never finding what she was looking for and met the messenger instead. Yet the message gave her a purpose the like of which she had never felt. She would fulfill it. For now, she said goodbye to the peaceful lands beyond the sea. To the gentle lowing of the cows and the warm rain. To the clatter of a young boy's shoes and the taste of her mother's apples. Goodbye to the tender care of the Martyr's welcome. Goodbye at last to Thia. She saw them all fade away behind her eyes, until all she felt was cold as she waited for morning.

VIOLET RODE A horse, a good horse, dependable. She had ridden Star since she was fifteen years old. Her gloves were wet from the rain, so she pulled them off. She pulled her hood up and looked back to a city of white. *No,* she thought. *Not my hood. Simon's.* She pulled away and looked at him. Hair plastered to his head, rain dripping from his nose. Hope surged in her chest, vital and unexpected.

"Simon," she said. Her voice was thin and weak. "Simon."

He turned and looked. "I'm coming for you."

"You mustn't." She told him about the ships, about the feint.

Simon hesitated, one hand on his reins.

"Trust me. Simon, please." She could feel herself growing stronger, feel Simon's magic flow over her like his warm cloak, warm and inviting.

"So we are two." He turned his horse back toward the city.

They saw everything, eye to eye, like this, the old man on the road had said to her. She smiled, finally understanding. Simon had not taken anything from her, he *was* the thing. Her partner.

But another magic, oily and nauseous, rose around her, winding along her skin. Simon's image flickered and faded in her mind.

"Simon…"

The magic crawled along her flesh in cold ripples, rushing into her ears and darkening her vision. Violet tried to rake it away with her fingers, but it inched forward, heedless, probing. It parted her lips with its cold, phantom fingers and slithered down her throat. Her lungs filled with icy fire. She screamed, scratching at her neck. "Simon!"

The green-coated man stepped forward in her mind, his smile proving his satisfaction with her pain. He brought his hands together and pushed. Power scraped at her, shards of cold that twisted her insides, threatened to rip her apart. She could feel his desire to destroy. He was a Peresine sorcerer, and she was a mage.

A mage, she thought, *with nothing left to lose.* She threw her senses out, grasping.

Simon's magic remained. It stirred everywhere around Violet. It had been there all along, even when she had felt the loss of it, following her from the farm to this clearing like her own hair, trailing behind her. It moved along the ground, danced along the waters of the stream, and rustled in the leaves overhead. As she felt it and reached for it, she understood it was not Simon's magic. It was her own, twined with his like sleeping fingers.

Violet drew on their strength and pieced herself together. She searched for every smell and sound of the clearing, the living warmth of the messenger's horse, and the light of the sun. She wove them into bright, strong armor. The sorcerer battered against it, tried to find a crack, searched for any way to get through to her again, but she kept him off. Her mind was clear. She had nobody and nothing to defend, no other duties to attend. She was free. She had made herself free. She returned his power against him. *I have defeated you already.*

His image wavered, then disappeared. Soon, the armies of the queen would descend upon his position. It was no longer her concern. Violet opened her eyes to the sunny clearing and got to her feet. She walked to the road, making no attempt to wipe the mud from her clothes and hair.

She would look even worse, she thought, traveling with the army.

It would be two weeks to walk to Korban, but she would not be walking. The mages would come for her. She took a step and felt dirt under her foot. One of her shoes had come off, somewhere in the muck. She kicked off the other and continued down the road, feeling the world alive against her skin.

THE TWO FACES OF WAR

ROB J. HAYES

GREEN FIELDS STRETCHED out before Bolin. They weren't suitable for camping, the ground too boggy and infested with leeches, but they looked peaceful from a distance. A sea of emerald rippling in the breeze, muted by moonlight and a sour state of mind. Bolin pulled the cork from his bottle and took a deep swig, wincing at the taste. He put the bottle down next to him and waited.

Heavy footsteps warned him of approach. He'd come to recognise the sound; ceramic armour clinking together, not quite rhythmic. Jun was limping again, his right knee always aching from the cold and the effort. Bolin didn't turn to watch the approach, nor give any sign he had heard the man. He just stared out towards the grassy expanse that lay beyond his little hummock.

Some warriors flowed like a stream over pebbles, some warriors crashed like a waterfall onto rocks. Jun did not sit gracefully, but collapsed in a barely controlled fall. He grunted at the impact, and then let out a loud sigh that was accompanied by his armoured plates settling against themselves.

Still, Bolin didn't turn to look at the old soldier but, instead, reached out a hand, and with a single finger, he flicked the bottle that sat between them. Jun reached for it and swallowed a mouthful, letting forth a sound that was part groan of distaste and part sigh of pleasure. Medicinal alcohol did not make for good drinking, but it did get you drunk. That was a big part of war, the ends justifying the means.

For a long time, they sat there in companionable silence, just watching the wind make snaking patterns in the long grass. Bolin picked at the dried blood under his fingernails and wiped his hands on his apron. It amazed him how he was always covered in other people's blood, yet Jun was nearly spotless. Some men carried the stains on the outside, and some men were drowning within.

Jun was the first to speak, his voice heavy and tired. He had a slight rasp on both his Ss and Ts, the product of an old shot to the throat that had never quite healed the way it should.

"I was in the thick of it today. A cavalry charge made a mockery of the shield wall, scattered bodies left and right, then pushed through. They opened up a hole, and the regulars filled it. We might have lost the battle there and then if not for my unit." His helmet thudded as he placed it on the ground next to the bottle. It was an ornate thing, the crest of the Praying Mantis on the forehead. Jun had once said it was passed down through his family, and now he was the last who would ever don it.

Bolin plucked the bottle from the ground and swallowed a mouthful of burning spirit, then he put the bottle between them before speaking. "Arrow wounds are one of the first things they taught us how to treat. Cut it out or push it through. Ignore the screaming and the blood. Let the brutes hold the patient down until it's done. Or until the patient is done. They never told us what to do when the arrowhead shatters inside the body."

Jun nodded at that, stretching his legs down the hillside and wincing at the pain in his knee. "Time loses meaning in the melee. Moments feel like eternities, hours pass by in a blur. The world recedes around you to a fine point. There's just you and the man in front, the one snarling at you over the shields. Stabbing, slashing. Crimson droplets flying all around. And the burning agony of keeping your shield up, arm shaking from the exhaustion. But you know… You know if you let the shield drop, even for a moment…it's not just your own death, but the man next to you as well. Hours or minutes, I don't know. Couldn't tell. And over all it, the captain yelling at us to keep our damned shields up."

Bolin tore up a handful of grass and crushed it as hard as he could in his fist, then opened it and let the breeze take the blades where they would. "It took four men to hold him down. Barely more than a boy, not even old enough to grow a beard, and four grown men pinning him to the table. I shoved a thong in his mouth and he glared at me, hatred in his eyes like it was my fault. As though it were something I was doing to him rather than saving him from. The others said it's often like that with arrow wounds. The patient never sees who kills them, or tries to, so they blame the first face they can. The first face they see."

Jun grunted, a sound that said he knew just what Bolin meant. No doubt the old veteran had taken an arrow before. No doubt he knew exactly how the boy had felt. "There's a feeling to a sword biting into flesh. Not the receiving end, mind you, that has a feeling all of its own. But holding a sword, swinging it and feeling it connect and sink into a man's body." Jun paused and let out a ragged breath. "The way flesh accepts a sword, pulls at it, almost sucks it in. It's sickening…and satisfying."

There was shame there, that much was obvious. Jun had been a soldier almost all his life, and judging by his greying whiskers and deep lines, it had been a longer life than some. Bolin had no idea how many times Jun had felt a sword part flesh. It was a number he had no wish to know and doubted the soldier knew himself. It was certainly enough to become good at it, enough to enjoy the sick feeling of power it gave. Pride and shame so often went hand in hand on the battlefield.

Bolin pulled the bottle close again and swigged from it, then passed it to Jun over his helmet. "I had to cut open the wound as the men held my patient down. He screamed so loud my ears popped. They say the thigh is good place to take a wound for the amount of muscle there. Less chance of hitting anything vital. But there's so much blood. I had to cut open the wound and reach inside, and it welled up and pumped out. So sticky and wet and coating everything." He looked down at his apron and the red stains there, some old and some new. "So much blood."

"I thought I was dead when the cavalry hit us the second time." Jun turned his helmet to face Bolin and ran a finger along the cheek plate. The metal was scored and dented, stark white underneath the flaking blue paint. "It was all the crush of the melee, and then it stopped, the enemy pulling back just seconds before the horses crashed into our lines. We lost a lot of men right then. Some I knew. Tengfei I'd known since we were kids, stealing apples from the market just to get through another day. Gone in a moment. Just gone." He paused and shook his head sadly. "I took a spear to the face right there. It knocked me off my feet, pushed me out of the front line."

"Are you injured?" Bolin asked, turning to look Jun full in the face. He had some purpling on his right cheek, spreading from below his eye all the way down to his chin. It looked like it hurt, but the old soldier smiled around the swelling. "I can look at it."

"Yes, I'm injured. But I've had worse. It could have been worse. The helmet saved me. It's just bruising, nothing is broken this time."

Bolin nodded at that. He knew often times the full extent of an injury only became apparent long after the fact, but Jun wasn't there for a consultation. Instead, he poked at the dinted face plate on the helmet and wondered at how such a thin piece of metal could have saved his friend.

"How's your neck?" Bolin said, turning back to the emerald fields ahead, but watching Jun out of the corner of his eye.

The old veteran stretched his neck first to the left, and then to the right, wincing and letting out a groan. "Fine. It's your turn, lad."

Bolin swigged at the bottle again before handing it across and continuing. "I had to dig into the wound. When we pulled the arrowhead out, half of it had broken away. There were shards of it in the man's leg still, and you can't leave it like that. The body won't allow it. It…sours and festers around the wound. So, I had to dig into his leg, holding the wound open with one hand and reaching in with the other. Pushing my fingers deeper into muscle while blood oozed up and…" Bolin felt a tap at his arm and looked down to see Jun holding out the bottle. He took it gratefully.

"It took me a spell to come to. A good whack to the head will do that to you, helmet or not." Jun rubbed the bruise on his cheek and grunted. "I can't even remember who picked me up. It was all a bit fast. The front lines were crumbling. A good cavalry charge is bad enough, but horses in amongst the fight… Nasty things, horses. Big enough to shove through a shield wall, heavy enough to trample of man to death, and the teeth… I've seen a horse bite a man's hand clean off before. By the time I rushed back in, our lines were strained to breaking. I pulled one lad from his horse, don't know what happened to him in the chaos. Then the horse went mad, kicking and stamping. Biting. I just hid behind my shield as it thrashed. I felt the thud as it went down, though, three spears buried deep in its neck." Jun fell silent and shook his head. Bolin handed the bottle back.

"He struggled the whole time," Bolin said. "Screamed and struggled. I could see the men were having trouble holding him down. I pushed deeper into his leg, following the mess the arrowhead had made, feeling with my fingers until I touched something sharp. I brushed against it and the screaming stopped. That was worse. The moment the screaming stopped, giving way to wide-eyed panic, I knew his time was running out. I pushed harder, widening the wound until I could grip hold of the shard, and then I pulled it out." Bolin paused just to breathe and dug his hands into the grass again, crushing it in his fists. "I lost hold of it twice, my fingers slipping in the blood, before I finally pulled it free."

A strong breeze rolled in, and Jun closed his eyes, raising his bruised face to the wind and smiling. "In the wake of the horses, the infantry hit us again." He shook his head, eyes still closed. "We had no time to reform and the lines were shattered. They were in amongst us and we were in amongst them. I barely remember it, just…swords clashing, wet *thuds* as they hit bodies. Screams, both from the dying and those doing the killing. Then *he* arrived."

Again, Jun fell silent, composing himself for the next part of his tale. Bolin filled the void left by his friend's words. "I had to go back in twice more, poking around inside the soldier's leg so I was sure I had all the shards. I did. I mean, I think I did. I felt his pulse slowing. The blood welling up out of the wound less and less. I felt him stop while I still had my fingers inside." Bolin wiped at his eyes with the back of his hand.

"Just as our lines were breaking, the Crimson Tide appeared. He swept in like a storm and I felt him pass. I was on my knees, hands wrapped around another man's throat, squeezing. I don't when or how I lost my sword, only that I was fighting for my life with everything I had. When I looked up from the body, I saw him. His cloak was as red as his name, fluttering around him and twisting in the wind. He had a sword in each hand and every strike cut one of them down." Jun let out a sigh and shook his head. "I've never seen anything like it, and this morning, I woke thinking I'd seen everything. He turned the tide all on his own, beat the enemy into a retreat. I think he might have chased after them, but the captain called him back to help out another section of the line. It put an end to the fighting, though, at least for today."

Bolin waited until Jun grunted and nodded his head. "In training, they said never to give up on a patient while the skin is still warm. So, I didn't. Even though I couldn't feel his pulse, and the blood had stopped. I pulled free the last shard of metal, and closed the wound as best I could. He didn't move after that. Even those holding him down gave him up for dead." Bolin paused and smiled. "But he was alive. Faint though it was, he held onto the spark and I didn't give up on him."

Jun let out a chuckle, and Bolin looked over to see his friend smiling back. Jun picked up the bottle and gave it a little shake, sloshing around what was left. He pulled free the cork once more and swigged, grimacing as he did. Then the old soldier held the bottle out to Bolin, who took it and finished it off. When it was empty, he threw it down the little knoll, watching it bounce and roll to a stop amidst an easy dozen just like it.

"Best get back, lad," Jun said. The old warrior, groaned as he pushed to his feet and placed his helmet back on his head. Then he held out a hand and helped pull Bolin to standing. For a moment, they stood there, hands clasped, staring at each other.

"I hope to see you again tomorrow," Bolin said.

Jun nodded. "I hope so, too, lad. I'll find us something better to drink." With that, Jun turned and walked away, back towards his camp.

Bolin watched him go for a few moments before calling out. "Do you ever wonder what it's all for?"

"What's that?" Jun stopped and turned back.

"Every day, you go out and fight. You swing your sword and people die. Every day I patch men up, sow shut wounds, and get them back on their feet. All so the next day they can go back out there and swing their swords so more people can die. Don't you ever wonder why? What is it all for?"

Jun smiled, his mouth just visible underneath the dented plates of his helmet. "The answer to that question is the same as it was yesterday."

Bolin was almost afraid to ask. "What's the answer?"

"I'll tell you tomorrow." Jun chuckled and turned away, heading back to his camp. turned his feet in the other direction.

GRANNIT

J.P. ASHMAN

WHAT A MAN would give for armour such as his.

'And you are?' the knight said, sun gleaming from polished plate.

'Grannit, my lord.'

'Granite, as in hard as?'

'No, my lord, Grannit as in…' Grannit held his hand out to the scribe beside the knight, beckoning toward the quill.

The snooty scribe pulled away, as if he might catch something, and looked to his liege lord before handing it over. Grannit nodded his thanks and wrote his name before the quill was snatched away.

'Where did you ride in from, Master Grannit?' the knight asked, clearly amused at the exchange.

'I walked in, my lord, from Rowberry.'

The knight's eyes widened almost as much as the scribe's had when Grannit had proved he could write.

'Grannit of Rowberry, then,' the knight said.

'Grannit of wherever you like, my lord, if it means I can fight for you.'

The whitest smile Grannit ever saw presented itself, along with a satisfied nod.

The knight stood, polished armour shining, surcoat almost as white as his smile.

'Sir Silver,' he said, holding out his hand.

Grannit took the offered hand and shook it once, as firmly as he could. The white smile intensified.

'Pleasure to have you with us, Master Grannit.'

'Pleased to be here, Sir Silver.'

Nodding at that, Sir Silver motioned to a large bell tent further down the lane. 'See yourself to the quartermaster and ensure you are outfitted in my colours. And see if they can't do something about your lack of arms and armour, too.' He winked, and Grannit was taken aback to find a gold penny in his palm.

The weight of the thing struck Grannit more than its brilliance, but before he could thank Sir Silver, the knight gestured to the next man, or boy, in the column. Grannit suddenly felt old at sixteen years. Most of the lads lining up to sign-on looked younger. Mind you, it was said that Grannit had aged two years for every one he'd lived. His craggy face aged through pox, as it was.

The quartermaster's tent was dark and stifling. Thick with the smell of oil, iron, leather, and farts, the last striking Grannit as he stood there, waiting for the fat bastard to notice him. Grannit cleared his throat for the third time.

'I heard your first cough, son.' A set of narrow eyes peered up. 'What is it you want?'

Grannit licked his lips before answering. *What* don't *I want? A full harness of plate like Sir Silver's would be preferable.* 'Liveried…clothes?' He was unsure what he'd be allowed, so he started with that.

A grunt was all he received in answer. A grunt and the loudest fart yet, followed by a sigh from the big bastard.

'I've a white tabard around here you can throw over your shoulders. That'll mark you as one of Silver's lads—'

'Sir Silver,' Grannit corrected. 'He's a knight, and a knight should be addressed correctly.'

The wheezing that followed went on long enough for Grannit to realise it was laughter.

'Ballsy bastard, aren't you? Sir Samorl praise you, son, but I like you. Fuck the tabard, you fight like you speak and you'll be lasting long enough to need more'n a damned tabard. Wait there.'

Cursing his outburst and offering a prayer to Sir Samorl at the same time, Grannit watched as the quartermaster shifted his weight over to a particular sack at the back of the tent. Rummaging eventually produced a blue and white striped gambeson, its diamond quilting sewn in blue stitching. Grannit gaped. It was less than he hoped for, but more than he'd realistically thought he'd get.

'This should fit you, lad.' The quartermaster held up the gambeson, which would surely come to Grannit's knees as well as his wrists. He hesitated before asking Grannit's name.

'Like the stone?'

Grannit managed to hide the sigh and merely nodded, eyes still on the gambeson.

'Well, Master Grannit, my name's Dell Taylor, but my mates call me Needles.' He patted his paunch with his lump of a right hand. 'An ironic name, I know, but it's aligned with my trade, I guess.' He grinned brown, rather than the white of Sir Silver, and shuffled over. Grannit noticed Needles' lame left leg for the first time.

Once the gambeson sat across Grannit's broad shoulders and hugged his chest, Needles made a rumbling sound and shuffled off to another sack. 'Belt!' he shouted, needlessly, waving a dark brown length of leather above his head before bringing it over. 'You'll need something to keep that gambeson tight about the waist; scrawny shit.' Needles grinned as he tied the belt, the elaborate knot looping through to hang barely below Grannit's business.

'It's not very long,' Grannit complained, looking down. 'Sir Silver's hung to his knees.'

'It's free, you cheeky shit.' Needles shoved Grannit by the shoulder and barked a laugh. 'Anyhow, Sir Silver's belt is plated in silver. I doubt you expected that as well, eh?'

Grannit smiled for the first time, but shook his head.

'Good. There's plenty of knights knocking around without the kit or coin of Sir Silver about their person. But who knows, son, you might make it up the ranks one day and be knighted yourself. Stranger things have happened, especially in these parts.' He winked and sat back onto his chair, sighing as the weight left his legs.

'I can only hope, Needles.'

'Needles?' The quartermaster laughed. 'Only my friends call me that, son. It's Master Taylor for now. Now, now, no sulking in here. I don't doubt it'll be long until we're glugging gallons of ale together around a fire.' It was Needles' turn to lick his lips. 'You've something about you, Master Grannit, and you'll do fine in this company if you keep that something about you at all times. Understood?'

Grannit smiled again and nodded. 'Understood, Master Taylor, and thank you.'

'No need to thank me, son, just don't rely on that padding too much, eh? It'll take harder hits than most people would think, but it won't save your life if the blow or thrust is right, or lucky.'

Grannit patted his chest and understood. 'Sir Silver said to pick up some arms and armour. He gave me this.' The golden coin gleamed despite the poor light.

'Shit a block of, well…granite, why not… He gave you that? Truly? I mean, I know he's richer than a dwarf and all, but…' Needles filled his cheeks and let the breath out slowly.

'Aye, Master Taylor, he did.' Grannit grinned and handed it over.

'Well, son, I ain't no smith, but I tell you something for nothing, a coin like this in my pouch ensures I'll see you right. He said arms *and* armour, did he?' Needles frowned whilst eyeing the gold penny.

Grannit confirmed it whilst looking about the tent. His hopes died a little as he noticed a complete lack of iron.

'Sort that face out, son.' Needles got to his feet with a groan, led Grannit to the tent flap, and pointed across the way. 'My mate, Trout, is a journeyman smith. I kid you not. Take this thong to him…' Needles held out an intricately twisted and knotted leather thong, and Grannit took it, confused. 'Take it and give it to young Trout. This'll show him you came from me, and he'll sort you out.'

'And the coin?' Grannit asked, staring from thong to penny, leather to gold, unsure whether he was being had.

'The coin stays with your mate Needles, son. And Needles sees his own are set up right.'

With a shove, Grannit stumbled out of the tent and into the sunlight, thong in his hand, his feet carrying him to the smoking smithy across the way.

PUSHING A SWORD into a man's chest, through iron links and the wool-stuffed padding beneath—not to mention through skin, muscle and between ribs before piercing the doings inside—was tougher than Grannit thought. The psychological barriers were almost as tough as the physical. Until the second man came at him, that was. The barriers fell away altogether by the third and fourth, but by Sir Samorl did Grannit's right arm ache. All the pell hacking in his lifetime couldn't have prepared muscles he'd never felt ache before from burning as he thrust and thrust and thrust some more.

'Bollocks,' Needles said to Grannit that night, whilst they sat around a fire, sewing clothing and skin, working burs out of blades and attempting to remove the rust that appeared after the lightest of rains.

Grannit looked up, the stitches pulling skin taught across his neck. He'd been lucky, his mates said. Lucky the lunge he'd almost avoided hadn't ran through his neck and out the other side. Still hurt like a blind barber had been at him though.

'Bollocks to what, Needles?' Grannit maintained his frown. He'd been surprised, then proud, then sick, then quiet after the battle, but after the stitching, and the small-beer they'd had their fill of, the stories had come out and he was proud again. So, to have his best friend call out bollocks to his story nearly had Grannit surging to his feet. Anyone else and he would have, blood still up after a day's bloody work.

'Bollocks, son, to a lifetime at the pell not helping you. War's a life-long business if you want to be a knight. You've spent barely a cycle of the moon with the earl's army and far less at the pell. 'Course your arm's aching. 'Course your sword felt like a log a short way into the scrap.'

'That won't last?' Grannit asked, dared hope.

Needles spat and shook his head, eyes on his bronze needle as it passed through leather, repairing the sole of Grannit's left boot. Not Grannit's original boot, mind, but half of the pair he'd taken from a corpse on the field.

'How long then until I can fight all day without my arm and shoulder and 'morl knows what else burning?'

A grunt of a laugh and Needles looked up. 'I never said that would happen, son. But did you see the knights? Did you see Sir Silver whilst on the field?'

Grannit shrugged and shook his head. 'No.'

'Oh, I guess you were busy. Well,' Needles began to explain, leatherwork needle jabbing at Grannit like a miniature sword, 'Sir Silver and the like train and train and train. They wear their armour almost all the time whilst on campaign, unless we're completely free of danger. They wear it and they fight in it, be it against the pell or one another. They practice with sword and lance and hand, on foot and from the saddle. Why?'

'So they can be the best,' Grannit said, easily.

Needles rocked his thick head from side to side. 'Yes and no. Of course, they want to be the best, but war, especially battle itself, isn't just the art of combat and strategy. It's fitness! A tired man might slip up, literally if he's too exhausted to stay on his feet. Your arm fails to lift that pig-sticker you got there…'

Grannit frowned down at his arming sword. He was immensely pleased with it despite it being at least one other's before he got his hands on it. Sir Silver's gold penny, given to Needles, had gone a long way. Arming sword and rondel dagger. Padded gambeson and kettle-helm. Grannit never expected to have such gear so quickly. All he needed now was some damned maille to stop his neck being opened up again in the future.

'If that sword,' Needles went on, clearly recognising the hurt in Grannit's face at the slight against his sword, 'lags your arm enough to miss a parry, you're for the dirt. Simple. If those legs of yours give out, bringing you to one knee like you're ready to receive a title, then your kettle-helm won't do shit all to protect the nut inside.' Needles mimicked a flailing fall as the firelight danced across his grimacing face. 'You bloody well fall flat in some of the shit weather we get up here on the border and you'll drown in the mud and puddles as lads from both sides scramble over you, taking you for a corpse. And what then, son? No knighthood for you, eh? No Sir Grannit of Rowberry then. No. Your boots are another's, as is your iron lid and your sharps.'

'Fitness keeps you going.' Grannit voiced his understanding. He may understand words, or enough to write his name and a few other bits, but life on the march and fighting, real fighting, not the sort he'd grown up with in Rowberry, all fists and sticks, was a continuous lesson.

'Fitness keeps you fighting, son. Fitness, the likes of which Sir Silver possesses, keeps a knight thrusting and hacking and slashing and jabbing. They move like a shade, flowing from one stance to another, working their swords or hammers or `morl knows what with both hands. Their legs move in practiced ways to put them where they need to be for strike or defence. But their fitness must allow it, Grannit lad. Their breathing and concentration must remain constant because you can bet your teeth that one slip up through exhaustion, just one, will be exploited by the bastard opposite or to the side. Armour may take a blow, but a knight on a knee has his soft bits prodded until he's pumping red across his shiny plate.'

Grannit watched as Needles pretended to jab his tiny bronze sword up under his arm, then his eyes before moving to the back of his knees and, finally, and with the most enthusiasm, between his legs.

'Jab, jab, jab,' he said, 'and the best knight is dead. Fitness, son. Fitness is what keeps you at it, bastard man after bastard hobyah after bastard adlet. And those latter foes, mark my words, they keep on coming even when they're stuck twice, even thrice.' He tapped below his eyes with his finger. 'I've seen the fuckers, son. I've seen them go at men, jaws snapping, spears sprouting from their backs like hedgehogs, with arrows making them look like my pin pads down here.' He pointed his toe at one, bristling with pins. 'What beats a mad foe like that, eh? Finesse with a sword or the fitness to keep on swinging it?'

Grannit nodded slowly whilst working his aching shoulder.

'The fitness, every time,' he said, eyes on Needles.

'No.'

Arm dropping by his side, Grannit's brow creased. He opened his mouth to speak.

'Both!' Needles cut in and corrected him. 'Deft skill and fitness alike. That's why a knight's a knight and you're just a lad with a sword—'

Grannit made to protest.

'—for now!' Needles added. 'For now, son.' And he winked.

THE DAY WAS hot, and it felt like the longest in Grannit's life. It's true that waiting in camps drags on, as does marching, but there's something about a battle that makes every moment feel like an age. Whether it's manoeuvring according to barked orders and tooting horns, or crashing into flanks and shoving and clambering, stabbing and kicking and slashing and, truth be told, biting, if it comes down to it.

Grannit's muscles burnt. His sword-arm felt leaden and his feet throbbed. He was sure his soles had worn through again. March leagues and they last...until the moment you need them. Mud sucked at his feet and hard edges poked through, catching and stumbling him in ways that would see him fall were he not an experienced, and fit, man-at-arms.

He swayed to the side to avoid an incoming spear thrust. As the shaft past him by, he grabbed it with his left hand and pulled its wielder towards him whilst stepping in. His sword pressed through the hobyah's stomach, which was a feat considering the muscle packed into that space.

Jaws gnashed at Grannit's face, but not for long. The length of the day led to many staggering and swinging lazily on both sides. Not Grannit. He pumped his burning arm, threshing the insides of the tall goblinkin whilst keeping its head back with a well-timed grab of the neck. He squeezed and he stabbed and he twisted his sword whilst choking the already dying hobyah.

The burn in his arms and legs and lungs was familiar now. He'd never lost it, he'd merely become used to it and knew, as Needles had told him again and again before he'd left the world via consumption, that Grannit would never lose that burn and exhaustion, not in battle where he'd be tested beyond anything he could put himself through during training. No, he'd never lose it, but he'd come to appreciate it, manage it, and when it counted most, push through it. He knew now, had done for some years, like Needles had said, that the burn was a good burn. That it was the growing and hardening of muscle. Grannit knew that after this fight, should he survive, Sir Samorl think him willing, he would be stronger and faster and fitter for it. As long as he didn't succumb to the softening touches of life as a soldier; strong ale and mead and over-eating as some men did when given the opportunity. No, Grannit knew that the pell and the yard and the battlefield itself was what he needed. Because, one day, he would become a knight. And he was damned sure he was close as he finished off the last hobyah standing and raised his longsword to cheers all around.

'STRING ME UP and let the rooks have my eyes,' Grannit said to Sir Silver as they walked from the burning village. It'd been years since they'd faced goblins and hobyahs, and this last fight had been a close call.

'How do you think I feel, Sergeant Grannit?'

Grannit looked sidelong at the greying—now aptly named—Sir Silver. 'Fair one, my lord. Fair one.'

Sir Silver smiled and stopped. It took three paces for Grannit to realise and retrace his steps.

'My lord?' Grannit asked, noticing the thoughtful look on Sir Silver's face.

'I'll not survive another fight like that, sergeant.'

Grannit frowned. 'Goblins, my lord?'

'Who or whatever, sergeant. I don't have the life in me to go on. I slipped, you know?' He paused, his rhetorical question seeming to stall his meaning. 'No...I stumbled. There was no mud in that village, so dry was this summer. There was nothing to catch my foot.' He looked down at his blooded plate legs and sabatons. 'My knee gave out as I stepped back, and I almost left you all to meet Sir Samorl.'

Grannit made to speak, to tell Sir Silver he was wrong, but the ageing knight—not a ten-year older than Grannit—held up his gauntlet to halt Grannit's words, gold-chased fingers splayed.

'It gave out because I've not the strength I had. I spend less time at the pell and at tilt, especially the latter, because it hurts my bones, sergeant. It hurts my everything. Old wounds and old bones and old muscles wasting away.'

'You put younger lads on their arses daily, my lord.'

Sir Silver smiled. 'Maybe, but lads looking to me in awe aren't goblins or adlets or other men trying to open me up, are they? The fight isn't the same in the yard as it is out here.' He waved his arm about, indicating the bodies and the smoke of war.

Grannit took a deep breath before he spoke, his heart pounding like it had been during the fight. Truth be told, he knew how the old knight felt. After all, Grannit must have been near on forty years by his reckoning. A bloody hard forty years, too, with less pampering than Sir Silver, not to take away from the knight's hard work at warfare.

'What are you saying, my lord?' Grannit dared ask.

Sir Silver smiled again, although there was less heart in it and more resignation.

'I've been asked to serve King Barrison in Wesson. In the palace itself.'

Grannit's eyes widened, and he filled his cheeks before letting it out. 'His retinue, my lord?'

The sudden, short laugh was a mixture of humour and regret. 'No, sergeant. As a captain of the wall. I should be honoured, really.'

Grannit swallowed hard. 'You should, it's a fine honour and a fine position,' he lied.

Nodding, Sir Silver shot Grannit a knowing wink. 'Thank you.'

I'd follow this man anywhere, Grannit thought, *but is this the end? Will he while his years away now, growing fat whilst ordering guards up and down a wall. Working out rotas and organising the repairs of crumbling crenellations?*

'When do you leave?' Grannit asked, not sure he wanted to know.

'Immediately.'

It was hard for Sir Silver to say that, Grannit could see.

'And so…' Sir Silver motioned for Grannit to kneel.

Grannit hesitated. His heart started anew and his stomach twisted. He'd fought his whole life for this moment. Literally. He'd fought and he'd fought. He'd lost friends along the way. Almost all of them. And, if he was honest with his own aching bones and stabbing wounds, new and old, the only man he trusted enough to call friend that remained in the world was the knight standing before him, ready to make Grannit his peer rather than his subordinate.

'My lord,' Grannit said, staying on two feet like he'd sprouted the roots of an oak, 'what happens if you do this? What happens to…this?' He indicated himself and Sir Silver. The two of them. Their brotherhood of pell and field.

Plate spaulders scraped across maille as Sir Silver shrugged.

'I guard a palace and our king whilst you march around Altoln, ridding it of this shite as a knight of the realm.' He pointed to the corpses all about. Corpses being looted and dragged off to pyres already lit.

Nodding knowingly, Grannit made a decision he never thought he would, or could. 'Then I cannot accept, my lord Silver.'

Sir Silver rocked back and made to protest, but for the first time in the decades they'd known one another, Grannit held up his hand and stopped the knight from talking.

'My lord needs a sergeant he can trust, and I need a lord I, too, can trust. My place is with you, Sir Silver. My place is at your side, in Wesson, if you'll have me.'

The uncontrollable smile that spread across Sir Silver's face struck Grannit more than any enemy ever had—and there'd been a few to talk of—but in a good way, of course.

'You mean it, Sergeant Grannit?'

'I mean it, Sir Silver.'

There was a pregnant pause filled with the call of crows and the sound of a victorious company making camp.

Both men clasped hands and pulled into an embrace before holding each other at arms' length.

'We'll show Wesson what real soldiers are made of, eh, sergeant?'

Grannit gave a wolfish grin. 'Oh aye, my lord. The bastards in Wesson won't know what hit `em.'

ASALANTIR FOREVER

STEVEN POORE

SILENCE RUSHES IN.

For a moment, Jin is certain she has died. She exhales raggedly, feels her heart hammering hard in her chest. She stares at the opposite side of the trench, then up at the muddy sky. The air is thick, flecks of earth, stone, flesh, bone, iron, and grit on her tongue.

She ducks back down. The assembled Pride stares at her. Peng, mismatched gauntlets, shoulders braced to carry the mining cannon. Kareem, the cannonball. Sails and his lances. Who the hell brings lances to a trench fight anyway? Pash and Harp. Spill. A random, nameless squire to a knight who didn't duck in time, now running with the Pride because she has nowhere else to go. Others Jin has picked up along the way.

Even a crafter or two, which'll be helpful if they ever get close enough to Asalantir to use the cannon.

'God's sainted shit, we're still here.' She grins at Peng.

Peng grins back. 'Never thought we wouldn't be.'

That's a lie, and they both know it. This close to the front lines, they're lucky to be in one piece, lucky to be alive, lucky to be recognisably human at all. The fortress on the hill, Asalantir, dominates the western horizon and overlooks the approaches. Put your head over the top at the wrong moment, or for too long, and it'll likely disappear in a sorcerous bolt. Or an arrow, hurled far beyond the normal range of a longbow by the damned devilish Hinyans on the battlements, taking an eyeball with hellish precision. Or one of the exploding stones that arc through the air with the grace and weight of a giant's bollock and send even plate-clad knights tumbling like rag dolls.

Or worse. Though Jin can't think of much worse than being here, now, in this place, at this time.

She risks a look. Sighs. Asalantir doesn't appear any closer. The last advance has barely advanced at all. Dozens of lives, maybe hundreds, all spent and wasted for a few poxy yards.

'Nearly there,' she lies. 'They're digging in ahead of us. We can wait here for a bit, then go once they send the knights through again. Then it's just a quick race to the next set of trenches…'

Collective groans. Nobody wants to think about open ground. Not with the Hinyans up there. And the Hinyans aren't even the worst of it.

Spill offers a flaccid skin. The Pride take a mouthful each. The last of the water. It tastes of dirt and death, just as the air does. Jin takes her share and washes out her mouth. She passes the skin to Pash, and a thought, a feeling, makes her frown. Like Pash is a ghost, like she's already left him behind. But there he is, chain shirt rusted, helm jammed tight over his ears.

Jin shakes it off. Curses, dire premonitions, like there isn't already too much magic on this battlefield. Sorcery in the very earth, in the air, clinging to the skin, deep in their bones. And the magic isn't trying to stick three-foot blades through her guts while she dives from trench to trench. Damn Asalantir, damn the Hinyans, damn the idiots who told her the war would be over in a season.

'Right.' She takes stock. If Asalantir is there, then the front is over there, and she remembers a connecting trench that ought to be over there, and that'll take the Pride straight up. No need to climb up and leg it. Hopefully. 'Sails, up front. Poke everything. Pash, push from the back. We need to hurry it up or the knights will roll right over us and leave us behind.'

Sails tips his lance, jabs everything in their path. Boards, corpses, things softened by mud. Some things can explode. Others can bite. Some do both. Left behind by retreating soldiers from one side or the other, or else catapulted in from the fortress. There's a use for lances in the trenches after all. Jin moves crabwise, back bent, peering past Sails, looking for the junction, hoping it hasn't been bombarded to shit. The Pride follows behind her, Peng and Kareem breathing hard with the weight they carry. The lost squire clanks through the trench, her armour gouged and battered. Jin glances at the planks that span the trench at irregular intervals—no movement up there, no sign yet of the knights.

A sharp turn and, suddenly, she can see the fortress, looming over the field. Distant shouts from the other side. Staggered flights of blind-fired arrows take the air—somebody's raised their head too high for a moment or there's an observer on the ground.

'Cover!' Jin shouts. The Pride ducks, raising shields if they have them. One breath, two, three...

Shafts clatter, bounce, hit the mud with wet thuds. Someone shouts.

'Move it!' Jin matches action to words. She shoves Sails, he keeps going for the next sharp turn, lance scoring a lengthy gutter in the floor of the trench. Peng and Kareem squeeze past her, the others, too, and then there's only Pash, pinpricked, legs kicking, the blood running out between his fingers as he clutches at his neck.

More shouting from up ahead—alarm, Hinyan voices. Pash is on his own—Jin pulls her stabbing blade and runs for the trouble. She pushes past Spill and the rest, and Sails is holding the Hinyans back with the length of his lance while Harp chants razor-sharp beads of energy into them. The enemy has a mage, too, and the beads spray out and up, and there's mud and stone flying all over the place. Jin roars the Pride's cry and surges down one side of the lance while the lost squire takes the other. They stab and hack furiously. The shouting might draw help from back down the trenches, or it might bring more Hinyans. Right now, this bunch are between Jin and where she needs to be, and she won't let them stop her.

The last few turn and run. Now, Harp's beads can cut them to shreds, and the Pride stomps the bodies into the ground as they overtake the Hinyans. The squire is grinning, Spill is limping, Peng's shoulder braces have been scored by Hinyan clawblades. Sails takes the lead again, and the Pride has fresh momentum. *We can do this,* Jin thinks. We can.

Harp grabs her shoulder. 'Something's wrong.'

That feeling she had earlier. Jin thinks a moment—it's gone now. 'What?'

'I don't know. Think we might have tripped something.'

'Magetrap? Early warning?' That would explain the enemy in these trenches. A counter attack.

Harp shrugs, unhappy. 'Can't tell. I don't recognise it. It's new. Could be a curse.'

And they won't know what it does until it takes effect. Jin gives her own shrug. 'This whole bloody war's a curse. Onwards. Take Asalantir, beat the curse, right?'

Harp pulls a face. 'Maybe.'

Jin elbows her way towards the front of the Pride. Scarred and blooded and almost past the point of no return. Kareem virtually glows with antici-pation, ready to be cannoned through the earth to Asalantir's great vaults, to open the way, to take the fortress from within. They have to get close enough to use the cannon, though, despite all the sorcery invested in this bollock-crazy weapon. Thus the Pride, one last time, one final mission.

This is the front line. The part of the field nobody owns, at least not for more than an hour at a time. Trenches collapsed by bombardments, blocked by corpses and the shattered debris of the farms and villages that once sat here below Asalantir. There are clawblades and shields and all sorts of sharp, rusty objects. You can shout to the other side, if you feel so inclined. Jin doesn't. The Hinyans have not long come over the top. There may be more of them.

'We're on time,' Peng whispers. She's checking the orders. Howls and steel clashing, echoing down the length of the battlefield. Somewhere else has a push on. It might be the diversion they're waiting for. Jin can't tell. She finds the crafters, makes certain their spells are ready. They're uncomfortable in leather and helms, holding swords and bucklers. Not something they've ever had to do before, but Jin doesn't want them picked out and picked off by the bloody archers in Asalantir. Robes and fancy torcs are too obvious.

It's quiet. Too quiet. Something's going to happen, any time now. Jin looks up, catches Harp's eye. Harp's frowning, too, attention fixed on...Sails.

The tip of his lance scores another line in the mud. Jin holds her breath.

The walls of the trench explode out. Vast jaws come together like *that*. Sails may be armoured, but he's still crushed like a swatted fly. The nearest of the Pride are covered by his sudden death. The trenchwyrm is gone, back into the mud, before anybody can do more than shout.

Jin wipes her cheek. 'Fetid cocks.'

'How did I know that was going to happen?' Harp mutters, perhaps not realising she has spoken aloud.

'Good question,' Jin says. 'Well?'

Harp hesitates. She's about to speak when the air is filled with horns, louder than any crafted explosion. Despite knowing this was coming, Jin winces, shrinks down. That's the power of the order to charge. Her ears ring so much she can't tell if the horns still blare or if she's gone deaf.

'The knights!' Peng yells in her face. 'The knights are coming!'

And now she feels it. Like a tremor building through the ground, driving even the hungry trenchwyrms down into the safety of deep earth. Pounds, tonnes, of ensorcelled armour, hurtling towards the front. Lances, swords, hammers, shields, the great push forwards. The one to get them over the lines.

It shakes her teeth. The crafters are pale, wetting themselves. They've never seen an advance from this side before. The lost squire whoops in delight, her fists in the air. Above the top of the trench. A sorcerously-enhanced arrow takes off one of her hands, but she's too caught up in her rapture to notice.

And that's the rapture the knights are caught in, too. They hurdle over the front line trenches like armoured catapult projectiles, the air around them bright with magic. They would sing if their throats weren't raw from screaming their blood-induced rapture. Huge, almost-human shapes, soaring through the air over Jin's head. An awesome sight.

The Hinyans fire in response. Sorcery erupts across the front. The knights' armour gleams, glitters, radiates colours there are no names for as battle magic ricochets off enchanted plate and mail. Shields absorb and reflect death rays, fireballs slide down chest plates like fat in a pan. Weird bulges form in the air as spells collide, and dimensions explode into life, evolve, and die again in half a heartbeat. Blinding flashes of infinity tear into the earth through withered spells, melt armour and cook flesh. If the knights themselves are awesome, then this bombardment is truly spectacular.

From a distance, of course. Preferably, the top of a mountain, in a different country.

Jin is counting. The Pride watches her. The lost squire, overwhelmed and berserk, vaults out of the trench and takes off after the knights, heedless of her injuries and lack of protective spells. She is lost in the spray of magic instantly. Jin counts down with her fingers. Four, three, two, one…

'Go!' Peng roars. 'Go, go, go!'

And they do. Over the top, at a slant to the big push, behind the last ranks of knights, the ones who maybe aren't quite so ready for a glorious death yet. The front is wreathed in a nimbus of sorcery. It has an almost physical presence. Jin feels it tugging at her, slowing her down. Peng is gleeful alongside her, Kareem and the crafters not far behind. They weave between fresh craters where the land still bubbles, trying not to notice the twitching limbs, the half-transformed torsos, the reanimating remains of the last wave before this one.

'Mage down,' Spill shouts. Jin peels away and looks back. There's Harp, hauling herself back to her feet, mud streaked down one side of her body. She limps forward a step, shakes her head, and waves Jin on urgently. Jin ignores her and runs back. Peng knows where they're going.

'No! Keep going!'

'How bad is it?'

Harp grimaces. 'Bad enough. I can't keep up.'

Jin shakes her head. 'We need you to fire the cannon.'

'No. Crafters can do that. Just remember to get the bloody thing right way up.' Harp pauses and looks up. 'Oh, shit. Not again. Jin, it's the magetrap— We triggered a time—'

'Incoming!' shouts Spill. Instinct takes over, and Jin dives. She hits the ground just as the ground explodes up to meet her, and she lets the impact carry her forward, rolling away from the new crater that was Harp.

She staggers up, glad of Spill's helping hand. Through unfocused eyes, she can see the Hinyans rising up from their trenches, going hand to hand with the surviving knights. Blurs of blood and steel and mercury. There's still a chance, still time to use the diversion. Jin holds onto Spill's shoulder, and they lumber back to the rest of the Pride, taking cover in another gully next to the shards of a shattered barn.

'I can see their trench,' says Peng. 'Easy run.'

Easy run. Jin nods. She isn't feeling it. But they are past the point of no return now. And if Harp was right, if the squad triggered a curse of some kind… She looks around at the others. 'On my count,' she says.

They charge the last yards, past the stakes, down the mud banks, stabbing and hacking and smashing the defenders with their bucklers. It's tight again, yet completely different to the trenches just a stone's throw behind them. And without Sails, the enemy is much closer, right in their faces. Jin pours all her energy into the fight, pushing for every step. The noise around her is deafening as Hinyan reinforcements arrive to repel the knights. She can't afford to get bogged down in that battle. She has to keep moving, keep the Pride moving at all costs.

At *all* costs.

Hinyan clawblades rip Peng's guts open. She falls, holding them with one hand, the other loosening the straps that hold the cannon to her shoulders. Spill takes the cannon while Jin decapitates the offending Hinyan with a stroke Peng would surely have applauded. There's not many of them left now. The crafters, Spill, Kareem, Jin herself, half a dozen others with names she never learned. They don't stand and fight, they just run and hack. Speed is all now.

They leave the knights behind. The sorcerers in Asalantir are focused on that battle, not on them. At last, the ground begins to shift, leading upwards towards the great hill itself. Here, Jin thinks. They must fire the cannon here, before it's too late.

'Spill! Kareem, you're up!'

The crafters set the cannon, with Kareem inside it. The big man glows with anticipation. Fire him through half a mile of earth, he'll be ready for the fight at the end. Asalantir won't know what's hit it.

'Trouble,' someone says. 'We're spotted.'

Here come the Hinyans. Jin urges Spill to hurry. Spill urges the crafters to hurry. Then the Hinyans are on them again, and this time it takes everything Jin possesses to keep them at bay. She feels the exhaustion.

'Fire!' shouts Spill.

Nothing happens. Jin glances over her shoulder. There is a tableau, moving as if part of a dream. Spill tumbles, pierced from the fortress. The crafters duck away from the cannon. And the cannon itself tilts backwards as Spill's body falls across it. The muzzle lifts, pointing up instead of down.

Oh shit…

Kareem launches into the sky. The cannonball soars—up, and up, higher than the towers of Asalantir. And then higher still. Kareem hasn't reached the top of his arc yet, and he's left Asalantir far behind. And now the mission is dead, and there's only Jin left.

She turns back and stares at the Hinyans downslope. They stare back, and the bravest amongst them start to shuffle forward, clawblades at the ready.

Jin lifts her gaze, looks across the front one last time. As more of the Hinyans advance on her, she sees a great fireball lobbed from the rear positions towards Asalantir. It looks like it's coming her way. And quickly, too.

Well, it could have been worse, Jin decides, as the heat and the Hinyans hit her at the same time.

Silence rushes in.

For a moment, Jin is certain she has died. She exhales raggedly, feels her heart hammering hard in her chest. She stares at the opposite side of the trench, then up at the muddy sky. The air is thick, flecks of earth, stone, flesh, bone, iron and grit on her tongue.

She ducks back down. The assembled Pride stares at her. Peng, mismatched gauntlets, shoulders braced to carry the mining cannon. Kareem, the cannonball. Sails, and his lances. Who the hell brings lances to a trench fight anyway? Pash and Harp. Spill. A random, nameless squire to a knight who didn't duck in time, now running with the Pride because she has nowhere else to go. Others Jin has picked up along the way. Even a crafter or two, which'll be helpful if they ever get close enough to Asalantir to use the cannon.

'God's sainted shit, we're still here,' she grins at Peng.

Peng grins back. 'Never thought we wouldn't be.'

TOWER OF THE LAST

STEVEN KELLIHER

MADREK MATTEO WASN'T an overly large man, but he cut an imposing-enough figure. He moved with a heavy sway, flashing a black cloak as he came up to the hewn marble of the southernmost gate of the citadel.

With a touch, the polished section eased its way forward, slipping through the humid air in a thick silence and easing Madrek's passage into a deserted courtyard.

Recently deserted, no signs of a struggle because there hadn't been one. Still, there were plenty of dead.

Madrek's boots breezed over the hem of a cloak dyed a darker purple than twilight. The royal purple of the tower's lord, known for his penchant for finery and plenty else besides. He passed several more of the former sentries before reaching a short staircase that spilled onto the patched yard.

"Such workmanship," Denali grinned by the doorway. He gazed admiringly up at the twin columns framing the stair and holding aloft a dazzling plaster tapestry framing some or another massacre. But whether he meant the plaster or the bodies he had made, Madrek couldn't be sure.

Madrek nodded curtly but didn't laugh or smile. He wasn't as mirthless as Kano, but the sun had dipped below the horizon, and his blade was still sharp. His mood was a hair trigger in all the best ways.

Just the way he liked it before a fight.

"Luck," Madrek said, clasping Denali around the wrist. The spearman didn't rise but it was no insult. He'd need every bit of his strength and wiles to make sure Madrek was the only one passing through the arch that night. His gleaming white teeth lingered in Madrek's mind as he made his way down a dimly lit hall.

Black porcelain masks inlaid with gold accents leered at his periphery, but his direction was forward. Forward, and up, up, up, as it always went in all the best and worst tales of yore and youth.

The long tunnel opened into an impossibly wide chamber whose ceiling Madrek could not see from the depths. Only the barest hint of upside-down spires hung from the darkness, like stalactites. Ahead, the oval yawning narrowed cleverly to form another short tunnel, which opened to the main entryway, Madrek knew.

In the center would be a wide spiral stair formed of polished ivory. This was the most direct route to the upper levels, and Madrek could just now make it out, gleaming in the artificial glow of mirrored candles. He wondered how many of Denali's gray beasts had died to make such an awesome, awful thing.

Although the most direct route should have been the most heavily guarded, the captain had learned long ago that daring had its place, and complacency its cost. In truth, Madrek felt bullish tonight. Whatever guardsmen, horrors or dark designs in store for him, nothing more than sharpening tools at the borders of his concern. They would be his whetstone before a true test appeared, and he meant to bear a razor's edge by the time that happened.

He met the first pair at the second level. No shouted warnings or bare steel, only the whiz and hiss of bolts darting toward him. One skipped harmlessly off his breastplate, the other off his drawn sword. His blade was wet and the two guards dead before another bolt sailed. Madrek was already past them before they fell, turning around a corner on the landing with little more than a swish of his blood red cloak and the errant *squeak* his boots made on the marble.

No longer dull and not quite sharp.

Before he rounded the next bend in the stair, he felt a familiar tug, like a slack rope drawn taut at his temple. He slowed, recognizing Chen's mental prodding. She'd gained the balcony at the height of the north tower faster than he could have hoped.

Madrek hissed out a low, steady breath, emptying his lungs and letting his eyelids drift closed. In an instant, he was around and up, racing to the third landing and drawing his blade. He tore out the flank of the man on the right in a crouch, felt the blade catch on the spine and stayed low for another blink, then shouldered the falling sentry into the one charging from the left. They went down in a tangled confusion of glinting metal and animal sounds, one choking, the other gasping.

He hadn't the time to finish them off, however, as he aimed his attention up and ahead. Another bolt streaked past, and he felt the wet burn on his cheek. He reached for his belt, drew and threw, and the sentry in the archway fell, clutching her throat and gurgling some curse Madrek wouldn't have paid any mind even if he could understand it. Behind her, a long chamber stretched away into the glow of candled chandeliers. A grand dining room of sorts, and soldiers—some armored and most not—pushed away their chairs in startled confusion at the sight of him standing and her falling.

Upward was the only way forward, and so he went.

Madrek darted to the left and turned again, taking the stairs three steps at a time as the clang of wall-mounted spears—now free of their catches—accented the dull thuds of leather boots on tile. He hadn't time to worry at the pursuit before he heard a loud *pop*, followed by a familiar sizzle, like steak turning on a spit.

And the first screams of the night echoed through the vast, decadent halls. Kano had made his entrance, and he was not known for subtlety. No pursuit but for the sounds of the dying would follow from the center stair. Of that, Madrek could be sure.

But he didn't allow his spirits to soar quite yet. Denali and Kano had done what was expected of them. They drew attention, and they drew it loudly. The undoubted scores who would fall to their blades were close to meaningless in the scheme of things, and the buzzing in Madrek's head redoubled as he climbed.

Chen was preparing to enter the spire. Her prodding intensified, forming into a needlepoint before disappearing entirely. She must be inside. At the top of the tower. In the Dragon's nest.

Not yet old and no longer young, Madrek was panting when he reached the final stretch of stair. He slowed enough to catch his breath, then crossed the threshold onto the landing. There was a conspicuous absence of resistance during the latter part of his ascent. Then again, it was said the black spire was the haunt of one of the king's most deadly servants. A war captain of great and terrible renown, known to friend and foe alike as 'The Last.'

A man didn't take that sort of name without earning it.

Kano had been sent on reconnaissance several times in the past month, eyes keen for signs of his passing. It seemed this warlord kept to his own, when he wasn't running the Dragon's bloody errands. Whatever the reason for his hermitage, Madrek intended to oblige him permanently.

When up ceased, Madrek found himself in a hallway that curved to either side, encasing a cylindrical chamber. The walls seemed carved of one massive block of obsidian, and the hints of screaming faces leered out at him like specters.

He reached over each shoulder and unbuckled his cloak, a useful thing to deter an aiming scout, but more harm than good in a duel.

He stood before stone doors dyed in deep poison lavender and steadied his breath.

Chen's mental rope hadn't gone slack—it was still drawn tight as razor wire—but she had stopped tugging him along, and Madrek wondered why, but he had paid for forward thinking in the past. Chen was the thinker, he the doer.

Denali would have shouldered the door to the right and tucked into a roll on the left, spear in hand, lips drawn back in a toothy snarl. Kano would have foregone a corporeal approach and snapped himself right into the chamber, sword drawn from a chandelier or some other perch on high.

For his part, Madrek strode forward, checked the handle, and eased himself into the room. To say the scene he encountered caught him by surprise would make a mockery of understatement.

Coming from the gray gloom of the entryway, his senses were assaulted by colors on the opposite end of the spectrum. Rose, coral and emerald stung him on the back of a warm blue-white glow. The room was tiled in swirling patterns. Small, spectacled pieces coalesced in the center of the floor around a dazzling star shape, while longer shards of polished stone speared up before curving around and in.

The whole room was a mosaic shaped like a flower. Like a tulip, to be precise.

Chen stood in the center of the chamber with another female. Unlike him, they both seemed the image of ease.

"Chen."

She regarded him almost absently, the ghost of her attention still focused on the curious girl beside her. And she was a girl, young as could be.

"That's a sharp name," the girl said, drawing them out of their mutual shock.

Madrek felt strange, but the feeling was passing. His initial shock at entering the chamber had given way to a dizzy sort of haze, and now that, too, was dissipating.

Chen gave a slight nod to put Madrek more at ease—it didn't work—then took a step toward him. "Madrek, meet Phenia."

The girl swept into a low bow, one string falling loose from her slight shoulder. "It seems I've found my prince," she said, smiling. "Too bad I've drawn the eyes of another."

Madrek gave her the barest hint of acknowledgement and kept his eyes fixed on hers as he addressed Chen.

"Is this a trick?"

"In the cosmic or literal sense?"

He looked at Chen. She shrugged. "I haven't put all the pieces together yet, but this little damsel might be just what we were looking for." She paused, "Rather, what we should have been looking for the whole time."

Madrek turned to regard Phenia, who stared back, aloof and unflinching. This time, he marked her hair, which shimmered between honey-light and deep amber. Her eyes were dark green, but the shards around the center reflected like gilded facets, mimicking the play of green and blue on the walls of the sun-lit chamber. She was undoubtedly young and undoubtedly clever, and she held herself with an amateurish confidence.

"Where is the lord of your keep?" Madrek intoned. "Where is your dark master? The one they call 'Last.'"

Her smile had faded, but she seemed unperturbed.

"Just where he's always been."

"And where might that be?"

"Not at home," Chen cut in. "'The Last' is a story. We never found him because he never existed."

Madrek's mind raced through the events of the past months. The men he'd released in exchange for information. Rather, the men he'd forced Kano to release. Bad men. Sick men. Alive men.

"Phenia Draeyna." Realization dawned.

He looked from one to the other. Chen's expressions were as easy to read as shallow tracks in a hurricane. But he saw it. A faint glimmer buried beneath shifting tensions. And he knew.

"The Daughter of the Dragon."

Phenia positively beamed. "Did my father send you?" she asked. If her sincerity was a mask, she wore it well.

Chen looked as if she were about to speak, but her eyes lost focus. It was a look Madrek had seen too many times before to ignore. She brought a finger up to her temple and squeezed her eyes shut while he waited on pins and needles.

"Kano is in retreat," she said. "He's drawn a sizeable pursuit through the north gate and intends to lose them in the marsh."

"How many did he kill?"

"Many."

"What of Denali?"

"He waits nearby, on the southern border of the grounds."

Madrek regarded the young girl—maybe not so young as her aloof demeanor suggested—and considered his options. Trouble was, most situations only left him with two.

To kill or not.

Chen looked at him earnestly, searching his eyes. That glimmer was still there, but it wasn't pity nor misplaced compassion that guided hers. That was Denali's bent. If the girl needed to die, Chen would be the first to swing the blade, the better to get it over with. This was something else. She believed the decision he made in this room would change the course of the war.

Right before their eyes stood a long rumored, rarely glimpsed, and never substantiated key to turning the tide, one way or the other.

The Daughter of the Dragon. Princess Phenia. Like a fabled maiden from the Tales of Longkeeping. And here she stood.

Here she stands.

If she was aware that her life tilted on the scales of his conscience, she gave no indication. Just continued to stare, curious and with a touch of naïve excitement.

Long ago, Madrek had been given a choice: a choice between a chain and a noose.

"Chain."

Chen's momentary disappointment gave way to the barest crook of a smile. She knew him well enough.

"No harm will come to you, child," she said calmly, extending her slender hand toward the girl. "But you will come with us."

Phenia seemed fit to burst. "We're going outside!"

"I take it you don't get out much," Madrek replied. He was already at the far window, searching the grounds for any guards Kano and Denali hadn't already dispatched. He sighed as he looked back at the girl and the woman who shadowed her, at the ceramic and jewel-encrusted chamber she would never see again.

"I have to admit, I was in the mood for a fight," Madrek said. "You sure 'The Last' is a story? Nothing more?" Phenia shrugged as if nothing had ever bored her more.

"You're always looking for a fight," Chen said. "Kano's just better at finding them."

She was right. "Hence, *worthy* being the operative word." She rolled her eyes at him, and he didn't blame her.

In truth, there were harder things than dueling legendary lords in fabled keeps. Madrek was the best there was with a sword in his hand. Now, as he reached out to take Phenia's thin wrist, he knew he held something much more delicate. Much deadlier.

He held the future and all its turnings.

"Right, then," Madrek said. "Let's move."

THE WAVING OF THE FLAG

THOMAS R. GASKIN

"YOU SEE HIS knife?" said Toris to Famastil as they looked upon their friend Peralis, lying on the ground with a crossbow bolt protruding from his neck. He also had a wound to his gut, partially exposing his intestines.

"Remember how he kept saying he couldn't wait to draw it, showing us over and over how clean and quick it pulled from its sheath, then began slashing away at thin air." Toris let out a slight laugh at the memory. "In fact, he showed us that with every weapon he had, remember? And now look at him, he didn't even use them. All that effort, all that skill and time that went into making him invincible. What was the point? May as well sent him into battle naked for all the good it did him."

4 years, 3 months and 14 days earlier…

"WE'VE GOT OUR war!" cried a young man as he ran through the village waving a poster in his hand. He bristled with enthusiasm, making heads turn.

"You hear? We've got our war. Pick up your arms, we're going to fight those filthy southern rekons!"

Toris stood high upon a cart as he helped his father unload sacks.

He didn't notice his father's expression, but it was like other fathers in that moment: sombre, regretful that they knew their sons would go off to fight in something they couldn't possibly understand.

But Toris smiled, he had dreamt of battle. Sitting high upon a field of bodies with his country's banner waving in the breeze.

Jumping down, he pushed through the throng of young lads surrounding the boy.

With his chin raised, the boy smiled as he read.

"Under the heathen oppression of the southern invaders, our mighty and noble King Gelmont II has declared war upon the nations of Asmog, Belliphia, and Zefrin, and their allies. All men ages of nineteen and above are ordered to go to their local mayor's office, where they will enlist into the military. Failure to do so will result in death. The crippled and elderly are exempt."

There was a moment of silence before the boy looked up at their eager faces.

"Well, what are you waiting for? Go, let's go!" he said encouragingly waving his arms at them.

There was chaos as the dozen or so boys scattered to their homes. Some fathers would try to grab them, but it was fruitless, the tension and propaganda of war had been building for some time, and they had all been waiting for this moment. But for Toris, he stopped among the stampede when he caught his father's sombre gaze. They stood looking at each other.

He didn't have a tear in his eye, but Toris knew he was feeling the pain.

"Father, I need to do this."

"I won't argue that, my boy. I just know that if…when you return, you won't be the same man who left."

"Of course not, Father. I will know far more by then," Toris said, beaming a grin as countless thoughts of action and adventure raced through his mind.

"Come, we have but one night, and I have a little extra coin, why don't we feast. There's something I want to give you."

His father climbed up onto the cart and placed his crutches to one side. Making a clicking sound at the mule with his mouth, they left the village towards the farm.

THAT EVENING, SITTING at the table as two small candles burned crisply through their wicks and illuminating the small space around them, Toris reached over for his fourth helping of honey roasted ham, butter, and bread. He even had a flagon of pale ale, which he didn't really enjoy, but seeing grownups drink so much of it made him swill the whole thing down as if it made him strong.

As the evening pressed on, Toris started to feel light-headed. Worried that he was becoming ill, he chose to ignore the strange sensation and kept gulping. But in his enthusiasm to eat a hearty meal, he didn't realise that his mother's dinner was untouched and his fathers was barely scratched at.

"Toris," his father said, eventually breaking the silence.

Toris looked up surprised, his cheeks filled with food.

"I will walk you down to mayor's yard tomorrow. We best be up early so we don't get stuck in a queue, eh? But there's something I want to give you from my war days," he said, rubbing at his leg.

It was a strange moment for Toris. It was the first time his father had talked about his time soldiering.

Reaching down, he picked up a long, wrapped object. The fabric looked old and worn and covered in dirt, like it had been buried.

Toris's eyes grew in wonder.

"When I went to war, my father gave this to me, and his father to him. I am now giving it to you," he said, reaching out with both hands like an offering to the Light God Tamelia.

Toris reached up and took it, but it fell into his chest under the weight.

His mother let out a whimper and excused herself from the table running into the bedroom.

"I suggest you go to bed now, son. Get a good night's sleep eh? I will wake you in the morning."

Toris smiled, praying his headache would be gone by then. He picked up one of the candles and made his way to his room and closed the door. Placing the wrapped object on his bed, he undid the stiff string. He was so excited that his grin could not spread any further across his face.

Pushing the object out like a bed roll, he was full of fascination, keen to see the shiny weapon which was sure to be revealed. But when it unravelled, when he saw the sword, his face contorted as he looked down at a battered and dark piece of steel covered in runes.

Wrapping it back up, Toris lay in bed and sulked, wondering why his father gave him such a hideous gift.

Present day…

TORIS BREATHED IN as he looked down the bloodstained trench of corpses. There was no one there. No one alive anyway. Spread around was an endless piles of bodies, lying in their last stance of battle as crows feasted upon an easy meal.

Asmogs, Belliphians, and Zefrinarians lie amongst his kin. Even a giant from the far reaches of the east was face down in the mud, his corpse peppered with arrows and spears, a mighty struggle to bring the godlike man down.

"What was the point in it all, Famastil, what was the reking point?"

4 years, 3 months and 13 days earlier...

"NAME?"

"Galaron."

"Age."

"Fifteen, I mean eighteen–I mean nineteen."

The officer looked over the table at the young lad. "You have to be nineteen to join the king's army, boy. On your way."

The boy named as Galaron looked defeated and went to leave before the officer spoke again.

"Try coming back tomorrow and next time, remember your age!" he said with a wink.

Galaron smiled and raced out of the office.

"Name?" the officer said, producing a fresh scroll.

"Toris," Father spoke. He had an arm around Toris's shoulder and held him tight. Toris didn't like it, it made him feel incompetent. Nevertheless, he knew his father needed this.

"Age."

"Nineteen."

"Do you have your own weapon."

"He does."

"Say your goodbyes and enter through the door. Name...?"

Toris helped his father hobble over to the side of the room. His father attempted to stand straight and placed his hands on Toris's shoulders, trying desperately to think of a thousand ways to explain everything he knew in that one moment. All he could manage was his mouth hanging open with his breath held inside.

"Goodbye, Father. I will be back soon," Toris said, uncomfortable with the situation.

His father tried to force a smile.

"You take care of yourself, son, eh?"

Toris pulled his bag over his shoulder and held his wrapped sword, walking to the door. He turned and gave a wry grin before leaving. The last image of his father was him still trying to smile.

Present day…

AMONGST THE THOUSANDS of flags waving in the breeze, one stood out for Toris; the one of his regiment.

"You know, I was looking at *that* flag before we charged. As the dawn sunrise lit up this world and thousands of people still lived, I looked at *that* flag and tried to work out what life was all about. Isn't it strange? Isn't it strange that you focus on a piece of fabric to work out what life is all about?"

Famastil didn't make a sound, clutching at the wound to his gut. The blood flowed less now.

4 years earlier…

AFTER THREE MONTHS of swinging a club at a post and marching out to the far reaches of the world, Toris stood in formation wearing nothing but the garb he left home in. With armour in little supply, he shuddered that he would be wearing someone else's if and when it became available. He looked below at the front ranks of clad men dressed from head to toe in steel and wondered which one of them he would be wearing.

But it was otherwise quiet.

He was distracted by the sound of a flag flapping chaotically in the breeze, and looking up, he saw a blue triangle upon a green field; his regiment's banner. With so many regiments formed so quickly, they were given basic shapes to identify them.

Toris had made an arm band to match it and stood proudly, but also a little nervously as were the other young faces around him, for the reality of this war was starting to sink in.

Before them, beyond the curve of the hill, a long horn blast rang out, followed by a deep drum beat.

His mouth went dry, and he felt light. Everyone around him did. The adventure he was expecting was starting to unfold and, so far, he wasn't enjoying any of it.

1 month later...

"WHAT'S THAT?" TORIS said, looking at several blue objects hurtling their way, leaving long mystical clouds of smoke. "Haven't seen catapults fire anything like that before."

His friend, Famastil stood next to him. They had seen battle but had yet to fight, and they knew that that day had now come.

"They're not boulders, Tor. That's magic." He immediately ducked behind a steel defence they had just captured. Toris followed.

The explosion was something Toris hadn't experienced before. It took a while for his mind to catch up. Opening his eyes, he looked around at pieces of body strewn across the ground. He saw an arm that looked like a giant had ripped it from its victim. The pure white bone stuck out amid the red and stretched flesh. All around were similar pieces of debris.

A cry rang out as hundreds of men charged forth from the trench before them.

Toris was clinging to the large metal object used to slow down their advance, but for the first time, the enemy were charging at them.

Seeing his brethren go down so quickly fuelled Toris with rage, and lifting his father's sword, he ran at them. He wasn't alone, and the two armies clashed.

Carnage was all it was as men fought one another to the death.

In the thick of it, Toris gritted his teeth as he was greeted by his first Asmog, standing there snarling with filed teeth to look like fangs, ready to run him through with his sword.

Toris threw back his sword, but something strange happened. The symbols on the blade glowed blue and the sword felt suddenly light. But he didn't linger on the strange sensation. As the Asmog threw his sword towards him, Toris slashed in a long arc, his own weapon suddenly as heavy as a boulder. It clashed with a deafening ring with the Asmog's sword, shattering it into pieces, much to the astonishment of both soldiers.

Toris lifted his blade up again and it became light as grass, he then swung again, cutting open the man's chest cavity, sending blood everywhere. Toris got his first taste of blood, the sticky metallic substance was something he would never forget.

1 year later...

WHEN A SNAKE catches a frog, the frog screams for the serpent has it within its grasp and its fate is already decided. It screams because it has lost control. It screams to beg for something to come to its aid. It screams because it is terrified.

For Galaron, a young boy who lied about his age to join the army, he screamed as he lay in the mud. The thick substance slowly consumed him. When he moved, he sunk quicker, when he stood still, he could do nothing but feel the heavy earth swallow him up.

Before him, way out of reach and on solid ground, stood his comrades, just watching, keen to help but helpless to do anything for he was too far away.

Galaron's screams and cries for his mother carried on into the night. Until they were cut short by a gurgling cry as the mud swallowed him.

For all the death Toris had seen, for all the people he had killed and lost, Galaron's was the worst.

3 years later...

"NICE HELM, TOR. Where did you get that?" Famastil said, looking at the heaume helm in his grasp.

With a cross running down the middle, splitting the faceguard into four sections, each quarter had a different set of shaped holes to let the owner see through.

At first, Toris didn't say anything. Standing in a mismatch of armour, he didn't really want to say how he found it.

"You heard what the commander said," he sighed, knowing that he would figure it out anyway, "don't bother waiting for armour anymore. Take what you find before the enemy does."

He sat down with a huff.

He was more toned and better built now, the body of war showed. Scars appeared on every exposed bit of skin. The sights, sounds, and smells around him didn't distract either. Not even the crying screams of men being mended.

His right arm had a pauldron and arm guards all the way down to his wrist, and he wore a thick leather gauntlet, his left arm bare. He wore a thick gambeson, which he had stitched together from three shredded ones, showing a mismatch of colour.

Famastil was dressed the same, but the opposite to Toris. They both looked down at the ground sombrely. They hated looting, but when the arrows came raining down upon them, anything they found was for the taking.

"How about this," Toris said, noticing his despondent look, "we make a pact. If either of us goes down, neither of us will be bothered if the other takes what we have."

"I don't think you'll feel much at all if you're dead!"

They let out a slight chuckle at that, receiving several strange looks as to why someone was laughing.

It had been a stalemate, but the attacking nations were gaining ground at the consequence of the vanguard where Toris and Famastil were.

"Ere up, here comes Delros," Toris said, noticing him.

Walking through the shambles of men he came, a hard-faced man carrying a warhammer over his shoulder and helm under his arm.

"Tomorrow, lads" he belted out, "is the big offensive, be ready. They'll be coming hard this time. The general has dished out extra rations for you all with his compliments."

"He said that last time and we didn't get anything," Famastil muttered.

"He looks well fed, though," Toris replied. "Why does he keep saying they're charging? Ever since we've started, that's all we've done!"

"Maybe they see them coming and send us out to stop them?"

"Maybe."

In that moment, Peralis came pacing through the crowd, trying not to appear too eager in front of the despondent and ill-equipped soldiers, yet he still had a skip in his step.

"Where have you been?" Toris asked him. Then he noticed what he was wearing.

"Just been up to the smithy's tent. Managed to get to the front of the queue this time." He beamed as his mates looked him up and down as if he were a beautiful woman, for the garb he wore was far better quality than anything they had.

"Look how well they pull out," he said, grasping his knife.

Present day…

TORIS AWOKE AND looked around. Everything was as it was before. The blood running through the trench had started to solidify. It was darker with night creeping over. He nudged Famastil. "C'mon, let's move."

Famastil remained seated.

"Fam? Let's go!" Toris said bluntly. "It's no time to muck about." He took hold of his friend's arm, and then noticed it, Famastil was cold.

Bending down, Toris looked into his friend's eyes and saw that there was no life. Toris had bottled up his emotions ever since he had left home, but now, seeing his best friend dead, was too much, and resting his forehead against Famastils's, Toris could hold it in no longer and wept.

A WHILE PASSED, and Toris heard voices above.

He dried his eyes.

"Rest a moment, my friend," he whispered. "I'm just going to see if there's anyone about," he said and gave his friend's body a firm reassuring hold.

Pulling himself up, he felt his stiff joints ache as he willed them to move from being in the same position for so long.

Bloodied, bruised, and tired, Toris pushed his way up the trench. Climbing over bodies of friends and foes, he willed himself on. It was steep, and he felt that just tilting his head back ever so slightly would cause him to fall backwards. But he clung onto the bodies. He didn't touch any mud. He had pretty much bathed in it all year, but it was nothing but a trench covered in bodies and blood now.

He pulled himself to the top, and stood looking at an endless sight of the same thing as far as the eye could see; endless armoured soldiers in their last moments of war.

"DO YOU KNOW what a pyrrhic victory is, Lembon?"

"No, sir."

"It's where the victory is overshadowed by the cost it took to get it. A cost that our boys took."

Tears began to form in the general's eyes, for the two people who survived that war stood upon the edge of the battlefield looking at the carnage before them.

Just then, they both braced themselves as they saw a Thi'Perian soldier climbing up the trench towards them. Caped in blood and holding a sword that looked like splinted metal, he had a rather relaxed guard before the two Asmogs.

"Kill him!" the general ordered, stepping behind his aid. But Lembon was weedy fellow, not a soldier, and he cowered away.

"Haven't enough died at your hand?" rasped the helmed warrior.

Removing his helmet, he looked at the two men. He looked tired and emotionless. "I've just heard what you've said. It appears I am all that is left of my nation and you of yours."

"Stand down, young man." said the general, trying to fill his voice with authority.

"I think between us, I hold the upper hand," Toris said, pacing forward confidently with his sword by his side. "But I want to ask you something." Holding back an emotional tear from his friend's death, he said, "I would ask my own commander, but he's dead. There he is down there." He pointed to the body of a man with his own warhammer buried in his skull. "I want to ask why you invaded. What was the point in it all? Did you get what you wanted? Is this…" he said casting an arm at the world around them, "is this what you wanted?"

"You're a soldier," spat the general, "and can't possibly understand the politics of war. But alas, you seem to lack even the most significant piece of information. It was *your* nation who invaded ours."

"Ha!" Toris laughed. "I think not. This is our land, we came here to defend it from you heathens."

"You filthy…!" the general went red with rage and lifted his sword to smite Toris, but Toris's reactions were far quicker.

He leapt forward and stabbed the general through the heart all the way up to the hilt. Grabbing the man's sword hand, he brought his face to his, showing him nothing but wrath as the general sunk to the floor, cold steel inside him.

When his soul had departed his body, Toris pulled his blade clear and looked at the aid, who went pale.

"You need not fear me," Toris said, calming himself. "I'm done." He wiped his father's blade clean with a rag.

"With respect, soldier, smite me down if you must, but the general is quite right." He pulled out a folded parchment.

Stepping before Toris, he showed a worn map of the world with hundreds of lines and three shaded areas.

"You see, soldier, the green represents your land, the yellow ours. The red is what you have conquered over the past four years."

"Four years?" Toris said incredulously.

Lembon nodded. "We have sent everything to stop you. We've lost two thirds of our male population. All we have left now are the cripples and the inept."

Toris looked at the map.

"Invaders?" he said, not quite believing it. "We've been told that you were attacking us."

"No, young soldier, that is not the case. Your legions marched forth, killing man, woman, and child. Our queen paid and rallied all our allies to amass against you. You and I are all that is left. Your king died this morning over there," Lembon said pointing to a far-off hill. "My queen died fighting him."

Toris looked stricken.

"I wish you well, soldier," Lembon said, handing him the map. "Take it, show your people what really happened here."

He left without a final word.

WALKING BACK THROUGH the village Toris grew up in, he was keen not to draw any attention to himself. He had removed his armour and placed it in a large sack slung over his shoulder. He wore a monk's cowl to cover himself with the map in his hand. Now, very worn, he had showed it to every town, village, and hamlet between the battlefield and here, telling people what had really happened and that they were now kingless. But with no other soldiers returning, he didn't want to come back in his garb with pride and joy that he had fought and survived the war when no one else had. So, with his head bowed, and trying not to let his armour rattle too much in the sack, he walked through the quiet streets of women and children as he saw his father struggle to lift the wheat sacks he hadn't sold that day into the cart.

"Need a hand there, mister?"

Toris spoke normally, although his voice was rugged and heavy, his father stopped, turned ever so slightly to meet its owner.

"Just heading home, stranger. Need a lift?"

"Please."

Toris lifted the last of the wheat sacks into the cart with ease.

His father let out a tear as he walked around the cart and climbed up, and sitting together, he held his son's hand firmly, not wanting to let go.

THE ART OF WAR

BRIAN STAVELEY

IN ALL HIS forty-seven years, General Dakash has never set foot inside the imperial gallery. He tells people this is because a warrior's place is the battlefield or the arena, fighting for his own name and the glory of his emperor. He tells people that he has no need to see the newest painting of him, no need to bask in the grandeur of the most recent sculpture. *I was there*, he says. *I lived it.*

This is both true, and not true.

He fought his first duel at the age of sixteen. Everyone expected him to die, including Dakash himself. The Mad Bull was older, stronger, the veteran of a dozen bloody fights. When he said he planned to cut Dakash apart one piece at a time, Dakash believed him. He couldn't sleep for weeks. He barely ate. When he wasn't trying to train, he stared at the wall, rehearsing the possibilities of his own annihilation. He considered running away. The other bhanti ran sometimes, if there was a fight they knew they couldn't win. Usually, if they made it over the walls or past the gate, they were brought back in chains and fed to the lions.

Even now, thirty-one years later, he can remember stepping out of the cool, subterranean darkness into the blinding light of the ring. He can remember the sun like an anvil on his face, the weight of his blades in his hands. He can remember the sound—so loud it seemed solid—pouring from ten thousand eager throats. He can even remember the Mad Bull striding into the ring, muscles and mustache oiled, each of his blades half again as long as those Dakash held.

What he cannot remember is what happened next.

One moment, he felt ready to vomit up his own heart. The next, he was standing over the Mad Bull's body, soaked in blood, a severed head clutched in his left hand.

His own unlikely survival terrified him almost as much as the prospect of his death. The other bhanti tried to talk to him about it, about what happened in the ring. *What came over you?* they asked. *You were not yourself. You were inhabited by a god of war.* They meant the words as praise, but Dakash could only feel an awful, twisting unease.

He grew up knowing he could not trust the world. When his parents saw he was a large child and strong, they sold him to be trained as a bhanti. Inside the camp, the young warriors betrayed one another daily—stealing food, sabotaging weapons, smearing the drinking troughs with shit to make the others sick. The owners in their seaside palaces would make bargains to see one fighter saved, another slaughtered, according to their own favorites and the whims of the crowd. It was not an accident that the Mad Bull fought with longer blades. Dakash learned early that the only person he could trust was himself.

And then that self became unknown to him. He felt like a man shipwrecked in the ocean. For days, for weeks, for a whole lifetime he had been holding on to a fragment of shattered mast, trusting it to keep him afloat, only to find it turn to stone in his grip. The danger and strangeness were no longer just outside of him, they were inside, too. The ugliness he'd known his whole life had grown in him like an organ.

Death would have been better, but he was too frightened to choose death, and so he continued to fight, continued to lose himself in the violence, continued to wake to awful slaughters he could not remember having wrought, continued to lose hold of himself, continued to kill and to win.

Eventually, he caught the eye of the emperor, who bought him, made him his personal champion, set him free, elevated him to the commander of the Raven Guard, decorated him with the armor of a Manjari General. At some point, the great artists of the empire, keen to curry favor with the throne, began to paint Dakash. Sculptors sculpted him. People came from Uvashi-Rama and the Vrishan Hills, Gosha, and the coast of the Ghost Sea to see him fight in the arena, and they went to the imperial gallery to see the depictions of his duels and battles.

Dakash never goes to the gallery.

He spends his time, when he isn't fighting or training to fight, as far from blood and battle as he can get, in a hillside villa above the city given to him by the emperor. There are vines there that he cultivates, and fruit trees. Even on hot days, there is a breeze. He trains with his sword or his bow on a large open patio, but the movement and effort feel more like dance than like fighting. He has killed, according to some accounts, over seventy warriors. He remembers killing none. The gaps in his memory terrify him, but for thirty-one years, what has terrified him more is discovering what fills those gaps. He's aware that it must be bloody, ugly. He's seen the bodies he leaves behind. As long as he doesn't have the memories, however, he can believe that the violence belongs to someone else. He can remain a man who raises grapes, who picks fruit, who sits on that patio in the evenings and watches the swallows carve their passage through the air.

Then, on one of those evenings, as the warm air is just going vague and pink, a shape approaches up the twisting road, broad-shouldered, broad hipped, a woman from the village at the foot of the hill that he knows well. Her name is Runya. She has a single mole high on her right cheek, and she can recite from memory all three epics. She sells his fruit in the local market and, sometimes, when her servants are picking it, filling wooden crates, then loading those wooden crates into wagons, Dakesh and Runya spend an afternoon together in his bed. Sometimes she spends a night.

On this evening, however, she comes alone—no servants, no crates, no wagons. When she arrives at his patio, she fixes him with her dark gaze and tells him something beautiful and awful: *I am pregnant with your child.*

His child.

He tries to imagine what this means, what it will mean. His own childhood was synonymous with fear, bafflement, suffering, desperate perseverance. He did not want to have a child because the world is cruel, and worse, because he fears he himself may be cruel. How can he be trusted to rear a child when he does not know his own mind or recall his own life? How can he trust himself?

Runya sits on the low stone wall, takes a peach from a basket, considers it a moment, then puts it back.

"What do you want to do?" she asks.

He shakes his head. "I don't understand."

"Do you want to raise the child together? Or shall I raise him on my own?"

"Him?" This, too, he cannot imagine. "How do you know?"

"I know. So, what do you want to do?"

He shakes his head again. When the only good things in the world were grapes and swallows and occasionally Runya's warm brown skin under his fingers, he could bear his own brokenness. How will he bear it if he has a son?

Runya watches him, one hand resting on her belly.

"You are not a bad man," she says.

She does not say, *You are a good man.*

"I am not sad to have you as the father of this child."

She does not say, *I am happy*, but she does reach out to him in the gathering dusk and put a hand on his knee. It would be enough, that hand, if he were a whole person. It would be more than enough. There is tenderness in her touch, and strength, and bravery—good lives have been built on less—but it is not Runya he fears.

He stands up, too quickly.

Her hand drops away.

"Can you come back tomorrow?" he asks.

She is angry—he can see it in the tightness of her face, in the way she wraps her hands around her middle once more—but all she says is, "What will you know tomorrow that you do not know today?"

THE IMPERIAL GALLERY is the private collection of the emperor, and for hundreds of years it was closed to all but the empire's most august citizens. Just before Dakesh's birth, however, in a gesture of civic magnanimity, the emperor opened the doors. Now, as Dakesh approaches the fountains fronting the building, as he walks between the massive sculptures of the snakes, grubby children race around his feet. Women and men, with enough coin to spend an afternoon away from their work, loiter beneath the willows beside the ornamental ponds. It is a fine summer day. Shifting leaves sift the sunlight.

Dakesh feels awful, hot and cold at the same time. His legs are weak, as though he has just recovered from a long illness. It is hard to hold a thought for more than a few moments. Sweat slides down his chest and back, soaking his tunic. He runs a hand through his thick black hair, and it comes away dripping wet.

The stairs are wide enough for an army to mount twenty men abreast. The general feels the way he feels when going to battle, only worse. There *are* battles inside, but these, unlike all the other fights of his life, he will actually see. The blood will be paint, the bodies marble, but he will remember them when he leaves the gallery.

He passes beneath the gilded, fifty-foot wings of a raven with the head of a man and the tail of a snake, steps from the sunlight into shadow and pauses. He does not have to do this. Unlike that fight against the Mad Bull all those years ago, he can simply leave. His villa is waiting high on the hill. Runya is waiting, his unborn son restless inside her womb. He closes his eyes, wipes the sweat from his brow, takes hold of his courage, and moves deeper into the vaulted space.

It is not difficult to find the room that bears his name. He had no idea it would be so large, no idea there was so much art. Twenty or thirty people occupy the space. They move between the works, pausing occasionally to exclaim at a particularly gruesome detail. He catches snatches of names he remembers: foes long dead, battlefields silent now, swaying with grass or wheat. From the doorway, he can see snatches of color in the great, gilded frames: flags waving above soldiers with spears, fires raging, red everywhere. He can still leave, but he does not. A sculpture stands just inside the door. Like a man in a nightmare, Dakesh steps forward, one stride, then another, until he is standing eye to eye with himself.

He was younger then, slimmer, stripped to the waist for his duel. His muscles strain inside the stone as he lifts a larger man from the ground with the two knives he has buried inside his stomach. The dying man is torn half open. His eyes are squeezed shut against the agony of his own ending, his teeth bared in a silent, unending scream. Dakesh is open-mouthed as well, but instead of screaming, he is smiling, or laughing, marble face a mask of bliss. The general stares at it a long time, then turns away.

For half the afternoon, he moves through the gallery, from one piece to the next. They are all different, and all the same. Here he is riding down a the last of the Saddha Usurpers. Here he is strangling a man with his bare hands. Here he is, ignoring the knife lodged in his shoulder as he smashes a man's skull to bloody pieces with a fragment of stone. In some poses, he is obviously victorious, in others, he looks close to death, but in every single one he is grinning, laughing, roaring with delight as he rips the life from his foes.

By the time he leaves the gallery, Dakesh has been clenching his hands so long that they ache. His back hurts from standing motionless. He can think only one thought over and over again: *A stranger lives inside me, an awful man I do not know.*

When he reaches his villa, the moon hangs above the vines, a slender crescent. It will ripen with the grapes. He sits on the patio watching it traverse the sky, rising, then falling in its ancient arc. He wants nothing more than to sit here, to watch that moon rise with his son, to drink with Runya the tart first pressing of the year's wine. Instead, when the light bleeds into the sky, he goes inside, finds a quill and two pieces of parchment. The first he addresses to the emperor.

If ever I have served you well, my lord, if ever I have brought you glory, please see to it that this, my villa, my wealth, and all my land passes to Runya the fruitseller.

The second note is even shorter.

If ever he asks, please, tell your son his father was a winemaker, gentle and foolish, of no particular repute.

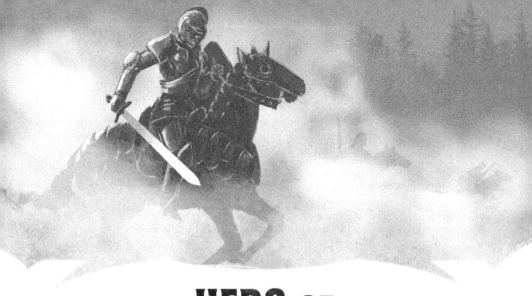

HERO OF THE DAY

NATHAN T. BOYCE

GOLFREY PEERED OUT into the dawn air, the morning fog settling on the meadow below. The poor fools following the bastard child of King Francis, God rest his soul, deserve everything coming to them today. Today, history will record the day King Menschel defended his crown.

The king and his captains met in the middle of the field with the potential usurper and his men. As if there was any point of this. If any of this could be averted with words, things would not have gotten this far. Golfrey looked at the king's lords flanking him and wondered, not for the first time, if his father knew about his existence.

His mother captured his dreams of his future when she spoke of Duke Welton's visit to the small, poor farm village in her youth. She wasn't naïve enough to think anything would come of it, and the purity of farm girls were often over-estimated. But she was very proud that of all the girls in town he chose her, even if only for a night. Every time she went to tell the duke of Golfrey, his guards would not give her audience. His mother remained poor but happy until the croup took her lungs last winter. She beamed in pride at her son when she passed, whispering with her last breath how noble he looked, just like his father. Today, Golfrey was going to prove his blood line.

He looked beyond the meeting of commanders where the opposing army gathered, a crowd of rebels about to meet their fate. Did they expect to take the field with only twenty cavalry? The king's horsemen alone numbered over one hundred. The thundering stampede of death would turn the tide this day.

Golfrey scratched at his chest through his wool tunic. His faded red blazon almost a pink compared to every other archer he stood beside. Their gold lions gleamed against the bloody background while his mewled in a placid yellow. The boys got him good on that one. He looked down at his hands. His blisters had healed from the concentrated lye they told him to use. It was supposed to get his uniform cleaner than the queen's under britches.

He did not imagine his service in the king's army to go so wrong. He was nobility after all, if not by title, by blood. He longed for his place with the footman, where glory and promotion, maybe even a title he earned on his own, could be claimed with skill of the sword and courage in battle. So what if he had missed when sheathing his sword. No one is perfect. It wasn't his fault his line sergeant stood behind him while the Duke Welton inspected him. It was a clean wound, right into his thigh. A few stitches and the sergeant could tell the brothel maids any tale he wanted.

If Golfrey were honest with himself, he did not excel in arms training. The bruises and cuts even with the wooden practice swords in the daily sparring proved to him how dead he would be if he were still among those footman he looked upon now.

The king and his commanders galloped back as the opposing leaders did the same. The banners blowing behind the king, glorious red and gold, claimed the land and its people. The might of the true king and his men.

Damn! His bootlace was untied again. Golfrey bent down to fix the loose ends, and his bow slid off his shoulder and into the dirt in front of him. He reached in reaction to grab it, the suddenness of his maneuver causing the strap for his quiver to slide down his other arm. He let his arm looped all the way through quickly, freeing himself from the restraining strap, and he tied his boot. Grabbing his bow, he stood. The strap, now around his waist, slid down all the way to the ground with the weight of his quiver.

Sigh.

No wonder even these archers made him the butt of every joke. Quickly, he stepped out of the loop and picked up his quiver, slinging it back in place.

"Sorry, Bart." Golfrey apologized. Banging his gear about while getting adjusted.

The flagged arrow whizzed uncomfortably close to his ear, its streamer sailing behind with the red and gold challenging the oncoming would be king and his army. A ploy, intentionally short to take the advancing footmen by surprise as the hail of arrows cast their bodies down.

The cadence of the drums startled Golfrey as the sharp staccato notes burst into the air. The footmen on his right all readied shields and swords in reaction to the commands given by the taught leather's call. The armored cavalry behind them gave no indication as to where they would move on the battlefield once the charge began.

In response, the opposite side of the field challenged the drums with their own ordered beats. The footmen in blue advanced. Slowly at first, then their pace picked up, eating away the distance of the field.

The king's drums pealed out again. His footmen getting anxious as the cavalry behind continued to remain motionless. Finally, with the last beat, the footmen began their march.

To battle.

The men marched towards each other, the crisp morning sun clearing the fog. Golfrey noticed every detail of the battlefield now. The men closing on each other. Stoic men ready for their chance at glory. He was surprised to see the trepidation in a few, and others with outright fear broadcasting from their faces.

The drumbeats picked up, and the walk moved to a slow run. With three quick taps off the rim of the drum, Golfrey readied his arrow and aimed for a long arc.

The usurpers horsemen began to advance, and Golfrey couldn't help but look at the king's own cavalry still motionless. While he was no tactician, it would seem the footmen would feel more confident knowing they had support. Even twenty mounted men could wreak havoc to the line.

"RELEASE!" the command came from behind him.

Golfrey let fly his arrow and nocked another. No point in trying to keep track of whether his aim was sure.

A glint of light hit his eye. He looked to see where the distraction came. On the left, past the trees, two hills met. He hadn't noticed the small earthen depression between the two until now, but every few seconds, a sharp glint of sun on metal caught his eye. He looked harder, trying to get more detail. Men on horseback flitted behind the small crease of earth quickly, as if galloping.

The usurpers true cavalry!

Golfrey looked back onto the battlefield as he let his next arrow fly on command. The screams below ringing in his ears now. Still twenty horsemen barreling down on the king's men. The opposing army had split down the middle, allowing the riders through. Behind the advancing armies, the battlefield already was littered with fallen men, pierced with a rain of steel and wood.

The usurper outplayed the king. If even half of his cavalry outflanked the men, the results could be catastrophic.

"Sir!" Golfrey yelled.

"Quiet on the line"

Stupid line sergeant.

"But, sir!" Golfrey needed to get his attention.

The fist on the back of his head sent him to the ground. Golfrey looked up to see Trenton. His line sergeant glowering at him.

"Shut your hole, ya' worthless string," Trenton ordered. His hand resting on his sword.

Golfrey scrambled to his feet and bolted, trying to get to the tree line.

"Get back here you tit-sucker! Cowardice is punishable by death!"

Golfrey didn't care. If no one was going to listen to him, he needed to do something. If Trenton followed him to kill him, at least he would know about the cavalry riding down behind the king. He could see the other line sergeants drawing their swords. He dashed to the left to avoid the first swing, but that only brought another sword in range of his stomach. A sharp pain deep through his left side. Golfrey cried out in pain.

He kept moving. He was clear.

Holding his left side, he could feel his life leaking out of him, sticky and warm. The tree line gave him cover and shade, but still he moved, ignoring the pulls of brambles and underbrush. Up ahead, a clearing of sun let him know he was nearing the edge of the small island of trees.

On the grass below, the cavalry came. Golfrey grabbed his bow and nocked an arrow. He pulled back. The pain on his left screamed as his finger touched his cheek. Where to aim?

His fingers let the string slide from the crook. He felt the slap against his armguard as he pulled another arrow. While he drew back again, he noticed a horse go down, his rider catapulted into the air in front of him. The cavalry behind did not have time to pull back before the horses behind trampled over the screaming man.

Another arrow gone.

This one missing the mark as it flew over the formation of riders.

Another arrow left his bow. This one managed to hit a rider in the side. Golfrey pulled another, but his hand waivered as he saw the formation turn in one fluid motion. Like birds in flight, the men moved their mounts towards the trees.

The nocked arrow fumbled on his resting hand. He could see large clods of earth pulled up under the weight of man and horse as they charged towards him. He felt a wave of dizziness come over him, and the bile in his stomach approach the back of his throat.

He needed to concentrate. Was that a red and gold lion coming at him from the corner of his eye? Concentrate.

He let fly again, but there was no strength in it. His arrow skittered along the ground before the oncoming death. He dropped his bow and reached for his sword.

Before the blade left its sheath, he felt the impact. The rider did not even bother trying to kill him with a blade. The earth spun. A red flash blasted through his eyes as pain racked his body. He didn't feel the impact of the tree behind him.

He tried to breathe. He tried to move. His chest groaned as he felt shattered bones grind against each other. He needed to breathe. The red foam bubbling from his mouth fell against his pink tunic. He NEEDED to breathe. The spasm is his chest pulled him onto his side, contracting and forcing splinters of his ribs through his lungs. Just one breath. Just one…

DUKE WELTON SAT astride his horse, Ironhoof, next to the king and looked down upon the havoc this day had wrought. Men had fought tooth and nail to survive down there. The line had held fast against the first charge of cavalry, and Lord Edmond should be proud. The command of the footmen was on him today, and his sacrifice would not be forgotten. The initial surge and energy of battle never lasted long, and the slugfest down there became a matter of endurance over rage. The numbers had favored the king.

The odor of blood and excrement hit him in the face.

King Menschel had acquiesced to letting the cavalry held in reserve to finish the battle.

Still, the king's lack of commitment had done its part to turn the battle. When the tree line on his left behind the archers erupted, the fact the horsemen were not already engaged allowed him to split his forces. As the cavalry in blue tore into the bowmen like a scythe through a wheat field, he gave Earl Graysmith the order to clean up what was left on the battlefield. The rest of his men went in to engage the flanking horsemen. If they had been able to get to the defenseless backside of the footmen, the mass of men would collapse and run, fearing their position had been overwhelmed.

Why go through the trees there? Had they continued to ride around, they could have taken King Menschel and his cavalry by surprise. The day would have been lost, and the usurper would have had his throne. With his men able to charge on the oncoming surprise attack instead, the clever strategy was evaded.

He rode around the area where his bowmen were ground down. All of them slaughtered save one, a line sergeant named Trenton.

"How did you manage to survive when all your men sacrificed themselves for their king?" the Duke asked.

Trenton kneeled. "I'm sorry, m'Lord. I wasn't around when my men were attacked. I was chasing a coward name Golfrey who ran. I was in the wood line when the assault occurred. In chasing him, I was able to see the flanking cavalry. After my sword took care of the coward, I used his bow to draw the charge towards me. They must have thought there was more than just me in the woods. They rode past me too fast for me to kill any more. They didn't even avoid riding over the coward I killed."

Duke Welton stared at his line sergeant in disbelief. "You have no idea what you have done. A lesser man would have just hidden in the trees until he was out of danger."

The duke didn't even bother with trying to ease Trenton as he stammered. A common man standing in front of a nobleman often became overwhelmed.

"You have saved the day, young man!" the duke said, trying to put his heroic sergeant at ease. "I will take you before the king and let him decide how best to reward a man with such bravery. I expect nothing less than a title and your own land to protect for his majesty."

Trenton stopped, looking up at the duke with a smile.

Duke Welton dismounted.

"As my personal thanks, I would like you to have my horse, which helped carry us to victory today, just as you did."

He took this amazing man and allowed him to mount Ironhoof, grabbed the reins, and began walking towards the king's tent.

SACRED SEMANTICS

NICHOLAS EAMES

BEFORE LEAPING TO his death from the edge of a steep bluff, Neph decided to offer a quick prayer to the Spider Goddess because a lot of devout men had died this morning, and it probably wouldn't hurt to introduce himself.

"Hi, Goddess. It's me, Neph." He belatedly remembered to take off his cap. There was mud all over it, which he tried in vain to brush off before clutching it to his heart and peering skyward. "It looks like we're done for. The six-leggers have us surrounded, trapped on this blasted hill, which the colonel said was impregnable, except it seems awfully... um, impregnated now."

He heard men shouting in the smoke behind him, followed by the *whapwhapwhap* of spinneret gun unloading in staccato bursts, then silence.

"I don't get it," Neph complained. "We did what the priests asked of us. We said the prayers, made the sacrifices—cut eight men into eight pieces and burned them in eight separate fires—and *still* the Sixers beat us. How? Why? Is there a lesson we're supposed to learn?"

Something exploded in his periphery, forcing Neph to squint against the glare. He sank to his knees at the bluff's edge. Smoke churned like soiled bathwater over the battlefield below.

"Maybe the heathens are right!" he cried. "Maybe you *do* only have six legs, and we eight-leggers are the ones who've got it all backwards. Or maybe you've got *seven* legs and we're all wrong, in which case we're fighting this Holy War for nothing!" He shook his head, despairing. "No. Nevermind. That's insane. You're a Spider Goddess, and spiders have eight legs. We're right, they're wrong, and we need to kill them until they understand. Until they see the truth."

Neph startled as a man on fire lurched past him and went screaming into the swirling abyss. Hopefully, the poor soldier had said his prayers *before* being lit up like a torch.

"Anyway—" the boy replaced his hat, "I'm gonna jump off this cliff. Kill myself. It might seem like a coward's way out, but if the Sixers take me alive, they'll torture me. Or worse, they'll *recondition* me. Strap me to a table and tell me a spider's only got six legs until I actually start believing them. And after that, they'll blind me, hobble me, and send me home, another false prophet doomed to starve on the streets, shunned by my own people." He spat over the brink. "Well, thanks but no thanks! I don't—"

A tickling sensation drew Neph's eye to his hand. Incredulous, he saw a tiny red spider skittering over his thumb. Was this a sign from the Goddess? A message of some sort? He'd been about to kill himself. Was this her way of telling him not to? He sure hoped so, because although death was preferable to capture, life was a great deal more preferable than death.

He brought his hand to his face. "Hey, little fella. What are—"

Whapwhapwhap—a spinneret gun went off right behind him. Bolts of searing white metal whizzed over his shoulder, so close Neph could feel the heat on his face. He yelped and scrambled to his feet, except one foot slipped on the mud-slick scree, and he went pitching over the edge.

He'd barely summoned the breath to scream when he hit the sloping face of the cliff. The impact forced the air from his lungs, but he managed a pained gasp as his plummet continued. The fog seemed to grasp at him as he fell, chilling and sticky, and then he was through it, watching the ground rush up to meet him. Except it wasn't ground. It was—

Water?

Neph went into the river, and river went into him. It filled his mouth, clogged his throat, and flooded his mind with the animal panic of drowning. Disoriented, he rolled and squirmed, unsure of which way was up, aware that the river was bearing him sluggishly along.

Was this some sort of joke? A cruel punishment for his sins? Had the Goddess—blessed be all eight of her legs—spared him from death-by-falling only to drown him?

Finally, his head broke the surface. He sputtered, gasped, flailed, and went under again. When he surfaced next, he made a concerted effort to *swim* (or something like it) toward the bank. A log bobbed past him, and Neph latched onto it, paddling with his legs until he ran aground.

Still clinging to his log, he gagged up a mouthful of mud and water. His tongue tasted like a copper shil fished out of a shit-trench, and he wondered what had fouled the river so thoroughly.

The answer was right in front of him. He was hugging a corpse.

After frantically kicking it away, Neph screamed for a bit, sobbed for a bit, then retched what remained in his stomach into the mud. As he lie there panting, he noticed several other bodies scattered along the bank, bloating and pale, many of them missing arms or legs or a combination of the two.

"What are you doing?" a woman's voice called.

Neph froze. Was it a friend? An enemy? There was no way to know since the heathens spoke the same language as those who worshipped the true faith. Hells, they even *dressed* the same. A Sixer's uniform was greyish-blue, while the one worn by Neph and his fellow Eights was bluish-grey. They'd looked distinct enough from across the battlefield this morning, but once they were doused in rain, or mud, or blood there was no telling the difference.

Why hadn't someone higher up thought to differentiate their own troops from the enemy? *We're nothing like the Sixers,* he fumed, *so why do we dress like them? Why aren't we wearing orange or something? Well, maybe not orange, but—*

"Aran!" shouted the woman. "Quick mucking about, will ya? There's Eights in trees over there. And a few left fighting on the hill!"

An enemy, then. A Sixer. Neph's skin crawled in revulsion.

"I'm just making sure this lot is dead!" said a boy's voice, disconcertingly close.

Through the bleary veil of half-closed eyes, Neph saw a pair of boots trudge into view and halt beside one of the corpses farther along the bank. Not content with simply inspecting the body, the boy—Aran, the woman had called him—stabbed it in the throat with his tarsus.

Neph might have yelped out loud because the boots suddenly turned and stalked slowly in his direction.

Oh, Goddess, he prayed, *what have I done to deserve such torment?*

He flinched as Aran's sword skewered another corpse.

Must you toy with me so? Am I nothing but a fly, doomed to wriggle and suffer for your cruel amusement?

The boots stamped toward Neph. Blood dripped thick as molasses from the point of his tarsus.

"Aran! Let's go!"

The boots paused.

Neph's heart leapt. *Thank you, Goddess. Bless you forever. I swear, I'll never—*

"Just one more!" Aran shouted.

Eight Hells! Seriously?

The boots stopped right in front of him, and Neph, seeing no other recourse aside from waiting to be stabbed to death, open his eyes and screamed.

The Sixer screamed back.

When both boys finished giving vent to their terror, instinct kicked in. Aran raised his sword to strike. Neph rolled as the point gouged the ground behind him. He kicked at the boy's knee and felt it snap. The Sixer collapsed on top of him, and Neph, with uncharacteristic ferociousness, grappled Aran's neck with one arm and squeezed with all his strength. His free hand groped at the boy's face, nails digging into flesh, clawing like an animal for no good reason except to cause pain to someone who'd been about to kill him a moment ago.

Aran bit him.

Neph howled in anguish, tightened his grip on the boy's throat. His enemy kicked and thrashed. He was bigger than Neph, who was weary from pulling himself to shore. Any second now, he might squirm loose, and then...

Without thinking, Neph buried his fingers in the boy's eyes. He felt the rubbery orbs burst into pulp as he burrowed into the Sixer's skull. The Sixer tried to scream, but Neph's arm tightened around his throat.

At last, after a final racking convulsion, the Sixer went still.

Dead. Neph's mind floundered, mired in fear and dawning horror. *He's dead. I'm alive. I'm still alive.*

Because you gouged his fucking eyes out, some unhelpful aspect of himself chimed in.

Neph rolled out from under the corpse. On his knees in the mud, he wiped his shaking hands off on the kid's uniform. The gooey remnants of Aran's eyeball clung to his fingers like the innards of a harvest pumpkin.

"Aran?"

Goddess, he'd forgotten about the woman! Frantic, Neph pried the boy's sword from his grip. There was a mandible pistol in a leather holster, which he grabbed as well. His eye snagged on the six-legged spider in tarnished silver pinned to the corpse's chest. He set his pilfered weapons down and unclasped it (no easy task for trembling hands), then tore off his own eight-legged sigil. He was busy fastening the heathen's pin over his heart when the squelch of footsteps sounded behind him.

"Aran, I—" the woman trailed off as Neph glanced over his shoulder. "What in the Six Hells is… Oh, Goddess, no. Aran!" She aimed the point of her tarsus at Neph. "Who are you? What happened here."

"I…uh…" It took an effort to pull his gaze from the Sixer pin on her chest. "I found him like this."

"You found him like this?" The woman looked deeply skeptical. She glanced at the boy and, judging by the expression on her face, just now noticed the gory mess Neph had made of his eyes. "What the actual *fuck*? Who did this? I swear on the Six Legs of—"

Neph shot her. The pistol kicked violently, and was so suddenly hot that it scalded his palm. He fumbled the gun, cursed under his breath as it plopped into the river, and shook his hand to cool it. He'd never fired a mandible pistol before—he'd certainly never shot anyone—and finally understood why the soldiers who used them wore leather gloves on their left hands.

He stood there for moment, gazing blankly at the river's current and trying not to think of the two people he'd just murdered.

His mother's voice floated into his head. "*It's not murder*," she'd told him when he'd expressed remorse over being drafted. "*The Sixers aren't people like you and I, Neph. They're Heathens. Sinners. You're not killing them, you're* cleansing *the world of their taint.*"

A devout woman, his mother. In truth, Neph had lived in fear of her for most of his life, though he missed her dearly now. She'd be proud of him, if he managed to make it home.

Screams and spinneret fire pricked his ears. He turned to survey the forest behind him.

There's Eights in the trees, he recalled the woman saying. "Well, then," Neph muttered. "The trees it is."

He stopped to loot the woman's pistol, making a point of not looking at her face, then straightened and set out for the tree line. He started out a sprint, but was forced to settle for a shambling jog. A few of his ribs were broken, Neph suspected, and he'd bruised his leg bad when he'd struck the cliffside on the way down.

To the east (or west—he honestly had no idea which direction was which) the battlefield lay beneath a shifting blanket of black smoke. Neph could see distant figures scuttling like ants, the bright flash of gunfire, the glint of wan sunlight on steel. The wreck of two spider tanks were burning, and a razorfly buzzed in the low clouds, though he couldn't know if it belonged to the enemy or not. The Sixers' razorflies were almost identical to those piloted by the Eights, save for the blasphemous decal painted on the side of their shells.

The forest didn't provide as much cover as he would have liked. The trees were tall and too-slender to hide behind in case he spotted the enemy. He heard distant shouts, and the successive *thwumping* of bomb clusters going off somewhere ahead.

Something chirped on his right. Neph spun, fired, and cursed himself for a fool when he saw the squirrel that had startled him. He lobbed the scalding gun at the animal, but it missed, as well.

The squirrel's chittering sounded an awful lot like laughter.

"Something funny?" he asked, knuckles whitening on his weapon's hilt as he started toward it.

"Hello? Help!"

Neph looked around, wishing to hell he hadn't wasted the mandible's shot on a fucking squirrel. There was a toppled tree nearby, a woman pinned on her stomach beneath it. She was wearing an Eight's blue-grey uniform.

Her cap had fallen off, and her muddied blonde hair was in disarray.

"Can you help me, please?" she prompted.

"Oh." Neph blinked, dimly aware of something clanging off to his right. "Yeah. Sure." He stabbed the point of his tarsus into the mud and knelt by her. "What happened?"

She looked at him as if he'd asked something idiotic (like how many legs a spider had, for instance) and blew a strand of yellow hair from her eyes. She was younger than Neph had first supposed. As young as him even. "A tree fell on me."

"I can see that," he said. He hooked his hands under the trunk and hoisted upward. His arms strained, his knees shook, and something in his lower back tore like a loaf of fresh bread.

"You're not strong enough," she pointed out.

"I'm strong enough," he assured her, failing to mask his sudden breathlessness.

"Maybe go get some help," she suggested. "I can wait."

"I don't need help," he snapped. "I just need a better—"

"Hurry!"

"Hurry? You just said—"

A beam of splintering energy missed him by inches. It carved through the tree in his hands, cauterizing the stump of both halves. Suddenly, he *was* strong enough to lift the tree off the girl. She scrambled out from underneath, and he dropped the trunk.

"Thanks. C'mon." She took his hand and pulled him off at a run. Neph yanked his sword out of the ground as they went by it, then made the grave mistake of looking over his shoulder. A behemoth crashed through the forest behind them, a mechanical monstrosity with segmented legs and clustered green eyes.

"A spider-tank!"

"It's malfunctioning!" she shouted over her shoulder. "Look at its head."

He did. The top of its head—where the cockpit should have been—was blown apart, smoking and sparking as the giant spider charged clumsily after them. Neph tripped over a tuft of earth, stumbling.

"Watch where you're going!" said the girl.

"You just told me to—"

"This way!"

She dragged him down a slope, toward a steep-sided cleft in the valley below. A pair of snarling lasers crossed overhead, sawing through branches, slicing through trees like a sword through shards of grass. The girl—Neph still didn't know her name—stopped short as one crashed down in their path.

"It's targeting matrix is fried," she said, yanking him along. "The autopilot has kicked in, but it thinks everyone's an enemy. We need to get away, or else damage it enough to override its survival scheme and trick it into self-destructing."

Neph was impressed. "How do you know so much about spider tanks?" he shouted, ducking as a stray laser tore a gouge in the earth beside them.

"I'm a driver!" she explained. "That was my tank."

Neph risked another glance over his shoulder. Four of the tank's eight eyes were cracked and damaged, while the other four rolled sporadically, firing beams of crackling energy at anything it deemed a *threat*. He saw the squirrel who'd tormented him earlier get caught by a laser's blast. *Good riddance,* he thought. *Little fucker had it coming.*

"How did you escape?" he asked the girl, who pulled him behind the sheltering bulwark of a grassy ravine. Whatever wrecked the spider's head should have killed her as well.

The girl stopped to catch her breath, swiping hair from her eyes and wincing as she pressed fingers to her ribs. "I wasn't in it at the time. I got out to pee, and the enemy ambushed us. Meleagant went crazy and wiped out both squads."

He'd meant to inquire who stops to pee in the middle of a battle, but she'd caught his interest on something else. "Meleagant?"

"My tank. We name them. Meleagant was a hero from—"

"The Anthrology, yeah. I know him."

She favoured him with a grin. "Pious, are we?"

His attempt to grin back resulted in a harried grimace. "My mother—"

The earthen bulwark exploded, showering them with dirt and stones. They crouched, huddled against the hail of debris. The girl smelled (not unpleasantly) like sweat and spring lilacs. Neph was suddenly conscious of what *he* must smell like: water-logged corpses, blood, the charred tang of pistol-smoke, abject terror…

It's a wonder she isn't gagging right now.

He considered offering up an apology, but the giant mechanized arachnid straddling the sky above them proved a more immediate concern.

Neph stifled a yelp and started to rise, but the girl clutched him hard, hissing into his ear. "Wait. It doesn't see us."

He squinted against the falling grit. She appeared to be right. The spider's remaining eyes looked everywhere but down, occasionally firing off random bolts of crackling energy. There was a spinneret gun on its abdomen, and Neph saw blood splattered on the fractured window of the rear cockpit. "So what do we do?" he whispered.

"We split up. You run that way." She glanced over his shoulder. "Distract it. I'll get on top and—"

"What? *Me*, distract it? Why not you?"

"Do *you* know where its OS hub is? Or how to disable its gyrospanner?"

Neph frowned. He didn't even know what an OS hub was—let alone where to find it—and couldn't have picked a gyrospanner out from a pile of coat-hangers. "Okay, fine. I'll distract it."

"You will?" She eyed him seriously.

"I will," he said, feeling inexplicably brave for the first time today.

The girl took hold of his shoulders. "You can do this."

"I can do this," he repeated.

Neph started to rise, but paused in a crouch. "What's your name?"

Her smile showed white through the grime on her face. "Tisca. What's yours?"

"Neph," he answered. He wanted to say more—to ask her where she was from, what House she belonged to, and why she'd come to war against the Sixers—but all that could wait. He turned, took a breath, and sprinted for all he was worth.

For a moment, all Neph could hear was his pounding heart, his huffing breath, and the snap of twigs underfoot, but then came the whir of motors and the raw sizzle of an eye-laser cutting across on his right. He dove as it passed overhead, then leapt to his feet and took off in the opposite direction. Another beam tore a vertical stripe before him. Neph sidestepped it, heard the canopy come crashing down behind him, and juked again as more lasers—three this time—cut trisecting paths ahead of him.

He dropped, skidding on his side beneath the lowest beam, closing his eyes against the glare of the blistering torrent.

The lasers disappeared. Neph lay on his face in the mud. His whole body ached. Something—the ground beneath him—was trembling.

Get up, he urged himself. *Get up! She needs you to distract it, fool, not lie here like a Sixer coward.* He rose, but his jaw remained pinned to the forest floor.

The tank—Meleagant—charged him. Its legs hammered the earth as it crashed through the brush. Its eyes pulsed red. Its pincers hinged open, coughing acrid black smoke as the chain-edged blades roared to life.

Neph briefly considered offering a prayer to the Goddess, but since she'd been actively trying to kill him all day, he decided on a wordless scream instead. He ran straight at the behemoth, sword raised, and figured that he'd at least die a hero's death, running fearlessly (well, *relatively* fearlessly) into the chainsaw pincers of certain death. He glimpsed a figure—Tisca—clinging to the tank's sternum, tugging desperately at a braided blue cord.

The spider collapsed, sloughing like a boulder behind a rising tide of black earth and wet leaves. Tisca was thrown from her perch, landing hard at Neph's feet.

"You did it!" he cried, kneeling beside her.

"…elf…uct," she murmured.

Beep went something on the tank's blasted console.

"Huh?"

Beep.

"It's going…"

Beep.

"…to self-destruct."

Neph's eyes went wide. He grabbed the girl by the collar and hauled her to her feet, then hurled her, stumbling, away from the crumpled spider. There wasn't time to take shelter, so Neph tossed his sword aside and threw himself onto Tisca, shielding her.

And he prayed, after all, that the Goddess would spare their lives.

Things got very bright and very loud. He might have screamed. He *almost certainly* lost consciousness. Eventually, Neph became aware of a shrill blaring in his ears. He'd closed his eyes at some point, and when he finally opened them, he found Tisca blinking up at him.

"We lived," she said, as though marvelling at something she'd once thought impossible.

"We lived," he breathed.

"You saved my life," she pointed out.

"You saved mine first," Neph said. He rolled off her and sat up. Pieces of charred scrap-metal lay scattered all around them. "Praise the Eight Legs of the Goddess!" he almost laughed for joy. "We lived! You did great, Tisca. I didn't think—"

"What did you say?"

"I said you did great."

"Before that," she snapped. "About the Goddess. You said, 'Praise the *Eight* legs of the Goddess."

"So?"

"So...she only has *six.*"

Neph opened his mouth to protest, but then (as if his mind was just now piecing together the events of the last few minutes) he recalled the *six*-legged tank she'd piloted plodding toward him, remembered that he was wearing an enemy soldier's *six*-legged pin, and realized belatedly that Tisca's uniform really was more of a greyish-blue than a bluish-grey.

His eyes strayed to the sword laying discarded in the leaves between them.

So did hers.

He leapt for it.

She didn't.

She drew the gun at her hip and shot him in the face.

HEAVEN WAS NOT at all what Neph had expected it to be. He was under the impression there would be sweet music in the air, silver webs spanning the sky, and that everyone he'd ever loved would be on hand to greet him with open arms.

Instead, he was chained by the ankle to a stranger while the two of them pushed a massive stone up a seemingly endless rise. And worse, the old man claimed he'd been a Sixer once upon a time.

"So why are we both here?" Neph asked him. "If the Spider Goddess has eight legs, I should be in paradise right now. And if she had six legs, which is fucking stupid, mind you, then *you* should be in paradise."

"Keep pushing," the man grunted. He seemed weary, as if he'd been here for a very long time.

"But I don't understand," Neph complained, straining under the weight of the stone. "Which one of us is right?"

His partner nodded toward the top of the rise. Following his gaze, Neph could make out a vast, horned shadow rearing against the glow of hellish fires.

"Neither," the old man growled. "She's a dung beetle."

THE WAR GOD'S AXE

ANNE NICHOLLS

"GOAT! WATCH OUT!"

Too late. The flashing hooves connected with Goat's shoulder, cata-pulting him head-first into the stable wall. His skull rang, sparks burst in his vision, then everything went black.

"Perrick, you idiot!" snarled Jash, hurrying to kneel by his friend's side. "What d'you go and do that for?"

Innocent as poison ivy, Perrick picked a bit of straw off his novice's robe and smirked. "I didn't do anything! Not my fault Firestorm felt like kicking out at a passing nutcase. Goat should know better than to walk behind a stallion, let alone a mad bastard like Firestorm."

"Ole Firestorm was fine 'til you spooked him. You done it a-purpose `cause he made you look bad in front of Presbyter Meran." As he spoke,

Jash tore off his sweat-rag and pushed a flap of Goat's scalp back into position. Blood poured out around it. "Go and get a healer."

"You can't tell me what to do! You're only an ostler, and he's only a Flatface who spouts nonsense in his fits of lunacy. And I'm—"

"You're an arrogant dick-head who's only down here as a penance. I know. I've heard it all before. I'm not leaving you alone with him so take your holy novice's arse over to the Temple and get a healer or your next punishment'll be back down the sewers."

"You wouldn't dare tell on me!" Perrick blustered, but his patrician face paled. He couldn't meet Jash's penetrating gaze. Everyone knew Perrick hated the smell of the stables at the best of times, but what made him retch now wasn't dung but acid fear. Under Temple law, the penalty for harming a citizen was a flogging in front of the altar. One stroke from each cleric on his naked, humiliated flesh. Powers only knew what the archbishop would deem a suitable penance afterwards.

"Goat's not even a citizen!" he exclaimed as a thought struck him. "He's a vagrant Flatface, mad as a kite in a storm! He babbles like a lunatic whenever the fit takes him. He's probably a traitor just waiting to let the tribes in at the gate."

Jash stood, walked over to the pitchfork he'd abandoned when Perrick had flapped his cloak at Firestorm and the stallion lashed out. He picked it up, walked slowly right up to Perrick and stabbed the prongs into the ground not a hair's breadth from Perrick's sandalled toes.

Perrick jumped back. Jash laughed up into his face. "Yeah, that's right. I never done nothing neither. But watch out who you go round calling a traitor. Goat's got no love for the tribes. When he was crippled, they exposed him on the steppes. It's a miracle he survived to get to Temple City. This…" Jash flourished the fork around at the racks of saddles, the hay-loft, and the horses, who were trampling nervously at the tension vibrating between the two men, "*this* is his home." With a final flourish of the pitchfork, he backed the bully out into the sunlight. "And don't take too long about it!"

"Shaman eyes!" Goat gasped. Thrashing, he tried and failed to sit up. Jash rushed back to catch him before he could crack his head on the stone. "Spying on us. Monkeys! Crawling up from below!" He threw his arm across his face as if he could hide. "Don't let them get me!"

Jash held him still, crooning, "What eyes? There ain't no eyes, nor monkeys neither. Sssh, Goat, it's all right. It's all right, me ole mucker." He stroked his friend's raven-dark hair that was soft as silk. "You just wake up now. It's only a dream."

Far from waking, Goat became more agitated. His mutterings slipped from the common tongue into something barbaric. He writhed and strove to break free. By the time the healer arrived, Jash, red-faced and dripping with sweat, was losing the battle to stop him flailing.

The healer was an impressive figure shrouded in satin that shone now emerald, now bronze. She paused, looking down at the two youths wrestling in the straw. With one gesture she stilled Goat into sleep. "You can let go now," she said, smiling at a gaping Jash.

"But-but you're a—" His tongue stumbled to a halt as his flush threatened to boil him alive.

"A what?" She cocked her head. "A girl? A healer? A Flatface? The only one who would come? Take your pick." Now she knelt, too. "Let the dog see the rabbit."

Such a homely phrase for such an exotic bird, thought Jash, pleased at the way her skilful hands tended her patient. Taking cloths and lotions from a belt-pouch, she cleaned Goat's bloody wounds. The only sound was his stertorous breathing. When she touched the jagged cut on his left temple, though, he cried out in his heathen tongue.

She answered it in the same. Pushing her damascened hood back the better to hear him, she crouched at his side, her voice soothing. Hypnotic. Goat talked on, more calmly now but disjointed.

Gradually, he rambled to a stop. Her eyes, dark amber flecked with green, smiled into his. He pressed her hand in thanks. His own fell away as he dropped into sleep.

"Powers!" she whispered. "We've got to tell the Temple!"

But outside, footsteps had already burst into a run.

GOAT WOKE TO a bucket of cold water sloshing over him. His eyes were gummed shut with blood. Outside, he heard trumpets blasting messages from one side of Temple City to the other. He caught shouting and the creak of carts. Dogs barked and children cried. In here, wherever here was, incense vied with the stink of red-hot metal.

He tried to stand, but the weight of clinking chains kept him trapped on a chair. Finally, one eyelid fought its way open. In the Temple, of all places. Right in the chancel, with ranks of priests, presbyters, and bishops glaring down at him from the choir-stalls. He saw his tribal axe talisman uncovered on his chest and groaned.

"At least get him something to drink!" snapped the healer. Goat turned stiffly, wondering why an imperious young woman in elegant robes was chained to a seat beside him. In the Temple. With…a full court? And the tribes about to burst upon them all! What were they *thinking?*

"Back with us then?" asked Jash's voice from his other side. "Just in time to—"

Goat couldn't turn his head that far, but he recognised the sound of a slap.

"You're wasting time!" the healer barked. "I've *told* you what he heard in his vision. The tribes are going—"

"No!" Perrick strode forward, posing in a sunbeam to fling out an accusatory arm. "*I've* told everyone you two Flatfaces and his bum-chum were plotting away in your jibber-jabber. He's even got the gall to wear his pagan trinket in our very own city! Why anybody trusted a couple of stinking apes running loose around the city in the first place when the tribes are practically at the gates I do not know, but you're not getting away with it." Preening for the Archbishop, Perrick folded his arms. "I've saved the city!"

"No, you haven't, you twat!" yelled Jash, exclaiming, "Ow!" as a Temple official clouted him on the ear.

"Your Holiness," Goat began, "I appeal."

"No, you don't. I find you most unappealing." The archbishop paused to collect the polite titters from his prelates. "Batzorig Chahotai, known as Goat, we of this city have housed you, shod you, fed you for seven years. And this, this *treachery* is how you repay our generosity!"

Goat worked desperately to moisten his dry throat. "I'm not a traitor! I'm trying to warn you, aren't I? I've done as much as anyone for this city. Since I first managed to crawl out of bed I've never taken a penny I haven't earned."

"Crawled out of bed? Were you too lazy to get up for a decent day's work?"

"No, Archbishop. My spine was broken and so was my skull, but I got myself secretly away to…to someone's riverboat, and from there to the Temple. I'm no traitor! I may walk like a crab, but without this place, I wouldn't be able to walk at all. This is my *home!* I've told you what I saw when the Powers touched me. The main attacks are from below!"

"Saw in a vision?" scoffed Perrick. "You're not sane, much less an acolyte blessed by the Powers. Who are you to have visions?"

"Novice," the archbishop growled.

Perrick sat down huffily. The archbishop pointed a bejewelled finger at Goat. "And why, Batzorig Chahotai, do you cover your real name with an appellation derived from the caprine?"

"I never done that!" Goat exclaimed. "I can't write."

Again the court's snickers echoed round the aisles.

"If it please you, your grace," said Perrick, once more standing up. "We call him Goat as a joke, sir. No? Nimble as a mountain goat, see?"

The archbishop sat forward with a rustle of slithering silk. "And that's funny, is it?"

"Well yes, your grace. It's ironic, isn't it?"

The archbishop looked up quizzically from beneath lowered brows. After a long, long stare, he waved an imperious hand. "Explain."

"He's a cripple, see?" Lacking any visible response, Perrick licked his lips and went on nervously, "Your Grace, he can hardly walk a step."

"I do see." The archbishop's voice was as dry as a desert. "My fellow prelates and I will long regale each other with your dagger-sharp wit."

"Look," Goat interrupted, dodging another blow from the guard behind him. "Please, your graces, I'm telling you! We haven't got *time*! Listen to those war drums coming in the distance if you won't listen to me. It's a *distraction!* Right this instant, there are hordes of Monkey Tribe warriors crawling through the caves under our feet! We're already under attack! We've got to—"

Perrick shouted, others shouted him down. Goat was too hoarse to be noticed in the din. Why wouldn't they *listen?* His knuckles whitened on the armrests as he struggled to break free. It was only when the dragon trumpet blared from the highest tower that the racket died to appalled silence.

Ever since news of the invasion had reached from one end of the valley to the other, one citizen from every household had been compelled to attend defence training. Only the archbishop failed to recognise the savage tune.

"That's an attack on the west gate!" exclaimed Perrick into the silence. "See?" He whirled to point dramatically at the prisoners. "Told you they were lying!"

But nobody was paying him any attention. Every eye watched as the prelate military jumped to his feet and hastily bowed. "Your Grace, by your leave," he said, but he was running as he said it. Towards the west gate, Goat noticed with a groan.

"That's not the main assault!" Goat croaked.

Yet, in the distance, rose the clamour of axes on shields and a battle-song that screamed death.

Several of the prelates were upright now, also begging their grace's pardon before they dashed out. "Novice master," the captive healer said to Goat in a not-quite-whisper. "Infirmerer. Quartermaster. And that fat one scuttling out, that's the chancellor. Bet he's off to bury half the treasury for himself!" she shouted after the fleeing figure. A guard cuffed her on the mouth. Spitting blood, the healer laughed. "What? No takers?"

The archbishop snapped his fingers. A maroon-clad mage stood up on the back row and edged along the seats. His gangling progress downwards made him look like some exotic cranefly.

"The mages at the back," the healer said out of the side of her mouth, "they're the powerful ones." Goat looked a question at her. "The ones who keep an eye on the lower ranks," she went on. "And that one taking his time coming down the steps so he can give us a good mind-probe, he's our tutor, Doctor Brainspoon."

"Really?" squeaked Goat, then cleared his throat in an ostentatiously deep way.

"No, that's just what we in the aspirant class call him behind his back. A long way behind his back, actually, because he can read minds. Well, tell truth from lies, anyhow."

Suddenly, the man called Brainspoon was right in front of her. "Indeed, healer trainee." He smiled, a rictus rather than an expression of feeling. She instinctively pulled back until her head was up against the carven wood behind her. "I can do more than tell truth from lies." She turned away, bravado overwhelmed by contact with the invisible barrier that slimed over her. Yet when she looked down, her glorious robes were unsullied. She, however, was limp as riverweed.

Goat saw how drained she was, and fear rode him, but in desperation, he raised pleading eyes to the truthteller's. "War's come to my home and yours, milord." He jerked his head at the high windows. "Can't you hear it? But if you go believing the main force is outside the west gate, you're a fool."

"A fool, eh?" Brainspoon's cold, skeletal fingertips skittered over Goat's forehead, turning him until they were locked eye to eye. Cold moisture that smelt of the grave coiled into Goat's nose, forced apart his lips, nipped at his eyes, and flowed horribly down his ears. Smothering his skin, probing and moving on, it seemed as though green tendrils were growing into the void between the worlds. Roots as fine as hairs grew to shatter the darkness until there was no part of him that Brainspoon didn't know.

The mind-reader concluded. "This is neither spying nor treason. It is simply a man with a timely warning." He jerked his head as though listening. Blenching, he said urgently, "Archbishop, since the healer reported his words, I've had students probing underground. Batzorig Chahotai, known as Goat, is telling the truth. There is indeed an army swarming the lower caverns. They'll be coming through our sewers. I had a message," he added.

The archbishop peered at him suspiciously. "I didn't see a messenger."

"You wouldn't, Your Grace," he said blandly. "The enemy's target access points are— Bring me a scribe." A youth bobbed up right under his nose. "Oh, you are one. Well get the lid off your inkpot, boy! Their target points are Saint Urtulin's Wash House, St Kalidor's Duckpond, and the Peak Forest Torrent. That's Torrent with two Rs. Well, go on, lad! Take it to the prelate military. You'll find him at the west gate."

The scribe scampered off, an inky cherub thrilled to be trusted with this vital mission.

"Whatever shall we do, Archbishop?" asked one of the remaining prelates.

"Stop panicking, man! We'll fight, of course!"

Above the rising hubbub, Doctor Brainspoon made a forceful announcement. Forceful but somehow intimate, as though he were whispering in each individual's ear. Breaking off the debate, they left purposely for their emergency duties. After all, they'd practised the drill until they could do it blindfold. Literally.

"Sir?" said Goat. "Doctor Brai— Doctor?"

"Two things, if I read your perturbation correctly."

"Yes, Doctor." Goat got the *read* part. What the perurberters were was anybody's guess.

"Earth wins."

Brainspoon raised a quizzical eyebrow.

"You know, Earth wins." Goat thrust his pagan war god's axe out. "See those four points? Oh, I haven't got *time* to explain. Just read my head again. Let me show you what you're looking at."

Once again, those chilly fingertips seemed to claw into his skull. For his part, Doctor Brainspoon felt as though he'd plunged into a whirlpool of rage and pain and fevered nostalgia. He merged with Goat, assaulted in each heartbeat by the memories of Batzorig Chahotai. His family. His happiness. His pride when he passed the Twelve Winters trials with little more than a frostbitten toe.

Unlike his cousin, whose mount threw him not a hundred paces from the starting point, jostled by Batzorig's pony, which skidded on a patch of ice. Cousin Dorbei never forgot the way Batzorig had run rings around him. And later, on a *friendly* hunting trip out on the steppes, Dorbei rode rings over Batzorig, cracking his skull and trampling his body into the sun-hardened ground. Forever after, e sworeBatzorig would be Goat the cripple. Goat the madman who raved at the moon. Goat the shunned. Except in the bed he shared with Jash, where he was Beloved.

But best was the plan Brainspoon found in the thoughts of Goat, the points of whose talisman summed up the arts of war: deception, dissension, destruction, and the deadly use of the elements.

THE HEALER—HER name turned out to be Astiviar—and Goat were freed but confined to the infirmary. Astiviar sutured and Goat carted away amputated limbs. Jash joined a reluctant Perrick and a cohort of Defenders in the caverns. They poured flaming oil upon the waters and terrible shrieks rose from the tribesmen in the sewers below. Then they tipped down an extinguishing mix of dung and urine from the tanners' vats to more screams. The last of the aggressors underground were hunted through the caverns.

The prelate military got a gong for his valiant defeat of a much smaller force.

The chancellor was imprisoned for theft, but he died before he could reveal where he'd hidden his plunder.

The arrows, axes, spears, catapult balls, and other materiel, as well as the need to rebuild the west gate and parts of the sewage system before cholera wiped out the survivors, put the exchequer into debt.

Taxes were raised, and the price of food rocketed.

Perrick was flogged in front of the congregation. He may not have liked the stables, but he *really* didn't take well to clearing half-burned corpses from the sewers.

Astiviar was made full healer, her tutor, Doctor Brainspoon, having declared her heroic labours over battle-torn soldiers as thorough a practical exam as they come. His name, actually, was Lervin. But that's another story, because even after war, life goes on.

Goat earned full citizenship that day. He even got it. Lots of citizens crowded round to congratulate him. Others wouldn't touch him with a yardstick.

But in the snug hayloft above the Temple's horses, Jash lay in the arms of his Beloved, Batzorig Chahotai, and they were content.

THE FEATHER AND THE PAW

BENEDICT PATRICK

An extract from the teachings of the High Corvae

THIS STORY TAKES place in the early days of the world, when the creatures of the forest had not yet lost the ability to speak, when dog and deer and man would tread alongside each other through the woodland, conversing happily about their hopes and misfortunes.

The Leone, the Lionfolk, had long been aware of the great forest that loomed beyond their southern border but had paid it little attention, instead choosing to battle with the Mice and the Owls for spoils and plunder, and taking up arms against the Serpents for their own survival. However, one day, word reached the Lionfolk that the forest had a people living in it. Word also reached the ears of the Lionfolk that these people had a ruler, a king, and that the people of the forest were prospering.

This forest had lain to the south of Lionfolk land for centuries, and they had paid it little heed, right up until the moment they learnt it belonged to someone else. Then, inevitably, the king of the Leone ordered his armies to rank up and march upon the forest's border. After all, if the forest held value for others, then there must be something inside it worthy of the Leone's attention as well.

Many in the Lionfolk armies were uneasy at the idea of approaching the dark forest. As children, the Leone had been brought up on stories of unnatural beasts that lived in the woods, tales of wolfmen and giant spiders that would carry away Lionfolk young if they misbehaved. Even among the adults, it had long been rumoured the woods were haunted. Settlements on the edge of the forest wisely chose to keep their farmland well away from the long shadows that the trees cast when the sun dipped in the sky. Children would go exploring, never to return. There was rumour also that the king of the forest was not human, that the people who lived under those dark boughs were in the thrall of a monster, a creature known as the Magpie King.

When word of these fears reached the ears of King Reoric of the Leone, he laughed, and then had a dozen of his soldiers flogged and humiliated for allowing bedtime stories to make them quake like children. He rode before his army, blond hair and bushy beard billowing in the wind, the rising sun reflecting off his golden breastplate, and his men felt inspired, ready to face whatever horrors the forest held in store for them.

This resolve lasted only until they came within sight of the forest itself, and within sight of the thing that was waiting for them.

There, perched on one of the treetops at the forest edge, black feathered cloak draped over his shoulders, the beak of his dark metal helm protruding forward like an accusing finger, waited the Magpie King.

The men of the Lionfolk army were uneasy at the idea of advancing further and, eventually, King Reoric travelled to the front line to investigate. The handsome ruler of the Lionfolk strode forward to confront the spectre that haunted his men.

"This place is not for you," the Magpie King said, haltingly, unfamiliar with the Lionfolk tongue. "This land, the forest, is not meant for you. Turn back."

Knowing he could not show weakness before his men, Reoric stood tall before this uncanny creature. He put his hands on his hips, threw his head back, and laughed.

"Be gone from here, monster," he told the Magpie King. "What once was yours now belongs to me. There is no army standing behind you, but you can clearly see the forces I have brought with me. Step aside and let me take what is rightfully mine."

The king of the Lionfolk raised his eyes to see the dark figure's response, but the Magpie King had already disappeared, slinking back into the trees of his home.

Confident his foe had retreated, Reoric made his way back to his command tent and gave the order to infiltrate the forest.

But the Magpie King had not given up. Instead, he had moved back to the safety of the woods, ready to put his plan into action.

The route into the forest had been clear, and the Lionfolk scouts had already determined a path for the army to take through the woods. However, when the soldiers approached the border of the forest, new trees stood where only a few hours ago there had been none.

This was the early days of the forest, during the reign of the first Magpie King, when the people of the forest still had the ability to command the trees. In order to impede the progress of his enemy, the Magpie King had ordered a host of old, vicious trees from the forest's heart to march to the border and to confuse the invaders. When the Lionfolk attempted to cross the forest border, they became lost in a maze of wood, and grew deathly afraid. The legends their parents had told them of that dark forest were coming true.

Not wishing to return to their commander in failure, the soldiers spent their day trying to push through the wooden maze but, eventually, as night began to fall, they made their way back to the king with their heads hanging low. When King Reoric heard what had happened, without speaking he grabbed a burning branch from the fire and carried it over to the forest border. He spent the night walking along the new border, touching the branch to the dry leaves of the new trees, the amber light quickly consuming all it found, sending a beacon into the darkness, a warning to the people of the forest for trying to oppose him.

By morning, the trees had retreated, leaving the Magpie King's forest open to attack once more. King Reoric again approached the forest to survey the border, and again the Magpie King was waiting for him, out of reach on the uppermost branches, watching and tired. Ordering the trees to keep the Lionfolk at bay had greatly drained the Magpie King's magic and left him fatigued. However, despite his exhaustion, the Magpie King raised his helm when Reoric approached and yet again addressed the invaders.

"The forest is not meant for you," the Magpie King said. "Order your forces to move back, and no further harm will befall you."

Yet again, King Reoric put his hands on his hips in a show of superiority, all for the sake of his men, and laughed at the Magpie King's orders.

"No more will be harmed? I see scratches on none of my men, but your forest has burned through the night. More than anyone here, you yourself seem to be the most affected by yesterday's events. This forest is meant for me and my people, and we will take it from you."

Reoric raised his head to see the Magpie King's reaction, but yet again the Magpie King had disappeared. Once more, King Reoric ordered his men to infiltrate the forest, the border of which was no longer protected by the moving trees. The men marched forward, determined to prove themselves after their failure the previous day.

However, this was in the early days of the world, when the animals of the forest still listened to and obeyed the Magpie King, and spoke to him often about their own worries and desires. As the Lionfolk soldiers penetrated the low branches of the woods, they found themselves under attack. Herds of deer burst from the undergrowth, heads lowered, antlers pointing at the weak spots in the soldiers' armour. Squirrels leapt from the tree tops to bite at the men and to scare their horses. A few unlucky Lionfolk even found themselves attacked by wolves yet, oddly, no casualties were suffered by any of the men as they ran from the animals, the wolves' jaws snapping at their heels. What did result from this assault, however, was a complete rout of King Reoric's forces. Untrained and uncertain how to act in such circumstances, for the second time, the men broke and ran back to their leader.

King Reoric was not impressed.

"Squirrels? The cream of my forces have been scared away by rabbits and squirrels?"

He immediately ordered for the demotion and humiliation of his highest-ranking officers, then took to the battlefield himself. He ordered his stable boys to follow him, bringing with them his prize hunting dogs, reared for generations in the royal kennels. These vicious beasts, already starved so King Reoric could use them for sport in his conquered woodland, pulled on their leads, barking viciously. When they were finally released, they ran into the wilderness, bloodthirsty howls signalling their location long after they disappeared into the forest's depths. They returned, eventually, gums bloody and stomachs full. Satisfied with his work, King Reoric returned to his tent, determined that tomorrow morning would be the morning he would claim what he came here for.

When the sun rose, for the third time, the Lionfolk troops approached the forest border. For the third time, the Magpie King awaited King Reoric's arrival, and the dark figure seemed even more fatigued and weary than the previous day, so drained he was by the use of his magic to speak to and command the beasts. He hardly had the energy to lift his head when King Reoric addressed him once again.

"The forest is not for you," the Magpie King said weakly, his voice just loud enough to be heard over the din of the assembled forces. "Turn back now, or I take no responsibility for what happens to you within my domain."

King Reoric again laughed in the Magpie King's face, but this time, his laugh held true mirth. The Lion could see that the woodland ruler had run out of tricks and would no longer be able to stand in his way. "No, it is you who have been bested, Magpie King. Today, the Lionfolk take what we came for. This forest, Magpie King, is not for you, not anymore."

The Magpie King, too weak to respond, crawled back into the trees.

King Reoric ordered his men forward, to enter the forest once more.

The Magpie King's forest was a wide expanse, and would take a marching army many days to cross it. The Lionfolk began the first day of travel nervously, worried that the Magpie King and his people would be waiting in ambush for them as they travelled deeper into those dark trees. However, as the day progressed and they met with no further opposition, the Lionfolk believed, just as King Reoric had said, that the Magpie King had exhausted himself, and that he had no further ways to stop them from entering his home.

This, in fact, was true. However, it was not the Magpie King the soldiers should have been wary of.

It began not long after nightfall. Men turned to talk to their companions, only to find them no longer there, presumably having wandered off close by in the woods. Those companions never returned. Squads of soldiers making camp became unnerved by what sounded like distant screams, only to be assured by their commanders that the owls of the woods were known to make unusual noises.

Not long after that, the monsters appeared.

For all of their lives, the Lionfolk had been raised on stories of the creatures that haunted the dark corners of the woods that lay to the south of the Lionfolk kingdom. Things that, for most people, live only in stories. However, for the people of the Magpie King's forest, the creatures from the stories were all too real. These things were the reason the Magpie King's people locked themselves in their cellars at night, spending the darkness quaking in fear at the beasts that stalked the forest, looking to take them from their beds.

The Magpie King's people had nothing to fear that night. There was new prey in the forest for the monsters to hunt.

Mother Web and her eight-legged children scuttled from their hidden lairs, pulling bodies back into them by the dozen, stringing helpless Lionfolk up in their larders, a feast that would last them for weeks. Giant, hairless beavers the size of horses ploughed through the undergrowth, their fangs capable of ripping through armour just as easily as they gnawed through wood. Winged creatures with exposed skulls for heads soared above the canopy, swooping down upon any lone men who thought they had managed to evade the rest of the unnatural attackers. These men were carried off through the sky, screaming, never to return.

Weary, brokenhearted, the Magpie King could do nothing but sit in his cliff top home and listen to the cries of the dying as King Reoric and his army were beset on all fronts by unnatural beings. The Magpie King had done what he could to protect the Lionfolk from the dangers that he and his people faced every night, but they had not heeded his warnings.

That night, the Magpie King wept.

In the morning, he returned to the forest's edge. The remnants of the Lionfolk forces had fled through the night to return to this place, and a few scattered fires showed where survivors had collapsed, exhausted, back to safety. The Magpie King perched on the same branch he had challenged King Reoric from the previous three days, and caught glance of an unusual sight. Just out of reach of the shadows of the trees of his own forest, an ornate banquet table had been laid. There was fine cutlery and tableware, jewel-encrusted canteens holding hot soups, a glazed hog decorating the centre, a pinecone shoved between its open jaws. Only one person sat at the table, already tucking into the kingly breakfast. On sight of the Magpie King, Reoric stopped eating, then stood to regard his counterpart. It was Reoric's turn to look weary, the left side of his face clawed and bloodied, but he gestured for the Magpie King to come down and join him, indicating a seat at the opposite end of the table, in a position of equal importance. Cautiously, aware that no other Lionfolk were nearby, the Magpie King descended from his perch. Standing beside the empty seat, the Magpie King stared at King Reoric, the curve of his dark helm directed like a dagger towards the man.

"This forest," King Reoric said, indicating the Magpie King's realm, a look of acceptance and sadness on his face, "this forest is not for me."

The Magpie King said nothing but sighed deeply.

King Reoric laughed, but this was not a deep belly laugh served to ridicule the Magpie King in front of an army of men. This was a true, tired laugh. This was the sound of a king finally realising his own folly.

King Reoric glanced at the Magpie King again. "We have begun things poorly," the Lion said. "Allow me to start over." Reoric indicated the seat beside the Magpie King, then spread his hand to the banquet table laid before them.

"Please, come join me for breakfast."

And that was the beginning of the great friendship between the Corvae and the Leone, the Magpiefolk and the Lionfolk, which has seen both peoples through many hardships and has endured up to this very day.

UNTIL THE LIGHT HAD FADED

GRAHAM AUSTIN-KING

"DOWN!" REANNE'S HAND flashed out, gripping at Ferrin's wrist hard enough to bring a hissed curse from his lips as she dragged him down beside the tree. Her eyes were enough to silence him, the anger at his whisper almost lost in her fear.

He edged closer, moving in time with the wind as it rustled the leafy canopy above to bury the sound of his passage. Reanne was carved stone, eyes locked on some distant spot between the trees. He twisted to follow her gaze, moving slowly enough that no eyes would be drawn to him. The light was already fading from the hour's sun, and the twilight gloom was a mess of twisting shadows. He watched in silence. The strain of this run was showing on both of them, but Reanne wasn't one to jump at shadows. One hand drifted to the ruins of his ear, fingertips toying with the scarred flesh until he caught himself and pulled away with a flush.

Reanne crouched in silence, one hand gripping at the glyphmarked rod at her belt as the other twirled the leather covering through her fingers. It wouldn't hold much. The power tended to ebb away, and it had been weeks since they'd been in a position to infuse it.

Ferrin fought down a sigh. There was nothing that he could see in the mess of trees and shadows but then, her eyes were better than his anyway. His hand relaxed on the hilt of the blackblade as he forced himself to calm. Tense muscles moved slower and speed was everything with one of the fae.

Reanne hissed out a long sigh and shook her head, close-cropped red hair looking almost black in the shadow. "I'm sorry, Ferrin. I thought I saw eyes."

He brushed the apology away. "Don't worry at it. Better to be jumpy than to have one of the bastards jump us."

She met his gaze for a moment, a wealth of pain and horror conveyed in a glance. They had both seen too much death and blood in the past few weeks.

"We should keep moving." Her voice was a mutter, robbed of any force or authority.

He grunted and followed as she rose and led off. They travelled with a distance between them, one crouching down and scanning the forest ahead before waving the other forward, leap-frogging their position until they began again. It probably made little or no difference. Any fae creature would spot them in moments, but it made him feel better.

Dense trees gave way to ferns, opening into an airy wood. It made for easier travel, but Ferrin could see Reanne's eyes darting about as she took in the trees. There would be little place to hide if they were to encounter fae or satyr. Fae'reeth were another matter, of course. There was no hiding from the tiny winged creatures.

Reanne pulled him from his thoughts, dropping down beside him into the cluster of ferns. "We should be able to see the towers by now."

Her voice was gruff, almost a growl, but it was nothing to the strain on her face. The young woman had been almost beautiful when they'd first met. Now it was portrait of pain and loss, painted in hard lines that made her look almost feral in the low light.

He glanced into the distance and grunted. "Hard to say, Reanne. Could be another couple of miles."

Her expression told him she hadn't believed him. He hadn't believed himself. She was right, they should be able to see them both by now.

The trees thinned as they walked until he couldn't lie to himself any longer. They were coming out onto the plains. Ahead of him, Reanne stopped, leaning against a tree with a gasp as she stared in horror.

The first step was hard, muscles battling against a knowledge he didn't want to have. The second was no better.

The plains stretched for miles, an island carved into this endless ocean of trees. It had taken centuries to create, with entire generations spent cutting and clearing. It had been the slaves at first. Then later, the freed humans when the accord had first been reached with the fae. The towers were easy to see, even in the twilight. They lay, twisted and shattered, strewn over half a mile.

"Lost gods, how?" Ferrin muttered. "They were at least two days behind us."

Reanne reached for him, her hard shell melting away for the moment at his shock. "I don't know. There are rumours, things I've heard over cheap wine and ale." She shook her head. "The towers are gone. Does it matter how the fae got here?"

He pushed past her, moving in a slow walk that soon became a jog, and then a dead run.

The towers were polished marble, capable of being seen in the daylight for miles, and still further when the moon touched them and the capture-plates fired. Now, the marble lay dead and cold in the growing darkness. The moon wouldn't rise for a few hours yet, but when it did, the towers would remain as cold as they were now. Their destruction was more than just a strategic blow, Ferrin knew. It struck to the very heart of this war. The towers and their capture-plates were the closest source of power this side of Tir Riviel. Without the capture-plates and the power they gathered from the moonlight, any glyphs would soon grow dark and useless.

Ferrin grimaced as he drew closer. The base of the tower was wrapped tight in thick ropes of ivy and vines. Black scorch-marks stood as mute testimony to the occupant's struggle. No fae would ever use fire. He came across the first body moments later, a woman ripped and torn. The death lacked any of the elegance a true fae might have brought to the battle. This was a satyr's work. Ferrin pulled his hand away from his ear with a curse.

As if the first discovery had somehow opened his eyes to the dead, Ferrin suddenly saw the field of rubble for what it was. Scores of bodies littered the earth, lying broken amongst the rubble. There were no fae bodies of course, no bloodied satyr corpses or fallen fae'reeth. His own blackblade was explanation enough for that. The war had grown vicious and desperate almost as soon as the fae had first attacked. No single human could hope to stand against a fae without using iron. Fehru, they called it. Impossibly rare, it was the metal of the blood, the tool of the damned. Even touching the substance carried its own death sentence among the fae.

He glanced at the blade in his hand. He hadn't even been aware he'd drawn it, but now he was thankful for the weight in his hand. The desire to kill, to stab and slash, seeking blood and pain and screams, was almost strong enough to taste. He glared out at the remains of the towers and the bodies surrounding them, wishing for a naive moment that the fae would return and face him.

"The village," Reanne said, a touch of impatience in her voice the only sign she was repeating herself.

"What?" Ferrin shook his head with a frown.

"The village, you old fool," she snapped. "We should check for survivors."

He glanced at the base of the closest tower. She was right, there was little point in checking here. No human would have survived either the attack or the tower's fall.

The village was visible from the tower, though still an hour's walk away. The road was well-tended and well-travelled. The tower would have been easily supplied from the village, and Ferrin knew many would have preferred to go to the tower directly rather than rely on old conduits to infuse their glyphs.

Reanne muttered to herself as they walked, avoiding his gaze and clenching her fist around the glyph inscribed rod that hung from her belt, and her own, shorter, blackblade. The fields were as well-tended and maintained as the roads, but it was a silence that told the tale. The village was undamaged, stone and wooden structures standing the same as they had for generations. Yet a silence drifted through its street, roaming the village and out into the fields. No snatches of conversation carried on the breeze. No hint of a baby's cry or a child's laughter. The village was missing any sounds of life, and the absence screamed out death's call. The village was a tomb, the empty houses headstones for the bodies that were just now coming into view.

The wind-tossed leaves rustled as Reanne knelt over the first victim. The skin was shredded, covered in hundreds of tiny cuts that had left the woman a tattered ruin. Ferrin grimaced at the sight and looked away quickly, standing over the body as his gaze scanned the field and outskirts of the village. The rustle came again as Reanne rose to her feet, dry leaves scraping against stone.

"Shit," he muttered as he took in the green and lush fields. The rustling came again, longer and harsher, becoming an endless drone. The sound of a multitude of pairs of wings pulling tiny bodies skyward.

"Trap-stones!" Reanne's voice was filled with an urgency as the battle-lust took her. He'd seen it before, men and women no longer even caring about the war or somehow finding peace, they lived only for revenge and for pain. He didn't have time to think on it.

The trap-stones were small, not much bigger than a thumbnail, and scattered easily. He kicked at the few that had landed too close together and fell back into a fighting crouch, waiting with blackblade in hand, for all the good it would do. Reanne stood beside him, pressed close within the centre of the web he'd create.

The drone grew louder, and the first of the fae'reeth became visible, spinning in a lazy dance as their swarm gathered.

"Come on!" Reanne screamed out at them, lips pulled back in a feral snarl as she braced herself.

The tiny figures ignored her spinning in their aerial dance that drifted towards them, unhurried. As if released by some silent signal, the cloud of fae'reeth split, tearing through the air with a chorus of tiny screams. Ferrin waited, teeth clenched as they drew closer. The keystone lay close to his foot, it needed only his touch.

Reanne glanced at him as the first of the fae'reeth passed over the stones. "Ferrin," she hissed.

He ignored her, watching the swarm draw closer, they would only get one chance at this. He felt the tug as a fae'reeth's tiny blade caught at his leathers, the blade too small to penetrate. Reanne cursed as a slash drew a red line across her cheek. "Now, Ferrin!"

Ferrin dropped, falling to one knee, and activated the keystone. Faint lines of blue light spread out between the stones, creating a web. Wherever the stones formed a triangle, howling winds rose from nowhere, tearing into the fae'reeth and throwing them backward. The tiny figures were tossed from triangle to triangle, hurled in twenty different directions as they passed around the network of the trap-stones, and the wind ripped at them.

Reanne howled, the scream an almost orgasmic release of triumph as she thrust the glyphrod forward, fingers tracing over the inscriptions. The blast of fire tore into the fae'reeth, moving almost like a hunting beast as it surged after them. The winds took it, and the cyclone became an inferno. Fire ripped through the tiny creatures like a spark in dried hay, touching their delicate wings and eating hungrily. Screams of anger turned first to pain, and then to panic as the winds carried smoking bodies through the flames spurting from the glyphrod, time and again, until bodies fell to the earth, blackened and charred.

Blue sparks flew as Ferrin caught a fae'reeth with his blackblade, the iron streaks running through the weapon exploding the creature into nothingness.

And then there was silence. The winds fell, and Reanne's flames guttered and died. They stood at the centre of a circle of destruction, the charred grass littered with tiny bodies. The carnage sickened him. The fae'reeth, their wings gone, looked like bodies of tiny children, scattered across the scorched dirt by some uncaring hand.

Grabbed at him, her face exultant. "Beautiful! Look at the little bastards. Look, Ferrin!"

He grimaced. "I am looking." His words might as well have been whispered. She was beyond hearing him. He tried again. "We need to get out of here, that wasn't exactly quiet."

"Let them come," Reanne said with a smug smile.

"Let them come and then what?" Ferrin snapped. "And then we have satyr and fae to cope with, or even more fae'reeth." He stabbed one finger at the charred earth. "Those stones are done, and I'm betting your glyphrod would struggle to light a campfire. We need to get out of here, now. This isn't about us, Reanne. Damn it, we don't have the right to choose our own end. Not anymore. Not with what we've seen."

He'd gone too far, he realised that as her lips grew pinched, and she turned away quickly. "I know my duty, old man."

He sighed and watched her stalk away until it became obvious she wasn't going to stop. A moment later, he followed. Lost Gods, he was tired. It was more than just the ache of strained muscles and a body abused.

They'd been running for four days now, but the pair of them had been scouting for weeks. Passing through the endless forests of the Realm of Twilight in search of the armies everyone knew would be coming.

Weeks of passing through woodlands in silence, working to mask any sound of their passage with the noise of the wind in the trees, or the rustle of an animal's passing. Weeks of not daring to speak any louder than the faintest whisper, with lips pressed to ear. And then they had found them. The army of the fae was an unnatural thing. The fae were unlike humanity in so many ways. Despite the social structure of the fae courts, and the rule of the Ivy Throne, the notion of fae grouping into an army was outlandish. It was unthinkable. And yet they had. The armies of the fae had struck like lightning from a blue sky. Villages and farms had been reduced to rubble as the blood flowed. Village after village had fallen as mankind fled before them, rushing to the perceived safety of the cities, and then there had been silence. The cities waited, listening to the tales of terrified villagers as messengers rushed back and forth between them, trading messages but little news. Until, one by one, the messengers stopped returning and the cities fell silent.

"We need to head further north," he called, breaking a silence that had been uncomfortable so long he'd almost grown to like it. We're south of the bridge.

Reanne glanced back at him and nodded, her gaze passing him to scan the distant tree-line behind them before looking back to him. He knew what the grimace meant. The woods had been filled with bird song, but the plains were quiet in comparison. With only the faintest of breezes tossing the long grasses, there was nothing to fall silent when the fae drew close. There would be no warning. He matched her glance back behind them, hawked and spat. "Let's go a bit faster. It's not like we can hide out here. We might as well run for a bit."

She nodded with a shrug and led off. Within five minutes, his legs were cursing his name, and his throat burned as he struggled to match her pace. The woman was easily half his age. Why had he ever thought they could be a good match?

The plains stretched on, long grasses split by the occasional copse of trees or low scrubby bushes as they cut across to the northern edge. The trees would swallow them again all too soon, and Ferrin looked to the twilight skies as they ran. True night would come soon enough, and their pace would slow to a crawl for the short time it lasted. Would it slow the fae? Individuals, he supposed. The army, though, they would not stop. The image of the thousands of fae, all clad in glamours of shining steel and marching in perfect time, haunted him. It was all illusion. Beyond the glamour and reaching to the discipline. When the armies of the fae reached Tir Riviel, they would descend upon it, screaming for blood until the last of humanity lay trapped in the breeding pens or bleeding in the broken streets. Mankind was doomed. The war had been lost the moment it began.

Their path cut across the corner of the plains until the trees took them again. The gloom between the ancient boles brought a sigh from both of them. The woods would slow them, but not even a fae could see through the forest.

"Reanne, stop a minute." Ferrin leaned hard against the tree, the bark rough against his skin. "Just give me a minute to catch my breath."

She smirked at him. "You were the one who wanted to run," she reminded him.

"I was a bloody idiot," he managed between breaths. "It's not like running is going to make a difference anyway."

Reanne stiffened. It was a small thing, just a tightening of the eyes and a pinch at the corners of her lips, but he knew her well enough to know what it meant. She was a believer. Lost Gods, after all this time, she still believed they could win.

"You don't know that," she said, the words clipped and rigid.

Ferrin blinked. "I don't know that? Are you insane, Reanne? Of course,

I know that. We're outmatched. They are fae. Even the weakest could empty a village on its own."

"Until we found the fehru," she said, drawing her blackblade.

Ferrin sighed. "And how much of that do we have? How many blades, Reanne? Twenty? A hundred?" He reached for her arm, freezing before he touched her as she glared at him. "We are not going to win this war, Reanne. We're going to flee."

She frowned, anger forgotten for the moment. "Flee? To where? There's nowhere in the Realm of Twilight anyone could ever hide from a fae."

Ferrin grimaced and shook his head. "It doesn't matter. I shouldn't have said anything. The point is that we're fighting and dying. We've lost too many already. This war needs to end while mankind still exists."

"That's never going to happen, Ferrin," she told him quietly. "The fae would never kill us all. We're too valuable for that. They need their breeding stock."

"The pens," he said, his voice soft but thick with disgust.

"The pens," she agreed, and the argument fell from him. He was old and tired, but she was broken. She had pushed her splintered fragments back into the shape of a person, but she would never be whole again.

She turned away from his expression and shook her head. "Come on, we need to be moving."

They abandoned stealth for speed, crashing through the woods like spooked deer. The conversation had been brief, but it had brought reality home to both of them. There was little point in hiding now. They either outpaced the fae or Tir Riviel fell, and with it, the last place any man could call home.

The bridge loomed out of the darkness between the trees. Dark metal girders had been worked into the thick wood, which stretched over the ravine in a structure that was as much a barrier as it was a bridge. The fehru had been added to the bridge over the months, preventing any fae from touching it. It was no barrier to the fae'reeth of course, but then nothing was.

Their boots *thudded* over the planking until Reanne stopped in the centre of the bridge at the silvery capture-plate.

"Now?" Ferrin demanded. "We're only a few hours to the city."

"It only takes a few minutes, Ferrin," she told him, kneeling to set the glyphrod in place at the edge of the plate. "It's the last chance I'll get to infuse it. We might still need it."

He scowled at that, knowing it made sense but not liking it any better. The glyphs shone as she traced her fingers over the capture-plate, siphoning off the energy it had stored from the moonlight and sending it coursing into the glyphrod.

The arrow was white, pale as sun-bleached bone, as it erupted from his thigh without slowing and buried itself in the bridge.

"Ferrin!" Reanne screamed, pulling the glyphrod free and rushing to him as he collapsed. Blood gushed from the wound despite his hands.

"Go, Reanne," he managed from between clenched teeth. "Just run."

She busied herself with the tourniquet, running the line around his thigh and working it tight until he gasped.

"Go!" he hissed again. The fae didn't miss, they both knew that. The knowledge was clear in both of their eyes as he looked at her. The arrow had taken his leg because the creature was playing with him. It had chosen to wound rather than kill because his pain would entertain. Another arrow could come at any second, and it would not miss."

"We can make it, Ferrin," she whispered, an urgent lie that convinced neither of them. "Just let me help you up. We'll get you to the city and you'll be fine."

"No." He shook his head.

"Damn it, old man!" she hissed, tears filling her eyes and speech. "I'm not leaving you here."

"Go," he said again, a low plea that cut through her tears. "They need to know. You need to warn them. There's a worldgate, Reanne. That's how we're going to flee. It wasn't ready when we left. They were going to use it to take us all to our homeland, wherever that is. There's no time now. We use it now or we perish. Get to Tir Riviel and tell them. Just go!"

She stared at him, eyes doubting for a moment as she rose to a half-crouch. "Take the rod," she said, pressing it into hands still wet with his own blood. "I can come back with help."

He nodded, knowing the words for what they were. "I'll hold, Reanne. I can do this. Just get to the city."

She glanced at the tree-line for a moment, and then ran. She could almost feel the arrow that would slam through her chest, but it never came. She was alive because the fae willed it, she knew. She thundered across the bridge and ducked down behind the support beam for a second before risking a glance back.

Ferrin lay where she'd left him, pushing himself up against a thick bar of iron as he readied the glyphrod. The fae stepped unhurried from the trees, long whitebow held lightly in his hands. She had no time to study the creature before others began to emerge, already sporting glamours of gleaming silver. It was the banner that made her run, the blue and silver banner of the armies of the fae, glowing bright as they carried it forth.

Fire blasted behind her, the light bright enough to carrying through the trees as she ran. She glanced back twice, screams filling her ears from fae and Ferrin both until she forced herself to stop. She would watch. She owed him this much. She would watch the flare of the fire until they took him, until the light had faded.

UNDER THE QUEEN'S THRONE

ED GREENWOOD

IT WAS NOT going well.

But then, in Forn's life, nothing much ever went well.

Never had. It was all the fault of the gods.

IT WAS THE gods who'd so regrettably taken King Savagrath, the widely-feared "Lion of Swords." Very suddenly, of heartstop, on his throne while feasting. Leaving no one to rule the fair realm of Syndaelia but his slip of a daughter, the Princess Aumalle, who'd known but fourteen summers.

And it was the gods who'd made King Tarathur of neighboring Amarrandaer a mad brawling bastard who lusted after the rule of the entire world, and so had a large army ready. Promptly on hearing of Savagrath's demise, the Amarrandans had invaded Syndaelia like a gleaming black tide—like every other soldier of Amarrandaer, Forn was daily kept busy repainting and polishing his rusty, mismatched armor to keep it the gleaming epitome of gleaming, glossy black—and conquered most of the kingdom. The princess, now Syndaelia's first ruling queen (and according to the priests, the gods were frowning hard at *that*), had proved of much sterner stuff than expected, riding to battle and fighting well, but the Syndaer were no match for the might and valor and ten-to-one superior strength of the Glorious Wolves of Amarrandaer, and had suffered bitter defeat after bitter defeat.

Until five months ago, when the Syndaer army had been driven into their last lair, and the army of Amarrandaer had begun its siege on that den. Raging against the soaring, ancient walls of fortified Syndrist, capitol of Syndaelia and seat of its kings (and, aye, its first ruling queen, now). If Syndrist hadn't been built atop a mountain, it'd have fallen long since, but the gods enjoyed their jests. The walls of the beleaguered Syndaelian city were old and thick and a-crawl with ancient spells no living wizard could now match. There'd be no getting through them soon.

Nor was even an army as vast and fierce and gleaming-armored as the Glorious Wolves of Amarrandaer likely to withstand a typically fierce Syndaelian winter, so there was no time to starve out the defenders, who, after all, had a spring-fed lake and extensive food cellars and a working farm, all within those mighty walls. So curt, simple, and identical orders had come down to even the lowliest Wolves.

"Start digging."

Which really meant mining solid rock, in small crews like the one Forn was part of: an officer—that was Marace, a lifelong sword in the army; an outlander mercenary—that was Yulusk, a brawny dark mountain of a man of few words who yet managed to be outspoken; and an everyday smartmouthed dog of an Amarrandan Wolf—and that was Forn.

Crew Carnelian been tunneling for almost five months now, and word had been passed down that the Syndaer had been detected tunneling to intercept them, so Forn and his fellow Wolves were forced to work in full armor, with weapons kept ready.

"Amazing how all our wizards don't have even one spell between them to break rock or move a single stone." Forn growled. Not for the first time.

"Fall silent," Marace told him. "Someone comes."

A light bobbed closer, far down the none-too-straight tunnel they'd carved out. Crew Carnelian took the opportunity to down picks and shovels, snatch up their swords and maces, and challenge the lone man approaching with a round lantern.

They knew who it was, of course. A superior officer they all detested, the swordlord Arangor.

As Marace had once put it, "There's one or two swordlords worth their badge. And then there's all the rest."

Arangor worked diligently at being all the rest, all day and every day.

"Crew Carnelian, attend!" he answered their challenge sternly. "I bring news!"

"War's over?" Yulusk rumbled hopefully.

Arangor ignored him. Arangor always ignored dusky outlanders. "Crew Garnet were friends of yours, aye?"

"Well, they owed us coin," Marace replied, "from our last night of throwing the crowns."

"Get used to not ever getting paid," Arangor told them, managing to sound gleeful and sinister at the same time. "Crew Garnet is no more. What's left of them has just been found in their tunnel. Gnawed to bare bloody bones."

"*Gnawed?* What was it, giant rats?"

"No. Usual-sized rats, but a salarking *army* of them. Enough to fill a tunnel with a squeaking, clawing rat wall, I'm told by our wizard who's best at the farseeing spell. So, keep your torches ready, lads, and be prepared to burn your way out!"

"That'll take all the air we need," Forn pointed out. "Can't we drown them instead?"

"Drown them? With *what?*"

"Wine. We'll need two casks. The big ones. If you rush them down here now—"

"You'll be blind drunk by evening bell," Arangor said coldly. "No wine."

"Sir," Marace firmly interrupted whatever Forn was trying to say next, "what makes rats band together in an army?"

"The spells of Syndaelia's evil wizards, of course. Somehow, those slumgullions have found or crafted magic that inflames the rats with bloodlust and a common purpose, and musters them together, and sends them a-slaying."

"Our wizards told you that, too?" Forn couldn't stop himself from asking.

"Stands to reason," Arangor replied icily. "*Our* wizards would never do such a thing."

"So, if we see this living wall of rats coming," Yulusk put in gloomily, from beneath his ever-present cloak of rock dust, "we're doomed, yes?"

"Pretty much," Arangor said briskly. "Right, men, warning delivered. I must hasten on. The other six crews aren't going to warn themselves, you know."

"No? You surprise me," Forn muttered, swinging his pick again at the rock face. Its backswing brought its sharp hind spike perilously close to the swordlord's nose.

Arangor swayed back with the swift ease of the longtime veteran, deftly kicking Forn's nearest ankle so the overbalanced soldier crashed heavily onto his back.

"Careful," the swordlord's voice came back to him coldly as Arangor marched away, back along the tunnel. "You could overbalance and fall, swinging wildly like that."

Forn wisely said nothing at all.

After a time, Marace muttered, "He's gone, lad. Pity you didn't swung a handspan wider."

"What?" Yulusk growled. "And leave Basilisk Cohort without its worst swordlord?"

Their shared chuckle was strained.

And seemed to end in a titter.

Crew Carnelian had time to frown, turn, and look before they realized the tittering wasn't coming from their throats, but from down the tunnel. And was swiftly building into a roar as it came closer. In a living, swarming wall.

"AUMERRA," RALANDRA SAID patiently, "I *am* digging, see? But I'm *not* going to stop complaining! We're all wizards, we could blast this rock to dust with one spell and float all the dust out of here with another and sit down to a two-day feast and *still* carve it out faster than we're doing with these old picks and prybars and shovels! Besides, what happens when we meet the Amarrandans? And they overwhelm us and invade our last refuge because *we* helpfully dug out their invasion route for them? Right here under the queen's very *throne!* This is stupid, I tell you! *Stupid!*"

"Ralla," the older mage said, not unkindly, "which of we three anointed wizards of Syndaelia is the oldest? And the highest ranking?"

"You, of course. I'm well aware of—"

"And *I'm* more than well aware of your arguments, having heard them so often these last few days. As it happens, I agree with them, but the queen's orders were very clear: dig to intercept the invaders and blast them when we see them."

Ralandra sighed. "May I point out that they have wizards, too? We may not be the ones doing the last and best blasting."

"I don't think they'll have to blast us," the third, youngest, and lowliest mage piped up. He was covered with sweat and rock-dust and had flung down his pick to wring his hands from the pain of all his breaking blisters. "Not when they can send their armies of rats to swarm us and bite us to bare bones!"

"*Doran!* We're not supposed to discuss that!" Aumerra snapped.

Doran rolled his eyes. "Or the rocks'll hear? Surely, they've already heard the screams of the wizards who got gnawed to death! And we don't even know what *spell* the Amarrandans are using to conjure the rats! Wouldn't it be more prudent—?"

"*I* believe it would be more prudent," Aumerra interrupted, in a voice that promised swift and cold doom was coming to argumentative young wizards of Syndaelia, and soon, "to *shut up* and swing your picks at yon rocks!"

"Ah, Merra," Ralandra replied in quite a different voice, plucking at Aumerra's sleeve, "I, ah, think it might be a little late for that." Letting her pick fall, she used her freed hand to point back down the tunnel they'd so laboriously hewn over these last however many days.

To where thousands of tiny eyes shined back the light of Aumerra's conjured magelight, and a tittering was rising. Higher it rose, eerily shrill and strong, as the rodents came charging, in a roiling, racing wall.

HISSEEL WAS THE size of a dozen young rats, and his snout was gray with age and white with small patches of mange he could never quite seem to get entirely rid of these days. They'd drag him down and eat him soon enough but, for now, they still obeyed and accorded him a bodyguard of ten veterans.

He looked down from his ledge at the bedraggled rats crawling and limping up to the outermost of his guards below, and then across the cleft to the other ledge where Ulmalask lay. The rival commander was as old and wizened as he, but only rated a bodyguard of eight, who warily stood ranks side by side with his own, in the cleft below.

"Halt!" came the barked challenge. "No closer!"

The foremost rat halted. "I come to report to Hisseel. Is he within hearing?"

"He is," the bodyguard made reply. "Speak."

"The siege is over. The Amarrandans are dying in droves from the plague we spread among them, and those who can still walk or ride are fleeing back home to their own land as fast as they can."

"So, we can eat all the Syndaelian humans now?" one of Ulmalask's guards asked hopefully.

"*What?*" Hisseel's head bodyguard roared into his face. "You idiot, that's our *winter food store* you want to devour! Foolbrains!"

"I'm not!" the other rat hissed. "The Old Wise Rat said the human spells made us *all* smarter! I'm no more a fool than you!" And he pounced, biting viciously.

In half a breath, the cleft was alive with snarling, shrieking, hissing rats and their bitten-out hair and their flying blood, too.

Hisseel looked over at Ulmalask. They regarded each other across the bloody mayhem and smiled.

"Back to normal. The human doom seems averted," Ulmalask observed calmly.

"So, we can get back to making war on each other," Hisseel agreed with a satisfaction he didn't bother to hide. "Ah, I *love* the smell of fresh blood."

GOOD STEEL

ZACHARY BARNES

MOST BIRTHS ARE bloody, but mine was not. That would come later.

I was born into fire and brightness, wrenched shrieking from the womb's warmth. Formless sleep to a splintered cradle. Then movement.

Taken up in grimy hands, inspected. Cold air stung my naked body for the first time.

Soon, I was in a metal bed suspended over the *crackle* of flames whose tongues licked my body. But that reprieve quickly burned away as that mounting heat swaddled me, melted through me.

I began to scream.

The heat withdrew.

Slowly—so slowly—that agony faded, replaced instead by a silence in which I existed listlessly, a place of waking dreams, of smoke and scrimshaw.

A hand descended. *Please*, I gasped. *No more.*

But I was lifted back to the torment of white-hot coals. I wailed and dreamt of the warm darkness of the womb, but the memory was already fading. Cold metal kissed my back now. Movement in the air above me.

The hammer's head cracked against my face, but the pain it brought was so sudden I could not even scream. Not at first.

It lifted. Fell. My body bent, buckled, deformed, leaving me gasping.

Returned to the coals. But now their heat was a numb, faraway throb that could not compare to the mutilation of the hammer. Back and forth, back and forth, until I was battered to unconsciousness. It was a welcome darkness.

I WOKE TO murmuring human voices. Something was quite wrong, and it wasn't just this raw new form. *Have I been impaled?*

Indeed, fibrous wood scratched at my insides, but before I could panic, its touch brought an alien consciousness abreast with my own.

I wasn't sure if you'd ever wake. It was the wood I heard, its every thought dripping with sap. *Or it you even survived...*

The voices above us paused, and we rose through the air.

Among the next string of words, one alone stood out. "Hoe."

We're named "Hoe?"

I suppose, the wooden haft thought. Its confusion matched my own.

But then, a new hand brushed against me, nail testing my sharpness. Calluses kneaded my body. I bristled at first, but then warmed to the grasp.

"It's good steel." Sturdy. Confident. "I'll take it."

It was a solid voice and stirred a wisp of emotion in my deep insides: happiness?

GOOD STEEL

THE SHED—OUR new home—smelt of sawdust and oil and musty earth. By my elbows I was hung, nestled against an ancient spade with gentle care.

Hello, the spade grunted once the door had slid shut.

Haft squeaked. Around us, scarred veterans lounged, peering at us from shelves and hooks. They were worn but clean, to a tool.

Don't mind them. This life'll become more familiar, the spade quietly promised. *Our work here is tough but fair. Even rewarding. And the farmer is a good man.*

I hoped he was right. For a time, at least, those words held true.

AT THE HEIGHT of summer, toiling beneath the sun's unbending beat, Haft and the farmer and I waged war, as we had the last three years. As I had come to expect, our enemy was strong, well-fortified, and vast in number, whereas we were but a single hoe in the hands of a single man. Yet each morning, our farmer bent to his task with something akin to relish affixed in his silent snarl. Swiftly, brutally, I rose and fell in his hands. *Crunch.* With expert ease, he turned my blade deeper into the sward. Cowering in a clod of dirt, the felled thistle surrendered, roots exposed, lacy petals all aflutter.

"Out you get, you shitter," the farmer grunted, grabbing the thorny carcass with one gloved hand and depositing it in the pail behind him. Victorious, he raised his eyes, wiped sweat from his grimy brow, and surveyed the length of his field. It was rife with the enemy, but he was as tireless as I was sharp.

We were taking our midday rest when the stranger came.

Haft grunted as the farmer's grip tightened.

"Hmm. Been a long time."

The stranger's breathing sounded in heavy response.

"Say what you came to say," our farmer said, brandishing us. The sweat of his palms tasted wrong.

"You know why I'm here."

"Aye." Our farmer was shaking now. "But I'm not fighting your non-sense war, not when I've got land to tend and a family to feed. That hasn't changed."

The stranger spat at the farmer's feet.

"That how it's going to be then?" Without waiting for a response, the farmer swung us hard, not with the solemn strength of the field, but something sharper, altogether deadlier. And, for the first time, I tasted the blood of a man.

A grunt.

I fell, bit into the dirt, and wished it could wash away this sticky, metallic mess. Haft cringed at the snarls and *thumps* above us before we were lifted into the air once more, but this time in new hands.

"Fucking coward," the stranger gasped.

Though I strained against the motion with every ounce of my being, my sharp edge, so meticulously honed, punched into the farmer's chest, through his ribs, and I felt his insides wash over me, arterial blood hot as it spurted into the air.

The stranger wrenched me free, left me to drip as he swayed and shivered and cursed.

He didn't clean us, was the only thought I could muster as the stranger bore us away. Away from the farmstead, away from those tough, yet caring hands, now cold with death.

By the time the stranger set us down, the farmer's blood had hardened to a crust along my edge and across my face. It itched, and to that itch, the nightmare of slopping guts held fast in my mind. As the days passed, the itch grew worse.

Other tools had whispered about this, but for so long, rust had only been a distant threat to me. Never had I known his gnawing rot, but I

met him then and realized with sinking finality that he was here to stay.
THE WAR CAME for us...or ~~we went~~ to it. Not some struggle against
the field's weeds, which we had played at before, but real war. Of men
cutting down men, of steel biting steel and sparking in anger and pain.
The stranger was no coward, as he would mutter to himself some nights.
I tasted blood again, the blood of a few men, and dulled myself against
armor—worse a feeling than skittering over any field-rock—but those
moments became a blur of hate and blood and violence.

It was not long before Haft broke. When the mace shattered him, he
wailed, louder a sound than he had ever made before, and then was silent.

That is when we fell, me and Haft's corpse. To the blood-drenched
dirt, buried edge-first. My rust-pocked face sank into the mire. A boot
crushed us, drove us deeper down. There, entombed in mud, the horror
above became a muted thing. My birth, the pain of exposure, of the forge,
rushed back, and then the glorious memory of soil's taste against my blade.
But the mud was bitter and cold.

I wish we could stay here, I muttered to Haft. *I wish we could die here.*
There was no reply.

Gradually, the angry footfalls passed, the gore dried under the sun's
kiss, and the carrion feeders gorged on flesh, leaving the bones to bleach
and sink into the mud as well. And the stranger did not return. Every
moment away from his darkening, hungering presence left an emptiness
in a part of me. He should have answered for what he did to the farmer.
For what he made me do. Instead, he was gone. Just gone.

MONTHS PASSED, PERHAPS years. I could not tell, not in the murk
and mire. My only measure of time was the slow-pain of rust devouring
my poll, my shoulder, my heel, crawling through my eye-hole, and rasping at my body.

Against the gnaw of worms and thrust of roots, Haft's body rotted away, but I could only happiness at his parting for I knew he had finally escaped this hell. Perhaps it was better that way. So, I lie, alone with my thoughts, and endured the peculiar torture of being eaten away little by little.

SCRAPE.

Boots?

Pressure above me. As the earth moved, the grasses' roots shivered in the wind. A lick of sun grazed my body.

Then the smooth touch of a hand, chafing at the orange-armored rust. With a squelch, I surfaced into glorious sunshine. A thumb brushed away sheafs of corrosion.

We departed that place.

Trepidation grasped me as I bounced in the saddle-bag. *No more blood. No more, I cannot taste it again.*

I was placed in liquid.

Not blood, but oil. Soothing.

Wire bristles scraped at my side, massaged at the rust, which fell away like scabs of dandruff. My worry fell away, too.

Then to the hone. I winced at the bite of the grindstone. It was a long-forgotten, yet welcome hardness, a welcome pain. Any pain would have been better than wasting away in a murky grave.

But the strangest thing by far was the fresh haft fitted inside my embrace. A young, new being, still strong with sap.

We were off, redolent with the smell of oil, of wood and dirt. The new haft quavered, cringed.

Be still, friend, I murmured to the haft as my newly-sharpened edge whistled through the air and sliced into the soil's familiar warmth with a glorious *crunch.*

THE COST OF POWER

ULFF LEHMANN

DRAMMOCH FELT OLD this morning. As was his habit since he had come of age, he had risen with the morning gong. And true to his ritual, he had washed and again determined it was more effective when he defecated before rather than after washing. Nothing had changed in his routine, yet everything else had. Or so he told himself.

Breaking his fast accompanied by a flurry of courtiers, he wondered if today was the day he would snap and break one of their necks. Even with everything all right, these sycophants found some obscure issue to piss and moan about. Usually, it was the same ludicrous thing, if only viewed from a different vantage. "Majesty, House Cirrain doesn't guard the highland passes." "My King, House Farlin's taxes are too high." "One of House Argram's men raped a villein's daughter."

"My lord demands a solution" was the usual ending of most of these litanies, and Drammoch had grown tired of it. If Wadram Cirrain had withdrawn his patrols, it meant serious trouble in the highlands. "Hire more guards," he told the lickspittle of the Drovers Guild. That was the easiest solution of the three. "As for Farlin's taxes, speak with the master of coin."

"What about House Argram?" demanded the third petitioner, a woman wearing House Trileigh's colors.

"I take it you have sought out one of Lliania's clergy?" he asked, finishing his porridge. The mere mention of House Argram soured his appetite.

"All the lawspeakers excused themselves, Majesty."

"All, eh?" *Nothing new there,* Drammoch thought. Duncan Argram the Elder made sure his men only raped villeins, a minor crime compared to raping a freeborn. How he loathed the system, the society he had inherited.

"A girl's life means less than a cow's if she is a villein," the woman said, her face betraying her rage.

Swallowing the rising bile, he stood. "Thank you for bringing this issue to my attention," he said. There was little else he could say. "I will have words with Lliania's justiciar."

"But, milord," the woman said.

"Thank you!" Drammoch repeated. Short of risking a war with House Argram, there was very little he could do. Noel Trileigh was his cousin, and he knew full well how futile these complaints were. Or were they?

ONE LOOK DOWN the lichen and moss-covered stairs that led down to Herascor city from the palace made the decision for him. "The long way to town it is, lads," Drammoch told the warriors of his guard. Waving over the ever-attentive cupbearer, Liam, he said, "Find the steward, lad, and tell him I'll feast on his balls if the stairs aren't cleared by noon."

Liam grinned, turned, and ran back to the fortress.

"Milord," Zamar said. For a moment, Drammoch had forgotten the Dragonlander even existed. "We don't have the time to visit the city today. The envoy from Danastaer is waiting."

Once more the king wondered how this outlander had risen through the ranks of his court so quickly. Always he was a hint more competent, a bit more effective than the person he inevitably replaced. Justiciar Padraig found the man truthful, not that Lady Justice's clergy caught all lies, and spies had uncovered no damning evidence against the man, either. Yet something felt wrong, especially since Zamar now held several advisory positions. "High Advisor Zamar," Drammoch said, "I leave the matter of dealing with the Danastaerian envoy in your capable hands."

Zamar bowed, motioning for some of his guards to remain. "Your wish is my command," drawled the southerner.

"Good, good," Drammoch replied. "Then take your black guards and shove them up your ass. My warriors suffice!"

He caught the hint of a smile on Zamar's face as the man bowed. *Pompous bastard,* the king thought. But for no,w the man had his uses. He watched as the Dragonlander and his black-clad guards headed back to the castle.

MOST OF HERASCOR'S temples to the gods were flashy affairs, polished marble and bronze and gold. To Drammoch, they looked like whores painted colorful to attract customers. The few exceptions were those temples dedicated to the gods of Justice, Death, and Knowledge, and it was the latter's library that was Drammoch's goal.

Chief Librarian Marghread was already waiting for him. The stout high priestess with her ink-stained lips and fingertips showed Chanastardh's king her respect by receiving him on the library's porch.

"You look as lovely as ever," Drammoch said, embracing his old teacher.

"And for a man who must lie to others most of the time," she replied with a laugh, "you are a pathetic liar."

Somewhere in the depths of the temple, he knew, one of the librarians was writing down their conversation. "I must speak with you," he said. "In private." He imagined the priest put the parchment they were writing on aside, to be picked up and written upon once more when their conversation was over. Now, that same librarian retrieved a fresh sheet of parchment, dipped his quill into the inkpot, and began to record some other event the God of Knowledge deemed important.

"HE'S COERCED MORE houses to his side," Isobal Grendargh, his trusted contact from Danastaer, said.

They were near one of the quays, a brisk walk from the library. Nearby, a pair of seagulls fought over half a fish some fisherman must have dropped, drawing people's attentions to the birds.

"And yours?" Drammoch asked. They sat with their backs to each other as was usual for their meetings. He wore different garb now, clothes Marghread had provided, clothes that turned the king of Chanastardh into an everyman.

"House Grendargh retains its honor," Isobal replied.

Before he could ask, the Danastaerian continued, "The southerner's envoy was captured, their tongues cut out, and before they died, they watched the dogs eat their tongues."

He shuddered at the image. "And you are certain they were his creatures?" Experience had taught him early not to mention Zamar's name. Common wisdom was wrong, magic and its users still existed. How else could the high advisor have known about meetings held and words exchanged?

"Aye," Isobal said.

"So, Grendargh stands alone," he stated.

Isobal's affirmative sounded resigned. "As do you."

"Go and tell Lady Bethia war is unavoidable," Drammoch said. He remembered the mistress of House Grendargh, her bubbling humor and her blunt honesty.

"And you?"

Drammoch scoffed, rising. "I won't avoid it." The fewer people who knew his mind and his plans, the better the chances for success. Warning at least one Danastaerian noble house lifted at least part of the guilt from his conscience. "What must be done will be done. Safe travels, my friend."

"And to you," Isobal replied. He thought he could feel her sketching a bow.

A slight turn of the head showed the woman had gone. Drammoch returned to the Library for his clothes, his guards, and, if all went as planned, for the wellbeing of his people.

All his people.

"FACT IS, WE lack the grain to feed all your subjects," Zamar stated.

Of course, they did, Drammoch thought, denying the glum certainty access to his face. In the past decades, he had learned to keep his feelings hidden from his council of advisors. Sure, they had all sworn an oath of loyalty, but as Justiciar Padraig was fond of saying, "No matter the words, most people look out primarily for themselves, fucking loyalty in the ass." And since none of her priests could foretell the future, oaths made in Lady Justice Lliania's name lost their relevance and strength after a while. Sure, they all would be judged after they died, but how many people thought that far ahead?

"We can send out caravans to our neighbors, milord," said Alsdar Millerson of the Merchants Guild.

Drammoch bobbed his head, regarding Millerson in his gaudy clothes. The merchants, of course, would demand an arm and a leg for the service.

Greedy cunts. For a moment, Drammoch considered shutting them all
into the dungeons until the investigations of the coincidental fires had
finished. He knew Zamar and his allies here at court were responsible
for the crisis, but as Padraig had so prudently said, it was no more than
a suspicion, really, and suspicions without evidence were little more than
Fiery Tales. Not that finding those responsible would replant fields or
rebuild and restock granaries in time for the coming winter.

Iomhar cleared his throat and pushed his chair back to rise and make
a statement. Drammoch regarded the High Priest of Eanaigh, Lady of
Health and Fertility, hope rising. Of all the people assembled here, he felt
almost certain Iomhar would remain on his side. Something, someone,
though, caught the Eanaighist's eye and, resignation plain on his face,
the priest sat down again.

A quick look around the table showed all seemed as it was supposed
to. Not that the king needed visual confirmation of Zamar motioning
for Iomhar to stop. Coerced, bought, or volunteered, in the end, it mattered little.

"We cannot afford your prices," said the master of coin. Fergus Carpenter was the oddity at the table. The man was more concerned with
numbers than politics. In fact, he was happiest when shut away with tax
and fief spending records, shielded from the world.

"You could pay in intervals," suggested Millerson.

"And have the crown be at your mercy?" Zamar snapped before Carpenter could reply.

"Besides," added Esaag Thorn, the master of grain, "we need more
grain than we first thought!"

Of course, they did, thought Drammoch grimly. Rats, locusts, mildew.
If it wasn't fire, it was something else. In a way he felt like a spectator in
a superbly scripted but shoddily acted play. All of these lines, the outrage,
the terrible news, would lead to one thing: War.

The setup was perfect, with winter looming near, the threat of famine would convince most lords and ladies to gather their warbands. And villein and freeborn would gladly go in order to lessen the burden on the taxed granaries, allowing their families a greater chance at survival.

He glanced at Zamar.

Did the Dragonlander suspect he knew what was afoot? Had he made an error the southerner was even now preparing to exploit? The board was set, the tiles assembled. Chiath was no game for the meek, and there was little he could do to change the course of history. Marghraed had made that clear.

"Danastaer," said Caitlyn, High Priestess of Lesganagh, the God of Sun and War. "Their harvest was great."

Of course, she was involved. One didn't plan a war without Lesganagh's blessing. And unlike most others, it didn't take money to convince the Sunpriestess of this war's necessity.

The Dawnslaughter some thirty years ago had driven the surviving Lesganaghists from Danastaer. The Lord of Sun and War's clergy had fallen prey to Eanaighist schemes. Most priests and their families were killed and the temples plundered, all because of the accusation of demonology.

That Caitlyn loved the idea of returning the Lord of the Gods to Danastaer was no secret. Most likely the conspirators hadn't even bothered to include her in their plans. Her ambition guaranteed cooperation. "We could return Lesganagh's faith to Danastaer whilst plundering their granaries."

"And every warrior falling on our side would save us coin and grain," stuttered the master of coin.

It took all Drammoch's will to not blurt out his surprise. Fergus sounded as if he truly was reading from a script, as if he had waited for a signal that was phrased in the vaguest of terms. How had Zamar coerced Fergus's cooperation? What kind of threats had been made to the reclusive mathematician?

To his left, Zamar scoffed. "A little crude, don't you think, my friend? To equate people's lives to mere numbers?"

Fergus now seemed on firmer ground, for he spoke with more confidence, "In the end, what counts is that we have enough grain to feed the people. If there are less people to feed, we obviously need less grain."

"Just make sure House Argram sends their worst," Padraig muttered. Of course, the justiciar was a practically minded man. Drammoch had little doubt Padraig was still on his side—Lliania would have struck him down had he betrayed his oath—but Padraig was also a father and husband. Maybe Zamar had got to the man's family.

The high advisor laughed. "My thoughts exactly. Let's rid ourselves of some Argram troublemakers."

"Troublemakers?" Padraig replied. "A drunk in a tavern leering at married ladies is a troublemaker. Let's call House Argram freeborn what they are: rapist bastards. I have sufficient complaints to have them volunteer one thousand warriors."

Had they got to Padraig or was the justiciar just doing something they had considered while deep in their cups months ago? Was there anyone left at court he could trust?

"I'll have High General Mireynh begin preparations," Zamar said.

"High general?" Padraig asked. "Milord, what is this? First a high advisor, now a high general?" He sounded sincere.

"Zamar?" Drammoch turned to look at the Dragonlander.

For a moment, the man's olive skin looked ashen, then he seemed to gather his composure. "Our army needs to act on one warleader's orders, not many. What other rank would convince a man like Duncan Argram to obey your orders? Milord?" Despite the outlander's composure, Drammoch thought he detected a hint of uncertainty in his stance.

Was the high advisor's hold over the court weaker than he suspected? From the corner of his eye, he saw two of Zamar's black guards taking a step forward. It was time for the lion to pounce, to show the pretender why he was king. "Your guards leave now." Drammoch growled.

For a moment, he saw the two black-clad warriors hesitate, and to reinforce his command, he inclined his head and four of his guards moved towards the high advisor's. He hoped Zamar was no fool, prayed to all the gods for the Dragonlander to comply. The play was hardly begun and he still had pieces to move, and if the conflict came now, with Zamar having more agents in place than he, all would be lost in a civil war.

Now his guards drew steel, the blades halfway out of their scabbards. The black guards' hands were on their weapons, waiting.

"Leave us," Zamar said, and while the royal guards' tense posture relaxed immediately, Drammoch noticed that despite the order, the black guards remained alert. Yet they obeyed the high advisor's order.

As the door shut behind the black guards, a breath he wasn't aware he had been holding escaped as a sigh. Even Zamar looked relieved.

"Next…" Drammoch cleared his throat and began again. "You would do well to remember that these chambers are guarded by the king's guard only."

"Forgive me, Lord King," the high advisor said, clearly rattled. "It shan't happen again."

"If Mireynh leads the army, my cousin Noel of House Trileigh is second in command," Drammoch said. Zamar had hired the mercenary general Urgraith Mireynh several months ago, and while the general's reputation was outstanding, the king knew too little to trust the man. "Noel has been at war and has more tolerance for, shall we say, people from the other side joining our cause."

The shift in Zamar's expression was minimal, but Drammoch had spent too much time with the man not to notice. If appointing Noel to the invasion force upset the advisor's plans, whatever they were, the Dragonlander's influence was not as far-reaching as Drammoch had feared. "A wise choice, Majesty," Zamar said. "Turncoats are a pesky subject with the high general."

Once again, Iomhar cleared his throat. Was there still fight in the old priest? Drammoch wondered.

"It displeases the Lady of Health and Fertility to see so many partake in yet another war," the Eanaighist said. "She needs be appeased if her priests are to join the army."

It took all Drammoch's restraint not to burst into laughter. Did Iomhar now take lessons from the Danastaerian branch of Eanaigh's church? The king understood the Lesganaghists were keen on undoing the Dawnslaughter in order to return the church of Sun and War to Danastaer. He also understood Eanaigh's healers did not lightly participate in any bloodshed, unless they were corrupt souls like Morgan Danaissan, the faith's High Priest in Danastaer. But to ask for donations, nay, bribes so boldly left Drammoch speechless.

"The crown cannot afford to grease your palms, Iomhar," Fergus Carpenter stated. "We need to purchase grain once the army leaves, even if they forage their way to Harail."

On whose side was the master of coin? Had Zamar really corrupted the man, or was everything the master of coin saying based on his precious numbers? Right now, Drammoch couldn't ask, couldn't test the man's—any man's—loyalty, and while it surely would ease his worries to have a rational mind such as Carpenter's on his side, he had to rely on his own judgment. For now.

Iomhar rose, furious. "Prayers, Coin Counter, I was asking for prayers. Over the past few years, attendance has dropped. The people feel less need to pray for health and fertility. Eanaigh notices, and while we caretakers do our duty, people have grown complacent. We don't need bribes. The healing business keeps our coffers from running empty. We don't need to appease the Lady. Our fields never suffered bad harvests!"

"We cannot force people to pray," replied Zamar.

At that, the High Priest laughed. "But you can force them to fight for you?"

The king regarded Iomhar, wondering why people had stopped praying. A mystery for another day. Today, he needed to set things in motion. He looked around and saw his cupbearer in his usual out-of-the-way spot. "Liam, remind me to have a proclamation drafted: mandatory prayer to Eanaigh before each official event." Turning to Iomhar, he added, "That's all I can do for now."

From the corner of his eye, he noticed Zamar tensing.

"The caretakers will join the army," the High Priest said, sitting down once more. Maybe Drammoch had misjudged him.

"It's decided then," Zamar said, sounding, if not looking, relaxed.

"It is," Drammoch confirmed. "Assemble the army!"

Numbers, he never would have guessed. It all came down to numbers. Who gained the most from the invasion? Who gained the most from people's deaths? What was a life worth when used to purchase grain?

His eyes followed the council members, wondering what each of them was willing to pay to keep their power.

For Drammoch, king of Chanastardh, the cost would mount higher than any of theirs. He was bent on changing his kingdom, do away with villeins and freeborn and nobility, and for that, nobility and freeborn and, to a lesser degree, villeins had to die.

He knew, for him, the cost would only grow.

But he was willing to pay.

THE UNDYING LANDS

MICHAEL R. FLETCHER

FAYAD SAT ON a wood bench beneath the great bowl of the Colosseum of Eternal Life, which was something of a misnomer because she was definitely going to die here. Above her head, great beams of wood formed a ceiling, separating her from the fifty thousand men, women, and children filling the arena's seats. Even from down here, she heard their screams and jeers, the roar as blood was spilled to the red sands of the arena floor. The cheered their favourites and mocked those they hated. From the rumbling up there right now, there was someone they really liked killing a lot of people they didn't.

And I'm going to be one of them.

Red sand from the arena floor rained down upon her as the crowd stomped their feet and chanted for blood.

Breathing deep, she inhaled dust and ancient straw, sweat and fear, and the desiccated stench of thirty years of death. Stacked shelves lined every wall beneath the great colosseum. The walls above, those confining the fighters to the killing floor, also bore shelves. Even the shit and piss rooms where the fans went to relieve themselves had shelves. Severed heads lined those shelves. There were so many they were crammed together, ear to ear. The oldest were bone and gristle, gaping sockets and grinning bone. The newest heads still blinked and looked around, mouths sometimes moving as they tried to speak or scream.

The one directly across from where Fayad sat was fresh indeed. The young man still had tears for crying. He sobbed and blinked, lips moving. His eyes stayed locked on her, and she could tell he was trying to scream. But screaming without lungs is a quiet affair.

"Don't bother," she told him. "Can't hear a fucking thing you're saying."

Eyes boring holes in her heart, his lips made quiet smacking sounds.

"Even if I could hear you, I wouldn't care," she added when his eyes became crazed and desperate.

Finally, sighing, she rose and turned the head so it faced the wall. The manacles binding her wrists and ankles left her just enough freedom to move in small shuffling steps.

"Sorry. Don't want to spend my last few minutes of life looking at you."

Collapsing back onto the bench, Fayad shook her head, stared down at the red sand and rotting straw beneath her feet.

How the hell did I get here?

She knew. She knew *exactly* how she got here. It was getting drunk and accidentally killing the duke's favourite nephew when the little shit grabbed her ass. And those with the temerity to annoy the duke were carted across two hundred miles to the Colosseum of Eternal Life.

She knew the history. Hell, everyone knew the history. Thirty years ago, a powerful necromancer named Leben cast the mother of all spells…

and fucked it up big. Instead of just raising the ancient army she knew to be buried beneath the red sands, she turned the land for fifty miles around into a zone of unlife. Anyone killed here became undead.

Leben succeeded at her goal. She raised a massive undead army replete with giants and dragons and giants mounted on even bigger dragons and all manner of nasty. Unfortunately, she also raised their general, some long dead demonologist who still harboured dreams of conquest. The general killed the necromancer and took his armies south, where he conquered the islands and gave birth to the Empire of Corpses. Rumour had it, Leben became his wife.

The land, however, remained forever changed.

Leave it to some enterprising asshole royal to see the possibilities. They built a gladiatorial arena on the site and let convicts fight to the death. Not being cruel—or so they claimed—they arranged for the chance of reprieve. Kill ten opponents in a row and you walked free. Once the live fights were done and only living dead remained, they let them fight it out on the arena floor. The more undead you defeated—defined as 'rendered incapable of further action'—the better your final resting place. Defeat ten or more, and they stuck your head on a spike where you could watch future fights, see the passing days and nights. The fewer you managed to maim before becoming incapacitated, the shittier your final resting place. If you failed to down even a single opponent, they stuck your head on a shelf in the shitters and you spent the rest of eternity watching people vacate their bowels. That was if you were lucky. The crowd got pretty drunk, and people liked to toss the heads into the shit pits and throw things at them. Since shelf space was limited and there were always new heads, no one complained.

Kill at least one. Fayad couldn't even pretend she had any chance of killing ten living opponents and being set free.

The crowd above roared as their current favourite murdered another opponent. Feet stomped, red dust fell from the ceiling.

Forever undying. A last bright moment in the sun, and then pain and blood and an eternity of misery.

Fayad glanced at the head she turned to face the wall.

Shit. She winced in guilt.

Motionless, forever staring at a wall. What would that be like?

Word was that when the skull rotted enough, the eyelids were gone, the dead lost the ability to blink, to close their eyes. They saw everything. And having your eyes rot to nothing or be devoured by insects was no escape. Empty sockets stared forever, all part of the necromancy twisting the land.

Fayad held her eyes open, staring at another one of the heads on the shelf across from her. This one had only grey shreds of tattered flesh clinging to it. Its scalp had slid off one side and lay puddled beside it, maggots, hair, and putrescence.

Eyes watering, she stared, trying to imagine it lasting forever.

Finally, tears streaming, she blinked.

I'll go insane.

Closing her eyes, she sat motionless. This might be the last time she got to enjoy darkness.

Above, the crowds roared, and then fell quiet.

They're dragging away the loser, shoving them in a cage with the other dead, saving them for the mad brawl at the end.

How many could she kill?

Well, so far in her life, she'd managed to kill exactly one person. While she'd meant to stab him—just a little—she hadn't intended to kill him. And since she hadn't known who she was stabbing, she hadn't meant to kill *him*.

The magistrate hadn't been much impressed with that defence either.

Fayad heard the shuffling steps of the kennel master before she saw him. He came down the steps one at a time, like a child afraid of falling. A big fucker, he was damned near twice her height, all fat and muscle and stupidity. Grey skin hung slack, his eyes yellow like rotting milk. Upon reaching the last step, he stopped and glared at the floor as if suspecting a trap.

"Go ahead," said Fayad, "take the last step. I promise you won't plummet to your death."

He stepped down, saying, "Plummet. Plump bits. Plumb it. Plum tits."

He minced over to Fayad, examining her manacled wrists and ankles.

"The magistrate changed his mind," she said. "I'm to be let free."

"Good. You seem nice."

"I am."

Grabbing the chain connecting her wrists he lifted her off the bench and into the air so she hung dangling.

"That's quite painful," she informed him through gritted teeth.

He turned her, looking her over from every angle and for a moment she thought maybe she was going to get raped before someone murdered her.

"No hidden weapons?" he said. "Sometimes they forget to search and I get stabbed." He pouted. "I don't like getting stabbed."

Still holding her aloft with a single hand, he lifted his shirt to show her the many stab wounds in his bulging belly. None had healed. None bled. Something white and glistening squirmed in one.

"You're dead," she said.

"No, I'll get better."

"Right. Good luck."

Putting her down, he shoved Fayad toward the steps. "Go." He pushed her again, sending her stumbling, and followed along behind.

"How long have you been down here?" she asked over her shoulder.

"What time is it?"

"Early afternoon," she guessed.

"What day is it?"

"Fourthday."

"What year?"

"Thirty-two fifteen from the fall of PalTaq."

"Oh. Then I don't know." He pointed up the stairs with a blunt finger like a boiled sausage. "Go."

Up she went.

"What weapon you want?" he asked from behind her.

"A ballista and a squad of the duke's Marching Dead."

"What armour?"

"Full plate and a shield wall."

"Fine."

"I'm not getting any of that, am I?"

"Nope. Just curious."

"Fuck."

"No thanks. Too small. Don't like skinny."

Cresting the stairs, he herded her down a long hall, pushing and prodding with that fat finger. Daylight turned the far end a blinding cloud of dust and sand. The crowd grew in volume with every step.

Boom! Boom! The stomping of feet.

"I like to give people some motivation to do well," he said. "It's sad when they die too fast. The crowd doesn't like it."

"I'd hate to disappoint."

"Some kids threw all the heads in the fourteenth shitter into the pit. They dropped stones on them until they sank."

"Oh." Fayad's guts turned to water and tried to escape south.

"All the shelves there are empty."

"Fucking fantastic. All motivated. Thank you so much."

Placing a monstrous hand on her shoulder, he dragged her to a stop. He turned her to face a table she hadn't seen. An assortment of crude weapons lay scattered on its surface. Rusty knives. Bent swords. A trident with only two dull-looking barbs. A leather whip.

"No maul?" she asked.

The big dead stinky guy looked her up and down as if judging her ability to wield such a weapon. "It's out for repairs."

Noting the rough shape of the supplied weapons, she wondered how many pieces the maul had to be in before it was sent for repairs.

"I'll take a sword and a knife."

"Going to unchain your hands and feet now," he said. "No stabbing, please."

"Yeah, yeah."

What would be the point? There was nowhere to run, and the big man was already dead. Putting steel in his belly would just upset him, and she figured she had enough problems already.

When he finished unchaining her, he straightened and flashed a quick smile.

"The fuck you grinning about?"

"My knees don't hurt any more. Neither does my lower back."

"The dead feel no pain."

"Every turd has a silver lining," he said, shuffling away in his mincing little steps.

"What do I do?" Fayad called after him.

"Go out and die. If you hide in the tunnel, they come get you and break a leg as punishment."

"Great." She had a thought. "Hey!"

He stopped. "What?"

"There's a head facing the wall. Turn it back for me, would you?"

"Okay." And off he shuffled.

Turning back to the bright light and chanting crowds, she shrugged acceptance and set off. Someone out there with a booming voice announced her crime and made accidentally stabbing an ass-grabbing prick sound terribly dramatic.

Was the duke's nephew here, somewhere in the Undying Lands? Some wealthy families built elaborate mausoleums—sprawling mansions—where their dead were held as pampered prisoners. No one wanted corpses running free, but many wanted to visit their deceased to ask advice or just visit missed relatives.

People, she decided, were short-sighted self-centred assholes. No one cared what the dead wanted.

The announcer wrapped up his spiel as she stumbled into the sunlight. Hot air, desert dry, stank of camels and sweat. Bloodstained patches of the red sand a darker crimson. The colosseum, packed to capacity, dragged her to a halt. Never before had she been the centre of attention for fifty thousand people.

Fifty thousand people came to watch me die.

Well, not just her. Her and a bunch of other poor bastards.

When the crowd spotted her, a slight girl of twenty, bent sword in one hand, rusted dagger in the other, they booed.

"Fuck you!" she screamed at them, voice cracking.

Though most couldn't hear her, they seemed to appreciate the sentiment. Across the bloody arena sands stood her opponent. He'd been hurt and limped forward, blood pouring from a long gash in his leg. His left arm looked to have been broken at the elbow and hung swinging.

The announcer went into great length detailing her opponent's many crimes. Apparently, he was a thief and a murderer, a pirate and a sellsword, a spy and an assassin.

Assassin. Fantastic.

"And this," concluded the announcer, "shall be his tenth fight today!"

Fayad's heart fell. She faced a man who already killed nine opponents. If he killed her, he walked free.

If? When.

He grinned at her, teeth bloody like he killed his last opponent by biting him to death.

One little girl who accidentally stabbed someone for grabbing her ass against a seasoned killer who was one more wee murder away from freedom.

The crowd were on their feet now, screaming, a deafening roar of blood lust. The sound felt like a crushing weight, like their hate sucked the air from her lungs. Blood! Blood! Blood!

They want him to win. They want him to kill me.

She saw it. She saw his perfect hair and his perfect, if bloody, teeth. She saw that cocky grin, the flat muscled plain of his belly. He was square jawed and handsome, roguishly so.

And Fayad was going to kill him.

He limped forward, confident in his victory. And how could he not be?

Fayad retreated, circling away, and again the crowd booed.

I'll let him bleed some more. Hopefully it would slow him, weaken him.

He followed, calling, "Keep running away and they'll put an arrow in you to slow you down."

Glancing at the towering wall surrounding the arena, she spotted the evenly spaced archers up there. They stood watching, arrows nocked but not drawn.

Shit.

Was he lying? Again, she circled away until the nearest archer raised his bow and took aim.

Scooting closer, she feinted a stab, staying well out of sword range.

Ignoring the feint, her opponent said, "Sorry, girl."

They circled, finding their range and testing each other's speed and strength. His long arms gave him a decided advantage. He also clearly knew a lot more about sword fighting. Her feints were usually ignored. When she did lunge forward in an attempt to stab him with her bent sword, her attacks were bashed aside with a speed and strength that threatened to send her weapon spinning to the sand.

Even limping, his balance was perfect. He moved with flawless grace. This was a born killer. Fayad, on the other hand, liked drinking in pubs.

She considered throwing the rusty knife at him, but had never thrown a knife before. The weight felt awkward in her hand, too heavy in the grip.

Knocking aside another clumsy attack, he lashed out, leaving a gash across her ribs. It burned like fire, and she staggered away.

The crowd roared, a deafening crescendo. Blood! Blood! Blood!

He attacked, a liquid blur of steel, following relentlessly. Her sword sang harsh discordant notes of metallic agony, the blade shedding bright slivers and bending under the onslaught. Once she started retreating, she couldn't stop. He pressed and pressed, driving her back. Blood poured from a wound in her side, sheening her belly crimson. A splinter of steel flew from her sword, cutting her over her left eye. Still he pressed, stabbing, slashing, ever forward. She blinked sweat and blood, burning her eyes, turning the world red.

He's not defending.

Not in the least. But his ceaseless attacks meant that if she launched her own attack, he'd cut her for sure.

Already cut. Must—

Fayad's sword shattered, the bent blade spinning away to kick up a plume of red sand.

"Fu—"

He stabbed her in the belly, ran her through.

Reaching back, she touched the blade protruding from her back. "Oh."

"Sorry," he said. "Life is war, and I'm a warrior. You…" He shrugged.

The crowd screamed and chanted, but they all seemed so far away.

He withdrew his sword, and she crumpled, knees folding.

Fayad lay in sanguine sand, her life pulsing out, adding to the many stains. Knowing it was pointless, she fought to stanch the wound.

He stood over her, tall and handsome and deadly.

"In other circumstances," he said, flashing an apologetic grin.

In other circumstances I'd have accidentally stabbed you in a shitty tavern.

"You're my tenth." He let out a long sigh. "I go free. The gods," he winked, "have found me innocent."

She blinked up at him, seeing him through blood.

Not one. She failed to kill a single opponent. They'd cut her head off and stick it in a fucking shitter where she could watch fat old men grunt out craps.

Forever.

Or at least until some bored kid tossed her head into the bog. Then she'd sink away, see nothing but shit.

How many heads were in there? How long did you have to be an undying skull sank in excrement before you went mad? Would insanity be an escape?

"Belly wound," he said, moving closer. "I didn't... That's a bad way to go. Long and slow."

Fayad showed her own bloody grin. "And you can't leave until I'm dead."

He limped closer, grimacing. "True. But I would save you the many hours of agony."

He's lost a lot of blood. He wouldn't last hours out here in the sun.

She coughed and pain tore her. Gods, it hurt so much.

He ran you through. You're already dead. Why fight it? Let him finish you.

An eternity in a shit pit.

Fayad groaned in agony. "Do it. Make it fast."

He limped closer. "I take no pleasure in doing this. Life is—"

"War, I know." She closed her eyes so she saw only his blurred form through blood and lashes. "Do it now. Hurts too much."

He raised his sword.

Lashing out with the dagger, Fayad slashed his hamstring, and he screamed. Leg buckling, he collapsed to land heavily beside her. She stabbed him in the chest, and he punched her, breaking her nose. For a moment, they wrestled, and then fell apart, gasping. Eyes streaming, Fayad's world smeared red sand and pain and blood.

The crowd fell silent, watching, waiting to see who still lived.

Fayad felt for her knife and couldn't find it. She'd lost it. Blinking away tears, she saw him beside her, blood pulsing from the wound in his chest. He lay blinking into the sky, watching a bird circle far above.

"Why?" he asked.

"Life is war."

"But you were already dying."

She coughed a wet bloody laugh. "In the Undying Lands, death is war, too."

"Ah," he said. "Fuck."

"I had to kill one person to earn a better resting place for my head."

"Only works if I die first."

"Belly wound," she parroted. "Bad way to die. Long and slow."

"Got me there," he admitted. "I'm going fast." He turned his head, studying her with dark eyes. "I don't envy you the next few hours. They won't end you early. There's no mercy here."

"Once you're dead, I'll end it myself. If I can find my damned knife."

"Not that easy." He shifted in the sand, grunting. "I think I landed on your knife." He rolled to one side, cursing in pain. "Get it."

Fayad reclaimed her rusting blade. She considered stabbing him again, but there was no point. He was definitely dying faster than she.

"How do they do it?" she asked. "How do they take the heads?"

"Couple living men in full plate come out with axes. It's the final part of the show, watching the dead get dismembered."

"Great."

"If you manage to kill one, they give you a job working for the colosseum. You get to see all the fights."

Fayad thought of the big kennel master, the way he stomped back into the tunnels, turning his back on the arena. "Oh, to dream." She looked around as best she could. "They're not here yet." The pain made thought difficult. She wanted to curl around her agony and cry.

"Soon," he said.

"Then we don't have time to waste."

"What?"

"The war isn't over."

Fayad killed him, stabbing him over and over in the chest until she got his heart. The crowd roared approval, stamping and chanting. Blood! Blood! Blood!

Now for the hard part. She turned the knife on herself, held it over her heart, cold steel pricking flesh.

That hurts already.

"Death is war," she said, driving the rusty blade into her heart.

She woke to find him standing over her, sword drawn, wounds no longer bleeding. Offering a hand, he pulled her to her feet.

"Tell me there's a plan," he said.

She stood, staring at the chanting crowd, the people who just watched her kill both him and herself and who apparently loved the spectacle. The world was grey, muted. She felt nothing, no pain.

"We fight our way free."

"Great plan."

"You have something better?"

"Nope."

At the far end of the arena, a huge gate rose. Two men in full plate, huge axes held ready, marched into the arena. The crowd screamed and chanted and stomped. Blood! Blood! Blood!

The dead don't bleed.

"We have two advantages," he said.

"Yeah?"

"Me," he winked, "and the fact that assholes in plate armour in the desert sun get tired fast. Make them chase you. If an archer hits you, leave the arrow in unless it's making movement awkward. Save it as a weapon for later when that shitty knife breaks. When you do fight, go for the joints, the neck. Cut and run. Let them bleed."

"When the gate opens again to send in more men, we have to be ready to rush it and get out."

"So, whatever happens, don't let them damage your lovely legs."

Fayad watched the approaching men. "What are you going to do when we get out of here?"

"Confidence, I like that. I thought I might ask if you wanted to go for a drink."

"The dead drink?"

"This one does."

Fayad laughed. "Yeah. This one, too."

THE FALL OF TEREEN

ANNA SMITH SPARK

Being an episode from the History of Amrath the World Conqueror
Empires of Dust

FIRE ON ME.

Fire. Burning.

Burning and its pain, pain on me, running everywhere all over. Running, running, burning, my whole body is fire and it hurts, it hurts. And I'm burning, and I'm blind, and all there is fire and burning everywhere, running everywhere, and I hurt, and I hurt, and I burn, fire on me, fire on me.

The walls are falling. The walls of my city of Tereen. One day, I would have been queen of it. White walls of white smooth marble. Clean and smooth and tall. Silver towers. Silver gates.

Falling.

Fire.

Burns.

A burst of mage fire. The earth shakes. The whole world is falling. The walls burn. The earth burns. White light. Ladders up against the walls, and the enemy comes scaling up them. Sword blades. Knife blades. Sharp killing blade-sharp eyes.

'They're coming! Hold! Hold! We can hold them! Take them! Take them down!' Ansel's voice. My brother. His face is bleeding. His hair is burning. He holds his spear and it shakes in his hands.

'Hold! Hold! Take them!'

Our spearmen push. Forcing them back. The enemy coming up at us. A wall of spears, pushing and thrusting at the enemy soldiers as they climb. Arrows shooting down at them. A rain of arrows. Thick in the air. The soldiers climbing fall back, falling out into nothingness, spinning, screaming as they fall. Blood, as they fall. I get one of them. Get my spear in his face. Under the helmet, where his eyes are. I feel it stick in there. I see him falling. The first man, I think, perhaps, the first man I have killed.

More and more of them. Coming up the ladders. Scrambling with knives in their mouths. Their eyes staring at us. They hate us. They want nothing but to kill us. We kill them and an eternity of them rise in their place.

Like locust. Filthy scrabbling insects. The army of Amrath. They climb the ladders. We kill them. They keep climbing. They mount the walls. More of them. Like insects. We fall back. We kill them. We are overwhelmed.

Their ladders stand on piles of corpses. There is a great deep ditch around the walls of Tereen, filled with sweet water. A ditch and a moat and walls of white marble, that we thought would be our defence. The stories came to us from Bakh. They dug a ditch there to defend their walls, deep and lined with stakes coated in poison, and the walls rising smooth and strong behind it, impregnable, out of the enemy's reach. Five men survived the destruction of Bakh. They told us the stories, that the army of Amrath took the peasants from the fields around and killed them and threw their bodies into the ditch, more and more and more of them, all the people of Raen who had surrendered to them, opened the gates and embraced them and crowned Him in gold. Every one of them they killed, and threw their bodies into the ditch, and they filled up the ditch with corpses, and their ladders and their siege engines came up to the walls, and Bakh fell in three days.

We heard the stories.

We did not believe them.

Five men, who claimed to be the only five survivors.

Absurd.

All of it.

Absurd.

They have carts with them our scouts have told us. When they have killed us every one of us, so they will use our flesh and our bones.

Mage fire. The mage lord Semserest moves beside me. Her hair is black with ashes, she stinks of sweat and blood. Her face looks like she is dying. She *is* dying. Her hands clench. She is dying in pain.

'I can't… We have to pull back, my lady,' she says to me. The walls shake around us. Stones falling. Her voice is choked like she has glass on her tongue. 'We have to…pull back. To the inner wall. We must.'

'No! No!' We can hold them. We can. We must. Our spearmen strike, pushing them off their ladders. Archers shoot down fire arrows. Our trebuchets loose over and over. They come scrambling up the ladders with knives in their teeth, and our swordsmen kill them and cut them down. We can hold them. We can.

A crash below us, against the gates. Semserest staggers backwards. All her power, all her magery, clenched tight holding closed the gates. She staggers. Her mouth is bleeding. Her face is grey as dying. The gates groan and creak and begin to break.

'We must fall back,' she screams. 'The inner walls. The citadel.'

'No! No! We must hold!'

A blast of mage fire sweeps over the walls. Our soldiers shriek and burn. Their hair is on fire, white flames like they are crowned in gemstones. Like the crowns we placed on His head. Their skin shines white and golden, lit up with fire inside them, bursting out of them., They open their eyes and their mouths and the flames blaze up out of them, and they writhe and tremble in the light as they die. Twenty of them. Thirty. The army of Amrath cheers. Scrambles faster up the siege ladders, over the walls. Mage fire explodes again and some of the enemy's soldiers themselves blaze up burning. Their swords and their armour glow like gems. The men behind them on the ladders laugh at their comrades dying. They come over the top of the wall and kick the burning bodies out of their path.

'Hold them. Hold them.' My brother's voice. Shaking. 'Hold. We can. We can.' The walls tremble. The walls, falling. Rocks and fire smashing against them. Tearing them down. 'We can! We can!' My brother's voice rises to a child's cry. I do not think I have ever heard anyone so afraid. He thrusts his spear at the enemy coming up the ladders. His spear shakes like a grass blade. They come over the walls, more and more of them, like insects, locusts, swarming gleaming silver and bronze. The army of Amrath. They cut my brother down.

We push back in disorder. Retreat! Retreat! Get back to the inner walls!

A crash from the gateway. A roar of thunder. Semserest sways. Staggers. Falls down bleeding. Smoke pouring out of her mouth. The gates below us shatter. The army of Amrath streams through into the city. The walls tremble. The walls burn.

Retreat! Retreat! Retreat!

THE FALL OF TEREEN

HE FIRST SENT envoys to us three years ago. Amrath of Illyr. The petty king of a small poor country at the edge of our world. We had a beautiful city, with strong gates and high walls and many soldiers. We said kind polite things to Him. Gave him gifts of silk, cloth, and fast horses. I sat at my father's right hand as we bade His envoys farewell.

The next year, His envoys returned to us. Balkash and Ander had fallen to Him. Balkash surrendered. He burned it anyway. Ander resisted. Her rivers ran red. Nothing lives now where her towers stood

We proclaimed Him king. We are not stupid. We made Him gifts of silk cloth and fast horses and a crown of diamonds. Our poets praised Him as master of all Irlast. I sat at my father's right hand and made a speech of loyalty to Him.

Raen surrendered to Him. Bakh fell to Him. He sowed the fields of Cen Elora with salt and human ashes. He poured poison into the River Malpath until the water turned black as pitch.

We proclaimed Him god and lord and emperor. We are not stupid. We sent Him gifts of silk cloth and fast horses and diamonds and gold and wheat and slaves and pearls and tin. I sat at my father's right hand and swore that of all that lives beneath the sun, I thought only and ever of Him.

He returned three weeks ago. Spread His army beneath our walls. A host in bronze and iron, uncountable as the stars in heaven. Soldiers from every country in the world, armed with spears and swords and great war machines, hungry for our blood.

They ride horses we gave them. They eat wheat we sent them. They forged the tin we gave them into bronze armour. His tent is silk cloth sewn with gold and pearls.

We were a city of blind fools.

We wept and despaired. We are not stupid. We sent out envoys, begging Him for mercy. I sat at my father's right hand and our people cursed me.

The envoys were sent back to us. Their eyes had been put out and their mouths sewn shut and their hands cut off and their flesh rotting off their bones.

We forged swords and spears. We prepared to fight Him. Every man and woman. Every child old enough to hold a blade.

Our city is burning now. All the world burns.

Retreat! Retreat! Dying. Burning.

He has breached our walls.

WE CRAWL OUR way backwards. The enemy floods into the city through the Skaen Gateway, through the Gate of the Tower, up their ladders, through the walls. The people have sworn to make them fight for every inch of our city. Every flagstone must be bought in blood and suffering.

We die.

We die.

We die.

They come flooding in.

'Pull back!' A voice that might be my father's. An old fat man wielding his father's sword. He will not even know that my brother is dead. 'We should surrender,' he said to me. We stood on the walls above the Skaen Gateway and looked at the army of Amrath spread before us, and he said that he and I should walk out alone and offer ourselves to Him. The king and the king's heir. Let Him torture us. Play with us. Offer ourselves to Him that the city might live.

His soldiers thrust their way into the city. Killing everything. The air is black with flies and crows. Mage fire. Darkness. Rocks loosed from their siege engines. White and red and black and green flames.

I do not think He would have kept our bargain, even if we had had the courage to carry it out.

We did not, of course, have the courage to carry it out.

———

THE FALL OF TEREEN

I RALLY OUR soldiers to me. Good strong fierce fighters with good strong bronze swords. We must get to the citadel. The inner walls. Bar the way to them. Resist! Defend! Hold them! We can! We must! We can!

Lies and bloody lies and cowardliness. I wish I had offered myself to Him for Him to play with. I would now at least already be dead.

And His soldiers are on me. The army of Amrath. Ten of them. Silver armour. Plumes on their helmets. They are covered, covered running with blood.

A sword comes up at me. It looks huge as mountains. The only thing in my world. I strike back. Duck backwards. My sword catches it. My whole body rings with the force of it. Clash of metal. Again. Again. There is nothing else left of me. My sword. My body, trying to fight.

Blood in my mouth. My blood? The enemy's blood? Strike and lunge and duck and strike and duck away. Clash of metal. Blood. Sweat. Screaming. My sword is the heaviest thing I can imagine. Killing. Trying to kill. All there is. All there is. All there is.

My sword meets the enemy. Cuts into him through a weak point in his armour. Killing. Trying to kill. Clash of metal. My body screaming aching. Swinging the sword mad and blind. And I get him. I feel it, the sword taming him. His body yields. Grate of metal, and then skin, and then meat. The enemy falls backwards. He's bleeding. Blood all over him. I taste it. Gasp at it. He dies.

Another two are on me. They have bloody swords. I want to beg for mercy. I hit at one. My blade bounces off his armour. Laughs at me. A sword flares up blue fire. Mage blade. Harsh sweet dry smell of hot metal. Swinging the sword again and again, and I begin to break.

My sword is hot from his fire. The hilt burns in my hand.

I drop my sword.

I run.

———

THREE WEEKS, AMRATH sat before our walls with His army. He made no move to attack us. Just sat there. His army squatting around our walls.

So, we sent out our envoys. And He sent them back, maimed. But He did not send us a message. What He wanted. He just sat. His army squatting before us. His siege engines glaring at our walls. So, my father and I considered offering ourselves to Him. Wondered if it was us alone that He wanted to hurt. He destroyed Bakh in three days. Bakh is a far greater city than Tereen. Thicker, higher, stronger walls. I think… I think it simply amused Him. To make us wait.

My father wanted to abdicate. An old man with a paunch and a pain in his leg. Crown me queen because I am strong and in my prime, trained as a warrior, even if a warrior who had never indeed raised her sword in war. My brother refused to allow it. Said he would dispute my right to the throne. The army of Amrath sat before our walls, and we argued which of us should die with a crown on their head.

'We have a king. A good king. Beloved by his people.'

'We need a king who is younger. Stronger. A king who can fight.'

'Very well, then. But Lendalla is a woman. I am a man. I should be king.'

'Lendella is a warrior as much as you are. Her arm is strong. And she is six years the elder. Since before you were born, she has trained to fight. To rule. To lead. Don't be absurd.'

'We should have raised our swords against Him years ago!' my brother shouted. 'As I said we should.'

We looked at him, my father and I. 'We should,' I said. 'As you said we should. But that does not matter now. And it has nothing to do with which of us should wear the crown.'

'Our father will wear it. Until he dies. Or I will take up my sword against you, sister. I will leave you and go over to Amrath.'

Our father did not abdicate. He strapped on his father's sword. Went out to fight.

My brother did not leave us. My brother held against them, as they came over the walls at us. Shrieking and shaking with fear, and he held.

My brother's hands shook on his spear haft. My brother shrieked with fear.

My brother is dead.

I RUN. WHITE fire and green fire and blue fire erupting around me. The whole city is burning. The fire is silent. Mage fire. Magic fire that is silent as graves. A woman runs past me. She is burning. The whole front of her body is blood.

I should have given myself to Amrath in offering. I should have tried to save my people. I should—

Why are we even fighting them? Fighting will only delay them killing us. Give them leave to kill us more slowly and in greater pain.

A good ruler would have spiked our wells with poison the day Amrath first drew up His army before our walls.

Let them kill me! Let me die! Get it done!

But I run through the city as it burns around me. Run past my people, fighting, dying, burning, dead.

A GROUP OF soldiers. Bloody. Soiled. They cry out my name, 'Lendalla! Our Queen! Our Lady! Your father is dead! We look to you now!'

We are almost at the gates of the citadel. The inner walls. Huge. Surely impregnable, even to Him. I am almost at their gates.

'What should we do, my Lady?'

'Die,' I cry to them. I wish I could kill them. Cut them down. I do not want to be queen. I do not want them to look to me. I am their queen. So, I wish I could kill them quickly. They would not suffer. They would be spared. That is all that is left that a good ruler can do.

I run. Leave them. Up so close in the shadow of the safety of the inner walls.

A group of soldiers. Bloody. Soiled. They are mired in filth to the plumes of their helmets. They are cut and bleeding. They hold out their swords. One of them has a baby. Holding it. He drives his sword into it. He raises his sword aloft. The baby is still alive. It screams on the blade.

They chant 'Amrath! Amrath!' They laugh.

A good ruler would have poisoned the city's wells.

I strike out at them. There is nothing else. The city is burning. The city is dying. I should have tried to save my people. I should have tried, even if I knew I would fail. Five of them. And I am alone. I have no sword. I strike out at them with my hands. I do not want to die. I want to go on living. Even for a few moments. But there is nothing else left now. Dying. Giving in to death.

WHITE LIGHT. MAGE fire.

I am blind and I am dumb and I am alight with fire, and it is all my world. Black fire. White fire. Every part of me burns.

The soldiers I am fighting fall dying. I fall with them. Burning, burning, burning in pain. Pain everywhere. Pain like water. Bathing in fire. Pain everywhere, drowning me. I burn. I burn.

The mage Kestel. Semserest's friend, Semserest's rival, Semserest's lover. She is burning the soldiers who are killing me. She is killing me. Defending the citadel. Defending our people. Killing me. Letting me die.

The enemy soldiers are dying. Kestel, my friend, you are winning! I think. There is so much pain. But I am dying, and they are dying, and there are five of them, and that is five fewer soldiers in the army of Amrath.

And that is all there is left now. To kill as we die. To hope that as we die we take them to their death.

I don't want to die.

Pain. Burning. My body. Burning.

Five soldiers of His army, dying.

My death is worth that.

White light. White fire. Darkness.

I burn. I burn. I burn.

The city is falling. Tereen, with her white marble walls, her silver gates, her silver towers. She falls. She burns. She is gone from the face of the earth. Her people murdered. Her towers broken. Her walls breeched. We wove silk cloth and bred fast horses. We worked gold and jewels, we fished for river-pearls, we mined lead and tin. Our fields were rich with wheat and barley. We worshipped the gods with kindness. All my life, I was trained to be her queen.

White light. White fire. Burning. The enemy soldiers burn and die. More come running. More and more, like insects. A flood. A plague-tide. The gates of the citadel are shattered. The inner walls run with blood.

Kestel screams. Her body breaks open. Shattered fragments like the gates. A thing like a man towering over her. His sword is blue with fire. His face is empty. His face is an empty grave.

Amrath.

He does not need to strike her. He looks at her and she is destroyed. Her body claws itself open. She dies before Him. Worship. Her body tears itself apart for Him, and she dies.

The city is burning. The city is dying. Amrath strides through it. Huge and terrible. A man not a man. God. Death. The houses fall in ruins. The ground gives way. At His glance, the flesh is ripped from our bones. The flames leap around Him. White. Green. Blue. Black.

I am burning. I lie in his fire. Death running, pouring, tearing over me. White light. White fire.

Darkness.

End.

The city burns.

The walls are falling.
There is nothing left.
No life.
No living.
End.
End.
End.

VALKYRIE RAIN

DYRK ASHTON

A short story from the world of Paternus

WE APPEARED IN the sky. Released by Hugin, the Raven, to rain down upon our foe. For a moment, we hung there, our armor reflecting the sunlight, gleaming stars of war. We continued the song to victory we'd begun before the "slip" from our world to Midgard, the world of the humans, but our voices faded.

The Vigrid Plain lay beneath us, vast and wide as the eye could see. Horizon to horizon, it seethed with the largest armies this or any world had ever seen. Comprised of every foul creature we knew, and some we did not. Monsters, hideous and huge, men and beasts, gods and devils of every kind. The sons of Múspell, the multitude of Surtr, master of our enemy, against all the assembled forces of the All-father.

Light and darkness played a shifting patchwork upon the land. The frozen tundra quaked and cracked, spewing magma and steam. Fields burned with flames that reached the sky. Whirlwinds of stone and pestilence laid waste to thousands. Conjured storms struck lightning into the throngs. In the far distance, a bright, blinking flash produced a column of cloud that billowed at the top, a mushroom-shaped mountain of smoke.

The icy wind that raked me as we fell toward the field of battle affected me not. Dropping from this height caused me no qualm. But for a moment, I was daunted and awed. Though I was not afraid.

WE'D FOUGHT NUMEROUS battles in that war. For two thousand years it had raged. But the enemy was cunning. They would appear from other worlds to slaughter, then vanish. They spread plague. They called to treat only to ambush and massacre without shame or honor. Now word had come that all of them had mustered.

Our allies were already fighting, we were told, but they were outnumbered. So, Odin had come for us. Heimdall had blown his horn. We gathered on the Bifrost Plain, eager, armored and armed.

Some had been calling this war the Second Holocaust. I did not know it then, but the battle we were about to join would be known as Ragnarök, and the Vigrid Plain upon which it was waged, Megiddo. This was Armageddon. And it already happened. I was there.

Some claimed it would be our end. The end of the world itself. *So be it*, I'd thought as I beat my sword against my shield. As we all did while the horn blew and the people chanted and the World Tree sang. If we were to perish, we'd take our adversaries with us. Every one of them, if we could. And it would be a glorious death worthy of story and verse.

I am Pruor, daughter of Sif, herself a daughter of Odin, the All-father.

My father was Thor, son of Odin and the Vanir giantess Jörd. I know no fear. I was made for war. Bred for it. Trained since my earliest memory. All of us had been. Death was our reason for living. Bestowing it upon others and claiming it for ourselves in combat. We were the Aesir of Asgard. The elite force to which I belonged, the Valkyries—Freyja's warriors. We were strong. We were proud. We were cruel. And we were coming.

NOW WE HAD arrived.

We overcame our initial shock and let go of each other's hands, held to facilitate the transfer between words. We drew our weapons and cried the cry of the Valkyries.

We fell through a murky haze, the rumble and crash of battle growing louder below, then ripped free to see a gaping chasm beneath us. Enormous, with edges like jagged teeth, and deep beyond sight. This was what we'd been brought to. A trap. We watched, helpless as much of our host disappeared into the abyss and others scrabbled at the edges only to be driven in by the spears of forces waiting along either side of the gorge.

Freyja, armored in white, her golden cape spread like wings, called out ancient words, and we were pushed by a powerful wind. I was not diverted sufficiently, however, and continued to plummet toward the yawning maw of earth. My nearest sister-Valkyrie, Róta, spun in the air and kicked me in the chest with both feet. The force was just enough. I landed on my back at the lip—while she plunged into the rift without a sound. I'd never liked Róta. We were all conceited and mean, it's true, but she'd been the worst agitator among us. I was stunned by her selflessness, but I shouldn't have been. She was a Valkyrie. Just like me. She'd just thought more quickly than I had. I vowed not to let her sacrifice go to waste.

I rolled from the edge, striking with sword and shield, chopping legs from under feral men, vulgar Blues, and rival Firstborn as well. The remaining Valkyries had landed around me, some on their feet, others directly on the enemy, already killing with efficiency and speed. I leapt up as the chasm was closing, trapping all whom it had claimed.

Just before it slammed shut, trembling the earth, Sleipnir, Odin's steed, came rocketing out on his great wings, Odin clinging to one back leg. We cheered as the All-father swung onto Sleipnir's back. He roared in rage, eyes glaring red, and they flew off into the smoke and dust of battle.

We had been betrayed. And there was only one who would do such a thing. I cast my eyes about but saw none of the second force of Aesir, which contained Loki and was to be slipped at the same time as the rest of us. Of course, it was him. And somehow, he'd convinced Hugin to do his bidding and release us above this chasm. Most of our force was gone before our battle had even begun.

I worried the greatest of the Aesir had fallen, but then I caught sight of colossal Freyr, riding on the back of his brother, Gullinbursti the Boar. And there was Heimdall, and Týr, and I thanked Sun and Moon and the World Tree, for I saw Thor, my father, bash in the helmeted head of a giant with his mighty warhammer, Mjölnir, and by his side were my half-brothers, his sons Módi and Magni.

But the fell voice of Surtr fouled the air, and we were cut off from them by a strafing line of flame that trenched the ground between us, burning hot enough to melt the earth.

At the call of Freyja, we regrouped just as a flock of shrieking wampyr descended. We took up our bows in unison and fired in rapid succession. Not one arrow missed its mark. In moments, the wampyr were done, lifeless in the dirt or flopping in the throes of death. We shouldered our bows, retrieved our blades, and advanced in formation with tactics we'd drilled a thousand times and more. Our martial skills were second to none and our armor and arms had been forged by Völundr, also known as Dvalinn. They were nearly indestructible, capable of harming even the eldest of our foe. The wings on our helmets were as knives, and we had blades at our elbows, knees, and heels.

Mighty warriors fell before us. But they came in greater numbers, including enemy Firstborn, older and stronger than we were, with armor and blades of equal quality. My shield was shattered so I drew my dagger to accompany my sword. Our ranks were thinned, and those who remained were separated, reduced to melee fighting. It no longer became an attack on our part, but simply a matter of survival.

I recall being struck by a powerful wind as Jörmungandr, the Wyrm, appeared before me, crushing scores beneath his massive, snake-like bulk. Loki rode upon his neck, with Hugin perched at his shoulder. And behind them came the host of Niflheim, the ghoulish legions of Hel. Jörmungandr spat his venom over a force of our allies, melting the flesh from their bones, then crashed off through the multitude, seeking other of the Aesir.

I spied Hugin in flight and put an arrow through his breast. He tumbled and slipped away. I gave chase after Loki's host the best I could but lost them in the mayhem and darkness.

As I battled on, I found fewer and fewer of those who fought for Odin. I know not when it happened, but I found myself alone, blinded by smoke and fumes, and even for me, fatigue began to set in and my mind began to fog. But I am Aesir, and more, I am Valkyrie. I kept fighting. Kill after kill, climbing over heaps of bodies and, sometimes, out from under them. This was not war. This was chaos incarnate. And we were losing.

I lost all sense of time. I knew only fury and blood and my own heartbeat. Just my heartbeat and I, my training and the fight. Parry, thrust, parry, cut, roll from the steps of giants, leap from the slash of sword and scythe, parry, thrust and cut. I only saw what was in front of my face, comprehended only the present. No future, no past. Just killing. Just now. And now. And now.

I had no knowledge of what was happening on other fronts of the battle. I did not see my father fall after smashing the skull of Jörmungandr, or Heimdall slay Loki at the cost of his own life. I was not there when Freyr was felled by a single stroke of Surtr's blade, when Týr and the demon-hound Garm took each other's lives, or when Fenrir swallowed Odin whole, and Vidar, rash and bold to a fault, seized Fenrir's jaw and tore his face apart.

I just fought on, alone in the fog and darkness. My sword lost, I killed with my hands, my teeth and my broken knife, shrieking in rage and madness.

How long this went on, I did not know, because the next thing I remembered was both my brothers, Módi and Magni, defending themselves from me with ruined shields and screaming to bring me to my senses. Only then did I see the sun rising through white mist and hear the sound of a horn of Asgard and the screech of the Falcon high on the air. The sounds of victory.

They led me through quagmires of gore, over piles of corpses, around dead and mountainous beasts of rotting flesh, to a high steppe where the survivors gathered. There Odin stood, his spear sizzling in his hands. He had not died, of course, regardless what the stories say.

Among those assembled were members of renowned pantheons from this and other worlds, all of whom I knew, at least by name. Even then they were legend. The oldest living of Firstborn, Odin's children, fathered by him under different names and in a variety of guises throughout the history of the worlds. They were the brothers and sisters of the Vanir of Asgard, and like them, they came in all shapes and sizes of half-man and half-beast. Although they were covered in mud, offal, and blood, their armor shredded or lost, they were magnificent nonetheless. But there were so few left. Untold millions had died in that war. At least a million in the last battle alone. Most of the Firstborn were gone.

And of the hundred thousand Aesir who'd gathered on the Bifrost Plain, only twelve survived. Seven men and five women, including myself.

But humankind was saved and freedom had been secured. Surtr had fled through worlds untraceable, along with a small band of his followers. Others of the enemy had scattered. Most were destroyed.

VALKYRIE RAIN

I was hailed a heroine of the battle, told I'd saved the lives of countless humans and Firstborn alike, and even Freyja herself. Odin congratulated me and my Aesir kin, taking us by the shoulders, kissing our foreheads, and granting us the right to live and roam where we wished, even there on Midgard, among the humans. And so we did.

But over the millennia, we grew arrogant, querulous, petulant, and cruel. Even more than we'd always been. We stole the names of prominent Firstborn long dead, bickered amongst ourselves, and manipulated entire human populations with brutality and deceit. The elder Firstborn began to look down upon us. They called us the *petit gods*. But we did not care, possessed as we were by our own hubris. Then, four thousand years ago, Odin stripped us of our weapons and honor for the part we played in bringing about the Deluge. We were banished from Midgard, exiled to live out our days in Asgard, which had been rendered bereft of life other than Yggdrasil, the World Tree, by Loki's hordes and profane sorcery during that final battle of the Second Holocaust.

NOW WE HIDE in the dark, beneath the roots of Yggdrasil. Surtr has returned and come to recruit us, murder us if we refuse. But we are not without honor, no matter what Odin and the others say. We denied Surtr our loyalty and sought refuge beneath the roots of the Tree.

We have ruled nations of men from high palaces, in Mesopotamia, in Helas before it was Helas, and in the most ancient Italia. We were the Wild Hunt, the Harii, the fighting Rudras and Rudranis, the fiercest of the Marutagana. We've been revered and feared by the proto-Celts and worshipped by primitive tribes who would become the Slavs. Deep in our hearts, however, we've always been Aesir of Asgard and Valkyries, the last of our kind.

But now we know humility, and we have learned the meaning of fear. Fear we will waste away here in the earth and die a pitiful death. No weapons in our hands, no enemy but darkness and disgrace. To simply fade without fame or glory, a whimper in the night.

BUT WHAT DO I see? The roots of Yggdrasil are parting, the sunlight of Asgard slicing the dusty air. Surtr and his followers are not there, but Odin himself. And up steps a short, stooped figure, the light limning her shape in a glimmering aura. A figure I would recognize in any form, place or time.

Freyja shakes her head, tut-tuts to herself as she looks upon our huddled and filthy bodies. She speaks in the old tongue, "There is a challenge before us, children. Perhaps greater than any before." Her eyes pass from one to the other of the men, who bow their heads in deference and trepidation. She acknowledges them, "Aesir of Asgard." Then she looks over the other women and, finally, her gaze rests on me. "And my Valkyries."

Tears fill my eyes.

"Are you ready to fight?" she asks.

Love and pride swell my heart. I raise my head, as do the others. I can see they feel it, too. We are forgiven.

And, *Hel yes, we are ready to fight.*

CHATTELS

STAN NICHOLLS

*FOR GENERATIONS, THE kingdom of Lyceria maintained an uneasy peace
with its neighbours, not least the formidable Eagamar empire. But a dispute
with the adjacent nation of Chessolm brought Lyceria's fall. In laying siege to
the city state, Lyceria rashly ignored a treaty between Chessolm and the empire,
a pact that existed because the legendary Ranald Amentinus resided in the city.
Amentinus was a holy man regarded by many, including the empire's elite, as a
messiah. There was even a widespread belief that he was an actual deity. During
the battle, Amentinus died. Whether from deprivations due to the siege, or at the
hands of a Lycerian warrior, as some said, no one really knew.*

*The empire's response was savage. Lyceria was annexed and citizens re-
maining within its borders, however young or old, were massacred or enslaved.
The survivors scattered. Stateless, branded outlaws, all other lands were barred*

from sheltering them. Lycerian became a byword for outcast, criminal, god killer.

The aftermath was a succession of wars. An incessant, merciless struggle between Eagamar and Lyceria's descendants that drew in other states as alliances were forged and broken.

After decades of chaos, a group of disparate but like-minded individuals formed a union. They were healers, driven by the principle of mercy, and they called themselves the League of Resolve. The League offered aid to all, soldier or civilian, irrespective of allegiance. As its numbers grew, and its impartiality proved steadfast, the League earned a measure of grudging tolerance.

Deras Minshal, a Lycerian, is a League overseer with no great love of wars or military of any stripe. His brother, Goran, is a fighter in the Lycerian ranks, and their different outlook led to years of estrangement. Until Goran was brought into Deras' field hospital suffering from terrible, disfiguring burns, which Goran swore were caused by a dragon despite the creatures being regarded as mythical. Cared for by Deras, but mostly by his aide, Velda Piran, Goran slowly mended, although forced to don a mask to hide his terribly scarred features. It was Velda who was instrumental in reconciling Deras and Goran, but tension still characterised their relationship. A situation made no easier as an incongruous romantic bond grew between warrior Goran and pacifist Velda.

When Velda was kidnapped by agents of the empire, the brothers had to work together to free her. In achieving this, Deras violated his own ethical code and killed one of the abductors. But he did persuade Goran to spare another. Goran's assertion that this constituted "Two miracles in one day" did little to assuage Deras' guilt at taking a life.

Nor did knowing that one death was of little significance in a world where conflict and slaughter held sway.

THEY STARTED TO see bodies before they reached their destination.

Men, women, and children were scattered in their path, and on either side of the broad trail, sprawled in the grotesque postures of death. Parties were sent forward to check for any who might be wounded and to clear away the rest. They found none living.

'Looks like they were cut down as they fled,' Goran remarked, 'and somebody made a thorough job of it.' It was a straightforward assessment, apparently devoid of much in the way of empathy. Though given his leather mask, it was difficult to tell.

Deras merely nodded. He had seen many atrocities serving with the League and thought himself impervious to shock and outrage. Not for the first time, he was wrong.

Velda, riding alongside them, looked as distraught as Deras felt. She exchanged a glance with Goran, but whatever passed between them remained the secret province of lovers.

Apart from the trio on horseback, the convoy consisted of upward of a score of wagons, each sporting the League's ensign; a triangle in a circle, green against a white background. And now, with corpses heaped ever higher on the road, they were crawling along.

'I was a little surprised that you came with us today, brother,' Deras remarked as they carefully navigated the carnage.

'Why?' Goran replied.

'Shouldn't you have rejoined your unit by now?'

'Anybody'd think you wanted rid of me.'

'It's not that. It's just—'

'General Dunisten's been charitable. He said I could stay with the League as long as I needed to.'

'We can't do anything more for your wounds. There's no reason for you to stay.'

'I think there is.' Goran looked to Velda. Again, they silently shared something Deras couldn't read.

'Could there be another motive for you sticking around?' he said.

'*Motive?*' Goran came back testily. 'That's a hell of a word to use. What'd you mean?'

'Well, it might suit your commander to have someone in our ranks to—...'

'Spy on you? That's bullshit, Deras, and you know it. If you think the League's that important, you're deluded.'

'I know there are those who don't like what we do.'

'And you number me as one of them?'

'The League's in a risky position, always has been. We have to walk a line that at times isn't clear, and we have to placate a lot of powers. If anything happened that might damage the League's reputation and it got out—'

'Like you killing a man?'

For a heartbeat, the remark rendered Deras speechless. 'You know that was—'

'Necessary, yes. But don't worry, I won't tell on you.'

'You've got a nerve criticising me when you've no end of blood on your own hands.'

'Now you're trying to deflect the blame. Anyway, I'm not criticising you. I think what you did was right.'

'I don't want your approval. Not for a deed like that.'

'You ended a bandit's worthless life and saved Velda. I reckon that's something to be pleased about.'

'It's not the way to solve problems. It's not...right.'

'It worked, didn't it?'

'The answer's not always the edge of a sword.'

'It was for that bandit. What else could you have done? Sweet talk him?'

'Let me spell this out, Goran. I don't want to walk your path. That leads to the kind of butchery we've got here.'

'I don't claim to be virtuous, and I've killed my share,' he swept a hand at the slaughter they were weaving through , 'but never like *this*.'

'Do you think you two could stop squabbling long enough for us to do our job?' Velda asked. She pointed.

The fortress they were heading for was coming into view. Its white stone walls were blackened by fire and breached in several places. The huge, ironclad gates were flattened. Plumes of acrid smoke still rose days after the fall.

'Looks like the empire threw everything at the place,' Goran said, his clash with Deras forgotten for the moment. 'What was the setup here? Nobody's told me."

His brother was having a harder time overlooking what had been said, but duty kicked in. 'This was a refuge for civilians, not an army post. That's borne out by how few soldiers' bodies we've seen. It was defended, but lightly. 'Cos who's going to attack a refugee sanctuary?'

'So, there was no military objective?'

'None. It's just the empire's way of cowing the people. Terror, plain and simple.'

The League's healers were climbing down from the wagons to search for survivors. As they fanned out, a party of around twenty warriors came into view. Their individual, non-regulation style of dress and discipline marked them out, as well as the bows and quivers each carried. Sight of their leader dispelled any doubts. Giant in stature, with a mop of crimson hair and a generous beard, Gled Brackenstall was easily recognised.

Greetings exchanged, Deras asked, 'Why are you here?'

'In case any of the empire bastards who did this are still around,' Brackenstall replied.

'You're here officially?'

'Sort of.'

'That thing about your band being an autonomous unit in the Lycerian army,' Goran said. 'You really dwell on the autonomous bit, don't you?'

They grinned.

'However you're here, we appreciate it,' Deras added.

'I think me and the band should go in first,' Goran suggested, 'and your healers can follow. But stay alert. Who knows what we might find in there.'

IN THE EVENT a few wounded were found among the many dead within the rambling fortress, Deras agreed, but there was no sign of empire troops.

Deras, Velda and Goran rummaged through one of the buildings in the fortresses' inner courtyard when Deras' young trainee, Ismey Cleam, came running for them.

'Master Deras! *Master Deras!*'

'What is it, Ismey?'

'In a...storeroom,' he panted, catching his breath, 'over on...other side.' He vaguely indicated the way he'd come with a flailing hand.

'*What* is?' Goran demanded gruffly.

'I can hear something in there. Maybe somebody buried, maybe... something else. But there's so much debris I couldn't—'

'Let's go,' Deras said.

They hurried over to what appeared to have been a storeroom before falling masonry had added to the jumble. Standing silently for a moment, they heard nothing.

'Could you have been mistaken, Ismey?' Velda wondered. 'Perhaps it was rats or—'

'*Listen!*' Goran hissed.

Deras said, 'I don't hear—'

'*Ssshhh!*'

There was a sound. A tiny rustle of moving wreckage and sliding rubble.

'It's coming from over there,' Goran decided.

They crunched their way towards a mountain of broken stone and wood.

'We're here to help!' Deras shouted. 'If you're trapped, take heart! We'll have you out soon!'

They listened for a response, but none came.

Several more League members, and a couple of the archer band, were called in to help shift the clutter. Eventually, they cleared down to a large piece of timber. Heaving it aside, they revealed two crouching figures: a young woman and a girl of five or six years. Both seemed terrified. They were dirty and exhausted, and the child's grimy cheeks were tear-stained. The woman held a knife and looked ready to use it, though her hand trembled.

The League healers in their grey robes, some hooded, archers dressed like outlaws and, above all, Goran's black mask and scarred arms were enough in themselves to frighten the pair.

Deras tried to calm the situation. 'We're not your enemies. We're the League of Resolve. We want to help you.'

The woman looked unconvinced.

'You won't need that,' Goran said, nodding at the knife.

'I think I might.' Her voice was hoarse, weary.

In a move too fast for any of them to follow or anticipate, Goran snatched the knife. Stunned, the woman pulled the child closer and shielded her as best she could, bracing herself for the expected retribution.

Goran stared at her for a moment. 'Here,' he said, handing back the knife.

She regarded it, perplexed, before gingerly accepting.

'What are you *doing*, Goran?' Deras objected.

'She has a right to defend herself. I reckon they've been through enough. Notice their arms?'

The woman and child had both been branded, and the child's brand was fresh enough not to have properly healed.

'So, you're slaves,' Deras said.

The woman slowly nodded.

'We oppose slavery,' he gently assured her. 'As far as we're concerned, you're free.'

'You don't understand,' the woman said. 'My...master won't let us go so easily.'

'Was he here, too?' Goran asked. 'Or did you get away before the siege?'

'He was here, along with some of his gang.'

'They're probably dead then.'

'I won't believe that until I see his body.'

'Maybe you'll have that pleasure. Either way, you're safe with us.'

'I wish I could believe that, too. You don't know what he's like.'

'Are you a Casimarian?' Velda said.

'Yes. How did you know?'

'Our people have certain similarities in appearance.'

'You're from Casimar?'

'Isn't it obvious?' Velda smiled. 'My name's Velda. What's yours?'

The woman seemed reassured by the connection, however tenuous. 'I'm Taryian, and this is my daughter, Kahlar.'

'And this slaver...?'

'Lusnaw.' She almost spat the name.

'Any idea where he's from?'

'Hell, I think.'

'Well, hopefully he's gone back there. I imagine you got away from him due to the siege?'

'In the chaos, yes. And I stole this from him.' She still clutched the knife, but no longer brandished it. 'I swore I'd use it on us rather than be recaptured. And Lusnaw won't give up trying to find us, believe me.'

'Why should he run the risk to regain one slave when there are plenty of others for the taking?'

'It's not me so much...' She sighed. 'The fact is, he sired Kahlar.' She glanced at the child and chose her words carefully, almost whispering. 'Not with my consent, you understand. But, however she came into the world, I couldn't love her more.'

'Of course,' Velda said.

'Lusnaw won't let her go. He wants a dynasty, and he sees Kahlar as a way of achieving it. I'm sure he has no feelings for her beyond that.'

'You're both under our protection now, Taryian.' Velda rose and held out a hand to her. 'Come on, let's get you two cleaned up.'

WITH SUCH WOUNDED as there were being tended, most of the rest of the day was given over to gathering dead for the funeral pyres. As night fell, the fires lit the entire area, issuing a reek that had many covering mouths and noses with strips of cloth.

Wearied by hours on duty, Deras left the tents of the League's field hospital to take the air, fetid as it was. He had a water bottle to his lips when he noticed something. Figures, four or five of them, outlined by the flames a short distance away. They were running. With the initial urgency over and most of the healers employed in feeding the pyres, running wasn't the norm.

He followed the group's progress as they threw their shadows against the fortresses' massive wall. Then he noticed two figures chasing them. One had the unmistakable physique of Gled Brackenstall. Deras figured that Goran was the other. He also realised that the pursued and the pursuers were headed his way.

The fleeing group were caught by the chasers a stone's throw short of him. There was no mild surrender. The intruders turned on Goran and Brackenstall and set about them.

Goran's sword took down one instantly, and he was swift enough to inflict a wound on another. For all his bulk, Gled was no less agile, cracking a skull with a mighty swing of his cudgel. As the fight boiled, one of the figures broke away. He ran towards Deras who, standing in shadow, wasn't easily seen.

The running man, well clear of the fight, stumbled and fell headlong. The sword he carried flew from his hand, bounced and landed a few paces from Deras. The healer quickly stooped and grabbed it. The fallen man was back on his feet, staring at the levelled blade. He was sweat-sheened, and his long black hair hung lankly.

'Don't move,' Deras said. 'Who are you?'

'Just somebody who wants his property back.'

'From that, I'm betting you're Lusnaw.'

'What if I am?'

'Slavery's not tolerated in these parts.'

'The empire says what I'm doing's legal.'

'What's common in Eagamar isn't always welcome elsewhere.'

'I just want what's lawfully mine.'

'Forget laws. What sticks in my craw is you thinking that *owning* somebody's your right.'

'You catching me or lecturing me?' There was a kind of languid insolence in his tone. He lifted a hand.

Deras took a step nearer and raised the sword.

'Steady.' Lusnaw scratched his head. 'So, what happens now?'

It struck Deras that he was asking whether he was going to live or die. He wondered if Lusnaw knew about the League's pacifist code and that death by the hand of a member was an unlikely outcome. *Unless the League member happens to be me,* he thought, remembering vividly the last time he pointed a blade at a man. There was no way he was going to repeat the outcome of that.

'You're scum,' he told the slaver. 'Get it through your head that it's not good, it's not moral, if you like, to *own* people. You don't own Taryian and Kahlar, and if you push the case, you'll regret it. You deserve something harsh for what you do. Show your face here again and you'll get it. Now go.'

Lusnaw didn't immediately move, and he wore a disbelieving expression. When he began to run, Deras caught a look of cocky triumph on his face.

As Lusnaw dashed into the darkness Goran yelled, *'Deras!'*

He and Gled had bettered the other slavers and were hurrying his way.

'If that's who I think it was, what the *hell* did you think you were doing?' Goran demanded furiously.

'Yes, it was Lusnaw. I warned him off.'

'Warned him off? You had him at your mercy! You should have killed him, man!'

'You know how I feel about that.'

'Why didn't you hold him for us to do the job then? Oh no, of course you couldn't do that, could you? My precious brother has his humanitarian feelings to take into account.'

'We're never going to agree on this.'

'You're damn right we're not! But if I get my hands on that slaver, I won't be dealing with him the way you would!' He turned his back and left with a doleful Gled in tow.

Deras was not in a jovial mood when he got back to his tent. Shortly, Velda arrived.

'You look troubled,' she said.

'You could say that.'

'What's happened?'

He told her.

'That is not going to make Goran happy,' Velda admitted, 'but you did the right thing by your own lights.'

'By yours, too, I hope.'

'Yes. Goran may be…important to me, but we see the world differently in some ways.'

He raised an eyebrow but let it go. 'How are Taryian and Kahlar?'

'Cuts and bruises tended, bathed and sleeping now. And I'd better get back to them. We're in the next tent, by the way.'

Deras thought about getting some sleep. Before he could do anything about it, Velda came back. She was pale.

'Come,' she said. *'Quickly.'*

In the adjoining tent, Lusnaw lay dead. The knife Taryian had stolen jutted from his back. A long vertical slash in the back of the tent was big enough for a man to get through. There was no sign of Taryian or Kahlar.

Goran arrived, ready to carry on the argument with Deras until he saw the slaver's body. 'So, he got his due after all. No point asking if you did this, Deras. And our guests have gone, I see. Well, good for them.'

'Shouldn't we search for them?' Deras said.

'Let `em be,' Goran told him. 'Taryian's shown she can defend herself, so they stand a chance.'

'We could have prevented this.'

'*You* could have prevented it, Deras, if you'd dealt with this piece of shit when you had the chance. Instead, you left it to a woman and child. How does that feel?'

Deras didn't speak for a moment, then said, 'It feels like a weight.'

And the feeling never really went away.

Chattels *is the latest in an occasional series of stories featuring the League of Resolve. The first, eponymous story appeared in* Legends, *edited by Ian Whates (NewCon Press, 2013).*

THE STORM

MILES CAMERON

THE ENGINEER WAS as tired as everyone else, and she wasn't inclined to listen.

'Sword, get your precious knights and take me that bastion. Today. I don't care how you do it or how many you lose.' The aristocrat wore only a frilled shirt and breeches, and she looked like an unkempt fop.

Ser Ippeas, by contrast, stood in the command tent in full armour; cuirass, tassets, leg armour, heavy shoulders, arms, and long-cuffed, fingered gauntlets that hid the dirt under his nails the way the cuirass hid the sand-scarring on his back.

The heavy linen canvas tent moved slowly in the fitful breeze. None of the breeze reached Ippeas at all. The Souliote officers wore light kaf-thans; the militia officers dressed casually, in the mix of local dress, hunting clothes from home and scraps of uniform that were the fashion for officers serving in the desert.

Ippeas forgave them. None of them were professionals, and no one had expected the siege to go on this long. He breathed carefully, and tried to stand like a steel statue, the sweat running invisibly down his body, down his legs under the cuisses, into the light shoes he wore under his steel sabatons. His stockings were soaked through, as wet as if he had crossed a stream. His armour would be rusting from the inside. It would be his penance to clean it. Penance for anger.

The other officers looked away. Their deliberate inattention said as clearly as words that they knew the engineer was giving a bad order, but they weren't the ones concerned.

Ippeas rested his arms on the quillons of his four-foot sword, setting the iron-capped point of the scabbard carefully on the Vicar's carpet. The sword wasn't a statement—or perhaps it was—but the truth was, he needed the support of the sword to remain standing at attention in armour after a night in the trenches. He took a deep breath. 'The breach is practicable, I agree.'

'So kind of you. You're a qualified engineer, Sword?' The engineer didn't sneer, but she made a face to the Vicar.

The Vicar ignored the expression. 'Why the *hesitation*, Sword?'

Not the place for anger. He spoke quietly, modestly. His people's lives depended on his not showing temper.

'The breach is fifty stades from the head of the approach. The approach is so ill-dug that I was fired on while crawling its length. The garrison has a culverin sighted at the head of the sap. My brothers will receive fire while they crawl down the approach. They will receive a load of scattershot in their faces as they rise for the assault. The survivors will have to run fifty stades across broken ground just to reach the foot of the breach.' His voice rose a little at the end and he clamped down. He found speaking to so many ranking officers not just possible, but easy.

It was like fighting. The waiting was worse than the moment of killing.

The Vicar swung his attention from the engineer to the knight. 'You went and examined the approach *in person?*' he asked.

Of course. Ippeas wanted to say it, wanted to let his scorn show.

But war was politics, just as faith was politics. Ippeas let his anger boil away. He pushed it aside with a brief meditation on the moment of Sophia's birth among men. He played the scene in his mind until anger was gone and only calm remained. The meditation, his most valued, took only the fraction of a breath to practice.

'Yes,' he answered.

The vicar swung indecisively to his engineer. 'Great Sword Ippeas is not a novice on his first caravan, Engineer. Perhaps the two of you can visit the sap in person and determine a new course of action.'

The engineer shook her head. 'Perhaps the great sword can plan the rest of the siege, as well,' she snapped. 'That bastion must fall today, Eminence. I have ten, or at most, twelve days until the rains come. Twelve days, or our summer and all our dead are for naught.' She shrugged. 'I have said all this before.' She looked tired and, suddenly, the Sword wondered if he'd misjudged the woman.

The engineer looked at the Vicar. 'You know what's at stake,' she said quietly.

A month ago, you let the Vicar waste our time building siege lines that would stop all the legions of the Pure, Ippeas thought. *His caution and your vanity have doomed this campaign. Now you seek to spend the lives of my brothers to retrieve your schedule.* But even as his mind formed the heated thoughts, Ippeas admitted their injustice.

The Vicar looked back and forth between them, his tired eyes and slack face clear signs of his mental exhaustion. Like most of his soldiers, he felt he should never have been given so high a command. He hated conflicts among his officers, but his very weakness made room for them.

Ippeas tried to feel compassion. This war was sapping everything; his faith, his vision of the people around him.

'How do you answer the great sword's observations, Engineer?' asked the Vicar.

The engineer drew a poniard from her belt and began to use it on her nails, which were black. 'I was in those trenches last night,' she said. 'The garrison kept up a constant fire, and we lost pioneers. The rest became…skittish.'

She glanced at Ippeas, searching for something, and then she shrugged and went back to her nails. 'The approach trench is not the best. But it can be done. Your armour will protect you from the harassing fire. And, to be frank, Sword, your brothers can take the casualties to reach the breach, and then storm the bastion. You and I both know it can be done. You are our best.'

The engineer winced, waiting for his response.

The Vicar raised his hand. 'Clear my tent,' he said to his senior Centark, and the man made a hand motion. Officers scattered.

Ippeas stood and waited.

The Vicar motioned for a servant to open his camp stool, and then he sat with a groan.

'All clear,' his Centark said. 'And a cordon of lobsters to keep `em out, my lord.'

Lobsters being the elite cavalry of the imperial army.

The Vicar nodded, spat, drank some water, and spat again. 'It has to be done today. The engineer is correct. But it could be done at dusk. Engineer, you could place mortars in the second line and use them to suppress the culverin.'

Ippeas was surprised.

And yet, the old man *had* been a fine soldier before he was promoted beyond his ability. The idea was sound. It didn't change the crumbling, shallow approach trench, but it would almost certainly prevent a charge of scattershot at the moment of crisis.

'Yes. It can be done.' The engineer opened a lap desk and began to write notes with a pencil.

Ippeas reminded himself that the explosion of one of their own culverins on the second night of the siege had killed the first engineer and all his staff. That the engineer before him had been a junior second, newly minted by the Arsenal. Nerves probably caused the woman's abrasiveness.

'Tell him,' she said to the Vicar. 'He deserves to know.'

The Vicar looked at an icon of the Eagle, one of the old gods he kept to look at in the privacy of his tent. He made the old Eagle sign. Then he turned to the sword. 'Do you know why we're here?' he asked.

Ippeas stood straight, despite the sweat and the fatigue and the flies. 'I was ordered here,' he said.

The Vicar made a face. 'Do you know why we are attacking *this town?*'

Ippeas might have shrugged. 'It is an important town to the *Pure*,' he said.

The engineer nodded. 'It's not just an important town,' she said. 'This is where the corrupt crystals come from. The source of the bone plague. The scourge of our magik. We *must* take it. Now.' She looked at the Vicar, who nodded.

'Lives are at stake. Not just our own, but perhaps the whole population of Hatti and Byzas. The refugees, the whole of idea of reform. Everything we stand for.' He shrugged, and stood, and looked less like a tired, incompetent old man. 'If you like, Sword, I'll lead the sortie myself.'

Ippeas managed to stand straighter. 'That is not necessary,' he said, suddenly appalled by the weight of responsibility. 'By the Goddess, I had thought this a routine...' he almost couldn't breathe. 'I accept. I thank you, Vicar, and you, Engineer. I sought only to protect my brothers from unnecessary peril.'

The engineer glanced at him once, this time, like a conspirator, or an actor in a shared play, and then went back to drafting notes on her lap desk.

THE SUN REACHED its height, and the sands reflected the heat, so that a naked man might die in a few hours and eyes might become blind by too much staring.

Ippeas was still in his armour. His feet were almost cold from the sweat pooled in his shoes. He had climbed the rampart of the first line to examine the ground in front of the bastion from the highest point in his lines. He looked at the ground for half an hour, trying to find another solution. Across five hundred paces of open ground, crumbling walls, and blasted sand, heat-shimmers made investigation almost impossible. So did sniper fire.

Below his feet, sweating pioneers in nothing but loin cloths and sweatbands hauled four big mortars down the ramp from the first line to the second. Ordinarily, neither army worked or fought much in the full heat of the day, and this activity would tell the garrison a great deal.

Nonetheless, the mortars would help.

He leaned out of an embrasure, staring too long at the white glare, so that his eyes began to water.

'Try this, Sword,' said an aristocratic voice by him.

Ponderously, he forced himself upright and turned. The engineer was offering a farseer, a long tube with crystal lenses. Ippeas had used them in training, but had never been able to afford one. He gave the engineer a glance, looking for mockery, saw none, and took the instrument.

'It was with the first engineer's equipment,' the engineer said in a conversational voice. 'Made by the Academy. Turn this knob.' Then she leaned out over the walls and roared, 'Hey! Broxo! Watch that number two gun! That sled is *not balanced.* I don't give a *shit* how often you checked it. Load it again. Do it right!' She pulled the canteen from the strap over his shoulder and took a slug, spat, held it out to Ippeas.

Refusing water in this army was an insult, sharing it a gesture of camaraderie. Ippeas's hand barely hesitated. He spat and then drank.

The engineer curled up into the patch of shade left by the jutting fascines of the embrasure. She was not a big woman, and she fit easily in cover where Ippeas would have stood out, armour and all. 'Looking for another approach?' she asked.

Ippeas grunted. He was trying to steady the farseer and adjust it. His arms felt like lead. He needed to get his armour off, to rest before the assault. There was sand between his arming clothes and his skin. The sand abraded the skin, and he bled. The blood attracted flies.

'I wanted to try having a word with you in private, Sword. I want you to understand.' The engineer's voice said she wanted Ippeas to understand things she couldn't put into words. Political things.

Ippeas got the tube focused. He looked at the head of the sap, the dusty sand there, then the scree of rock—shale, it looked like—just beyond. No wonder the pioneers had given up.

He swept the farseer back and forth over the ground in front of the breech. Just to the left of the hole in the wall and collapsed rubble pile that led like a ramp up and into the bastion, there was a wide patch of desert grass, *raknard,* the hard, spiky leaves sticking up like arrows. The grass came up waist high. He followed the edge of the grass back towards his own lines until if petered out in the shale. The grass got within twenty paces of the breach.

A ball thudded home in the fascine by his head. Then he heard the shot.

'You've found something.' The engineer got up out of the shade next to him. 'Let's move.'

'There's desert grass growing at the base of the bastion,' Ippeas said. He handed the farseer to the engineer. They crawled to another lookout. Then, while the engineer looked, Ippeas continued, 'I can have my men put sand cloaks over their armour. We crawl up from the base of the east trench. You drop a mortar round short—right in the basin, there—to make smoke. A handful of my brothers demonstrate in the approach trench—that's where they expect us, so that's where they should see us.'

The engineer shook her head. 'They'll see you. You didn't like fifty stades of open ground, now you're crawling a hundred stades just to get to the grass.'

Ippeas pulled off a gauntlet and used his cuff, brown with dirt, to wipe sweat off his face. 'All too possible. In the hands of Sophia. But scared men keep their heads down below their walls. Or they fixate on the first enemy they see.'

The engineer was stretched full length on the parapet, heedless of snipers, farseer to her eye. Two balls struck the gabion next to her, and she didn't flinch. 'I can get my best pioneers up in the angle. They'll make you a gravel ramp and a covered entry to your line of— Well, to the way you'll crawl. I see it. Good eye.'

Ippeas couldn't resist. 'Engineering is taught in the Academy,' he said.

The engineer rolled on her back and slithered off the parapet. 'Fencing with great swords is taught at the Arsenal, but I don't claim to be an expert,' she said.

Stung, Ippeas withdrew a step. 'I meant— No, my tongue ran away with me. I apologize.'

The engineer raised an eyebrow. 'Father, I have an abusive tongue, as any of the brothers in my many schools can testify. I came up here to try and avoid open enmity with you. You seem competent. We're right on the edge, Father. Win or lose, it'll be the next few hours. If you take me this bastion, I'll take the damned city. You can have the credit.'

Ippeas wasn't used to being called *Father*. He was a priest, but none of his order would ever call him by other than his rank or his real title—Great Sword. The engineer called him Father as if he was a country prelate.

Was the aristocrat mocking him? 'I prefer you call me Ippeas,' he said. 'Ser Ippeas, if you wish to be formal.'

The engineer shot him a grin. 'I'm a Kallinikas,' she said. 'Collateral line. Distant cousins. All that crap.'

'You have the look.' Kallinikoi were one of the imperial houses. They were blond and dark-skinned, robust, given to heavy mouths and big noses. This scion lacked the size, but she had the dark skin and blonde hair. Her breasts showed in sweat through her shirt; her filthy shirt, which had a fortune in blackwork embroidery at the throat and frayed cuffs. She had a pair of pistols, in her sash like a pirate, and a heavy arming sword.

'Did you get my point about the siege?' Kallinikas asked.

Ippeas looked out over the besieged city, at the bastion standing in the bright sun with the gash of the breach spilling its walls like the intestines of a wounded animal. 'Myr Kallinikas, I will take this bastion with my brothers, or die in the attempt. At last light.'

Kallinikas shook his head. 'You Magdalenes are scary. Don't die. Just take the fucking bastion.' She paused. 'Call me Fresa. Myr Kallinikas sounds too much like we're in a fucking ballroom.'

She leaned over the parapet and motioned at a sapper. 'No,' she yelled. 'Follow the fucking rope line!' She spat. 'More water, Father?'

IPPEAS STOOD AT the head of his company. He had forty-three brothers fit for duty. They stood in their armour, their hands crossed on their sword hilts. They wore plate armour from head to toe. Every brother had a baldric holding a pouch of grenadoes, a pair of heavy pistols clipped to the strap by their hooks, and a heavy silver match-case up at the shoulder. The match-case held the slow-match to light the grenadoes. The pistols would make noise going up the breech. The heavy swords would do the work.

Every man had a sand cloak wrapped tight and secured by cords to his baldric. There was no point to throwing the thin *khatan* cloaks over their armour until they were ready to crawl. Cloaks and armour weren't friends.

Ippeas told off five brothers for the feint. He hardened his heart and chose almost at random. Almost. He didn't choose any of his best.

'Go to the base of the approach trench and wait. Then move up and down the trench. Expose yourselves as much as you can with sense, common sense, my brothers. The Goddess will not expect a display of bravura. She will expect an attention to deception. Am I clear?'

All five brothers raised their visors in salute and nodded in agreement.

He saluted them. 'Go in the name of Sophia and her Good Sister.'

'Amen,' said the whole company together, a hushed and potent sound.

They expected that he should speak. He was the sword. The priest. The word in the mouth of Sophia.

Except that he'd been in the desert for a year, had risen to command as better men died in sorties just like this one. His faith in Sophia was shaken, and his faith in his training and his army was fading. Speeches before action seemed childish.

Once he would have greeted this moment with joy.

He looked up at the company banner. It showed the Good Sister holding aloft the sword of the Sophia, with the words 'Penitence is our Glory. Glory is our Penitence.'

Once, the words had brought a chill to his spine. Now, they seemed like the thoughts of someone who had never seen a battle.

'Brothers,' he said. He probably paused too long, thinking about his brothers and what a debacle would do to him, and them. A long line of corpses stretching back across the desert to the bay where the galleons had dropped anchor when they brought the war home to the enemy.

He raised his voice. 'You know your places. You know your skill.' He looked up and down the ranks, saw Clestes and knew from his face that he had gauged the mood correctly. 'People depend on us. Let's go take the bastion. For the Good Sister.'

A growl rose from the company.

He led them into the trenches.

Dusk was falling with all the rapidity of the desert. The sky was red, full of light, but already the base of the trench was indistinct, and men tended to stumble. Looking at the western horizon, a man could *see* the approach of night.

Ippeas thought he had fifteen minutes. He looked at the heavy silver timekeeper that he had hung on his baldric. His timing was exact, but all guesswork. And having guessed, he now suffered from all the nerves of command.

The first mortar fired, seventy paces to his right. The explosion was loud, and a few grains of sand fell down the nearest trench wall. The round had dropped short, just as Ippeas had asked. A pall of smoke hung over the open ground.

'Here we go,' Ippeas said, catching the eyes of his Justicars. Thirty-eight pairs of arms fastened their *khatan*s at their throats and replaced their gauntlets. They reversed their pouches and baldrics so that the pistols and the match cases sat on their backs. Thirty-eight visors slammed shut together.

Clestes watched them and raised his hand for silence and to indicate that the brothers were ready.

Ippeas raised his own hand in the gloom and dropped it. Clestes was right behind him as he scrambled up the new-built gravel ramp and flung himself onto the sand. And then he crawled.

Crawling in armour on sand was faster than crawling without armour. The breastplate served as a sled. Hands and feet pushed, skittering like the limbs of a scorpion. Ippeas pushed on as hard as he could, his thoughts so concentrated on the timing of his movements and the orderliness of his brothers that he forgot to fear the fusillade of firelock shots that might announce that his ruse had been discovered.

He made it to the edge of the sand grass. The bastion loomed like a great black claw over his right shoulder. His breastplate was full of sand and something was biting his neck.

Clestes came right up next to him in the grass, and they crawled side by side through sharp leaves, which bent under the weight of their armour but never broke. Other, stronger brothers pulled ahead of their mates, spreading into a rough line. Every man had his place, but the order didn't require that a movement like this be disciplined.

A mortar fired behind them, and the culverin overhead answered with a roar. But the ball wasn't meant for them. It vanished into the gloom at the head of the sap and threw up a cloud of dust and debris around the approach trench they had not used.

Ippeas rolled onto his back, drew off his gauntlet, and raised the dial of his timekeeper to his eyes. The gloom was already deep, and the drift of powder smoke deepened it. And something of its impenetrable quality told him that their own magickers were practicing an illusion. He pushed the dial almost inside the eye slit of his burgonet.

Exactly on time. His breathing was labored. He was sweating out all the water he had ever drunk. He rolled back onto his breastplate and faced Clestes. Then he reached with an unguantleted hand up into his pouch for his tinder kit and struck a spark on char cloth, held the glowing ember to the slow match dangling from his shoulder.

Clestes held out his match, and Ippeas lit it, murmuring the bene-diction of fire as he passed the sacred ember, as if they were thurifers in chapel. Clestes took the fire and passed it to the brother next to him.

Ippeas unhooked the clasp of his *khatan* so that it would fall away when he rose to his feet. Then he pulled his pouch and pistols to the best position for climbing the rubble pile of the breach.

When he looked back, he saw Clestes doing the same, and beyond him, an empty field of desert grass with dozens of tiny spirals of smoke rising in the still air. The image of the smoke spirals froze in his brain, and he felt as if he was in deep meditation. Thirty-eight burning matches, their locations marked by the tiny spirals of smoke.

The mortars fired again, and then the culverin, a shriller bark now that the big gun was hot. Men were screaming in the bastion as the mortar fire grew more accurate, and a woman was screaming out in the trenches where the culverin had found at target. Darkness was minutes away.

'I hear the Sister calling me,' Ippeas said. Aloud. The words were ritual. Hiding was all very well, but the bastion was already dead. Even if the garrison awoke to their presence this instant, his brothers would carry it. They were already close enough to the breach, too close to be stopped. He was calm. He might die, but his job was done, his gamble won, and nothing remained but the will of Sophia. He stood.

Thirty-eight voices spoke together, neither hushed nor loud. 'I hear the Sister calling me.'

His hand seemed to raise of its own accord. Then they were running through the smoke.

Ippeas was the first to the angle of the defensive ditch. He slid down the angle into the ditch on his arse, collecting gravel and sand under his backplate and a host of minor abrasions that he ignored. He ran along the base of the wall, headed for the rubble ramp of the breach, looked back to find the ditch already full of his steel-clad brothers. They were readying their grenadoes. Clestes threw his high, and it went well over the wall and burst. Other brothers, the strongest, supported him.

Ippeas led the smallest men along to the base of the rubble pile and up the ruin of the basalt wall. There would almost certainly be a gun trained on the lip of the breach. Ippeas didn't plan to go straight into it. Halfway up the breach, hidden from the defenders by the outward turn of the wall, he led his handful across the rubble pile to the right, around the point of the bastion. A few hands over his head, the culverin bellowed defiance, sending its heavy stone ball into the attackers out beyond the approach trench. Four mortars fired together in return, their balls passing high overhead to land in the bastion almost together, followed by a volley of explosions and then more grenadoes from Clestes. Still, Ippeas climbed. He was directly under the embrasure of the culverin. He looked at his party below him on the face of the bastion, motioned to his junior justicar, and Dodes pulled himself up to the other side of the embrasure.

In the bastion, they could hear the grunts of the gun crew hurrying to load, the calm tones of a sergeant or officer speaking to them in Safi.

Ippeas made a motion and drew a grenadoe form his pouch. Dodes did the same. He pressed the fuse against the burning match in his match case. Ippeas matched him, gesture for gesture, so that their timing was exact. Fuses were only reliable with the will of Sophia, but men had to make the effort to gain the blessing. An apt sermon.

Ippeas risked a glance from his lit fuse to the silver forms of his brothers climbing the breech. In the dusk, they looked inhuman, and hard to see; mirrors of the sky above them. But quick. Each of his Justicars had done their duty.

Grenadoe burning away, the two of them crouched, counted with fists, and threw. Both grenadoes sailed through the embrasure to land inside the bastion. The first explosion threw sand over them where they had flattened themselves against the wall's timber reinforcement. The second was larger. A plume of sand and smoke rose on a fist of fire and drowned them in fury.

As soon as the first wash of fire was gone, Ippeas forced himself to his feet and drew his pistols. 'Magdelene!' he shouted. He was in the embrasure, he was jumping down into the bastion, he was down on his face, pain like the spread of lightning in a night sky from his right leg, and then he was up again. His pistols were empty—he had fired them—when? And he drew the greatsword. His brothers were flooding the breech, and his own party had swept the crew of the culverin away and butchered the crew of the light gun covering the lip of the breach all in the moments he had been down. He found the bearer of the company standard and roared for his knights to rally, rally at the standard.

The garrison attempted a counter-attack.

It was classic defense, the right response, but too slow and without much heart. The plate armour of the brothers brought its own terror. Their repute brought more. The counter-attack fell on the center of an ordered line.

Ippeas killed a man with the point of his sword, parried a bayonet thrust at his left-hand brother, took his great sword in both hands, and used his sword's sharp edges to slice away his opponent's fingers where they grasped his firelock. The soldier dropped the weapon, already screaming. Ippeas beheaded him on the backstroke, his head already turned, looking at his line.

The counter-attack broke, survivors fleeing into the city-ward edge of the bastion towards a low door.

Ippeas had no need to order a pursuit. Despite their armor, the sand, and months of deprivation, or perhaps because of them, the brothers were men conditioned to physical excess. They ran the garrison down, pinned them in the corner of their bastion, and butchered them. The survivors of the garrison ran through the low door at the back of the ruined bastion. A few were caught at the door, but the rest burst through, into the open ground between the bastion and the city. In the gloom, Ippeas could see a sally port set in the city wall. Open.

His heart almost stopped.

'On me!' he called. 'Follow me!'

As they emerged into the brick-lined ditch, the garrison on the city walls began to fire into their own, but the fire was sporadic, indecisive. Crossbow bolts rattled around them, and a harquebus ball shattered stone. Scattering fire.

'At them!' Ippeas called.

With a clang, one ball punched Clestes from his feet.

Ippeas wanted to scream. He felt as if he had been hit himself.

But he ran on. His company followed. They ran on to where the survivors of the garrison of the bastion pressed to enter the sally port door set low in the city wall. There was no covering fire from the walls. The embrasures next to the sally port were empty.

Now that he had made it this far, it seemed insane that he and thirty brothers would enter. *The enemy would cut them off and seize the gate behind them, kill or capture them all as trophies, and recapture the bastion.*

Ippeas thought of the trail of dead brothers that had brought them to this point, twelve days from the rains. Of the *kuria* crustals, poisoned to kill the poor.

Then there was no thought, no prayer, no meditation. He was in the knot of desperate men at the sally port. He thrust, he cut, he thrust again, pushing forward every attack. His sword was gone, in a dying man, and he had a dagger in his fist and a clubbed pistol, and then just his metal-clad fists and the dagger. Then he was through the door and up the narrow stairs on a carpet of bodies, and blow after blow landed on his armour and was turned. A pistol shot caught the comb of his helmet, and the force of it dislocated his jaw, but he pushed up another step and his latest victims fell forward onto him; he lost his balance. He fell back a step, caught himself, lost his dagger in another victim but held the body before him like a pavise. With his free hand, he fumbled a grenadoe from his pouch and kindled it with his *will*. He tossed it underhand.

He felt the blow of a weapon into the body he was wielding, and then the force of the grenadoe's explosion threw him back two steps into his brothers behind him.

They climbed over him, their boots pressing against his breastplate as they climbed. Then gauntleted hands were helping him to rise.

Ippeas followed his brothers past the top of the stair.

Dodes was first onto the landing. 'You, you, and you, up and onto the wall. Hold the wall over the gate.'

Ippeas swatted his shoulder armour, and Dodes turned, his helmeted head inhuman in the fading red light. But the justicar recognized him. 'Sword.'

'Hold the gate,' Ippeas ordered. 'Send whomever is last in line down there back, back to the mortar line. Tell them we can take the city right now.'

Dodes saluted.

THE STORM

'The rest of you, on me. Pistols loaded. Justicars, count heads and tell me who's gone. Share out your grenadoes. Everyone needs at least one.' ·Above them, where Dodes had led the first three brothers, there was a scream and the sound of fighting.

Chaerax—not a justicar, but a very steady brother—appeared from the stone steps. 'Clestes was hit. He's down but watching the gate. My mess has all its grenadoes.'

'You're with me, then. Everyone loaded? Brothers, I hear the Sister calling.'

Then they pushed through the door, off the wall, and into the town.

There were soldiers in the street, with firelocks. They were ready for the attack, and yet not ready, green soldiers with no experience of close fighting. Ippeas was the first through the door in the wall, and a harquebus ball rang on his gorget, pushed through it, and was stopped by his breastplate. He himself was punched to the ground as if by the hand of a giant, but his brothers ran over him—again.

He tried to breathe, failed, tried harder. Managed to lift a readied pistol and fire it at the shape of a firelock man across the street. Drew part of a breath. His chest was on fire. Broken ribs, and his breastplate dented so that the ribs couldn't move back into position.

Farther away, up the cobbled street that led to the citadel, the sounds of panic began. Screams.

The pain was rising. Ippeas fought it with all the tools he had—meditation, endurance, prayer. None was sufficient. He clawed at his gorget, couldn't make his hands work to open the buckles. Couldn't even shake the gauntlets from his wrists.

His brothers were all past him now, flooding out into the street. The firelock men were dead or broken. Mostly dead.

He lay in torment.

Then fingers popped his burgonet clear of the gorget and opened the gorget. He felt the pressure ease on his breastplate as his eyes grew dim.

Then his vision tunneled. It all looked a long way away.

He felt the breastplate go, the soft release as the ribs were allowed to float back, the flood of pain, and then the ease. He could breathe. His peripheral vision began to return, and then his hearing.

The first thing he saw clearly was the engineer, Kallinikas, stepping through the door above him. Behind him was a Souliote officer, another woman.

'You got my message,' he managed.

'I didn't need an engraved invitation to your party,' Kallinikas said with a bow. She had a savage smile, and her arming sword was red. 'You going to live?'

Brother Lineas, one of the hospital brothers who served in the ranks, stood over him. 'He's been hit twice. I am ordering him from this combat.'

Kallinikas rubbed her chin, watching the Souliotes spill out the door and begin forming by tent groups and then by companies.

Kallinikas knelt down. 'I think we can do it. Will your brothers obey me?'

Ippeas pulled himself to his feat, despite a frown from the hospital brother. 'They will' he croaked. 'Lineas, get Dodes off the wall. Myr Kallinikas, please send two tents and an officer to relieve them.'

Justicar Dodes appeared. He was covered in blood. He looked as if he had bathed in it. 'Great Sword?'

'The hospital brother orders me from the field. I cede command to you and ask that you obey the engineer. Kallinikas.' Ippeas was losing any ability to function.

Dodes touched his visor in obedience. He immediately faced Kallinikos. 'Your orders?'

Now a flood of soldiers were coming up the corpse-choked steps as fast as they could; Byzas militia, and then lobsters on foot, men and women in black armour with heavy swords. They formed across the street and vanished into the town.

Something was on fire.

Ippeas couldn't go down the steps. The tide of soldiers was rising, like sand in an hour glass, and then he began to fall. He caught the stone of the wall, and there was a hand under his armpit.

It was the Vicar.

A voice said, 'My lord, we have taken the sea gate,' and then he was being carried. Carried out along the glacis, out past the bastion, and a long column of soldiers was waiting; a troop of City cavalry sat on horses, watching.

The city was falling. He could hear the screams, and he tried to pray for them, even those who served the Pure.

Because a city taken by storm was hell on earth. And hell had come to Antaikeos.

SHORTBLADE

BRANDON DRAGA

O'DEN STOOD OPPOSITE his opponent. The visor on his helmet was down, obscuring his periphery, but in that moment, his task was singular. His right hand gripped his trusted sword the way his father had always taught him. He took the plough stance, placing his right foot forward, holding the buckler up in his left hand to sit proudly next to his weapon.

Without allowing his opponent even a breath, O'den pushed off his right foot and sprung forward, pulling his sword arm back and dropping it. He could see his opponent drop their buckler and await the thrust. With a wide grin hidden beneath his helmet, O'den quickly feinted, swinging his sword arm up and stabbing downward, right where a chink in the armor would leave the spot between the neck and collarbone exposed.

The strike connected with ease, causing the ramshackle stack of buckets to collapse from the relatively humanoid-looking facsimile in which they had been placed. O'den immediately stepped away from his fallen foe and resumed the plough stance, at the ready should the stack reassemble.

Behind him, he could hear snickering. The other junior guards were spying on him again.

"Saving the town again, Overhill?" Bannick's voice was shrill, nasally, and insufferable, like what might have happened if an arcanist were able to cast a spell on a stoat that gave it a voice. O'den turned to face his tormentor and the other two cronies. To his credit, Bannick's voice lent itself well to his face, beady eyes and weaselish sneer mocking O'den from behind a slender, upturned nose. To either side of Bannick were Kennor and Ramin. If Bannick was a stoat, Kennor was a burly badger, and Ramin a fish of some kind. O'den didn't know fish as well as he knew beasts, but he was certain there was one as ugly as Ramin.

"You three are supposed to be off this shift today." O'den removed his helmet and stared at each of them, trying to speak with an authority he knew he didn't have over them.

"And you're supposed to be cleaning this stable, not playing make-believe," Kennor retorted.

"I finished cleaning an hour ago!" O'den shot back. "And I'm not playing, I'm training." He didn't know why he bothered saying anything. They were doing it on purpose, and it wasn't the first time.

Bannick laughed. "Training. Of course, how stupid of me! I forgot we were in the presence of Sir Shortblade, the great halfling knight!" Each of the bullies dipped an exaggerated bow.

O'den felt his grip change on his guards' baton, clenching it as though it would fly from his hand otherwise. He struggled to not crack all three of them across the backs of their heads, knowing full well that the reprimand for undue use of force was not worth the fleeting satisfaction it would bring. "Look, would you three just crawl back under your rocks until you need to frighten children in the streets again?"

"Or what?" Ramin's flat, rotund face looked up with the smug satisfaction of someone too stupid to realize they'd just been insulted. "Are you gonna go tell your daddy on us?"

"I won't need to." O'den scowled. "You're all likely to get caught by the captain being useless on *his* time, and then you'll deal with him anyway."

"Aww, look at you, calling your daddy 'the captain', all professional-like." Bannick brought a hand up to pinch O'den's cheek, which he deftly swatted away.

"Well, he is." O'den felt his blood begin to boil.

"Yeah?" Kennor chimed in. "You would say that, seeing as he got you this job."

"Oh, and your dad didn't do the same for you?" O'den was indignant. "At least I respect the position! I don't just treat it as some punishment because I couldn't hack it as an army brat!"

"Why you half-sized little shit!" Bannick and Ramin both held the stocky young man back. "At least I get to try! At least my dad is tall enough that he won't be old and grey, breaking up drunks and shooing vagrants the rest of his life!"

O'den saw red and started toward Kennor. True, halflings were forbade from army service due to their size, but that never stopped O'den's father from reading, something most army men lacked. He studied combat voraciously and encouraged his sons to do the same. O'den readjusted the grip on his baton once more, preparing to show Kennor some of what he had learned.

"Stand down, guards!" a voice boomed from the entrance of the stable that froze all four of the boys in their tracks. "That will be quite enough from the lot of you!" Footsteps clacked on the clay floor, approaching all of them. "In formation, eyes on me." it commanded, and as quickly as the three bullies were able to untangle themselves and make an about-face, O'den was beside them, straight-backed, eyes forward as Guard Captain Odo Overhill stood before them. For being taller than only O'den, the captain of East Fellowdale's City Guard cut every bit as imposing a frame as anyone in the Ghestal army that O'den had ever seen. Arms as thick as a smaller dwarf's bulged out of his mustard tabard, only barely contained by the plain white undershirt beneath. His black, close-cropped hair added to the statuesque sternness of his pursed lips and focused, piercing blue eyes.

Out of the corner of his eye, O'den caught Bannick open his mouth to speak, but a quick silencing gesture from the captain forced the boy's jaw closed so fast anyone who didn't know better might mistake Odo for an arcanist. "You three: out."

The boys all but sprinted from the stable, and the captain turned to face O'den. Were Odo Overhill his father in that moment, and not the captain, he would have anticipated a lecture about not losing his temper, about personal honour over social standing. He had heard the lecture more than once back at home. In that moment, however, Odo Overhill was not O'den's father, but his captain. "How long ago had you finished cleaning this stable, Junior Guard Overhill?"

O'den swallowed hard. "Um, about an hour ago, sir." His voice cracked mid-sentence, and he cursed himself inwardly.

"And have you yet taken your midday meal?"

"No, sir."

Odo nodded. "Very well. Either consider this your meal taken, or dock one hour's pay in the ledger when you are finished your shift. If you are bereft of work here, you are to relieve Guardsman Schellek from his duties at headquarters. Am I understood?"

O'den bit back every thought running through his mind then. He had performed his assigned duties quickly and efficiently, was practicing the martial techniques his father had taught him, and his reward was a fine, an empty belly, and the remainder of his day spent washing dishes. Defeated, he nodded, belatedly adding, "Yes, sir."

"Very well." Odo nodded and turned on his heel. "put away those buckets, and then you are dismissed." With that, the captain left, and O'den did as he was bade, allowing only a few frustrated tears to roll down his cheeks now that he was alone.

O'DEN'S HANDS HAD long since wrinkled as he finally placed the last of the cups to dry on the rack beside the basin where he had stood for hours. His feet were sore, and the wash pit behind the city guard headquarters' personal bar smelled of stale beer and sweat. Had the dishes not been so constant in coming to him, he would have been happier scrubbing every inch of the small room just to be rid of the odour. He reached for a nearby rag, trying futilely to dry his hands with the already soaked piece of cloth. Too tired to even bemoan the fact, O'den simply resigned himself to hanging the rag on the side of the basin, climbing down from the step stool that he had been standing on, and shuffling out to the small taproom in front.

All but the candles at the front entrance and the bar had been extinguished. Balfram, the old, willowy barkeep sat on the patron's side of the vacant bar, quietly sipping from a tankard. "Oi, Overhill!" he called over to O'den and motioned to the casks opposite him. "Pour yourself one, won't you? I'm near sauced, and I'll neither be a lone drunk nor will I waste a perfectly good ale!"

O'den smiled at Balfram. Surely one drink wouldn't dull his senses. He grabbed a copper half-pint mug and filled it at the nearest tap. He sat behind the bar, opposite Balfram, and the two clinked drinks. The ale had a roasted malt taste, better than the table beer Father kept back home.

"Y'know, I want to thank you for taking Schelleck's place tonight." Balfram took another sip. "I know this is a pretty shit job, but I swear you're the only one of the juniors who gives a damn when you do it."

O'den sighed. "I just wish I could do more, you know?"

"And wind up dead before twenty in the process? Ain't worth it." He took another drink and leaned in. "Y'know what I heard? That ship captain who's docked here? The king's top one, or whatever."

"You mean Admiral Deuen?" O'den corrected.

Balfram nodded. "Her, yeah. The elf. Well, Orram was in here earlier, after doing his rounds out at the docks. He was talking some nonsense about one of her crew looking shady, caught him speaking Majad to people."

Any inkling of an effect the beer was having on O'den dissipated at that. "What?"

"Right?" Balfram shook his head. "I wouldn't want to be within a mile of whatever nonsense is going on there."

"Well, did Orram tell anyone anything?" O'den stared in disbelief. "That crewman could be a spy. Deuen could be in danger. Hells, Deuen could be in on it!"

"Calm down." Balfram lowered his hands soothingly. "No sense jumping to conclusions. Speaking Majad ain't a crime, and do you really think any soldiers'd go snooping about King Meklan's top ship captain's—"

"Admiral's." O'den reminded Balfram a second time. "Anyway, isn't it at least worth investigating? Can't we round up some other guards to head down to the docks?"

"Pfft." Balfram waved away the idea. "No way anyone'd be willing to go snoopin' round the docks in the dead of night looking for trouble. Not for what we're paid."

O'den deflated some, knowing the barkeep spoke the truth. His stomach knotted, a thousand thoughts racing in his mind. Through the din, however, his father's words from his training broke through.

"You represent this city, her guard, and this whole kingdom at all times."

"I've got to go." O'den looked up at Balfran, putting on the best smile he could at that moment. "Try to catch a coach back home before it get's too dark." He drained the last third of his beer in a single swallow and slammed the mug on the bar, hopping off his stool and running for the door, calling back belatedly, "Thanks for the drink!"

O'DEN LOOKED RUEFULLY at the motley assortment of weapons
and armor in the City Guard's armory. If he survived tonight, he had
every intention of petitioning to upgrade the collection to more than
just army hand-me-downs.

"Don't bother." Odo's voice behind him made his blood run cold,
startling him enough to cause him to jump. He turned slowly to see his
father standing not six feet away, his face betraying nothing.

"Fath…er…Captain!" He fumbled a salute, fighting to not let the
nervous quaking in his feet give way to the rest of his body.

"At ease." Odo said calmly, although dropping the salute was the
only thing about O'den at ease in that moment. "I caught Balfran as he
was stumbling out of the tavern. He mentioned that some rumour had
you spooked."

O'den swallowed hard. Of course, he'd been caught. He told the
captain, his father, everything he'd been told by Balfran, and his plan to
do something about it.

Odo nodded as O'den spoke, the words pouring out as though his
mouth was an upturned bottle that had just been uncorked. When he
had finished his mumbled explanation, Odo was silent a moment longer,
looking to the ceiling of the armory when he finally did speak.

"So, you thought to infiltrate a royally-commissioned vessel with
little grounds to do so, with nothing more than speculative hearsay to go
on, telling no one, not even considering that backup might have been a
wise consideration?"

O'den didn't answer initially, worried that the question might be
rhetorical.

"I asked you a question, O'den."

"I…" O'den tried desperately to formulate a cohesive response. "Sir, all due respect, who would I have recruited for backup?" His mind told him to just shut up, but his mouth ignored the warning. "This job is just an easy pile of coin every week to nearly everyone. I know full well that doing this could either get me thrown out of the watch or thrown into a cell, and who else is going to take that risk? Captain, our kingdom, my kingdom, is in the middle of a war right now, and if there's a chance I can do anything to help my kingdom I'm going to do it, consequences be damned!"

There was a painful stretch of silence between the two. O'den kept his eyes locked on his father, who after too long, started to walk toward him. O'den braced himself for the inevitable, for Odo grabbing him by his shirt, chastising him for being so reckless, and all but dragging him home. It was much to O'den's surprise, then, when his father walked right past him, to the back wall of the small armory. O'den turned to look as Odo pulled two leather jerkins down from a rack, took a small pocket knife from a sheath at his waist, and began to cut away at them.

"Mail and plate wouldn't do us any good." he said as he worked. "They're too damned noisy and cumbersome." He tossed one jerkin to O'den, having carved about four or five inches off the bottom of it. "Put it on." he said, starting on altering the second. "It's meant for elven women, so it'll fit better than anything else here, but don't bank on it stopping anything more than a glancing blade."

O'den, stunned, did as he was bade. He looked over to see that Odo had done the same and was in the process of cutting the excess pieces of leather into four long strips. Odo beckoned O'den over when he had finished, and proceeded to wrap the strips around their forearms and palms. "Not as good as proper bracers, but they'll be better than bare flesh." he explained. Once finished, he motioned to the wall of weapons nearby. "Choose what feels best." he said.

O'den walked over to the wall and picked a modest-looking short sword, barely longer than a dirk, but as long as the hand-and-a-half swords

Odo had commissioned for them to train with at home. He felt it in his hands, noting the obvious difference in balance between this and what he was used to. All the shields, he knew, would be too unwieldy for him.

Odo came up beside him, taking a spear from the wall and snapping its haft so that it was better suited to his stature. "Consider it yours." he told O'den, nodding to the sword. "You'd best name it."

"Halfblade." O'den said without a moment's hesitation. His father looked at him speculatively, and he smirked. "'Weakness is but a construct, a spy supplanted by the enemy to cast doubt on the battlefield. The cunning soldier will root out this enemy spy, finding strength within it, turning it back on his unsuspecting foe with thrice the efficacy.'"

Odo nodded, clearly impressed. "Darro's *On Warfare*."

"A classic," O'den remarked.

"It is." Odo motioned toward the exit. "Now let's see you put those words into action."

O'DEN WAS NEVER much of a fan of East Fellowdale's docks, especially at night. They smelled of fish, musk, and salt water more often than not, and the lack of lamplight threw strange shadows, making the whole area feel ominous. It didn't help that, in this instance, there was the silhouette of the HMS *Seahulk* taking up what felt like half a block of the southern end of the docks. The ship was touted as King Meklan's great naval achievement, the ship that would carry all the arcane and military power Ghest could muster overseas, striking Majad and ending the now three-year-long war between the two. It was the closest O'den had been to the vessel since it docked over a month ago, and seeing it now, he regretted not having done so under more favorable circumstances.

"Keep your eyes on the street." Odo's voice snapped him out of his bout of reverence. "We see a half-orc linger more than three breaths in front of that ship and we move."

O'den nodded and refocused, scanning the area as the pair of them crouched in the nearby alleyway. After little time, a slight, silhouetted figure made his way down the gangplank of the *Seahulk*, pulling up the hood of his cloak just late enough for O'den to notice his greyish-brown skin and pronounced, underbitten teeth.

O'den made to move, but Odo raised his arm to stop him. "Not yet." he whispered.

They waited until the half-orc had made his way nearly a block north-ward before pursuing, quickening their pace as he turned down another of the district's ill-lit side streets. Using their relatively small size and quiet footfalls to their advantage, O'den and his father beset their quarry quickly. O'den charged the half-orc in the backs of his knees, sending him face-first to the ground. He made an effort to draw something from his hip, but Odo's reflexes were quicker. The elder halfling leaped forward, landing on the hand reaching for the weapon, planting his knee into the small of the half-orc's back and grabbing for his off-hand, clasping the wrist and twisting it around his back.

To his credit, the half-orc didn't cry out. O'den focused on binding his legs, hearing him mumble something in Majad at them.

"You're in a very precarious position right now." Odo spoke through clenched teeth as he fought to keep their captor pinned. "You're one wrong word from the pair of us turning you over to the militia, so if you've got anything to say that you think might be of value, I suggest you say it in a language I understand."

The half-orc muttered low once more, and O'den saw his father twist just enough on his restrained wrist to get a reaction.

"The satchel!" the haf-orc gasped between shallow breaths, his voice thick with his Majad accent. "The letter inside!"

Odo looked to O'den, then to the bag slung around their captor's shoulder, and nodded. O'den opened the bag, rummaging through until he felt a rolled-up parchment. He pulled it out and unfurled it. The writing was in the careful, trained hand of someone with a good education, but was all in Majad.

"What does it say?" O'den asked as he tried to parse the foreign script.

"I do not know." the half-orc replied. "I have no letters. I believe it is for Warlord Ankhul. She means to betray—" the sentence was clipped short with a sharp intake of breath, and O'den looked up from the page to see Odo putting pressure on the half-orc's wrist once more.

"Treason?" His father's voice was calm, which O'den knew too well to be a bad sign. "What reason do I have to believe such allegations coming from a Majadi we caught skulking around in the night?" When an answer was not immediately given, O'den heard the half-orc cry out in pain. "Four seconds or you never use this arm again," his father warned coldly.

"I am a fisher!" The half-orc growled, struggling. "I do not care for soldiers and their wars, Majadi or Ghestal!"

"We're all tired of war." Odo replied.

"Not Deuen," the half-orc retorted. "She thinks talks of a treaty are weak, calls your king Meklan weak. She sets a trap."

O'den continued to look at the parchment, trying desperately to make out any of it. Something about all of this felt off. "Where were you taking this?" he asked.

"A merchant, Broschk." The half-orc panted. "Is Majad-born, but Ghest is her home. Can read and write both."

"O'den looked at his father. "Captain, what if he's telling the truth?" Odo made no move to relent.

"Father..." O'den tried not to sound as though he were pleading.

With that, Odo looked sidelong at O'den for a breath, then released the half-orc, rolling off his back. "Fine." he said simply. "You'll escort us to this Broschk. You try anything, I'll climb up that skinny little frame and slit your throat."

The pair of halflings quickly bound the half-orc's hands and unbound his feet. "What is your name?" O'den asked.

"Thakrach," he answered as he shakily got to his feet. "Thank you."

"Don't thank me yet." O'den raised an eyebrow. "You're still well in the woods as far as I'm concerned."

The clicking of hard-soled boots on cobblestones stopped the trio in their tracks.

"In the name of the Ghestal Royal Navy, I order you to halt." O'den turned to see a short, slight woman standing at the entrance to the alley. In addition to the hard-soled boots that were the source of the steps, she wore a long cutlass on her hip, her dark hair pulled into a tail that sat atop her head, flanked on either side by the tips of her pointed elven ears.

"Admiral!" Odo calmly snapped a salute, and O'den followed suit. "I am Captain Odo Overhill of the East Fellowdale City Guard. My junior guard here was alerted to some potential suspicious activity in the vicinity, and I was accompanying him here to investigate."

The admiral stepped further into the alley, the light from the main street keeping her face shrouded in shadow. "In that case, you have my thanks, Captain. This man in your custody is in my crew, and I suspect he has been involved in a plot to sabotage the *Seahulk*'s upcoming mission." She stretched her arm out toward them. "Kindly turn him over to me."

O'den looked at his father, who looked at Thakrach, and then back to him. "Admiral, with all due respect, we were in the midst of our own investigation into the matter. If you would like to accompany us in—"

"Your diligence is noted," Deuen cut Odo off, her annoyance just clear enough that O'den could tell that she was trying, poorly, to hide it. "However, this is a matter for the Royal Navy, *not* a pair of city guards. You are relieved."

O'den looked to Odo, whose eyes had narrowed. "Admiral," he began with the sort of calm that gave O'den the chills "I have made my career keeping the streets of East Fellowdale safe. If there is a plot afoot in *my* city, then it is *my* matter, regardless of who might be masterminding it."

Deuen put a hand on the hilt of her cutlass. "I'm afraid I take umbrage with your tone, Captain."

"And I with your pensiveness, Admiral." Odo retorted, the grip on his spear tightening. "Perhaps there's something to that letter your crewman gave me after all."

Despite the darkness, O'den saw the admiral's eyes widen in a flash of anger. She unsheathed her cutlass and darted forward. O'den watched, forgetting to breathe as time seemed to slow down. There was something off in Deuen's stance as she charged toward Odo. Her left shoulder was too far to one side, her centre of gravity was off. It was almost as if…

O'den drew Shortblade just in time as Deuen feinted and changed direction, swinging her cutlass sidelong to *clang* against the short sword's flat. O'den parried and ducked, gripping the blade with both hands to deflect another attack, and another. For as certain as he now was that the admiral was guilty, he didn't dare press an attack on someone who so greatly outranked him.

Remaining on the defensive was tiring O'den out quickly, the admiral's greater size allowing her to put more power into her blows. She raised her blade up and prepared to swing, and though O'den raised his own blade in a cross defense, he knew he lacked the strength to hold her back. Before she struck, however, O'den heard a loud *thunk*, saw Deuen's eyes glaze over, then watched as she collapsed at his feet, unconscious.

Behind her stood Odo, his spear held blunt end up, his mouth pursed into a thin, stoic line. He looked at O'den, who had lowered his sword and was staring at his father, mouth agape.

"Damn coward." Odo spat in the direction of the unconscious admiral. "I don't care if you're the king himself, you try to harm my boy and I will be swift in my retribution." He looked back at O'den. "You did well, but your offense was nonexistent."

"I know." O'den said apologetically. "I just… You can't blame me for not wanting to attack the king's top admiral."

Odo nodded thoughtfully. "About that…" He motioned to Thakratch, who hurried over.

"Turn around." Odo instructed, and Thakratch complied and was released from his bonds as a result. "We don't need her going anywhere." Odo explained as he bent over and began using the straps to bind Deuen's hands and feet. "I have a feeling that the admiral has quite a lot to answer for."

"I WOULD LIKE to make one thing perfectly clear," Odo's voice carried through the chill winter air in which the new recruits stood, all the way to the rear ranks where O'den stood. "Despite what you all may have heard, war is still very much upon us. It is my job to prepare you for that, and it is a job I take very seriously."

O'den had heard the rumours. He had wished that they were true. Unfortunately, however, after Admiral Deuen had been implicated in a plot to have the *Seahulk* attacked at sea, it only furthered animosity by both kingdoms. Acts of war had only been on the rise in the six months since.

"So, if you think the soldier's life is in some way easier than tilling fields, or hauling fish, or slaving over an anvil and forge, then my job is two-fold, and I will not relent until each and every one of you is not only willing to fight and die for your kingdom, but that you'll all be too damned good at the former to have to worry about the latter."

O'den smirked at that. He had seen the sort of training Ghestal soldiers were used to, and he had lived the sort of training his father had expected. A lot of these recruits were in for a world of hurt.

"Beyond all else, know this: you are the first in a new, proud tradition. Every other soldier in Ghest will be watching. Indeed, *all* of Ghest will be watching. But you will show them that you are capable, that you are brave, that you have every right to serve your kingdom that they do." There was a cheer that echoed across the field where Odo made his speech, five hundred halflings calling out their assent. It sent a chill down O'den's spine.

SHORTBLADE

Odo dismissed the assembled crowd, all of whom then split into their respective units. O'den climbed atop his pony and watched as one hundred halfling men and women formed in ranks in front of him. He fought a grin as the unit, *his* unit, saluted him.

"Ladies and gentlemen," he called out to them, "welcome to the Ghestal Second Halfling Infantry, welcome to the Shortblades."

"Thank you, sir!" they called out in unison.

O'den's smile broke through at that. "You're welcome. Now let's get to work."

RENDERED CHAOS

D.M. MURRAY

THERE'S SOMETHING ALTOGETHER mind-bendingly disappointing about being woken up in the middle of a sex dream.

That was the overwhelming notion that stabbed into my mind when that bloated old fuck Corporal Winston ground the sole of his boot into my bollocks.

"Wakey time, Sontino, you piece of shit." Winston's ravaged voice was never the sweetest caress one needed when birthing the mother of all hangovers. "Every morning," Winston growled on, blazing spears of cruel sunlight finding their mark in my eyes, "you wake up humping your cot. Must be feeling it bad. Fucking over-sexed, sun-baked Aneochins."

I rolled my tongue about my sour-as-shit mouth, furry as week-old mouldy cheese, and not tasting much better. I rubbed at my burning-dry eyes and looked at the piggy-face of Winston. Baby-sitter number one. Dog-wanking prick.

"Been out here, what, three weeks? Crying out for some velvet, are you?" Private Broochman piped up from the upturned bucket he sat on by the entrance of the tent. Baby-sitter number two. Not quite having achieved the rank of dog-wanker, but certainly with aspirations.

I fixed a greasy smile, ignoring the growling sickness in my belly. "Why don't you two fret less on me and concentrate on fucking yourselves?" Broochman was right, though, it'd been three weeks. Three weeks since the archduke had sent my happy existence of painting, and then fornicating, with the wives of absent military officers into the shitter. Three weeks of mud. Three weeks of shit rations, even worse brandy, and worst of all, no velvet worth the fucking that wouldn't give me the cock-rot. Actually, no, worst of all was storming into my tent to crown my hangover like the mother of all shitting hangovers.

"Where's DeVerocci—" The tall young officer looked every inch the hero. The prick. Long-blond hair kissed the silver markings of captaincy on his epaulettes. No doubt my face being the only one not as pale as the risen moon was all the answer he needed. He strode forward, ignoring the lazy salute of Winston and Broochman. "Sir," Captain Hero said, fury simmering behind his good manners. These people and their fucking manners. "You, sir, are a scoundrel."

Been called worse. Captain Hero was shit at this. I pointed at my chest and pursed my lips in my best feign of innocence. I mean, I didn't know the man, but chances are I'd fucked his wife, or sister, or even his dear old mother. Innocence was lost on me, and the two or three fading and not-so-fading bruises about my face were testament enough that others agreed.

"Sir," I said, attempting to stand, a smooth smile dawning on my lips.

"Sit down!" Captain Hero snapped.

My arse hit the cot hard.

"You, sir, have dishonoured my sister."

Sister! A first for this week.

"And by dishonouring her, you dishonour my family. I would have hers, and our honour restored with your life, if it weren't for the fact the archduke is so a fan of your work."

"He does quite like my—"

"Shut the fuck up!"

Winston and Broochman sniggered behind Captain Hero. Winston's glee in particular making me wished I'd fucked *his* sister. Though, that again would mean an inevitable run-in with the old cock-rot, as no doubt the man's sister was the most rancid whore in Warungsland.

"As I cannot take her honour back from you in blood, I shall take it from your hide."

"Sir, if you feel I must present my arse to you, I'm sorry to disappoint. Whilst I understand the predilections of the officer class, and despite my reputation for being a prolific lover, it's not a preference of mine. Can't you just rough me up a little?"

Captain Hero's face plumed red, and his mouth gaped open and closed. "That's not what I meant."

I stood, sympathetic smile curling beneath my sweat-beading lip. "Why, of course you did."

Captain Hero's fury drained from him now, caught off-guard with my well-timed accusation of a preference for buggery. I presented my chin and placed a paint stained finger-tip to it. *Tap, tap. Thump.*

The blow sent me corkscrewing in a spinning haze of stars, and then down. Down into my cot. Down into my side-table of empty bottles and spent cigars. Down into my tubs of paint powders, spent canvases, and down into a black void of pain and disafuckingpointment. How had it come to this? I was perfectly happy painting, drinking, and fucking myself into a courtly stupor. And now I'm here, on the outskirts of the Highlands, to capture for posterity glorious battle art of the Warungsland's army repelling the Antellenians. I rubbed my aching chin. Bollocks to this.

YELLOW-BOG-STAR FLOWERS BRUSHED against the ankles of my boots as I crested the wooded hill. Scouts reported no Ant soldiers, so I made my way up. Winston and Broochman huffed behind me, hauling canvases, easels, and satchels full of paint powders, brushes, and charcoal.

"Chop, chop!" I called to my mules.

"Fuck yourself, Sontino." Winston grumbled.

"However could I do that when I'm spending all my fuckery time with your mother?" I ignored the grumbled insults from the rear and stepped out between two red-barked pines and into the little glade. Bright purple buds bloomed about the summer heather in a meadow flower mosaic. I'd rather be painting this merry scene than battle.

"Those mountains look like tits." Broochman's just-a-man voice pipped behind me, followed by the clatter of him dropping easels and the bag of paint powders.

"Careful!" I said, looking at the mountains across the valley.

"Called the Twin Sows." Winston grunted, tossing the equipment on top of Broochman's abandoned heap.

No point calling out these two pricks any more. Either too stupid or too much a pair of arseholes to care different. He was right, though, Broochman, the Twin Sows did look like a pair of tits. Tits. I shook myself out of my reverie and studied the landscape below. More of a portrait man. I guess that told when I sent my first work back to the Archduke. *'Not grand enough. More action. More visceral.'* So here I was, atop a windy hill in the Highlands, freezing my own tits off in this shit-stinking weather the Warungsland folk called *summer*. I pulled a hairless paintbrush from my pocket and mouthed it, teeth finding familiar pits and grooves as I took in the land. Heather-clad drumlins ran down from the foot of the Twin Sows, purple gleaming with yellow. About the only thing of brightness and beauty out east.

"Shitting weather." I set up my easels, careful to fix the legs into the ground. I fitted my canvases in place. Five easels, and five canvases. *'Give me the art of war,'* the Archduke told me. *'Give me glory, and gore, and the divine beauty of it,'* he demanded. *'Give me it all, and you shall be returned to court.'*

The clouds rolled slow overhead, ugly and dull like the skin of a day-dead fish, all lustre and promise gone to shit and leaving nothing behind but wasted glamour and the promise of disappointment. Beneath the drumlins, the ground evened off into the valley floor, a dull carpet of hummocky grass, beaten and bent over by the easterly wind. The grey sheen of countless little mirror pools played out the reflection of the ugly sky, leopard-spotting the ground either side of the worming meander of a small ox-bow river.

I laid open my paint pots and mixed my palette. An unpleasant task owing to the colours in this place. Greys. Or browns. Or the yellow-greens of a fading bruise. There was about as much charisma in this palette as there was in that mouldering shit-and-wine stinking tent I shared with those two guardsmen. So, about the same as a dried-out turd.

I took a moment and sketched out the backdrop, making sure I'd at least one good landscape canvas to capture the meeting of the armies. After all, the archduke would be keen I show he'd offered terms before slaughtering the Ants.

The mirror pools drew my attention for a moment, and I wondered just how deep those little bog pools were. Armoured men falling into deep pools leads to one conclusion. I opened a sketch book and began to scratch down an image that played in my mind. Bright strobes of light cutting though the shades of water before losing out to the inexorable depth. In the midst, the hero of the piece descended, sleeping the long sleep. His armour gleams in the water, and his white cloak floats up and out behind him like a phantom reaching up to haunt the valley.

"Shit." Winston's voice sounded from behind. "Tie a pencil to my cock and watch me dry-hump your canvas, bet I'd do better than that." His reeking breath strangled me from over my shoulder.

I turned and offered the meat-headed prick my best *fuck yourself* smile.

"Corporal, whilst I respect and, indeed, value your critique, it would be altogether more helpful in maintaining the atmospheric stability favoured by my paints if you were to take your shit-stinking breath away the fuck somewhere else."

He sloped off to the edge of the glade and leaned against a tree, fixing his piggy-black eyes on me. I duly extended my middle finger in his direction and flashed him my most disarming smile. The prick.

I closed shut my sketch book and returned my attention to the valley floor. A herd of deer grazed to the east of the river. The stag raised his dozen-pointed antlers, cocked his head, and turned his bearded neck to the south. I followed where he looked and saw them. Five thousand men according to the scout reports. Five thousand Ants marching inexorably towards a hungry Titan. Why the Antellenian's believed they could just carve off the Highlands was beyond me. Yes, there's the rumour of gold in the mountains, but fuck me, they were never equipped to deal with the Warungsland Army. Idiots would all die. The stag bellowed, his breath pluming out around his head. The harem bolted towards the woodland fringing the hill I stood atop.

Noise drew my eye to the north. A whinny of horse, and the slow, grinding clamour of Warungsland's finest. Ten-thousand cavalry, archers, and foot. I'm a lover, not a fighter, but even to me it was simple arithmetic.

I sketched the formations underneath the two colossal tits of mountain and watched as the white-cloaked Warungsland general rode out to meet his counterpart. The offer of terms the archduke wanted. Easy. Utterly rejected as fuck by the outnumbered Ants, naturally. Ants, much like their crawling namesakes, haven't much in the way of brains, and so they can't see when they're utterly, hopelessly defeated.

"We're fighting!" Broochman squawked, fingers tapping his sword belt. He may be a lowly private, but that boy, well, captain of stating-the-fucking obvious.

RENDERED CHAOS

I BROUGHT THE optics to my eyes and peered into the valley. The heavy cavalry of the Warungsland force would hit them any moment, white cloak's billowing out behind them like a host of vengeful phantoms. The horsemen crashed into the Ants' pikemen with a thunderclap that could have roused the dead. It sure as shit roused the hangover in me. I swung my optics along the line and picked out my frozen moment.

A white horse reared, back hooves planted in the heathery ground. Front hooves rose above the grimacing Ant pikeman, birthing a jump that the horse would never see through. The Ant's leather round-cap had slid down over his eyes. Shit gear for shit soldiers. Fair is fair. The man's gritted teeth bared in the moment. White knuckled hands gripped hard at the mid-shaft of his pike as he drove it between the shoulders of the great beast. The rider, with silver armour gleaming, had the look of the most pronounced disappointment on his face. I imagine he thought it rather unfair that a mere Ant foot soldier should have him so rudely unhorsed and most likely cleaved into the dirt.

I lowered my optics and wasted no time in sketching the moment onto the canvas. I worked fast, ignoring the bleating of dying men in the valley below.

"We're fucking smashing them." Winston's ugly voice sounded as he looked down at his comrades tearing through the Ants. He clapped a heavy hand onto my shoulder, sending one of the horse's rear legs askew. "Fucking well smashing them, eh, Sontino?"

"Corporal," I turned slow, "would you ever piss off?"

"That's right, you Aneochins are lovers, not fighters."

"Quite correct." I turned my attention back to the canvas, correcting the askew leg by building up the heather about it. "Now off you fuck."

"Greasy prick."

"Greasy from your mother's cunt."

Winston lumbered past the easels and pissed over the crest of the hill. No doubt that was as helpful a contribution to the fight that bloated arsehole would ever manage.

I finished my work on the clash of cavalry and pikeman, and then raised my optics, searching for my next frozen moment. No shortage of options. My view alighted on a riderless horse galloping past two foot-soldiers locked in a dance so lacking in love, it would seem it would end in someone's death. Well, war is war. Hand's gripped hard on the opposing arms. Weapons trembled above each of the men's heads, the tremor running down and into the strained faces of each.

A Warungsland horseman galloped past, and the Ant axeman released his grip of the swordsman's hand. With confusion dawning on his face, he tried to stem the bright blood that spurted from where his arm had been severed at the elbow. The Warungsland swordsman waited, almost respectfully before he shook himself, realising where he was. With a double-handed cut, sent the axeman thumping to the ground, his lower jaw flying to join his lower arm. The instant the swordsman struck, a spear met him above his hip, just under his breastplate. It jerked him off his feet, and he crashed to the ground like a sack of marionette dolls. The Ant spearman's shaft jolted and snapped, courtesy of the riderless horse bolting back where it had started from and riding him down.

"Fuck me." I blew out wine-stinking breath and tried to process what I'd just seen into a painting. Never easy, deconstructing such intensity into a single scene. Archduke wanted visceral, fuck the old crow, he can have it. I worked fast. The riderless horse colliding with the spearman. The spearman sticking the swordsman, and the swordsman felling the axeman. Sheer and utter bloody madness.

A palsy had worked its way into my hand. Could've been either the wine, or the chaos below. I stepped to the third easel, and raised my optics once more. The Warungsland foot pressed, filling the holes the cavalry punched into the Ants like sickness into a rent in the flesh. It was terminal. A rout. The mass of the Warungsland forces was turning the Ants around and pushing them up onto the heathery drumlins at the foot of the Twin

Sows. They'd grind them into the mountain.

"Look at `em fuckers!" Broochman yipped, pointing to the small groups of Ants that had avoided the press. "Making a break for it."

"They'll be ridden down." Winston laughed as he lit a thin brown wrap of mulch-leaf, sending out yellow plumes of smoke above his head.

Didn't matter a shit to me if the Ants ran. Didn't matter if they lived or died. Simply characters lost from the canvas now. I raised my optics once more, sweeping their view into the melee at the foot of the Twin Sows.

A man lay on the heather clutching at his knee where the rest of his leg used to be. He howled as the awful wound bloomed red on the blooming purple flowers of the heather. Holy hellfire how he howled. Bellowing louder than that stag earlier. He was trampled to silence by the press of Warungsland foot. One of the foot was taken down by an axe to the neck. Not severing the head, but not failing at its work either. Made a right mess. He fell and was lost to the press. An Ant soldier, stepping backwards, took a shattered spear shaft in the groin. He bent over, and was clattered groundward by a flash of silver. A metal-rimmed shield pushed out of the press, deflecting an Ant sword thrust before swinging back and clattering the man in a spray of blood and teeth. Another strike of the shield obliterated the Ant's nose. He fell and was joined an instant later by the Warungsland shield-man, his world turned to shit by a hammer to the chest.

Ravens gathered overhead, reapers come to feed on flesh and claim the souls. I added them to the canvas. Black wraiths circling a tombstone-cold sky, bearing witness to the birth of new spectres to this unwelcoming land.

I had one more canvas to work at. I picked up my optics, searching for my next scene.

Broochman roared. A sound like that leaves little room for question. I dropped the optics. Four blood-spattered, wild-eyed Ant soldiers stood chest's heaving and weapons drawn.

"Fuck!" Winston scrambled at the corner of my eye. The sound of metal grinding as he pulled his sword free.

"Shit! Shit!" Broochman yipped, fumbling the grip of his shield and dropping it as he drew his sword. Clumsy fucker.

I eyed the nervous looking Ants. Their dark-metal swords were edged with a red glimmer. I saw the droplets of blood still wet on their faces. Other men's blood. I stepped backwards and sure as shit, tripped over my paint box. Fell right onto my arse. They stepped further into the glade. Maybe we could just let them past? Maybe we could be civilised about this whole—

The Ants attacked, pairing off on Winston and Broochman. I would say my pride was hurt that they didn't see me as a threat, but I'd neither a weapon, nor was I within sniffing distance of their wives.

Winston ducked a swipe from an Ant sword and lashed his own blade across the man's thigh. A crescent of red sprayed out from the slash, and he dropped. Winston spun and blocked the thrust of the other Ant.

Broochman howled for help as he was pressed by his two. He crouched behind his round-shield, breath hissing between clenched teeth.

I started to shuffle backwards. Maybe they wouldn't notice. Maybe by the time this was done, I'd be halfway the hells away from this cauldron.

Winston had the second Ant in a grip, the other man grunting like a drunk humping some velvet up an alley. Then the Ant fell away, and Winston's sword slid red from the man's chest.

"Behind!" I shouted to Winston. Too late. It was Winston's time to grunt. Heard so many soldiers say, '*Never leave an enemy behind you.*' Winston took thigh-struck's sword right through the back. He turned around, all slow like dying men seem to do, and prodded his sword point into thigh-stuck's neck. Was almost as casual about it as I'd be dipping my brush into paint. Winston fell onto his knees, and I swear, before he toppled, it looked for all the word like he just called me a cunt.

Broochman was on one knee, swords battering his shield to kindling.

He rushed a jab around its edge. Got lucky. The sword punched into the Ant's gut. The man cried, and Broochman poked his head out. Not the finest of brains in young Broochman's head. Actually, not much brains in his head at all after that. The second Ant's sword split Broochman's head, spraying blood and brain across the glade.

One Ant remained standing. As it would happen, I was sat on my arse, mouth hanging like, well, like Broochman's after that sword brained him. Four men lay dead, and one squealing, his life half-drained into the bleak, hungry ground.

The Ant shouted something to his injured comrade, then hawked a lump of his finest cheddar and spat onto Broochman's ruined head. The private's tongue poked fat from his mouth like a hung toad. I tried my old trick of closing my eyes and hoping when I opened them the hatchet-faced old troll I was fucking had turned into a beauty. Didn't work. Never worked, and this ugly prick was still eyeballing me. The Ant licked the spray of blood off his lips and walked towards me. Time slowed. It slowed as the Ant flicked his sword, sending an arc of tiny rubies sparkling in the grey daylight. It slowed as his old leather boots with the toes sticking free pressed down on the heather. Time slowed as my bowels twisted, and I shit my pants. The Ant pulled back his sword arm. Cold, hard, sharp and fuck-ugly steel raised ready to cut me open. No more painting and poking for me. As luck would have it, the Ant turned around towards the edge of the glade. That herd of deer from the valley came bursting out of the treeline. They sprung over Broochman's hung-toad corpse, crashed into my easels, and trampled gut-struck into the heather with a retching noise. Something bellowed, and the stag burst through the trees and into the glade. The beast's tongue lolled as it bounded my way. The Ant looked back at me, his mouth framing an O. It framed fuck-all apart from a, '*Whoop,*' and a gout of blood. The stag dropped its head and rammed antlers up into the Ant's body, lifting him off his feet. He was shaken about, all bloody vomit and jumbled words, then was cast to the ground like the wasted remains of a doll unfavoured. The deer bounded out of the glade, leaving me alone save for the heather, meadow flowers, and corpses.

I SCRAMBLED UP on wobbling legs and puked onto the feet of the gored Ant. Winston's accusing eyes stared blankly as I stumbled to my toppled easels. A hand grabbed at my boot. A bloody hand, staining my Ferocci Leather boot. Fucker.

"Help. Me," the voice called in a mangled attempted at Warungsland. Ugly fucking language at best, but even worse on the tongue of this dying Ant. Would've thought being gut-struck and trampled by deer would kill a man.

"Get off. These boots are expensive." I shook off the man's hand. Hell of a dirty face he had. All hollow-eyed and hungry. I looked about, saw Winston's sword, and picked it up. In fairness, I'd probably look more comfortable holding a horse's cock, but needs must. I jabbed it into the Ant's chest. The tip didn't go far. "Fuck." I avoided the man's eyes and leaned down on the handle-end, pommel, whatever. The wretch wheezed and gagged his way into death.

I turned back towards my easels and saw a troop of Warungsland foot come into the glade.

"Boss!" a soldier called back over his shoulder. "Painter's alive. He killed the Ants!"

I puffed my chest, good and bold, and gripped the blood-stained sword like a hero. I think. Soldiers rushed into the glade from the wood now, laughing and cheering. Quite the nice feeling, as it happens. Soldiers picked up my easels. Blood sprayed across the worked scenes of violence. Great splatters of dark, and thin lines of bright red speckled the artwork. Never had my paintings been so alive, rendered so by death. If that crusty old fuck wanted visceral, well, he had it. A couple of back slaps tore my attention from the canvases. Shouts of, 'Hero,' set me grinning. I was there. This would work well for me. Warrior Poet. Hero of the bedroom and the battlefield. Wielder of brush and steel.

THE BEST AND BRAVEST

ML SPENCER

SILENCE SHATTERED, THE quiet of the morning fracturing like glass.

The cry of a war horn rose out of the gray stillness of the forest. The call was answered by others, some not so distant. Michel cast an anxious glance over his shoulder at his father. The old man didn't react, just kept his heavy stare fixed on the ground ahead of his horse. The slight breeze faltered, and then died off completely.

"Over there, sire." One of the baron's knights pointed into the forest with a mailed hand.

Michel stared into the shadows of the surrounding trees but could make out nothing. Just a thick veil of fog that hung like a curtain between their own party and the defenses of Brouette. The fog encased the forest, smothering the dawnbreak.

The baron shifted in his saddle. He scratched his whiskered chin, eyes narrowing as they scoured the mist. Jean de Verglas was not a large man, but his burgundy surcoat and the sword at his side made up for what he lacked in stature. He scowled, swiping a dark lock of hair out of his eyes.

He grumbled, "They cower beneath the mist. Make ready."

Michel wondered at the baron's words as he swung from his horse's back. If Brouette's men were using the fog as cover, then why signal their presence by sounding horns? The discrepancy made no sense, adding yet another texture to the layers of anxiety he already felt.

He left his own mount where it stood and untied his father's best warhorse, leading it toward the group of knights gathered at the front of the column around the Baron de Verglas. Michel didn't dare look the baron in the eye as he moved around his tall stallion. He could feel the man's cold stare lingering on him, following his every motion.

He stopped at his father's side, holding the stirrup for him to mount, then handed the old knight his shield and lance. Bernard de Torleaux gazed down at his eldest son with a look of calm assurance and gave a slight nod. To Michel, his father's bright eyes seemed much too youthful for his age-worn face. He moved with a grace that was unaffected by his years, bringing his lance up smartly as he eased himself back in the saddle.

"Have a care," Bernard said under his breath. "I mislike the feel of this place." He reached down and clapped his son on the arm. Then he kicked his horse toward the forming line of cavalry.

Michel stared after his father, feeling his nerve wither. Bernard was an accomplished knight. In his youth, he had accompanied the great King Roland on his last foray into Khash. Bernard's experience across the sea made him a fair judge of the portents before a battle. Michel had great confidence in his father's judgement. If the old man was troubled by this field, then he had every right to be afraid.

With deep misgivings, Michel led away the plow horse his father had ridden on the journey, heading back toward the jumbled collection of squires at the rear. The countryside around Bélizon had been Michel's home all his life, but this forest was strange to him. Yesterday's march had brought their small warband deeply into a part of the county held by the Baron de Brouette, Verglas's sworn enemy. Generations of feuding between the two noble houses had begun over some small offence no one living cared to remember. Regardless of reason, enough blood had been spilled over the past two centuries to darken the ground of the woodland that formed a natural barrier between their holdings.

Michel pulled himself back astride his horse as he watched his father position himself in the line of knights making ready for the charge. Footmen ran forward to assemble in a disorderly throng behind the mounted cavalry. More horns brayed out of the roiling fog, closer than they had been before. Another noise rose as well: the constant swell of echoing thunder.

Ahead, in a clearing through the trees, the mist yielded before a ragged line of enemy horsemen. The sight made Michel's throat go dry, a shiver tracing the small of his back. There were many more knights than he'd expected. Brouette's numbers far surpassed their own. The baron himself sat astride an elegant warhorse, distinguishable by the emblem of Brouette on his surcoat. He bore no lance, but held a sword raised at his side, his tapered shield marked with the insignia of his house.

"Hold," Verglas commanded, slamming his helm down over his face. Behind him, the baron's young standard bearer fidgeted anxiously, the boy clinging to the staff in his hands with what looked like a death grip.

The horses tossed their heads and danced in place, the jingle of tack upsetting the silence of the woodland mist. One stallion broke forward, its rider having to fight to bring it back in line with the others. An uneasy stillness encroached, charged with compressed tension. It was as though time itself was wound tight as a spring, stretched and ready to snap.

Brouette's men formed up in one long rank at the edge of the clearing.

Michel searched behind the line of cavalry, scanning the mist for signs of footmen but seeing none. Perhaps they were back there somewhere, hidden under the gray cover of fog. Or perhaps they were somewhere else entirely.

A small group of riders had positioned themselves off to one side of the field, almost invisible in the roiling mist. There, astride tall horses, sat two knights wearing mantles of pristine white emblazoned with the splayed emblem of the Order of Syre. Michel could only stare at the two undead knights in bewildered horror. He'd only seen their kind once before in his life.

The Knights of Syre were a mystical order composed entirely of the risen dead, unholy paladins sworn to the service of Syre even beyond the grave. But neither of the two wights looked ready to add their skill to the impending fight. They held themselves aloof, watching with ice-dead eyes the two forces squaring off at opposite ends of the clearing.

Verglas bellowed out the command to advance. The line of horses started forward, breaking toward the enemy. Brouette's cavalry advanced at a trot, their lord allowing his knights to draw abreast and overtake him. The forest rang with the thunder of hoofbeats, the clamor of men and arms, armor and tack.

The distance between the advancing forces narrowed. Both lines broke simultaneously into the charge, their knights dropping lances. Michel gripped his horse's reins as he watched his father's destrier career ahead of the others, directly toward the center of the enemy.

Just as the opposing lines closed with one another, every lance pulled sharply up.

The ranks of horse converged, parting again as Verglas's knights continued past their foes at a gallop, quickly swallowed by the fog.

Michel's mouth hung slack in confusion. He took an anxious step forward, his concern deepening. As he watched, every man of Brouette wheeled in unison, doubling back with swords drawn toward the only knight left behind on the field, the only man whose lance had remained couched throughout the whole of the charge.

Bernard de Torleaux cast away the shaft and drew his sword instead, wheeling his horse around as Brouette's men encircled him in a slowly constricting ring. The old man glanced around and, realizing his plight, raised his sword and shield. He wound his blade as his horse turned a slow circle in the center of the clearing. Throwing back his head, he gave a fierce war cry.

Then the ring of knights imploded.

There was a torrential hail of falling steel, the vicious crunch of armor yielding beneath the honed edges of blades. A blood-curdling shriek that ended in a gurgle. And then the riders fell back, scattering into the forest at a gallop. Soon, the clearing was empty, save only for the mist that groped over the ground and the prone figure sprawled like a sacrifice on the grass.

Michel kicked his own horse forward, driving his heels into the animal's flanks. He pulled up just enough to drop from the gelding's back, breaking his fall with his palms. He staggered the last few steps to his father's side, collapsing next to him on hands and knees.

There was surprisingly little blood. Bernard had fallen beside his slain charger, one leg still thrown over the saddle. His fine hauberk was scored in a number of places, the steel rings yielding to the fury of the blows inflicted on it.

Michel released the helm from his father's head, setting it gently aside. Bernard's blue eyes stared up at him, still young-seeming in his aged face. His lips were parted slightly, as if ready to offer a chance thought or wonder at a fleeting marvel that had just occurred to him, as Bernard so often liked to do. But no air moved past his lips. There was no breath or life left in him.

Michel could only shake his head in confusion and denial. He didn't understand. His mind fumbled desperately for an explanation. Why, out of all of Verglas's men, had his father alone been singled out to die?

"A shame," commented a voice above him.

M L SPENCER

Michel raised his head to stare into Verglas's arrogant face. The noble lord had brought his horse up, unnoticed, and gazed indifferently down from the saddle. His narrow lips were pressed together, as if he found the sight of the corpse distasteful. He sat his destrier stock-still, holding the reins primly in a black-gloved fist.

Michel glared up at him, trembling with rage and grief.

The sound of hoofbeats made him turn. The Baron de Brouette had doffed his helm, holding it in the crook of his arm as he reined his mount in. He wasn't much more than Michel's own age, his blond hair worn tied back. His face was gravely set, an expression akin to regret moving behind his eyes as he gazed down at the fallen knight.

"It would seem that my men lack the will and heart to fight you this day," said Verglas, offering Brouette a smile that looked more like a sneer. "I concede you the field. Bravely won."

Michel watched Brouette's eyes narrow as they rose to consider the man who was his enemy. But though the young lord said nothing in reply, the look he offered Verglas was one of contempt. Michel looked down into his father's death-pale face, fighting back the threat of tears. His whole body trembled, his emotions raw like an open wound.

He couldn't understand what had happened, why his father had been left behind on the field. But the lack of concern in his liege lord's eyes, the derision in his voice, left little room for doubt.

Somehow, for some reason Michel couldn't fathom, his father had been murdered.

He didn't realize his hand was moving until he felt his fingers close around the hilt of his father's sword, fallen at his side in the grass of the meadow. He drew the sword toward him, fingers tightening on the hilt. He lifted the blade off the ground, testing its balance in his hand.

"I say before these witnesses that the house of Verglas is reconciled with the house of Brouette," the Baron de Verglas announced from his horse. "My noble lord, let there be no further hostilities between us from this day hence."

Michel's grip tightened around the hilt of his father's weapon until the entire sword shook just as violently as the rest of his body. He didn't look at Verglas. Instead, Michel gazed down at the trembling blade, eyes focused on a gleam of light reflecting off the oiled metal. He had never noticed before how silken were those melded folds of steel, how elegant the many traces of color that were a natural part of the sword's texture. How perfectly good the hilt felt in his hand, how keen were the edges of the blade.

"Your requirements have been met," he could hear Verglas saying, as if from a distance. "Here's the poor soul you wanted. Now, good brothers, if I might remind you of the promised letters."

The baron's words moved past Michel without context or meaning. They spoke but said nothing, absorbed by the wandering haze. Around him, the forest seemed to groan, a breeze stirring the leaves with a gasping sigh of air.

Michel lifted the sword, cradling the hilt against his chest as he gazed into his father's staring eyes.

"This was not what we agreed," said a rasping voice that sounded older than dead. "We asked for your bravest and your best. But what we have witnessed today appears nothing more than the calculated murder of an inferior knight."

Turning, Michel found himself staring into the grisly face of one of the undead knights he'd glimpsed before the battle. He had no idea as to the wight's purpose. All he knew was that his slain father now seemed to have a champion, someone to defend him, if only with the force of accusation.

The Baron de Verglas sneered. "Perhaps your duties in the afterworld have kept you away too long, good brother, if you fail to distinguish between murder and simple incidence of casualty. Or could it be possible that you have never seen combat? It is, after all, difficult to gain a good sense of a battlefield if your back is turned to it."

Michel felt a sharp pang of outrage at the insult. His trembling fingers clenched the cold hilt of his father's sword. He didn't know he was rising from the ground until he found himself standing, his father's sword clutched in a double-fisted grip. He took a step toward Verglas, drawing the blade back over his shoulder.

For the first time, the baron seemed to take note of him. The nobleman frowned, a look of confusion passing over his face. The expression broke into a thin grimace of amusement.

"What is this?" The baron barked a laugh, indicating Michel with a sweep of his gloved hand. "The boy wants to make a fight of it!"

The baron's knights regrouped about their lord. Not one looked amused. The eyes of the men shifted nervously between Michel and Verglas, their expressions tense and uncertain. Many had been friends of his father. They all knew him well.

"Ignorant boy." Verglas dismissed Michel with a scowl of contempt. "Men of noble birth do not cross swords with the likes of mere squires."

Michel clenched his teeth as his cheeks flushed scarlet. His father lay dead at his feet, and the hilt of Bernard's sword felt lovely in his hands. The baron's arrogance filled him with a white-hot fury that took him well past reason. Michel stood with his sword swept back over his shoulder, but he couldn't bring himself to let the blade fall. The baron was mounted and unarmed.

"Give over the blade, son."

The command startled him. Michel glanced up into the corrupted face of one of the undead knights. The wight had somehow managed to dismount and come up silently beside him. He was standing with a skeletal hand open and proffered. Beneath his rotten boots, the grass withered and turned black.

Michel relaxed his grip on the hilt. But he couldn't keep the rage of grief from his face. He stared helplessly, unable to comply. What he saw in the wight's face shocked him. It was a look of sympathy, of understanding. The paladin gazed at him for a long minute, eyes like mirrors of clouded glass. Then he commanded again:

"Give over the blade, son, if you wish to seek the justice of Syre."

He reached up and gently eased the hilt from Michel's grip. The knight lifted the sword before his gray and desiccated face. Then he angled the weapon in front of him, staring down the length of the blade. Seeming satisfied, he stepped forward and slipped the sword under Michel's belt, where it hung dangling by the crossguard.

"Kneel you down, son, and let your eyes and hands be lifted."

Michel stared mutely into the knight's skeletal face, comprehension failing him utterly. But something about the wight's undead stare compelled Michel to do exactly as he bade. He dropped to his knees beside the corpse of his father. He raised his hands and stared straight up into the gray and dismal sky. His eyes blurred, filling with tears. Ashamed, he wiped his face.

The wight gazed down at him and said, "Swear you to give defense to the poor and weak and combat treachery all the days of your life, and even after, into death?"

"I so swear it." A shiver ran down Michel's neck as it finally occurred to him what the knight was doing.

Nodding curtly, the paladin stepped forward and, with an open hand, struck Michel soundly on the side of the head. Reeling from the *colée*, Michel gasped as the knight took his hand in his bony fingers.

"Arise, good knight."

As Michel rose unsteadily to his feet, he could hear Verglas blurt, "What mockery is this?"

It was the other Syric knight who responded as he drew his horse up at the baron's side. "You said you would not cross arms with a squire. But a knight now stands before you demanding the justice of Syre. What is wrong, my lord? Surely you have nothing to fear from the likes of a mere boy?"

For moments, the Baron de Verglas glared silent hatred into the wight's dead eyes. Then, with one swift motion, he swung his leg over his stallion's back and dismounted, drawing his sword. He held the blade at a threatening angle as he turned his body to square up with Michel. He ran his gaze over the youth with a look of disdain.

"Your father was my sworn vassal," he said, hefting the weapon in his hand. "For that reason alone, I will give you this one chance to kneel and pledge me fealty."

"It was murder." Michel heard his own voice as though it were someone else's, the words sounding distant and foreign to his ears.

The baron looked at him, raising his sword and licking his lips. He mumbled under his breath, "Of course it was."

And then the blade was falling.

Michel stumbled back as a blur of steel sliced toward him. Clumsily, he freed his father's sword from his belt and managed to bring it up in time to parry the next strike. The two blades met with a ringing jar that shuddered down the length of Michel's arms, nearly wrenching the hilt from his grasp. Michel staggered, barely avoiding another hissing slice.

He found himself forced backward across the field to maintain his range, working his arms furiously to keep time to the nobleman's press. Each parry he made was a fraction too slow, each attack an instant too late. He lost more ground, retreating under a hail of relentless blows.

Michel was no stranger to the sword. But for all his years of practice, he was hard-pressed to defend against the baron's assault. Verglas moved in quickly, pressing him back with calm, precise attacks.

Michel deflected a thrust, swept his sword back, and then let it fall with all the weight of his body behind it. Verglas merely brushed his blade aside. Angered, Michel lunged forward and pressed a rapid sequence of attacks that kept the lord moving but left nothing for defense.

Seeing an opportunity, the baron thrust his blade in low, dipping beneath Michel's guard and cleaving upward toward his stomach. The youth spun away as the blade's edge scored his front. A thin line of blood appeared across the fabric of his shirt, spreading quickly over the wool. There was no pain. Verglas's steel was wicked-sharp.

Shaken, Michel barely managed to bring his sword up to parry the next slice aimed at his chest. The baron's steel shrieked up the length of his blade, scraping all the way to the crossguard. Michel reached out and caught the man's hand with his own, driving the pommel of his hilt into the baron's face.

Verglas cried out as his head snapped back. Michel raised his sword and brought it down with every ounce of strength left in his body. The blade took the lord at the base of the neck, tearing through his shoulder and parting the riveted chains of his hauberk.

Michel wrenched back on the hilt to free his blade. Verglas slumped forward against him, mouth open, eyes wide and startled. His hands went limp. The sword dropped from his grasp and fell beneath him as his knees gave way. Inelegantly, the Baron de Verglas doubled over, slumping to the ground.

Michel stood, gasping for air, staring down at the corpse in numb disbelief. His father's sword trembled in his hands, his chest heaving with the force of each drawn breath. His legs were shaking and weak, his flesh ablaze with a sudden, searing fire. Staring down at the baron's sprawled form, Michel lowered his sword arm to his side.

An armored fist slammed him full in the face.

The blow spun him around, taking him to the ground. Opening his eyes, Michel saw the baron's men hovering over him. He tried to rise, but found he lacked the strength for it. He didn't care what they did to him. He was too tired, too grieved. So, he lie there, staring into a turbid sky barely visible through the trees, blinking slowly.

"Help me," he whispered.

"I am," came the reply. To Verglas's men, the undead knight said, "Let the worms have the father. We asked for your best and bravest. There he is. Deliver him unto us."

Without hesitation, Verglas's men fell upon Michel. Their gauntleted fists rained down on his armorless body, their boots taking him in the sides, chest, and head. A crushing heel came down to pound molten fire into his groin.

Overhead, mist swirled through the forest. A gentle breeze stirred the fog, moved the age-old branches of the trees. The new spring leaves whispered as they trilled on the boughs, their song a breathless sigh.

In the remote distance, a hawk shrieked, but the youth did not hear it. His mind had slipped somewhere far beyond hearing, beyond knowledge of pain or grief. Beyond awareness. His thoughts, like the mist, swirled away in a churning grayness that was strangely, mercifully, comforting.

EXHIBITION

BEN GALLEY

ON THE BATTLEFIELD, time is not made of minutes and hours. It is measured by the incessant throbbing of a muck-smeared skull. It is another bead of sweat invading the eye. It is the count of bodies lying bloody behind you. There is no now or later, only death or survival. Time has no place on the battlefield. It lends its mantle to carnage and skulks on the fringes, waiting to matter once again, when all the blood has spilt.

The ground vomited another puddle of brackish water as I pivoted. His broken sword-tip whined past my ear, robbing hairs from me. Blood spattered in my face as my blade slashed his poorly leathered belly. Boggle-eyed, he sunk to the mire, screaming at the sight of his guts splayed across his muddy palms, steaming in the dawn's cold.

I considered his neck, but his iron collar would have notched my sword. I left him to his wailing as a lance sought to skewer me.

In that tightfisted world, that ring of fog and shrieking steel, my existence was no more complex than who could kill who. My only struggle in life was being faster. Better. It was a terrifying simplicity, and I clung to that throbbing in my forehead, a constant reminder of what side of existence I danced on.

Winter trees cast skeletal shadows on the haze where the enchanters had begun to put their fires to work. The slate-grey fog took on a sickly glow, undulating between green and the yellow of bile.

A pitiful wail cut the din of cursing and dying as the bog swallowed a man whole. Just a fatal misstep on poorly chosen-ground. No glorious sweep and clash of gleaming ranks, this. There was no more glory to be found here than in a tavern-brawl in a swamp.

An axe came spinning for my legs. A sidestep, and it cut the turf from a mound behind me, lodging in the skull of a corpse. Those who think there is peace in death on the field of war are sorely mistaken.

My new enemy came hunting for me, spiked fists raised, mist spiralling about his chains and leather plates. A roar sprang from his foreign tongue as he reached for me. I cut it short, taking a smart step and burying my sword up to the hilt in his chest.

The roar withered into a gurgle, but the blaze in his eyes refused to die. His fists fell on my shoulders, seeking my neck. The iron gauntlets locked together, pinching my skin. I seized the crossbars of my sword and wrenched. Crimson poured down its channels, wetting my hands. The man gripped only harder. I choked.

As I felt my chest burn, I twisted the blade, again and again, until I'd bored a hole so big in his chest I could have used him as a window. Only then did he falter, eyes rolling up to bloodshot whites. He collapsed on his side, his face in a murky pool and his gauntlets still at my neck. I could breathe, but I thrashed to be free. He held me tighter than a jealous lover.

EXHIBITION

Emerald fire bloomed behind the fog. Thunder rolled across the marsh, and with it, a hot breeze that made the walls of my small world billow. With it came bodies: some mere shadows arcing high through the mist, others crashing into the masses like ballista bolts. I spied one still wriggling as she flew, her legs enveloped in fire. A nearby bog saved her bones, and her landing showered me with stinking water. When she reared up, she was still screaming. I saw the water bubbling around her, and a green glow between her thrashing.

She reached for me, and I saw her eyes burning with the same sickly flames. As her clothes began to fall to flakes around her white skin, before the fire turned it black, I saw the brands across her chest. It was then I heard the meaning of her screeching. Not for her own pain, but for mine, and the colour of banner we shared.

'I-I can't hold onto it! RUN!'

Slippery hands wriggled my sword free, slicing my palms in the process. With desperate pants, I hacked at the corpse's hands. My peripheries worked for me. My gaze was locked on the enchanter, now consumed by her green fire. Her eyes glowed white through the conflagration.

I felt the pop of a wrist coming loose, and I tore myself free. Stumbling over dead legs, I scrabbled away on my backside, face full of horror. *To be cheated of life through no fault of my own...*

Time came for me then, showing me with glee how little sand remained in my hourglass. So little, and yet the grains fell like snowflakes. I spat curses until I felt something burst from my chest.

I stared down at the bloody spearhead, decorated with scraps of something vital. A vein stretched against the barbarous hook, still pumping with my blood. I looked up at my killer to find not a cold grin, but a gawping mouth of blackened teeth. His eyes were not for his prey, but for the enchanter. In my chest, I felt something snap.

The blast consumed us both, green fire so hot I felt the flesh peel off my bones before it reduced me to ash.

VOMIT CHOKED ME. I bucked against callous restraints. Icy water drowned me in wakefulness.

The voice boomed through my senses. 'Untie her.'

I was loosed, and before my eyes could make sense of my surroundings, I reared up and tumbled to a heap against cold stone. I felt rough robes against my skin. No press of sweaty armour. No wet boots and dawn-chill. No ache of sword in my hand. By my knees, my fingers found themselves. I felt flesh, not charred knuckles. That world had faded, though the throbbing still reigned in my head.

I opened my eyes to see dusty sandstone, dark with the sweat from my face. I took a breath, choked, and spent a while hawking up more bile.

The voice floated to me, heavy with condescension.

'Another wasted meld, novitiate?'

I looked past my shoulder to the cot where the bundle sat. I remembered the smears of black soot on its fabric, and this time they made me shudder. *What had I expected?* To survive longer than she had? That was not the way of the meld.

'You wish to paint nothing?'

Tracing the tangle of tubes past the sinuous flasks and lamps, I looked to the balcony high above me. Candles glowed along its edge now. It must have been night beyond the shuttered windows. Their flickering did nothing to illuminate the tuton's face. He paced, betraying impatience.

With a snarl, I forced my legs into working order. My bare feet slapped the stone. I snatched the brushes from the table. The paints waited for me, refilled and glistening.

I forced my eyes to focus on my canvas. My neck crunched as I toured its expansive edges, somehow releasing a pressure in my head.

Paint slopped as I went to work. Great arcs of colour obscured my previous efforts, wiping out gleaming generals and captains with mean streaks of my brush. I chose a bog-brown and decapitated half an army with a sweep of my hand. There came a tut from above.

'Another try, novitiate?'

'You asked for perfection, tuton. I intend to provide it.'

Only the brush of his bare feet answered me. The weight of the days spent in that hall lie heavy between us. I could feel his irritation wafting into my paint and vomit-smeared pit. It only served to drive me on. I stabbed my brush into a slate-grey and bound my scene in oppressive fog.

Time once again faded into meaninglessness as I painted. I was no artist. This was not love of my craft. This was yet another battle. A toil for my own betterment, not the canvas'. My only audience was the critical eyes above me. My only exhibition a final test that I was currently failing.

The drudgelings came twice to change the candles while I worked. I did not realise until I tore myself away from my canvas and saw the burnt-out husks of wax beside new red pillars.

'There, tuton. I am finished.'

I saw dark knuckles slide into the light and grip the balcony railing firmly. His hooded figure angled forwards to pass judgment of my efforts. My legs shook not through nervousness, but from exhaustion. My eyes snuck around my pit, looking for water.

He took so long to decide, I began to judge with him. The artist will always see what the viewer does not. Not more or less, but as though viewed at a different angle. The light didn't show me perfection, but every bump of overzealous wash of paint, every betraying shadow of my past attempts. Staring at my scene of fire and fog now, I wanted to snatch up a candle and burn it.

Like a coward, he offered the verdict up to me. 'Why do you think it is a fit offering?'

I was thankful I faced away from him. My bared teeth took some time to hide. 'It depicts valiance, tuton. Camaraderie. I understand now the art of war is not about tactics, nor the well-trained army, but about the prowess of each soldier.' I hurriedly corrected myself. 'The *heart*, rather, of each soldier.'

'Hm.'

Even from such a curt response, I knew I had failed once more.

'Again. Show her valiance!' His bellow was many-voiced, echoing about the hall. I stared up at him as the drudgelings came from their hatches to drag away the cot and its burned bones. He turned away from me, disappearing from view. I did not like to linger on the great paintings beyond his perch. Even then, as I scanned their multitude, hauntingly illuminated by their own candles, I saw them moving. I tore my gaze away and turned back to the contraption.

In place of the bones, the hunched old goblins wheeled in a body bleached grey by death. Rot had already claimed him. His stench mixed with the reek of the paints, and I gagged while they prepared the wires and leathery veins. Behind the grille in the wall, the cogs began to spin. I felt the sweat gather on my palms as I heard their teeth crunching.

Again.

The drudgelings shepherded me towards the table. Shrugging off their filthy, withered hands, I took the position on the table, face thrust through the hole at its head. I arched my shoulders, breath short and sharp, and listened to the insidious dripping of the bottles.

When the cogs came to a clanging stop, feet gathered around my head once more. The straps were tighter this time, and when they showed me the silver bowl with its dark, viscous liquid, I betrayed myself with a convulsion.

I knew it was pointless to hold my breath, but I did it anyway.

DARKNESS, BROKEN ONLY by shafts of dusty sunlight, betrayed gaps in a gate. They lit slices of my crowded surroundings: a spiked helmet decorated with cat skulls; lips shivering with nervous prayers; armour plates like palm fronds.

The stench of sweat stung my nose. I felt an oppressive lump in my throat as I took breath. A cough took me, and I was cursed in hushed voices. I reached to thumb sweat from my eye and felt the bush of a beard in my hands. A spear was firmly gripped in the other.

Past the huddled figures before me, I saw shapes scattering in the slits of daylight. Shrieks filled the air. There arose a boom from below, and my new world shook violently.

Sunlight blinded me. Were it not for the savage shoving from behind, I would have shrunk into a ball, all my training forgotten. I blamed the exhaustion.

I found stone beneath my boots and screams of war pushed me on down a thin causeway. I glimpsed a battle raging far below. Ranks sprawled across a scrub plain dotted with the graves of waterways.

'Death!' came the chant, rising from the soldiers around me. I looked for an enemy but saw only flashes of coloured silk and heard high-pitched screams. I watched a man wade past me, his scimitar raised high. It flashed in the hot sun as he swung it. A splash of blood followed its arc.

A woman burst from the crowd and flew at me, sharp nails spread like claws. She ripped a chunk from my cheek before my reflexes threw her aside. Before I could pin her, an axe found her spine, and she tottered over the side of the causeway with a thin shriek.

'Death!' roared the soldier before storming on. I followed dumbly in his wake.

A pair of doors had already been smashed through, and I marched over their remains into a room choked with silk curtains and polished furniture. A score of women were pressed against the walls, fending soldiers away with fire-pokers. A handful of guards toiled alongside them. The soldiers sought them with spears, impaling them against the marble.

Despite my revulsion, I fought with them, finding a convenient excuse in the futility of fighting the meld and the possibility a lesson. I lashed about half-heartedly with my spear, knocking a guard off his feet before turning to run an escaping woman through. I had thought her another guard. She took my spear from my slack grip, painting a bloody streak across the rug before dying.

An explosion ripped a nearby door in two, and I saw silver-armoured soldiers flooding into the room. The tide turned immediately and violently, sweeping us onto the causeway. My body proved itself a coward, ducking lances and pounding the stone to stay ahead of the flood. I wondered if all of us were, when death is close and the odds are stacked high. If valiance can't save a man, maybe cowardice could.

A trip slew me. A silk-draped corpse, a spear through her belly, avenged her death by sending me spinning over the edge of the causeway. I saw the desert plains yawn before me and felt my heart attempt to flee from my mouth.

The ground was a hungry beast, rising to me with relish. It took an age to fall, and while I roared with useless rage, I caught the sight of others falling around me. We met the ground with great clouds of dust. Merciful deaths, far too merciful for killers such as us. For we were no soldiers.

AGAIN, I CRAWLED from my table, bile-splattered and reaching for the brushes. I tottered to the canvas, decorating it in vomit before any paint found my brush.

I sprawled across my art, showing it no mercy, drawing fierce grins and pale faces with crimson makeup. I painted silks stretched over the sharp, purposeful lines of spears. I let blues bleed into the yellow of the sandstone. I let the scarlets spread. Hate was a colour I used often. Splendour was used sparingly, saved only for the shining suits of armour at my canvas' core.

I do not know how long I spent on those gleaming characters, but I know I bent the whole scene around them. Every other figure in my painting fled from them, including a marauder with a dark bush of a beard. They had no faces in their helmets, unlike the gawping, grinning villains at their feet, cowards scrambling to be free. The borders of mist from my last attempt still clung on in that sandstone room, as if I had no stomach to paint the rest of the contemptuous scene.

The tuton barely had the patience for another failure. His eyes had begun to glow.

'Again!'

'Let me finish!'

The drudgelings came forth to bind me with tough leather and cold buckles. I batted away their scaly hands. 'I can finish!'

'Sometimes it takes fire to paint a masterpiece, novitiate. Again, I say!'

Another body came, small as I in stature and covered in cloth.

Tuton's voice bounced from the walls, condemnation coming in waves. 'You would waste a decade of training? The sourest insolence!'

The wood was slimy from days of sweat.

'No! Let me paint more!'

'You would fall at the final test?'

'No, tuton. Don't put me in—' The clang of cogs drowned me.

'It was but a simple request! Paint the art of war!'

My eyes bulged as they pressed me to the hole. 'And I was trying!'

'Failing!'

'I don't know what you want from me!'

'All we have ever wanted, novitiate. Success.'

I roared all the way into the bowl of grey slop.

INSECTS DRONED ABOVE. A shameless wind whined across the grasses. Somewhere overhead, I heard the clack of leafless branches duelling. Now and again, a distant groan, or choke, and then silence again.

My eyes were caked in muck. I prised my eyelids open and lifted a head that throbbed once more, though this time with pain, not life.

I watched the bloody water rise around the weight of my palm, then around the other. The very mud itself bled a reddish-brown; part earth, part army. When I pushed with my elbows, pain scorched my side. I realised I was contributing to the boot-churned mire.

The wind blew again, eager to chill me. I felt its northern heritage against my shaved scalp, no different from my own hair outside the meld. I wondered which I felt more: my exhaustion or this body's.

I shivered now, half-bloodless and pressed against the squelch of mud. I pushed again and felt the weight of something against my legs.

Turning my head, I met the skewed stare of a dead man missing his lower jaw. The other way lay an unknown, face so deep in the mud I thought them decapitated at first. Fidgeting my feet told me more bodies lay behind me. Soft skin clinging to hard bone. It was unmistakable.

I crawled. That was all I had to offer life: two elbows and some strength left to use them. I gave thanks for my cold-bitten nose, and how it fended off the stink of those around me. Small mercies count for a lot, when mercy is all you depend on.

I cursed the tuton with each effort, foreign tongue spitting ill-formed words. My profanity startled a seagull, come to pick at the bodies. It backpedaled, cawing harshly.

The next time I planted my elbow, the ground moaned. A strong grip—the strength only a dying man has—encircled my wrist. I stayed still, watching a patch of mud crack into the white of an eye, a bloody smear of a mouth, the pink of a throat.

'S-save me.'

I felt the need to save myself overpower me, and I freed myself with a kick to his man's shin. He gasped, falling limp, and I felt a shame envelop me. Though he still blinked at me, I kept crawling, shuddering from more than just scold and blood loss.

A scorched crater beckoned me inwards, and I curled into a ball in its cradle. The black earth smelled acetic, rotten. At its centre, a burnt skeleton was frozen in some worship of the sky.

'Another!'

Rough hands grabbed the nape of my clothes and hauled me back to the mud. The pain in my side brought fireworks to my eyes.

'Fucken' 'shield-brat!'

The cold steel found my throat before I could bleat a word. I felt no pain, just the warmth escaping me. I refused to breathe, to drown in my own blood. I clawed for eyes, kicked like a mule, and yet it changed nothing.

'Die, heretic.'

Before the darkness claimed me, I felt their rough hands begin to search and paw at my body.

THE LEATHER WAS loosed from around my wrist. I felt my limbs tumble to the floor, painless in the absence of sensation. I blinked, seeing the huge canvas tipped on its edge. The paint had ignored gravity, falling sideways as if blown by a gale.

I felt the cold of stone against my temples and put the world back upright. I stayed there, my knees, shivering while I stared under hooded brows at the hateful creature the painting had become. It was like no enemy I had ever fought. The more I swiped my brush, the more skin it wore, the more armour I pasted onto it. I wondered how much I'd have to chip away to find out why I had started fighting it in the first place. *A decade of training…*

He must have felt me sway. He spoke to remind me he was there.

'Show me. A final chance.'

I raised a knee. My hand found a scattered brush, and I swiped it from the stone.

One step. I took a moment to gather some saliva.

Two steps, and I was angling the brush at the canvas like a lance.

Three steps. My knees found the stone again, scraping the skin away. I was still too numb from exhaustion to notice.

I raised the brush to paint the air, and while it danced, I reached up and snapped its neck. Green paint smudged my palm. I smeared it across my face.

The pause was so pregnant I expected a roar of indignation to break it.

'You wish not to paint?' came the question.

I felt like laughing. All I did was choke and spat something red to the stone.

'There is no point, tuton.'

'Because you cannot do it?'

I found my humour, letting loose a cackle as sharp as napped flint. 'No. Not because I cannot.'

Finding my strength next, I stumbled over to my canvas and lay my hands on the darkest paints I could find. With great windmill swings of my arms, I drowned my painting. When the containers were empty, I took my hands to it, smearing it across every part I could reach.

When I was done, and panting like a hound, my backside found the floor again. I didn't want to look at him. His hidden face wouldn't have shown me the displeasure I wanted to see. I had failed, and that I wanted to burn out, not wither away. And besides, I might as well have danced on my way down to meet death. It was the last chance to do so.

'Explain yourself, novitiate.'

'Because, tuton, it can't be done,' I gasped, laughing some more. 'Because there is no art to war.'

For an age, he left me there on the cold floor, staring at paintings that held nothing but shaking heads and disappointed shrugs. If I'd had the saliva, I would have spat at them.

The tuton's answer, when it came, was a slow clap. I heard the shuffling of drudgelings and felt myself being dragged across the floor.

'Well done, novitiate. Well done.'

FLESH AND COIN

ANNA STEPHENS

THEY CALLED HER Stoneheart. And they didn't smile when they said it. Didn't mean it as a joke or a mock. They Named her in the old way and there was nothing she could do about it. Can't argue getting a Name, but of all the Names she'd hoped for herself as she made her way into the ranks of mercenaries, as she climbed those ranks like ladders, Stoneheart wasn't one of them. Quickstrike, Spearfast, Steelwill, those were Names she could be proud of, Names she could wear like a badge, carry like a banner. Not Stoneheart. Not cold and hard and without mercy or regret.

Stoneheart. But what could she do other than smile, big and bold and mocking, chin up and a challenge in a cocked eyebrow. Stoneheart, aye? Sure you want to find out just how stony?

But right now, Syl Stoneheart had more pressing concerns. She crouched with her company on the western slope of the ravine, scrunched in among the boulders and scree, two dozen women and men in scuffed leather and ragged shirts, chainmail muffled under jerkins, spears and bucklers plain and functional. Nothing fancy. Nothing shiny or noisy. Just quiet, grim-faced folk in a quiet, grim ravine on the road to Talannest.

Syl hated ambushes more than she hated stupid fucking Names. Too many things to go wrong. Too many unknowns. And worse, too much time sitting, waiting, thinking about all the things to go wrong. The boulder was cold beneath her cheek as she rolled her head up to peer around it. She could see a quarter-mile before the twisting road vanished around an outcrop. Every stride of that quarter-mile was empty. Empty as her purse until after this job was done.

A guarded wagon will traverse the ravine an hour before noon. Bring me its contents and I'll give you a bag of gold.

Tinker's words echoed in her head. She'd asked him what size bag of gold. On reflection, she should've asked what size guard. Still, she'd the numbers to see this through and another tale to add to the Stoneheart's glory.

The company opposite was silent and invisible. Or gone, she supposed, quelling the urge to spit. Wouldn't surprise her if Garn Spineless had lived up to his Name and fled with his fighters. She'd have to be the Stoneheart if he had. Have to be ruthless if she was to get this done with only half an ambush team.

And done it had to be. Her belly was emptier than her purse, and her company, while not yet muttering, had taken to exchanging meaningful looks when they thought she wasn't looking. A crew that did that was a crew only days away from meaningful words with their commander, and after that, there was nothing for it but meaningful fists and terminal knives. The Iron Blades were a good company. She'd no desire to be gutted by them. Or forced to do the gutting herself.

There was a clatter of stone behind her, a muffled curse, and Syl reached back an open palm in question. Renn slid to her side, well down on his belly where he was hidden. 'Rock scorpion,' he said. 'Dealt with.'

Syl stuck up a thumb, eyes fixed on the path. Still empty. She let out a soft breath and sat back, checking her crew for the twentieth time. Rock scorpions. Just what they bloody needed. Syl had seen men die from rock scorpion stings, black and screaming as their skin split from the swelling. Like watching someone get turned inside out.

Spineless cawed like a dying rook, and Syl's fists clenched as she looked to the road. There. She reached back again and found a part of Renn, shoulder or knee, squeezed twice, paused, then once more. He shifted from beneath her hand, back to the others to pass warning.

Long minutes crawled by, slower than a long death, before the clop of hooves and creak of harness echoed up the ravine. They were cautious now, alive to danger, archers on the flanks, the wagon in their midst. Syl cursed silently when she identified the guards—the Bleeding Eyes, led by none other than Etta Scarlet herself. *Just what I fucking need. Still, had to happen sometime, I suppose. Old scores and all that.*

Whatever was in those barrels stacked so ostentatiously on top of the wagon, Syl knew it wasn't what they'd been hired to steal. They were close now, and Syl could see the unease in the guards, the distinctive red makeup across their eyelids and noses highlighting the flickering of their eyes as they scanned the high scree and rock walls hemming them in. Etta didn't hire fools, and if she did, word had it she killed them herself. They all knew this was ambush territory. Syl could see it in every taut line, every horse's snort, every jerky twist of the head. It was also the only decent road to Talannest.

Garn's dying rook called again, and straight away the Eyes reacted, half closing in around the wagon, the rest in squads of three, bows drawn and aiming for the rocks on both sides.

Come on, Spineless. Now would be good. Garn had the better eyeline, so it was his decision when to trigger the ambush. Soften them up with volleys, then pelt down the slope and take it hand to hand with the survivors. Chances were, the Eyes would press forward rather than try and manoeuvre the wagon around to flee back the way they'd come. Soon as they started running down the ravine, they'd run slap into the third company Syl insisted on recruiting, never mind that it would reduce their cut of the takings.

All rested on Spineless moving his fucking arse, though, and so far, Spineless didn't seem inclined to do so. Syl didn't want to have to take on the Eyes alone, but the Stoneheart had a Name and a reputation to uphold, coin to earn to fill an empty purse. The Stoneheart would give the order even if Syl wouldn't. That's how it worked with Names.

The quarry was deep into the ambush zone now, moving at a trot, keen to be out the other side. And still nothing. Not an arrow, not a war cry, not so much as a fart on the wind. *Spineless, toothless, cockless old bastard. Fucking loose.*

Syl ground her teeth together. The front-riding Eyes were almost out the other end of the ambush site. Much further and they'd have ridden straight past Lobb and his squad, as well, and the lot of 'em would be left hiding in the rocks and stroking their cocks. Those who had them.

Not today, Spineless.

'Arrows.' Syl hissed, low and urgent, and her dozen archers slithered into position. 'Now,' she added, not bothering to wait, not giving Garn another second or the Eyes any more time to exit the ambush. Arrows arced up to kiss the sky and fall humming, whining, screaming to find marks in seven Eyes, one horse, the wagon itself, and one entirely innocent rock by the side of the trail.

More in the air, and more, and arrows coming back the other way now, random, without targets. Just loosing and hoping, trying to disrupt the Iron Blades' rhythm. Still nothing from Garn, though, and Syl wondered if she'd been listening to a dying rook after all.

She thought about abandoning it, running the way Garn must've, but it was too late. Besides, she was a mercenary, and a damn good one, her crew, too. She was the fucking Stoneheart.

'We go,' she said, low. 'Count of twenty. Archers, keep their heads down. One. Two. Three…'

The wagon had stopped, and a couple of Eyes were rolling barrels off the top, the others hunkered down in whatever protection they could find, behind boulders or shields or the wagon itself, loosing back where they could, mostly just hiding. With arrow shot only coming from one side, it wasn't that difficult to avoid. Piss and vinegar, but they looked a sloppy crew of amateurs in front of Etta.

'Take the loot,' an Eye called, gesturing at the barrels. Syl huffed a laugh through her teeth– eleven, twelve, thirteen–but it faded when the barrels came rolling in their direction, all the way to the edge of the road. Her gaze wandered the path, and she noted that now all of the Eyes were huddled behind the wagon with their horses, as far from the barrels as they could get. And that one was standing, smoke and yellow streaming from a fire arrow.

Syl's eyes darted back to the barrels. 'Get that fucking archer now!' she screeched, not bothering with quiet, and three arrows arced into the air, but the one on fire was already flying in the opposite direction, trailing smoke and spitting malice. 'Down!'

Syl hunched small and panicked behind her boulder, knees by her ears, arms over her head. The explosion rocked the ravine, shook the ground, and started several small avalanches of loose scree and pebbles. A shockwave of burning barrel splinters and rock shrapnel burst up the slope, and something laid open the back of Syl's hand, stung her ear sharper than a wasp.

Horses screamed and careened madly down the trail, and there were shrieks as Blades were caught in the blast, and one deep, ululating wail that spoke of injuries Syl couldn't cure out in the wastes, and probably not even if she'd been a surgeon in Talannest. Hooves faded into the distance, most of the screaming stopped, and a sort of quiet fell.

'Still alive, Stoneheart?' came the deep, amused voice of Etta Scarlet, bane of Syl's former existence. The voice that still made her cringe inside. 'That you making that sweet music?'

'Alive. Armed. Pissed,' Syl yelled back, checking as many of the Iron Blades as she could without giving away her position or letting any part of her body show past the protection of her rock. Her hand was bleeding good, hot and sticky, the fingers slow to respond.

'On a job, as it happens,' she shouted, 'and I know the real cargo's under the awning, so how about you drag it out and leave it with us? No more fighting, no more killing. You can be about your day with no hard feelings.' She squinted up at the early sun. 'Isn't it past time you were passed out drunk somewhere?'

'That sounds like a plan, Syl. A real good plan, and aye, I've got a thirst brewing. Just one problem, you don't count that most of our horses have bolted.'

Syl's guts tightened. 'Yeah? What's that?' she called, peering up the ravine for Lobb and his fighters. Plan or not, you hear fire barrels go up and you come running. Friends need you. Hells, even acquaintances, even people who were mostly enemies, needed you when fire barrels were in play.

'Me and Spineless and Lobb don't want you to have it.'

The words dragged Syl's full and disbelieving attention back to Etta standing concealed at the edge of the wagon. They wouldn't. They fucking had.

'Etta, Etta,' Syl yelled after a long pause, 'the drink's made you a fool. You really think they'll honour the bargain? You should know better than to trust scum like them.' Silence answered her, and Syl took the reprieve to pass her orders with a series of simple gestures.

'You're saying they double-crossed me?' Etta called eventually.

'Why not? They have me. Probably just waiting for us to wipe each other out, then claim the booty for themselves.'

'They wouldn't,' Etta said, but there was doubt in her voice now. Doubt was dangerous on a battlefield. Doubt was deadly.

Syl laughed and held up three fingers to her Blades. 'Wouldn't they?' Two fingers. She rolled onto her hands and toes. 'So where are they then? Haven't killed us, aren't aiding you.' One finger. 'They're on your side, why aren't I dead?'

She didn't wait for an answer, instead bunched her fist, and her archers loosed three quick volleys to keep their heads down and kill the wagon horses–*best hope the cargo's lightweight*–and Syl was up and running, dodging boulders, skidding through scree, using the butt of her spear to leap over rocks, mouth stretched and a howl tearing its way out of her throat.

The Iron Blades were with her, as always. Whatever their opinion of the situation, when the Stoneheart called the attack, the Blades attacked. There looked to be a second of genuine surprise from the Bleeding Eyes, but then they were racing into a ragged line.

A savage grin split Syl's face as she vaulted the last rocks down to the road, landing in a spray of dirt and shrapnel and punching her spear tip into the groin of the closest Eye. She felt the blade lodge in, and then skitter off the bone, dragging, cutting deeper, and wrenched, twisting as she did. The Eye shrieked and flailed a longsword at her, but Syl was way out of reach of the blade and the woman's leg was already buckling. Syl punched it in again, gut this time, and left the Eye to bleed, scanning the battleground for Etta.

Is it finally time for that reckoning, Etta Scarlet? Finally time to see who's got the bigger Name?

There. Backing slowly away from the wagon, two Blades hunting her. She was about to tell them Etta was hers when a man charged her, looking ridiculous and embarrassed with red paint on his face, caked into eyebrows that were a weapon in themselves, though the sword he swung was no joke. Syl batted it aside, but he was quick, so she ducked back out of range, skipped sideways when he followed, whipping the spear around her so fast it did the job of a shield, then stabbing out with the butt and crunching it into his sternum. Blow like that didn't need a blade on the end. She heard his chest crack, and he crumpled, wheezing, sword drooping and free hand pressed to his chest. His mouth gaped for air his lungs wouldn't take.

Syl readied the death stroke, paused at the call of a sick crow. 'You fucking wouldn't,' she whispered. But Spineless fucking would. He was. Arrows rose into the sky, humming like massive, pissed-off bees, and fell indiscriminately among Iron Blade and Bleeding Eye alike. Syl ducked beneath the big man as he slumped, felt the impact as three arrows took him in the back. Those had most definitely been aimed at her.

'You traitorous bastard dog!' she screamed in Garn's direction. She crawled from beneath the corpse, found Etta, raised her chin.

Etta scowled, nodded. 'Deal.'

'Archers. Volleys!' Syl spat. 'Stand with the Eyes,' she added, and the Iron Blades disengaged and formed up alongside the men and women they'd been trying to kill a second before. The Eyes moved just as swiftly, as though it'd all been rehearsed.

Oh, aye, if this'd been rehearsed, I wouldn't have seven crew dead that I can see from here. And Garn would've been spitted on my spear arsehole first a long stretch of day ago.

'You coming out, Garn, or do we need to come in there and drag you out?' Her shout was all bravado—chances of anyone climbing into that mess of scree and boulder with the intention of coming out with captives was slimmer than a starving snake—but it was worth a try.

'I think not, little girl,' Garn yelled, and Syl's eyes narrowed. 'Not unless you're thinking of dropping those trousers and giving me a seeing to.'

Syl sighed. 'Yeah, that one never gets old.' She raised her voice. 'How about you drop yours first and I ram my spear up your shitter?' Instead of a reply, there were arrows, and the Blades and Eyes scattered for cover.

Syl snared Renn's gaze. A flick of the fingers and a jerk of the head, and the man grabbed two more Blades and slid behind the wagon, then ducked into the rocks on Garn's side of the ravine.

'They're keeping us here,' Syl whispered at Etta as they crouched together behind the dubious shelter of a dead horse. 'Waiting for Lobb's crew is my guess. I've sent Renn to scout, but a perimeter'd be a fine idea about now, aye?'

'You're a backstabbing, crooked-dealing little bitch, Syl Stoneheart,' Etta said, and the line of her shoulders spoke of her defeat. 'This a double double-cross? Knew of Garn's deal with me, did you, then offered him a sweeter purse to kill me?'

Syl's mouth was hanging open. 'Aye, and get my own killed alongside yours? Gods, but the drink's rotted your brain, Mother. This isn't a double-cross. Whatever we've done, no matter the blood in our past, I wouldn't set you up to fall in front of your crew. I'm Stoneheart, aye, but I'm not a cold heart. Or a cunt,' she added.

More arrows killed the conversation. Syl's stomach churned. Etta really thought her capable of that? They hadn't spoken much in recent years, true enough, and the words they had said had been bitter and full of sharp edges, but still…Etta was her mother.

She chanced a glance over the saddle. There were men picking their way out of the rocks on the opposite side of the ravine, now. Garn and his crew coming to end it.

'Pity,' Etta said.

'What is?'

'This'd hurt me less if you had betrayed me.' Etta's knife took Syl in the gut, the point penetrating the jerkin, sticking in the chainmail, and then, mostly because Etta was hammering on the hilt with the heel of her other hand, sliding-squealing-grating through into flesh.

Syl gasped in a breath and found both her hands on Etta's, straining away even as Etta strained in. 'What?' she managed, and then groaned, the sound as long and protracted as the blade's slow path through her flesh.

'You really thought I'd forgiven what you did, girl?' Etta grunted. 'You killed Dyran. You killed him, and then you walked away like you'd saved the world.' Her breath was liquor-rank. 'Had this coming a long time.'

It was a long knife, and a lot of it was inside Syl now, hot and cold and sharp and liquid and pain, dead gods, the pain. Fire chased ice chased molten steel in her gut, and Syl's strong hands were so weak, slipping from her mother's, implacable, unstoppable.

She wanted to remind Etta that Dyran had been a flesh-peddler, snatching and ransoming important people's children. That he'd deserved every hour of the death she'd given him when she'd seen what he did to those whose families couldn't pay. But the knife had taken her voice, just as surely as it was taking her life, and the words stuck in her chest.

'I have a reputation, little girl, forged from my years with Dyran.' Etta hissed. 'And the Bleeding Eyes have a reputation. So expect no mercy, daughter mine, expect no leniency for your crew. They all die here. With you.' Etta snorted and a faint smile crossed her face. 'I'm a poet.'

'Poet, is it?' Syl groaned. 'Then rhyme this.' The last of her strength went into ramming her knife up under Etta's chin and into her spine. Missed the joint that would've killed her instantly, but caused a fair amount of surprise so she at least stopped pushing the dagger into Syl's gut. Etta's hands rose to her throat and a look of pure panic crossed her face. Jugular. Red, gushing death. Only Syl had missed that, too, on account of being skewered like a rabbit, so the blow, while serious, hadn't yet killed Etta.

'Can't be having that.' Syl grunted, slapped Etta's hands away and waggled the hilt of the knife, sawing the blade left and right, hoping something inside would snap and kill the old bitch. Something snapped, and Syl was coated in hot, sticky red.

Shouting, the pounding of feet, clash of weapons and grunts of pain as the Iron Blades and the Bleeding Eyes started killing one another again in response to the bloody tableau of mother and daughter and dead horse and red. Lots of red.

And then Renn was there, planting himself over Syl and kicking Etta square in the face, sending her over onto her back. 'Blades!' he roared, 'protect the Stoneheart.'

More arrows, a shriek of pain from close, so close, and the edges of Syl's world turning black. She clutched Renn's leg, tugged on his trousers. 'What?' he snarled.

'What's…cargo?' She panted as a horrible emptiness found her.

'Fuck should I know?'

'Show…me,' she demanded. Her hand fell limp. Opposite, in a tangle of smeared red makeup and greying hair and bubbling pink froth, Etta watched her with dead eyes in a dying face. She seemed oddly triumphant.

WHEN IT WAS over, when Spineless's crew had fled and Lobb's had been cut down to a man and the Bleeding Eyes had thrown down their weapons for mercy the Blades didn't much feel like giving them, Renn opened the hidden door in the side of the wagon. He peered into the gloom, knife held tight in his fist.

'Gold?' Syl coughed, still hoping even now.

'Not exactly.' Renn's hand trembled, and he sheathed the knife. 'Come to me,' he said, 'and I promise you won't be hurt.' There was movement, a shift of material, a whimper, and the girl wrapped her arms and legs around him as he lifted her out. He looked to Syl.

'Tinker's not having her,' Syl managed. Her gaze wobbled across the kneeling Eyes. 'This what you do now?' she panted. 'This how you line your pockets?'

'We ain't pure and principled,' a grizzled woman shouted back. 'Gotta eat.'

'Us too. But Tinker's still not having her. Children are not currency.' Renn's eyes were cold. 'Then it looks like we need us a new leader,' he said. 'And as I'm carrying the cargo, guess that makes it me. Three days to Tinker's hideout and the gold, lads and lasses. Or you can stay with the dying.'

The Iron Blades looked between the two, Renn standing tall, Syl lying in a pool of her own blood. As one they moved to Renn's side. The Bleeding Eyes scrubbed the paint off their faces and followed.

'Bye then, Stoneheart,' Renn said.

Syl waved a bloody hand. 'Shit,' she said.

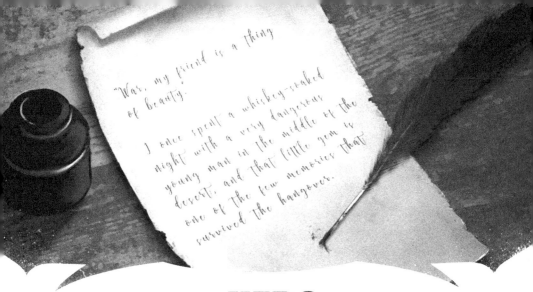

THE HERO OF ARAL PASS

MARK LAWRENCE

"WAR, MY FRIEND, is a thing of beauty."

I once spent a whiskey-soaked night with a very dangerous young man in the middle of the desert, and that little gem is one of the few memories that survived the hangover.

"To war is human. To run away is sublime," was my reply. Though in truth, the very best escape artist arranges to be carried away, ideally by a horse. Running involves entirely too much effort and is best avoided unless the only other choice is a camel.

I am Cardinal Jalan Kendeth, the highest ranking cleric of the Church of Roma in the entirety of the New World. Also, prince of Red March, favourite grandson of the Red Queen, marshal of Vermillion, and hero of the Aral Pass. This is my last will and testament. I entreat whoever finds this document to carry my bones from this miserable cave and have them returned across the ocean so that I may be interred in a mausoleum of sufficient grandeur on the banks of the Selene.

Forgive my shaky hand, but even now the bear is tearing at our barricades and...by the sounds of it...has eaten another of the trainee priests. I worry it will not be long before we run out of neophytes...

"God damn it!" I dipped my quill into the pot to discover that the ink had run out before the trainees.

I held the parchment up and blew across the glistening words to dry them off. The writing was rather shaky, but the bit about the bear was artistic license. I've met a couple of bears in my time, and whilst the main thing to do is have someone else fight them, the next thing on the to-do list is getting the hell out of there. Writing wills doesn't enter into bear wrangling at all.

No, the uneven calligraphy was all down to the ministrations of my native guide, a delightful creature named Ashley, blessed with long golden hair and an open mind.

"Like this, my lord?" She looked up at me. "Have I got it right?"

"Mmmmm." The part of me that wanted to shout, 'I'm a bloody cardinal! It's EMMINENCE!' and the part of me that wanted to remind her that 'Prince Jalan' and 'Your highness' were acceptable alternatives, were all drowned out by the part of me she was getting it so right for.

The bit about the cave was artistic license, too. But I did have trainee priests waiting for me downstairs in the tavern's main room.

To properly fake one's death requires a number of key ingredients. There's the manner, which is where the bear and the cave come in. There's witnesses. And three of my six young neophytes would serve to see me heading off into the mountains for forty days and forty nights of fasting in the wild. Then there are accomplices: the three fakes among my half-dozen trainees who would accompany me into the wilds, and then go back to their lives a few dollars richer. And finally, physical evidence. This to be provided by my hastily written last words and the judicious scattering of assorted bones. To which end I'd recently added grave-robbing to my long list of sins.

With all that in place, I felt I could safely slip away and return incognito to the empire without attracting unwanted attention from the pope, or the steward, or the young emperor, or my grandmother. After that, it would simply be a matter of digging up some buried assets and finding a suitably relaxed city to retire to.

One more ingredient was needed in this case, however. When dealing with unreasonably suspicious minds like those of His Holiness and the Red Queen, you also need something extra. The new pope has a particularly low view of me, one for which I blame his lowly origins. Those popes given the office to compensate some thwarted royal ambition, which frankly is almost all of them for the last few centuries, are much more relaxed about the sort of indiscretion that had seen the current incumbent exile me to the New World. Aristocratic popes, like me, see no reason why the inconvenience of holy office should stand in the way of life's pleasures. And to be fair, in my case, the nuns involved all held similar views. But, no, Pope Gormless, as I like to call him, took a very dim view of things and made all manner of dire threats concerning my fate if I returned before having converted the last heathen on these shores.

So, what you need when dealing with unreasonable suspicion is something in your death note that proves your desperation, something which shows that when the words were written you were utterly convinced that the end was mere moments away. Something you would never normally do.

And for me that vital ingredient, my friends, is honesty!

And so it is that with a distinct sense of peevish reluctance I commit to parchment the true tale of the Aral Pass, the military engagement on which my legend rests. The firm foundation upon which Prince Jalan the Hero stands defiant! The big lie that supports a whole series of increasingly bigger lies.

...Even now the bear has poor Stefan. I write with his screams ringing all around me. Would that I could forsake my holy vows and take up arms against this ravening beast. But alas, mine is the way of peace and I must arrive before God with clean hands and a clear conscience.

To this end, I offer my final confession. The true tale of my deeds at Aral Pass.

I would paint you a picture of that day, but I fear my palette lacks sufficient red to do it justice.

The Aral Pass runs through a particularly impassable ridge of mountains in the Tannerack range some twenty miles past the border between glorious Red March and the barren wastes of our sworn enemies, Scorron. Dying in the mountains close to this border has become somewhat of a tradition for the young men of both nations over the past eighty years, ever since Duke Micerow of Scorron allegedly made a disparaging remark about Prince Golloth's latest mistress. This sparked off an exchange of rhetoric that eventually reignited an ancient dispute over the ownership of various barren peaks in the Tanneracks.

Nobody actually fights on or defends the peaks themselves. War in the mountains is all about taking and holding the passes. And so, for those of us of a fighting age, attaining true adulthood required a rite of passage wherein we fought for the right of passage through some shitty mountain passes.

"VOLUNTEERS?" COLONEL ARTAX surveyed our ranks from the back of a horse far too big for hill riding, let alone daring the high passes. He had a grim face, bushy moustache, and terrifying pale eyes, his stare made all the more unnerving by a scar dividing his eyebrow and cheek. I happened to know he got it falling drunkenly onto railings at the palace as a young man, and that he fell into his current rank in a similar style, pushed by his father, the Duke of Arrais. But even so, he looked born to the part.

"I'll do it." I stepped forward, damned if I were going to call him 'sir.'

Artax ignored me and continued to scan the ranks. "These reports are credible. This is a serious assignment."

Silence reigned. Well, apart from the ceaseless complaints of the wind, the snorting of horses, feet shuffling, armour clinking, throats being cleared…more artistic license. More accurately, I should say that we had us a moment of relative quiet.

We all knew that the reports weren't credible. Artax was only acting on them because my grandmother had his predecessor horsewhipped through the streets of Vermillion last summer for failing to pay attention to the local scouts.

"Nobody?" the colonel asked.

I coughed loudly.

"Very well." He rubbed at his moustache and turned that stare of his my way. "Captain Kendeth will lead a party of twenty skirmishers back along the flanks of Mount Sorrow and Mount Crimson."

Captain Kendeth! I avoided spitting, just barely. I had somehow traded Prince Jalan Kendeth for Captain Kendeth. It was grandmother's doing, of course. The Red Queen held firm opinions about earning privileges, about starting at the bottom and working one's way up. All kinds of nonsense about learning in the field. It's very easy to have such notions when you're warming a throne with your arse.

I lifted my arm so the rag-tail bunch of peasants and criminals under my command would follow me, then led them from the ranks to assemble at the rear. Of course, I'd been the only volunteer. The front row along which Colonel Artax's pale eyes had wandered were all the sons of nobles hoping to make a name for themselves, and news of a Scorron Army approaching the Aral Pass had set them polishing their mail like madmen. Which, of course, is precisely what they were. The real insanity in them was not so much the idea of gambling their lives against a chance of social advancement. Which, although stupid given the odds and the stakes, does at least have a prize attached to it. The insanity was that they genuinely seemed eager and excited by the prospect of standing in line waiting to see if an arrow would hit them, and then hacking at other men with a razor-edged piece of steel, hoping to cut off something vital before the other man could cut off something vital from them. Come dawn tomorrow, the Scorrons would make their move and a fair few of those who could have been scouting the hinterland in my place would be dead or dying instead.

There are easier ways to gain the reputation you desire. Lying is a good method. So is buying it. A sensible mixture of the two and you can write your own legend, in red ink rather than blood.

In any event, while the regular cull of Scorron and Red March's most stupid and violent nobility was taking place, I would be rambling across the lower slopes miles from the action.

I led my boys away from the final preparations, reflecting that perhaps the Scorron war was just Grandmother's way of getting rid of those young lords with the most violence and ambition, avoiding having to deal with them herself later. A series of quiet murders in well-appointed bedchambers would have been a lot simpler, though, and would have wasted far fewer peasants.

"Not worried about missing the big show, Captain?" That was Sergeant Thrum, a veteran of twenty years with a more impressive collection of facial scars than the colonel, and all of them allegedly earned turning live men into dead ones.

"Well, obviously I would love to be holding the pass with my brothers in arms, Sergeant." I raised my voice for the men trudging behind us in a column, spears across their shoulders, helms hanging on their backs. Despite the elevation, we were all sweating in the sun and the windborne dust coated us like a second skin. "I'd love it! Just...stabbing my sword through those Scorrons, can't beat the feeling! The smell of burning flesh, all that...stuff." Glancing back along the line, I caught a few doubtful looks. "The thing is..." I raised my hand to halt the column and to give me time to think what the thing might be. "The thing is... You, Jemins isn't it?"

"Ives, sir!"

"Yes, Ives. Of course. From Hannar province isn't it?"

"Sarteth, sir."

Fucking peasants. I drew a deep breath. "What do you think we're out here doing?"

"Following orders, sir!"

"Yes, but what do you really think we're doing. Speak freely, Jemins."

He glanced at the sergeant, who gave him a small nod.

"Staying out of trouble, sir! And keeping the old b— I mean, her majesty happy, sir!"

I shook my head with that slightly pitying air my older brothers used so well on me. "War, my lad, is a science."

"I'm twenty-seven."

"The *speak freely* bit is over now, Jennings." He might have six years on me, but I was a good six inches taller and a prince, so I'd call him a lad if I felt like it. "War is a science. In these mountains, a military force is a pressure exerted on the terrain. Where it goes is all about the passes. Which ones are open, which are closed, and about when that changes and what new options it puts on the table. If we were to run around willy nilly, we'd get ourselves bottled up and slaughtered in no time. Maps, lad! It's all about maps."

"Sir!"

Maps are a particular interest of mine. A map tells you where the escape routes are. In every situation, a wise man, or a coward as they are sometimes known, first wishes to identify the escape routes. One is essential, two are better, three begin to feel comfortable.

Now, while my contemporaries were sharpening their swords, polishing their armour, and boasting over how much blood they were going to spill, I had happened to be making a careful study of the maps in Colonel Arkax's tent. The great Vermillanise painter Steffano Kensio had been commissioned to draw them, and they were a spectacular work of art capturing every wrinkle and fold, even the way the sunrise catches on the snowclad peaks and throws the mountainsides into fingered shadow.

More important than the aesthetic quality for me was, of course, the information relating to the best ways out of danger. And in addition, the wise man will look to see not only how he may extricate himself from the poor choices of his friends and allies but also to see how his enemy might come at him. Hence, I knew with certainty that the ragged little goat-worriers who had been taken on as army scouts at the Red Queen's insistence were lying their flea-bitten arses off when they reported Scorron cavalry in the Haimar Gap. A close study of Kensio's beautiful maps allowed me to state with scientific certainty that no plausible route existed by which such a force could have reached that location without falling foul of our sizeable reserve around Hawk's Peak.

"The maps tell me that these local scouts need to be taken seriously," I lied. "Contrary to camp gossip, they are not miserable sheep-fuckers out to get extra pay by making up new threats that urgently require their nephew be given a scouting job, too." I looked slowly along the line of men queuing on the narrow track. "There is a very real chance we will run into Scorron cavalry in Haimar Gap, and it is our solemn duty to keep them there. If those bastards get a chance at the rear of our lines in Aral Pass, we could lose the whole show." I managed not to smirk. "So, lads, onward and downward into danger!"

AND JUST LIKE that, I was walking away from what looked like being the sharp point of the whole summer's campaign, with twenty seasoned spearmen to protect me should I happen to encounter a particularly gruff goat.

"We'll break here for lunch." I sat back on a suitably sized boulder.

Sergeant Thrum approached me, lowering his head and his voice. "We've come less than a mile, sir."

"And we have a long way to go, Sergeant! No point exhausting the men just before a battle. Now, where's that cheese? And did we bring the wine?"

"I don't think we did, sir." The sergeant paused. "And it's hours yet `til noon. The sun's only just—"

"Lunch!" I repeated in my best princely roar and waved for the men to sit.

It turned out that there *was* wine and, as the only royalty present, I took charge of it. The cheese wasn't too bad, some kind of rustic creation, and whilst the bread did have roughly the same consistency as the boulder I'd jumped onto, it was far from the worst meal I'd had since joining the army. I hadn't joined of my own free will, of course. My father had made it very clear that the Red Queen expected it of me. And when that didn't work, six large soldiers had dragged me from my rooms at the palace.

IT WASN'T UNTIL about half an hour later, with a piece of the alleged bread poised before my lips, that my attention was drawn to motion at the corner of my eye. Mouth still agape, I turned my head. Horsemen were approaching. We weren't talking scrawny locals on those wiry little steeds that look to have been crossbred with mountain goats not too many generations back. No. These were Scorron knights on big black destriers that looked as though they had just ambled off the tourney field. Five of them.

"Fuck me," I managed to swear softly.

I saw dust rising further down the valley, as though these might be a patrol ahead of a much larger force.

By sheer chance or, as I would later claim, brilliant strategy, from the horsemen's angle of approach, the boulder on which I sat effectively hid the twenty men lined up behind it sitting on the path.

"Fuck me…" I slithered bonelessly from the boulder to join Sergeant Thrum, who looked up at me, brows raised in question. I began to unbuckle my armour. I pay as much attention to being able to escape from armour as I do to escape routes in general. Armour says 'I'm going to stay here and fight you.' That's the main point where I disagree with armour.

"Look," I said, attempting not to sound terrified. "The most important thing to do when we spot the enemy is to make sure that Colonel Artax knows their number and disposition. It's something that requires an officer's eye." I slipped out of my breastplate and set my helmet beside it.

"I…" He swallowed his mouthful. "Guess so." A pause. "Sir."

"Right you are then, Sergeant." I tugged my padded jacket over my head, then patted him on the shoulder. "My advice is to stay low until they're right on you." And with that, I took off running, slipping and sliding as I avoided the men on the path.

"But what—"

A cry rang out from one of the Scorron knights, answering Thrum's question for him.

I began to sprint. Fortunately, my seating requirements had seen us halt in a part of the valley-side strewn with boulders both small and large. When it comes to running away from horsemen, or indeed battling them with spears, you can't pick much better ground than a cross-slope studded with boulders.

Behind me, the sounds of distant galloping became louder with distressing rapidity. Then the howls as twenty spearmen broke from cover at short notice and arrayed themselves in the paths of the surprised knights. I didn't look back. It just invites a broken ankle, which is never conducive to running away.

I'm pretty good at running, though I've never enjoyed it. Riding is a whole different thing, but my grandmother had essentially eliminated the Red March cavalry. Centuries of tradition, honour, and excellence all ploughed under at the whim of an old woman. Apparently, cavalry weren't 'suited to the wars in which we expect to find ourselves.' So, here I was on foot, being chased by horsemen who merely had to lean from the saddle and lop off my head while passing by.

As the cries of wounded men and animals grew more distant, a worryingly persistent *thud-thud-thud* of hooves began to emerge from the cacophony. I skidded to a halt behind a chest-high rock in order to assess my chances. And also to breathe. Running uphill is a real pain.

Two of the knights had circled round my men and continued in pursuit. The three who didn't were down already. My men may have been peasants and cutthroats, but they were also experienced soldiers in the Red Queen's Army of the North and, thanks to my fine military judgement, facing the enemy on ideal ground. Worryingly though, the dust cloud that had been far off now looked ominously close. I kept on running, weaving around rocks, zigzagging, doing what I could to avoid getting a set of hoof prints up my spine. I heard one of the riders go down, the clatter of weaponry drowned out as the poor horse started screaming. The second rider slowed his pace, not wanting to have his horse break its leg, too.

Sweat-drenched and panting, I came within sight of our camp, the cooks, smiths and other followers milling around their shelters. The boulders were thinning out, and behind me, the rider had begun to pick up speed. I guess it had just become personal because if his goal was to stop me telling anyone about the Scorron horsemen approaching, then riding a Scorron horse after me into camp was probably much the same thing, whether I survived or not.

I opened my stride, beginning to sprint. I wished dearly that I'd had the presence of mind to throw my sword away, but drawing it whilst running for my life just wasn't possible and I had to let the weight drag at me.

I did manage to snatch the knife from my belt. The camp got ever closer, closer. An amazed audience now watched my approach. Whores from Madam Shi's tent stared open-mouthed, their paints and brushes forgotten. A boy chasing an escaped chicken abandoned the pursuit. A fat cook's lad stood just ahead of me, round-eyed. The thunder of hooves reached the level where I knew the stallion must be breathing down my neck. I shaved past the cook's boy and heard him go down behind me. A moment later, I was through the entrance to a mess tent and out the back, having slashed an exit with my dagger while the knight got fouled in guy lines and whatnot.

A whole tent failed to stop the bastard. He came thundering on, trailing lines and tent hides. Absolute terror gave me fresh wind. It wasn't just the knight, though he was bad enough on his own, but the hundreds of friends he had undoubtedly brought with him.

I ran on, my vision starting to pulse red, heart pounding, gasping like a landed fish.

And then, saints be praised, the lines of my lovely army. And still the bastard was coming.

"Run!" I found more breath. "Out of my way!"

I forced myself through the back lines. "Move! Get out of my way!" I drew my sword and hammered on the back of helms with the hilt. "Move!"

It seems clear in retrospect that the thunder of my heartbeat in my ears had taken over from the horse's hoof beats sometime earlier. But all I could think right then was that the mad bastard was chasing me into the ranks of my own army, a sea of backs all presented to his sword and mine the only one he wanted. I needed someone to stop him.

"Kill the bastard!" With elbows and shoulders I dug deep, worming my way through the lines. "Move! Make a hole!"

And suddenly, the press of men gave way and I was stumbling into space. I found myself face to face with a spike-covered, half-naked lunatic who had somehow run himself neck-first onto my sword.

The main force of Scorrons had attacked up the pass in my brief absence like the treacherous foreigners they are. The Scorron Razor-Men had led the charge, terrifying madmen covered in sharp metal and eschewing armour for defensive purposes entirely. They take some drug that makes them foam and howl. Some set themselves aflame with alchemical mixtures, and all of them want nothing more than to throw themselves amid the enemy and wreak a red ruin before they die. It's a famously intimidating sight, and until the moment an unarmoured prince of Red March had fought his way through his own troops to get at the Razor-Men, the intimidation tactics had been working. Colonel Artax's men had been in retreat on both flanks.

My inadvertent stupidity reminded my fellow men of the Red March of the similar but intentional stupidity that had brought them here in the first place, and with wild cheers, they charged after me.

MY MEMORIES OF what follows are disjointed and largely absent. War is a red haze punctuated by horror and death. It's a sequence of things that no human should ever have to know are possible, let alone see or have happen to them. War is neither a science or an art, it's a fucking mess, and the only sane response to it is to run fast in the opposite direction. If we all did that, there wouldn't be any more.

MONTHS LATER, I found the great painter Steffano Kensio in his airy studio in Vermillion, a place of high windows and light overlooking the Selene. I took with me a small, stained section of the map he had drawn for Colonel Artax, who we buried under a mound of stones overlooking the Aral Pass. I asked the venerable Steffano how it was that the Scorrons had reached the Haimar Gap on warhorses when his map had shown no possible way for even a well-prepared group of unencumbered mountaineers to get there from the Scorron-held territory. Steffano, an elderly man with a bush of wild grey hair, hummed and harred and waved a loaded paintbrush at me before settling on, "All those squiggly bits, dear boy, it's very messy up there. Every artist takes a bit of license in these matters."

I punched him on the nose. I may have broken it. But it was wartime, and war's hell.

I PUSH THE parchment back across the table. Night has fallen. An oil lamp burns beside me, though I have no memory of lighting it…or there having even been a lamp. Ashley has fallen asleep on the bed, an inviting collection of curves, light and shade offering up hints of her mysteries. If I had the talent, I would paint her here and now.

Instead, I force my gaze back to the pages that have held my attention for so many hours. With a sigh, I carry them to the fireplace. The Aral Pass still has its hooks in me after all these years. It had dragged me back wholesale, and I had bled again, this time in black upon parchment. I had wanted honesty, but sometimes you can have too much truth. Especially if you're supposed to be being attacked by a bear…

I consign the pages to the flames and watch as they are taken from the world. Tomorrow I will try again. Something shorter, less honest, and more believable.

ACKNOWLEDGEMENTS

PETROS TRIANTAFYLLOU

I KNOW THIS part may seem boring to you, so I'll try to keep it as short as possible, although there are many people who deserve to be mentioned.

To begin with, I would like to thank all forty authors who helped create this anthology. Each one of them spent dozens of hours creating the best possible version of their stories, and they did it for free, albeit for a good cause. This anthology exists because of them—I did nothing more than bring them together.

Of course those forty authors aren't the only ones who brought this anthology to life. There are four generous people that deserve equal recognition for their work. Tim Marquitz, Jason Deem, John Anthony Di Giovanni and Shawn King, thank you for your amazing work with editing, interior art, cover illustration and cover/interior design respectively.

I would be amiss if I didn't mention Adrian Collins (editor of *Evil is a Matter of Perspective*) who inspired me to create *Art of War* and gave me valuable advice, and Ulff Lehmann who gave me the final nudge into starting this project.

Most of the aforementioned forty authors of this anthology are part of a larger group (one hundred authors) who took part in another charity action from BookNest back in January called BookNest's Fabulous Fantasy Fundraiser (BFFF), in which we raised $4,400 for Doctors Without Borders. Since that was the success that led into this anthology, those one hundred authors deserve to be mentioned as well.

To go even further back, there was one person whom without BFFF wouldn't be the success it ended up being, and that's Laura M. Hughes. Thank you, Laura, for supporting me and BookNest all the way from BFFF to *Art of War*.

And to complete the reverse domino, I would like to thank Agnes Meszaros who first nudged me into creating BookNest. Everything that followed is a result of this action.

Of course BookNest isn't just Petros. A dozen other reviewers have helped the site grow, and although they come and go, they are still part of our family. Thank you Katerina, Petrik, Celeste, Mary, TS, Charles, Michael, and everyone else who's no longer with us.

Last but not least, there's one person who has supported me throughout the years like no one else has. I wouldn't exaggerate if I said that I simply wouldn't be here if it wasn't for Mark Lawrence, and therefore it is only proper to dedicate this anthology to him. Thank you, Mark. For everything.

Finally, many thanks to all those people who supported *Art of War* by giving it early reviews, spreading the word, or simply buying a copy. A fair number of them are part of four groups that I'm proud to be a

ACKNOWLEDGEMENTS

part of: Fantasy-Faction of the amazing Marc Aplin, Grimdark Fiction
Readers & Writers of the ever-amusing Rob Matheny, Fantasy Buffet,
and finally r/Fantasy. Thank you, all of you, from the bottom of my heart.

-Petros Triantafyllou

Made in the USA
Las Vegas, NV
04 March 2021